BUY IN. CHECK OUT.

BUY IN. CHECK OUT.

Where Thinking Stops and Life Begins

CAM CHAMBERS

To Robert, my father, and Lorinda, my mother.
For breathing life into me. For your unconditional belief in my dreams.
And for every moment you nurtured my creativity before I even knew what to do with it.
This book exists because of you.

ACT I

The Price of Admission

The illusion of freedom will continue as long as it's profitable to
continue the illusion. At the point where the illusion
becomes too expensive to maintain, they will just take down the scenery.
– Frank Zappa

CHAPTER ONE

Consumer Warning

Advertising is the rattling of a stick inside a swill bucket.
– George Orwell

Elise stared at the computer screen, her reflection a ghost in the black glass. The gray morning light slipped through the office blinds casting thin stripes across her desk. A Prison. That's what this place had become. Each day felt longer than the last, the minutes dragging like dead weight. The office felt claustrophobic.

James was dead. Three months gone and the weight of his absence pressed against her chest like a stone she couldn't push off. Three months, and she still caught herself reaching for her phone to text him. It was worse in these quiet moments, the sound of the office life fading into the background as her thoughts clawed their way to the surface.

The monitor covered her face in pale blue light, revealing the shadows etched beneath her eyes. Her inbox sat open, untouched, its subject lines like landmines waiting to explode. Her fingers hovered over the keyboard, but for some reason refused to type.

Somewhere in the back of her mind she heard James's voice. Steady and calming, reminding her not to let things pile up. She blinked hard, her vision blurring, not from tears, but from exhaustion. The kind that seeped into your bones and sat there.

A sound broke the silence, a mechanical noise followed by the soft hiss of silk rubbing against leather. Elise looked to her left. Amanda Singh, ever-perfect Amanda, sat upright at the next desk, adjusting her posture with a fluidity that was almost inhuman. Her Aether band pulsed at her neck. The glow calm and soothing, like the heartbeat of something alive.

Elise's fingers drifted to her own neck, bare and seemingly unremarkable. What it would feel like, she wondered, to wear one? To surrender to its gentle guidance. To let it carry the weight of every decision she'd been too tired to make. But the thought turned her stomach, and she let her hand drop, the rebellion against it instinctual, almost primal.

Her eyes moved back to the screen just as an email notification popped up, the subject line ruthless. *Final Notice: Tuition Payment Overdue.* Harper's school. Again. The words blurred together, but the meaning was clear. Sympathy only stretched so far, and Elise had already exhausted hers. Her finger trembled as it moved toward the mouse.

"Elise!" The knock of knuckles on her desk made her flinch. She looked up to see Ness standing there, perfectly dressed and manicured as always. Her Aether-free neck caught the office lights, a rare sight these days. Despite her upbeat tone, the way she shifted her weight gave her a restless energy. "You know Powell's calling an emergency all-hands, right? I heard it's something big from corporate."

Before Elise could respond, her phone buzzed. She glanced down, her pulse jumping at the message from an unknown number.

You may be in danger. We need to talk.

Her throat tightened as the office seemed to close in around her. Another soft chime from Amanda's Aether filled the air, followed by her perfectly synchronized posture adjustment. Elise's eyes moved to Ness, still hovering, her head tilted in concern.

"You coming?" Ness asks.

Elise nodded, standing on legs that felt like they might give out at any moment. She gripped her phone tighter, its edges digging into her palm. The world became unfocused as her fingers hovered over the screen.

Who is this? What do you mean? she typed, the message barely coherent as her pulse continued to hammer in her ears.

Three dots blinking, mocking her, as they disappeared then reappeared with maddening slowness. Finally, the response.

Your husband's death.

A chill ran down her spine. Her thumb trembled as she typed back, desperation seeping into every letter.

What are you talking about? Who are you?

Someone who can help. Meet me tonight. Don't tell anyone.

Her stomach twisted violently, her mind grasping at the absurdity of it all. It felt wrong, surreal, like a poorly scripted thriller. Yet, something about the specificity of the words clung to her, wrestling with her logic. She stared at the screen, her thoughts colliding as she began to type another frantic response.

"Elise!" Ness's voice interrupted, yanking her back to the office. The sound grated against her raw nerves like sandpaper. "Let's go."

Clenching her jaw, Elise locked her phone and shoved it into her pocket, its weight far heavier than the plastic and metal should allow. She followed Ness out of the cubicle, her steps unsteady as she tried to shake the words from her mind, but they clung to her like a funky smell.

As they navigated the labyrinth of desks, Elise's attention hooked on the glowing Aether bands wrapped around her coworkers' necks. Each one pulsed in perfect harmony, their lights flickering in shades of blue, silver, and gold. They sparkled like jewelry, but the precision in their synchronization felt chilling. The bands weren't just adornments—they were declarations of allegiance to something much larger, more insidious.

"Gorgeous, aren't they?" Ness whispered, catching Elise's eyes. "I've been saving up. Well, trying to. Seems like we're the only ones without them." She laughed it off, but Elise recognized the hidden anxiety in her tone.

Elise forced a tight smile, though her jaw felt locked in place. She'd heard it all before, the endless comments about how much easier life could be if she just joined the tide, let the current carry her. Her eyes moved back to the bands, shimmering with crystalline curves that caught the light like prisms. For a brief moment, she wondered what it might feel like to wear one, to let it hum against her skin, to give herself over to its promise of guidance. The thought left her cold, her hand instinctively brushing her bare neck.

Ahead, the frosted glass walls of the conference room came into view, the distorted shapes of the gathering crowd inside giving the space an almost dreamlike quality. The buzz of voices grew louder, a mix of excitement and speculation that set Elise's nerves on edge.

Her phone seemed to grow heavier with each step, its presence against her thigh inescapable. She pulled it out, glancing down as if it might have more answers waiting. The thread of messages stared back at her, vague and ominous.

Elise's heart beat violently in her chest as Grayson Powell stepped forward, the glow of his Aether band casting subtle golden hues across the room. The two corporate reps next to him looked eerily similar, their identical gold bands blinking in a slow rhythm. They didn't look at the crowd, didn't fidget, didn't blink often enough. They stood there like extensions of the machine Powell so effortlessly represented.

"Good morning, everyone," Powell began, his voice smooth as silk. It carried just the right mix of warmth and authority to draw everyone in without giving them room to question. "I won't keep you long, but I'm excited to share some groundbreaking news about our partnership with Necessity Mart."

11

He paused, letting the anticipation build, his eyes scanning the room with a calculated smile. "Actually, it's more than a partnership. It's a commitment... A commitment to embracing the future of optimal living."

He waved to the screen behind him, where bold white text over a black background came into view: *TRANSCEND THE ORDINARY.*

The words seemed to vibrate slightly, though Elise wasn't sure if it was the screen or her own straining eyes. The room got silent, the weight of collective attention pressing down like a physical force. She looked around, catching glimpses of her coworkers leaning forward in their chairs, eager, attentive. The buzz of excitement hung in the air.

She tried to focus on Powell's words, tried to tune into the presentation that had everyone else hanging onto every syllable. But her mind tugged relentlessly toward her phone, still in her pocket, still warm against her leg. The messages sat there like burning coal, whispering with possibilities too dark to ignore.

Unable to resist any longer, she slid her phone out, keeping it low under the table. Her fingers moved before her mind could catch up. *Where do you want to meet?* she typed. The question felt heavier this time, as if she were carving it into stone instead of tapping it into glass.

Three dots appeared, vanished, reappeared. Each blink sent her heart racing faster.

The old rail station. 8:30 PM. Don't let anyone see you.

Her breath caught in her throat. The old rail station—abandoned, decaying, forgotten. A place that no one had any business being, especially at night. Her stomach turned as she pocketed the phone again, her mind a storm of questions she couldn't afford to answer, not now.

She swallowed, glancing up from her phone. Powell rambled on, talking about "proactive wellness monitoring" and "unprecedented benefits." The screen shifted to show infographics: bars rising, scores climbing, smiling faces glowing with the subtle light of their Aether bands. Around her, those same bands glowed in quiet harmony, wearers unconsciously straightening their posture, deepening their breaths, adjusting their movements in unison. It was mesmerizing and sickening all at once.

Elise's phone buzzed again—the vibration rattling against her thigh. She didn't want to look down, but she did.

Don't be late. And don't tell anyone.

Her fingers tightened around the device, blood draining from them as she stuffed it back into her pocket. Whoever this was, they were pulling her deeper into something she wasn't sure she wanted to uncover. But the promise of answers, of finally understanding what happened to James, was a hook she couldn't ignore.

Powell's voice faded to background noise, the words blending together as her mind spiraled toward the rail station.

The lights flickered to life as Powell wrapped up, illuminating the room in harsh fluorescence. The sound of conversations started immediately. Elise stood quickly, eager to slip away, her chair scraping quietly against the floor. But just as she took her first step toward the door, Powell's voice cut through the crowd.

"Elise? A moment."

She froze, pulse hammering against her ribs. Slowly, she turned, locking eyes with him. His Aether band glowed... bright, steady, watching. As if it could sense her unease.

He drifted closer, tablet in hand, his movements unhurried. "Your numbers for Q3," he began. "I'm worried about you, Elise."

Her mouth opened, but he didn't wait for a reply. His eyes softened just enough to mimic concern. "I know these past months haven't been easy. James was..." He hesitated, choosing his words carefully. "... he was a good man, Elise. And I see how hard you're working to keep things together."

He swiped his tablet, turning it toward her. Cool blue graphs came to life, their dips and valleys like accusations. "But I can't help noticing a trend," Powell continued. "You're scattered. Distracted. This really isn't like you."

The glow of his Aether pulsed gently, its rhythm syncing unnervingly with his words. He leaned in slightly. "Have you thought that maybe you're carrying too much alone?"

He tapped the screen again, pulling up a new set of metrics. "Your natural ability is there... brilliant analysis, attention to detail... but it's fractured now."

"I'm managing," Elise replied.

Powell shook his head, his expression almost pitying. "You're surviving," he corrected. "But you could be thriving."

From his jacket, he pulled out a brochure, sliding it into her hands. The cover showed a serene woman bathed in soft light, her Aether glowing a tranquil blue. "The Aether isn't just about productivity," Powell said. "It's about finding balance. Something I think you could use right now."

He flipped the brochure open, pointing his finger at the financing options that were laid out in pristine columns. "The company has programs to help with the initial investment," he added. "I hate seeing one of my best analysts struggling when

13

there's a solution right here." His tone was sincere, almost fatherly. "Just... think about it. For your sake."

Elise forced a smile. "I will."

Powell smiled back, a practiced warmth that never quite reached his eyes. "Good," he said, tucking the tablet under his arm. "Because we want you at your best, Elise. And if there's anything else you need... really, anything at all, you know where to find me."

As he walked away, his Aether glowed steadily, its golden light fading into the crowd. Elise gripped the brochure in her hands, its glossy surface covered in sweat. She shoved it into her bag and slipped out of the conference room, her thoughts already spiraling back toward the rail station and whatever answers might be waiting there in the dark.

Elise looked at her phone, her fingers flying across the screen as she typed a quick message to Maggie about being late for Harper. The send button clicked, and the message felt heavier than the text itself, an echo of their last fight hanging in her mind like smoke in a closed room.

She could still see Maggie's face that night, illuminated by the glow of the TV Harper had been half-watching. Maggie's voice had risen above the sound of the show. "You're smarter than this, Elise," she said, her tone somewhere between frustration and pleading. "Can't you see what's happening? They're not just selling convenience anymore... they're selling goddamn control."

Elise tried to brush it off, deflecting with something about priorities and survival. But the words stuck like a thorn. Maggie had a way of speaking truths that festered under the surface. Truths Elise didn't want to acknowledge.

She checked the time: *4:45 PM*. The numbers blurred for a moment before coming back into focus. Less than four hours until she's supposed to meet a stranger in the shadows of a forgotten rail station to discuss her dead husband. The kind of place where bad things happen. Where no one will hear you scream.

She locked her phone and stood, the world tilting slightly as she took a step forward. She exhaled, her breath shaky but determined. Whatever this meeting is, truth or trap, she'll be there. She has to be.

As she grabbed her bag, Maggie's words whispered in the back of her mind like a ghost she couldn't shake. *Can't you see what's happening?* She pushed the thought aside, but it clung to her, following her out of the office like a second shadow.

CHAPTER TWO

Damaged Goods

We are made to be consumers, not citizens.
– Vance Packard

Elise's fingers gripped the steering wheel until her knuckles ached, the dim streets stretching endlessly ahead like the ribs of some ancient, slumbering beast. The old rail station stood at the edge of her vision, a jagged black smear against the winter night. She turned into the lot. The air felt wrong, a truth she wasn't ready to face.

What the hell am I doing here?

The thought surfaced uninvited, but there was no answer. Only the echo of her engine as it idled. She passed beneath a rusted archway, the faded words above it nearly erased by time. The lot ahead was a mixture of broken asphalt and growing weeds, empty except for a single dark blue Buick LeSabre parked in the corner like a predator.

Her phone buzzed on the passenger seat, startling her. She grabbed it, her breath visible in the chill air.

Park by the maintenance shed. Southwest corner.

She followed the directions, the shed appearing from the shadows as her headlights swept across it. The structure was small, its concrete walls cracked and its roof partially caved in. A rusted *NO TRESPASSING* sign dangled from a bent nail, the red letters so faded they looked like old bloodstains.

Killing the engine, Elise sat in silence for a moment, her breath shallow. Every instinct screamed at her to leave, to turn the car around and drive back to the safety of light and warmth. Instead, she grabbed her phone, typing quickly.

I'm here.

The reply came right away.

Platform 3. Stay in the shadows. Leave your phone.

She peered at the abandoned platforms ahead. They stretched into the darkness, broken rails and overgrown tracks swallowed by the night. A single security light flickered in the distance, its orange glow stuttering like a dying ember. The platform was barely visible.

Her fingers hovered over her phone, her mind still racing. She should leave. Call someone. Do *anything* but step into the black unknown. But then she thought of James, his voice on the phone that final night, raw with pain and something else… something she hadn't recognized until now. Fear.

She tucked her phone into the center console and pushed the car door open. The creak of the hinges echoed, ripping across the emptiness. The ground shifted under her boots as she stepped out, each step a quiet betrayal of her better judgement.

Ahead, a shadow detached itself from the darkness near Platform 3. The light from the flickering lamp revealed a figure standing just outside its reach. Medium height, heavy coat, face covered by an old baseball cap.

"Mrs. Winters," the man said, his voice rough and low, just loud enough to reach her ears. "Thank you for coming."

She stopped several feet away, the icy air burning her lungs. "Who are you?" she asked, her voice steadier than she felt.

"Miles Whitaker." He didn't move closer, keeping himself partially veiled by the shadow. "I was hired by your husband's firm after… well, after certain patterns raised concerns."

Her breath fogged in the frigid air. "What patterns? What are you talking about?"

"A Storage unit. Do you know about it?"

"No," Elise said slowly, her heart pounding. "I don't… What does this have to do with James?"

Miles shifted slightly. "It was discovered after a break-in. Professional job. Whoever it was, they knew exactly what they were looking for." He pulled a manilla folder from inside his coat, holding it toward her. "These were taken the day after. The locks were disassembled, not broken. Security cameras disabled. Precise, clean."

Elise hesitated before reaching for the folder, her fingers trembling. She opened it, the photos inside were harsh against the dim light. Metal shelving lined the walls of a standard storage unit, plastic containers stacked neatly. But her eyes were drawn to the metal cases, several lying open and empty.

"What were they looking for?"

Miles shook his head. "That's what I've been trying to figure out. The unit was rented under the name David Marshall, but the payment card traced back to your husband's firm. He visited multiple times before his death… always between two and four in the morning."

The photos suddenly felt heavy in her hands. "He said his migraines were getting worse," she mumbled, more to herself than to him. "He'd go for drives sometimes... said it helped clear his head."

Miles rubbed his jaw, the faintest trace of sympathy on his face. "Three days before his accident, James accessed highly sensitive files at work. Files he had no business seeing. Whatever he found, may have put him in someone's crosshairs."

Elise stiffened, the air growing colder around her. "He was distracted," she said, the words tumbling out like a defense she didn't quite believe. "He was stressed, sick. That's why he crashed. He... he blacked out—"

"Or someone made it look that way," Miles interrupted. He took a step forward, the light catching his face for the first time. His face was bony, worn. His eyes dark with years of knowing too much.

"They're still looking," he said quietly. "Whoever broke into that unit didn't find what they were after. And until we figure out what your husband uncovered, you need to be careful, Mrs. Winters. Very careful."

The wind picked up, whipping through the empty platform and scattering leaves and papers in chaotic spirals. Somewhere in the distance, a train whistle cut through the night. Elise wrapped her arms around herself, suddenly aware of how exposed they were.

"What do I do now?" she asked.

Miles handed her a burner phone. "I'll contact you. Keep it charged. Keep it hidden." His voice dropped lower. "And think back to James's last trip. Anything strange... anything that didn't add up. It could be the key."

As he turned to leave, Elise called after him. "Miles! NovaShield... they're fighting my claim because his body was never recovered. Could they be involved?"

Miles hesitated, his shoulders tense. "At this point, I'm not ruling anything out." He glanced around the dark lot. "But whoever's behind this, they're thorough enough to make murder look like an accident."

And with that, he disappeared into the shadows of Platform 3, leaving Elise clutching the burner phone, her mind spinning. The security light flickered again. In the distance, the train whistled again—longer, louder.

The drive back felt unreal, like moving through the aftermath of a bad dream. Each streetlight burned too bright, their beams stretching across the dashboard in warped, jittery patterns that made her uneasy. Elise gripped the wheel tighter, but it didn't stop the tremor in her hands. Her thoughts collided in a chaotic loop: the storage unit, the break-in, James's late-night visits, and that last, fractured phone call. It was too much, too fast, and it all felt like a thread she couldn't stop pulling.

Her phone buzzed in the console, the sudden vibration yanking her back to the present. She flinched, almost swerving before she steadied her car. A quick glance at the screen made her heart sink. Maggie.

Where are you? Harper is getting restless.

Reality clawed its way back. She was late. Far too late. Her stomach tightened as guilt and panic twisted together. What could she say? How could she explain the surreal horror show she'd just walked out of without sounding unhinged?

Her thumb hovered over the keyboard, the pressure in her chest building. The truth wasn't an option. Not yet. Finally, she typed.

On my way. Traffic.

She hit send before she could second-guess herself, the lie glaring back at her from the screen. It felt flimsy, too thin to cover the dark, splintered edges of everything she now carried. But it was all she had.

As the message delivered, Elise looked at the clock. The numbers smeared into a haze before coming back into focus. She pressed harder on the gas. The empty road unraveled, a thread pulled loose from the fabric of the night.

By the time Maggie's house came into view, Elise felt as if she'd been holding her breath for miles. The small, familiar home sat stubbornly in the dark like a relic, its edges soft against the glow of a world overtaken by technology. The sight grounded her, if only for a moment. A strange mix of dread and relief passed through her as she parked, her hands still gripping the wheel even after the engine went silent.

Inside, Maggie's house was as unchanged as its exterior. A controlled chaos of activist flyers scattered across the coffee table. An old mug of tea delicately balanced on the armrest of the couch. The TV played quietly in the background, a news anchor speaking urgently about data harvesting and corporate overreach.

"You're late," Maggie said, her tone carrying the edge of a long day. But her irritation faded the moment she saw Elise's face. She tilted her head, her eyes narrowing. "Everything okay?"

"Fine," Elise said too quickly, brushing past her sister into the living room. "Just... work stuff. The usual."

Maggie wasn't buying it. She leaned against the doorframe, her arms crossed. "You look like you've seen a ghost," she said.

"We should go," Elise replied, ignoring the question. Her voice was tight, short, leaving no room for further questioning. "Harper, pack up your things."

Harper appeared in the hallway, her backpack dangling from one shoulder. She hesitated, glancing between her mother and her aunt as if sensing the tension in the air.

Maggie approached Elise, lowering her voice. "You're scaring me, Elise. You'd tell me if something was wrong, right?"

"Of course," Elise said, forcing a smile. The lie stuck in her throat like glass, but the truth was too dangerous, too raw, to share here. She adjusted her purse, feeling the weight of the burner phone pressed against her hip like a loaded gun.

Maggie didn't look convinced, but she let it go. For now. Her eyes lingered on Elise as she walked Harper toward the door. The air outside felt crisper somehow, the darkness wrapping around them as Maggie stood in the doorway, her worry apparent.

In the car, Harper slumped against the back seat window, her breath fogging the glass as she traced lazy patterns in the condensation. Elise glanced in the rearview mirror, trying to will herself to focus on her daughter, but her mind was still caught in the shadows of the rail station.

"Mom?" Harper's voice was quiet, hesitant. "Katie got her Aether today. Her parents surprised her after school."

"Mm-hmm," Elise mumbled, her words automatic, detached.

"That makes twelve kids in my class now," Harper continued, undeterred. "Mr. Roberts keeps saying how they're showing 'exceptional focus metrics.' Whatever that means." She paused, her finger stopping mid-pattern on the window. "Today, at lunch, they all sat together. Their bands glowing the same color."

Elise felt the words like a distant echo, their weight dulled by her swirling thoughts. James's last phone call kept replaying in her head—his strained voice, the mention of switching hotels, his growing fear.

"Mom? Are you listening?"

"Yes, sweetheart," Elise said. "The Aether thing is just… complicated."

They turned onto their street, and Elise's grip on the wheel tightened instinctively. Something was wrong. The porch light was off, a small detail, but one that sent a prickle of unease down her spine. She always left it on. And the front door… the front door was slightly cracked, the outline of splintered wood visible even from the car.

She felt nauseous.

"Stay in the car," Elise said, her tone making Harper sit up straighter.

"Mom?" Harper's voice cracked, the fog on the window clearing as she pressed her hands against it.

"Just stay here."

Elise stepped out into the cold, her breath quick and shallow as she approached the house. Each step cautious, the crunch of the pavement beneath her boots impossibly loud.

The door creaked as she got closer, swinging slightly on its hinges. She saw it clearly now, the wood around the lock splintered, as if pried open.

Her hands trembled as she grabbed her phone and dialed.

"Nine-one-one, what's your emergency?"

"Someone's broken into my house," Elise said.

"I need the police. Right now."

Behind her, Harper pressed her face against the car window, her wide eyes locked onto the house.

Elise stepped away from the door, her mind racing with everything Miles had said.

This is a message.

Her heart thundered in her chest as she continued to put distance between herself and the house. Somewhere in the distance, a dog barked, its howls fading into the night. She gripped the phone tighter, her breath visible in the cold air. The shadows seemed to reach for her from every corner.

∞∞∞∞

The flashing red and blue lights cast harsh shadows across the neighborhood, turning every color darker, more sinister. Harper clung to Elise's arm, refusing to stay in the car now that the police were here. Elise held her tightly, as much for her daughter's comfort as her own. Across the street, Hannah and Rob Suarez stood on their porch, their faces unreadable behind the glow of their Aether bands. Rob leaned on the railing, his stance casual, but his eyes never left Elise.

Two officers emerged from the house, one nodding at the other. "All clear," one of them said. "You can come in now."

Elise hesitated before stepping forward, Harper still clutching her side. The house felt foreign as they entered, like it had absorbed the violation. Drawers hung open in the kitchen, and cushions were tossed across the couch. Yet nothing seemed to be missing. Her laptop still sat untouched on the coffee table, its screen dark. Harper's tablet was still plugged into the charger by the TV.

"Doesn't look like they took anything valuable," one of the officers said, flipping through his notepad. "Probably just kids or someone looking for easy cash... prescription meds, maybe. It's not uncommon."

Elise nodded, but her focus was elsewhere. She drifted toward James's office, her steps slowing as she reached the door. Her breath caught in her throat. The room was unrecognizable.

She had kept it exactly as James had left it. His coffee mug still sat on the desk, his papers neatly arranged, the framed photos on the shelf dusty but undisturbed. Now, the room was a mess. File folders scattered across the floor, their contents spilling like guts. Drawers had been yanked out and dumped.

Elise stepped inside, the officer's voice a hazy noise behind her. "Can you tell if anything's missing?"

"I... I don't know," Elise stammered. "I haven't touched anything since..." She trailed off, her eyes locking on James's coffee mug, now lying on the floor, a ring of dried residue marking where it had once sat.

Harper lingered in the doorway, her small body stiff with tension. She stepped inside cautiously, her eyes sweeping the mess. When she spoke, her voice trembled with anger. "Dad's office... they fucking ruined it."

Elise's head jerked, startled by the rawness. Harper stood there with her hands balled into fists. The word hung in the air, defiant, and for a moment, Elise couldn't bring herself to correct her.

She turned instead to the officer, who seemed unfazed by the outburst, his tone professional as he flipped through his notepad. "We can dust for prints," he said, "but in cases like this, it's usually opportunistic. They hit a few houses, grab what they can carry."

Elise barely nodded, her eyes drifting back to Harper. Her daughter's hands had unclenched, but she still stood stuck, her eyes locked on the mess. Elise crossed the room, placing a hand on Harper's shoulder.

"I'll fix it," Elise said softly, though she wasn't sure if she meant the room, the night, or something much bigger. Harper didn't respond, but she leaned into the touch, the defiance in her posture turning into something more fragile.

"Mom?" Harper tugged her sleeve. "Can I stay at Ethan's tonight? Please?"

Elise turned to her, saw the fear in her eyes. "Of course, sweetheart. Go pack a bag."

As Harper disappeared upstairs, Elise reached into her pocket and pulled out the burner phone. Her hands shook as she typed.

They were here. James's office. What were they looking for?

Miles responded right away.

Don't touch anything. And don't sleep there tonight.

As Elise walked Harper to the Suarez's door, the neighborhood felt even darker. The Hestia Hub's automated lights came to life as Hannah greeted them, her smile warm but slightly strained.

"She'll be safe here," Hannah said as Elise thanked her.

Elise hugged Harper tightly before turning back toward her car. Each step away from the Suarez house felt heavier, the distance between her and her daughter stretching like a black hole.

Her phone buzzed in her pocket, a message from Miles.

Room is booked at the Mayfield. Key card waiting at the front desk. Don't use your credit cards. Don't tell anyone where you are.

Elise stopped in the driveway, her eyes drifting back toward her dark house. The broken door still hung slightly cracked.

A low rumble caught her attention. A car idled at the end of the block, its headlights off. Elise froze, holding her breath. The car crept forward, its windows tinted so dark that they reflected only the streetlights as it passed.

Her pulse thundered as she followed its slow movement.

The license plate was missing.

Elise stood, frozen, her eyes locked on the taillights as they disappeared around the corner. She let out a shaky breath, realizing she'd been holding it. Every nerve screamed for her to move, to get to the safety of her car, to vanish into the night before whoever was inside the vehicle decided to come back.

She slid into the driver's seat, locking the doors. The burner phone buzzed again as she started the engine, but she didn't look at it. Not yet. The dark streets ahead felt endless, and the weight of unseen eyes pressed against her like a cold hand on her back. She drove into the night, the sound of the car's engine still lingering in her ears.

CHAPTER THREE

Fine Print

The big print giveth and the small print taketh away.
– Tom Waits

The hotel room suffocated her, thick with bleach and cheap air freshener. Elise sat cross-legged on the creaky bed, her laptop perched on her knees. Daylight fought its way through the poorly drawn curtains, revealing the frayed edges of the carpet and the slightly peeling wallpaper. It wasn't quite a prison cell, but it didn't feel far from one.

Her screen blinked with the countdown timer for the Project Harmony announcement. The seconds ticked away, slow and methodical, as though mocking her. Elise rubbed her temples, her fingers brushing a wrinkle etched there by stress. The sound of the laptop fan filled the room, its monotonous noise a strange comfort in an otherwise silent space.

The video stream stuttered to life. Mayor Langston stepped to the podium, his polished smile shining, but it was forced optimism. His voice carried through the speakers. "Today marks the dawn of a new era for our city. With Project Harmony, we are building communities where every citizen can thrive."

Behind him stood the Necessity Mart executives, each a portrait of corporate efficiency, their Aether bands glowing in rhythm. It was all too perfect, too rehearsed. Elise couldn't help but notice glaring anomaly. An empty chair at the far end of the stage. A subtle power play, or the calculated absence of someone who didn't need to be there to command authority? She frowned, knowing exactly who wasn't there. The elusive CEO of Necessity Mart, the shadow pulling the strings.

Langston's voice grew louder. "Project Harmony will transform neighborhoods, embedding cutting-edge technology to optimize every aspect of daily life—energy, security, wellness. This is not just an initiative. It's a movement."

Elise shook her head. To the crowd, it was a promise of progress, but she saw something darker. Gentrification disguised as philanthropy. Control veiled as innovation.

A knock shattered her focus. Her chest tightened as she looked at the door.

"It's me," Miles said through the wood, his voice hoarse and urgent.

Elise hurried across the room and opened the door. Miles stepped inside, tugging the curtains shut, in a quick, almost frantic motion. His face was pale, his guarded demeanor from the previous night replaced with something else... fear, maybe.

"What's going on?" she asked, taking a step back.

Without answering, he dropped his worn duffle onto the bed, unzipping it. From its depths, he pulled out a handgun, small but intimidating.

"What the hell is that?" Elise said, with a slight panic in her voice.

Miles held out the gun, his hand trembling just enough for Elise to notice. His eyes, dark and certain, locked onto hers. "It's yours," he said. "Because after last night... you're in it now."

She raised her hands. "No. No way. I don't know how to—"

"I'll teach you," he said. "We don't have time to argue."

Elise stared at the handgun as he held it out, her chest tightening. The polished metal caught the dim light like black ice, heavy with implications she didn't want to face.

Reluctantly, she reached for it, her hands trembling as she gripped it awkwardly. It felt foreign, the kind of weight that didn't just settle in her palms but sunk into her chest, dragging her deeper into the abyss that had slowly taken over her life. It felt like James's death all over again. Miles crouched next to her; his movements calculated but patient.

"Safety's here." His fingers tapped a small notch. "Don't touch the trigger unless you mean it. And for the love of God, don't point it at yourself."

She nodded, her throat dry. Her fingers clung to the gun as though it might bite her if she let go. Carefully, she placed it on the nightstand, her heart pounding as if it had absorbed the weapon's potential.

Miles straightened, his eyes scanning the room. "Sterling Ridge," he muttered, almost under his breath.

"What about it?" Elise asked, folding her arms.

He turned toward her, his face shadowed but adamant. "I'm heading there today. James's accident... something about the report never added up. I have a few old contacts in the local PD who might talk if I push the right buttons."

Her stomach twisted with the mention of Sterling Ridge. That name was an open wound, bleeding memories she wasn't ready to confront. "Where James—"

"Yeah," Miles interrupted, nodding. "Unless you don't want me to."

For a moment, she couldn't speak. The words tangled in her throat, fighting with fear and a desperate, gnawing need for answers. Finally, she forced them out. "No. We need to know. Just... be careful."

Miles gave a bitter smile. "Don't worry about me. I'm already on borrowed time." He tapped the pill organizer in his pocket, the pills rattling. "Might as well make it count."

Elise opened her mouth to respond, but her phone buzzed on the nightstand. She glanced at the screen, Maggie's name glowing back at her.

Daniel won't listen. He thinks optimization is the only answer. Call me. Please.

Her sister's stress bleed through the screen.

"Everything okay?" Miles asked.

"It's Maggie," she said. "She's..." Elise trailed off, shaking her head. "It's nothing."

Miles hesitated, then nodded slowly. "I'll let you know what I find." He turned for the door but stopped with his hand on the knob. "One more thing. That break-in, it wasn't random. Whoever it was …. They wanted something specific."

Elise felt her pulse spike. "What? How do you know?"

"I don't know yet," he admitted. "But I'll find out. Lock this place up tight. Don't let anyone in you don't trust."

The door clicked shut behind him, and the room felt emptier, darker. Mayor Langston's voice continued in the background, filled with promises of "optimized living" and "unprecedented progress." The words felt like oil slicks, shiny but toxic.

Elise stared at her reflection in the blackened screen of her phone. The weight of the gun on the nightstand was too much, a silent reminder of how far she had fallen from the illusion of harmony her life once pretended to be. She exhaled, forcing herself to move, to focus, to be anywhere but trapped in her head.

∞∞∞∞

Hours later, the world hadn't stopped spinning, but it felt more coordinated, choreographed almost, as she stepped into the polished sterility of the OptimumCare building. The conference room stood at the end of the hallway like a courtroom, its frosted glass hiding faces she barely recognized but knew she'd be judged alongside.

The room was brighter than it needed to be. The overhead lights bled across the polished glass table. Elise settled into a seat near the middle, her back stiff against the chair. The air held a quiet tension. Around her, glowing Aether bands pulsed softly—the lights reflecting off the table, reminding her she didn't belong. Not yet.

Grayson Powell stood at the head of the room, his Aether band glowing gold, an unmistakable badge of his superiority. His eyes cut through the room, pausing briefly on Elise. Her bare neck stood out, a glaring void in a sea of conformity.

"Congratulations to all of you," Grayson began, his voice smooth as polished steel. "You're here because you've proven yourselves as innovators, leaders, and problem-solvers. This division isn't just a new department; it's a new frontier."

He pointed to the screen behind him, where bold white text on a black background read: *Wellness Claims Solutions: Leading the Optimization Revolution.* Beneath it, an outline of objectives scrolled across: *ThriveWell Initiative Launch, Integration of Aether Metrics, Optimization Score-Based Policy Adjustments, Data-Driven Claims Processing.*

"This team," he continued, pacing the room, "will be the cornerstone of OptimumCare's future. You'll oversee ThriveWell, a program that redefines how wellness is measured, rewarded, and integrated into insurance. Necessity Mart's Aether technology allows us to track real-time metrics—sleep quality, physical activity, stress levels, and more. This will give policyholders direct control over their health outcomes."

Direct control. The phrase stuck in Elise's mind like a splinter. Control was such a simple word, so easy to disguise with layers of reassurance.

"But," Grayson added, his tone shifting slightly, "it's not just about data. It's about creating a system that encourages, and... when necessary, enforces better habits. Policyholders who meet their Optimization Scores will unlock benefits like reduced premiums and enhanced coverage. Those who don't..." He let the pause hang just long enough. "Well, there are penalties in place to ensure compliance."

His smile was warm, but his words carried an edge. Around the table, Elise noticed the slight shifts in posture. People leaning forward, some nodding with thinly veiled enthusiasm, others rigid with unspoken apprehension. Her pen hovered over her planner, the phrase *enforces better habits* etching itself into the margins of her thoughts.

Grayson's voice cut through her haze. "Each of you has been selected to lead this change. This is a unique opportunity to shape the future. But it will require adaptability, dedication, and alignment with our goals."

Elise's chest tightened as his eyes locked onto hers, the weight of his words settling like a lead blanket. He moved on quickly, but the moment lingered.

The slides shifted again, this time showcasing salary increases and perks. "Each member of this team will receive a 10% salary increase, as well as first access to exclusive Necessity Mart wellness initiatives," Grayson said.

The room erupted with mumbles of approval and a collective exhale of relief.

"Additionally," Grayson continued, his smile widening, "we'll be implementing Aether use among all team members. This isn't just a professional tool. It's personal. To lead effectively, you have to lead by example. Familiarizing yourself with the system firsthand is not optional."

The finality in his voice didn't leave much room for argument. The slide on the screen changed again, showing testimonials from Necessity Mart executives, their praises glowing as brightly as their Aether bands.

"Now," Grayson said, leaning casually against the edge of the table, "this is your chance to ask questions. Let's talk about expectations, goals, and how we're going to make this division the crown jewel of OptimumCare."

A woman near the front, her blue Aether glimmering, raised her hand. "What happens if policyholders can't meet their Optimization Scores? Will there be any flexibility?"

"Our system is designed to be supportive, not punitive," Grayson replied smoothly. "That said, the data is clear, when individuals fail to meet their goals, it's often due to a lack of engagement. The penalties are there to incentivize progress, not punish failure."

Another hand went up. "What's the timeline for implementation?"

"Great question," Grayson said. "We are looking to hit the ground running. We'll be rolling this out immediately."

Elise tuned out the rest, her pen moving idly across the planner, sketching shapes. The room buzzed with an almost intoxicating energy of progress. But beneath it was something else, something insidious, like the sound of a distant engine reviving toward an unseen cliff.

As the meeting ended, Elise gathered her things slowly, her colleagues filing out in neat pairs, their glowing Aether bands casting halos in the muted light. Her bare neck burned under an imaginary spotlight, a sign of resistance... or inadequacy.

"Elise," Grayson's voice stopped her at the door. "A moment?"

She turned, her heart sinking as he approached. His smile was weak, more predatory than kind.

"You're stepping into a leadership role here," he said. "I know you'll rise to the occasion. But to lead effectively... well, you know what's expected."

Elise forced a smile, *is this déjà vu?*

"Of course."

"Good. Let's make this a success."

As she walked into the hallway, the echo of his words followed her. This wasn't a promotion; it was a litmus test. And Elise wasn't sure if passing would save her... or destroy her.

∞∞∞∞

Elise stepped into the Wellness Claims Division like a diver entering cold water, every sense jolted by the atmosphere. The room had a mechanical vibration that seemed to emanate from the walls themselves, a background rhythm of keyboard clicks and the subtle, hypnotic pulse of glowing Aether bands. It wasn't chaos, it was order, too perfect, too polished. Rows of workstations stretched out in symmetry, each one a glowing node in the vast nervous system of OptimumCare's technological ecosystem.

Her new desk was pristine, its glossy surface reflecting the overhead lights with a sterile shine. The ergonomic chair adjusted automatically as she sat, shifting to align her posture. Elise let herself stiffen against it, her movements deliberate, cautious of surrendering even this much control.

Alan Pierce from IT hunched over her terminal, his lean frame tight with concentration. His faded graphic t-shirt and scuffed sneakers stood out in the sea of polished professionalism, but his fingers told a different story. They moved over the keyboard like a pianist playing a complex musical composition, each tap precise. The screen flickered to life under his hands, revealing a maze of data points— optimization compliance rates, real-time Aether usage, penalty matrices in bright reds and clinical greens. The dashboard danced like a heart monitor for lives under surveillance.

"ThriveWell isn't just another interface," Alan muttered, mostly to himself. His voice was almost appreciative, as though he were handling something alive.

The interface expanded, showing layers upon layers of data, pulsing like veins, pumping information through the division's collective bloodstream. Elise watched, her stomach knotting at the sheer scope of it. Lives reduced to flickering pixels, decisions and behaviors converted into numbers that decided insurance rates, benefits, futures.

Alan's phone buzzed. For a moment, his face softened, the mask of tension slipping as he answered. "Hey, Mom," he said, stepping away. "Did you take your afternoon meds? The ones Dr. Simmons prescribed?" His voice was warm, patient, a contrast to the precision of his movements just moments before. Fragments of humanity slipping through.

When he returned, the silence between them hung awkwardly. Elise noticed the absence immediately—his bare neck. It was a glaring omission in a world where Aether bands glowed like halos around nearly every collarbone.

"Getting mine this afternoon," he said quickly, his tone brittle with forced humor. "IT department mandate. 'Full system integration,' they call it." He managed a weak chuckle. "Can't support the systems if you're not part of them, right?"

She didn't answer, and he didn't wait for one. His attention returned to the screen, where the data continued its relentless dance. Client harmony scores flashed, some rising and falling in real-time like stock tickers.

"Any questions?" he asked, looking at her. His voice carried more than a polite inquiry—it was a plea, a fragile bridge toward understanding, toward something more human than the coldness of the data surrounding them.

Elise shook her head. "I think I'm good for now, but I'll let you know."

"Sounds good," Alan nodded, but his movements were too quick, as if eager to escape the moment. He grabbed his tablet and shuffled away, his shoulders tight as though carrying a weight he didn't want anyone to notice.

Left alone, Elise returned to the screen. The endless movement of data stared back at her, cold and impersonal. Each number represented a life—breaths measured, movements monitored, choices scrutinized. It all seemed so clinical, yet each calculation had the power to alter someone's reality, to dictate whether their day ended in relief or ruin.

Her eyes dropped to her hands, resting on the edge of the desk. How many small compromises, she wondered, did it take to become fully integrated? To let the machine swallow you whole, piece by piece, until the line between human and data blurred?

The pulse of the room continued around her, the soft glow of the Aether bands reflecting off the glass walls like ghostly fireflies. Somewhere, someone coughed. A keyboard clacked a little too loud. The illusion of harmony was perfect, until you listened closely.

Elise adjusted her chair manually, forcing it back from its auto-aligned position. A quiet act of rebellion, so small it felt insignificant. But even as she straightened the papers on her desk, she could feel the eyes of the system. Always watching, always waiting, for the next inch of surrender.

Work. School. Home. Different settings, same machine. Compliance wrapped in new slogans, control disguised as progress.

∞∞∞∞

The sun dipped low in the sky, bathing the glass shell of FutureReady Academy with a fleeting golden hue. Elise crept forward in the snaking pick-up line, her car crawling in sync with the vehicles ahead like part of a giant, restless organism. The school's exterior was pristine, every window polished to perfection.

Her eyes caught the bold banner near the entrance: *Partnering with Necessity Mart for a Better Future.* The slogan's cheerful confidence felt more like a command. Everywhere she looked, the logo lurked—on water bottles dangling from kids' backpacks, posters taped to the doors, even stamped onto the sides of the school's recycling bins. Necessity Mart was everywhere, its presence inescapable.

Finally, Harper emerged from the crowd, her ponytail bouncing as she trotted toward the car. Elise leaned over, unlocking the door with a distracted smile. Harper climbed in, the loud slam of the door breaking the quiet rhythm of the waiting line.

"How was school?"

"Good," Harper mumbled, already digging through her bag. "Remember I was telling you about the new program? We had an assembly today. Wish you'd been there. They talked about the Aether and how it's helping students and stuff."

Elise nodded absently, her thoughts already tangled on the day's events. Harper's voice faded into the background, blending with the low rumble of the car's engine. The lines from Grayson Powell's presentation at work replayed in her head. *Encourages better habits... incentivizes progress... enforces compliance.*

As the car idled in the school's lot, Elise pulled into a parking space to check her phone. A familiar voice cut through her haze before she could look at the screen.

"Mrs. Winters! Elise!"

She looked up to see Dr. Carmen Delgado, the school counselor, approaching with brisk, purposeful steps. Her warm smile was almost too polished, as though it had been rehearsed in the mirror.

"Do you have a minute to chat?" Dr. Delgado asked, her tone inviting but insistent.

Elise hesitated, her grip tightening on the steering wheel. She looked over at Harper, who was already absorbed in her phone. "Sure," Elise said, stepping out and closing the door behind her.

Dr. Delgado led her to a quiet corner near the entrance, her heels clicking softly against the pavement. "I just wanted to check in," she began. "I know it's been a tough year… losing James, adjusting to everything. How are you holding up?"

The question landed like a stray bullet. Elise straightened, reflexively smoothing her jacket. "I'm… hanging in there," she said. "It's been an adjustment. For both of us."

Dr. Delgado nodded, folding her hands in front of her like a therapist ready to deliver bad news. "I can imagine. And I know things can get tight financially, especially with everything that's happened. I wanted to talk to you about some options that might help."

Elise blinked, the shift in tone catching her off guard. "Oh. Um… Harper mentioned something about a scholarship program?"

Dr. Delgado's smile widened, a little too bright. "Yes! The Horizon Scholars Program. It's a fantastic opportunity for select students. Full tuition coverage, plus an Aether device to help them stay on track."

Elise forced a polite smile, though something about the phrasing prickled at her. "That does sound like a big help. Things have been… well, you know how it is."

Dr. Delgado leaned in, becoming more insistent. "You'd be surprised how involved Necessity Mart has been in programs like this. They're deeply committed to shaping the next generation, giving students the tools they need to thrive. For example, the Aether is revolutionary. They monitor academics, wellness, even social interactions, ensuring kids stay balanced in every aspect of their lives."

Elise's stomach twisted. She nodded anyway. "We've just partnered with Necessity Mart at my job, actually. Big program for policyholders. It's… a lot to keep up with."

"That's exactly my point." Dr. Delgado's eyes sparkled. "They're everywhere because they care. The Horizon Scholars Program empowers families while streamlining student success. Of course," she added with a delicate pause, "participation in the Aether program is a requirement, but the benefits far outweigh any adjustments."

Adjustments. The word clung to Elise like a cobweb. "What kind of adjustments?" she asked, unease crawling up her spine.

"Nothing major," Dr. Delgado assured her. "Students wear the Aether during school hours. It integrates with our monitoring system, tracking attendance, focus, and stress levels. It's all about their wellbeing."

Elise forced herself to nod, though the thought of Harper being constantly tracked made her chest tighten. "And privacy?"

"Absolutely," Dr. Delgado said. "The data is secure and used strictly for support. It's also a safety measure. If a child were ever in an emergency, we'd know exactly where they are."

The word *emergency* lingered, resurrecting images of the break-in at her house, the feeling of being watched.

Elise swallowed.

The thought of Harper being tracked felt both comforting and oppressive.

"Thank you, Dr. Delgado. Let me think about it."

Dr. Delgado handed her a glossy brochure, the Necessity Mart logo embossed neatly in the corner. "Take your time, but don't wait too long. Spots are limited."

As Elise walked back to the car, her thoughts tangled like headphone cords, the pros and cons knotted together in a mess she couldn't quite unravel. Each step felt heavier, as if the weight of the decision pressed down on her shoulders. The brochure in her hand seemed to pulse with the promise of solutions, but also with an undercurrent of something else she couldn't quite put her finger on.

Harper looked up from her phone as Elise slid into the driver's seat.

"What did Dr. Delgado want?" she asked curiously.

"She wanted to talk about the scholarship program."

Harper's face lit up. "So... can I do it?"

Elise gripped the steering wheel, staring out at the banner above the school entrance. *Empowering the Next Generation*, it promised in bold letters. The words felt heavy, as though daring her to make a choice she didn't fully understand.

"We'll see," she said finally.

As they drove away, Harper continued excitedly about the program, her enthusiasm filling the car. But Elise couldn't shake the shadows trailing behind her. Every decision seemed to lead closer to a future that felt less like progress and more like a trap.

∞∞∞∞∞

The drive home from FutureReady Academy crawled through the sluggish arteries of rush hour, each stop-and-go a test of Elise's patience. Her fingers tapped against the steering wheel erratically. Beside her, Harper was scrolling through her phone as if the world outside of the car didn't exist.

Billboards towered above the traffic, their glowing screens shifting and reshaping with every moment. A confident woman in a tailored suit stared down from one of them, her golden Aether band glowing on her skin like a medal of honor. The tagline beneath her flawless grin read: *Elevate Your Presence. Own Your Future.*

Elise sighed as another billboard lit up, the message pointed directly at her: *Unlock the Potential in Your Career.* The image switched, this time showing a kid grinning beside a championship robotics trophy, the caption: *Optimize Your Child's Academic Success.*

Not even the car was safe. The playlist paused abruptly, hijacked by an unskippable ad. The narrator's voice relentlessly blared through the speakers: *The Optimization Revolution is here! Are you ready to take control of your future? Join the millions already thriving with Aether.*

Elise groaned and lowered the volume. "Guess we don't get a choice, do we?" she muttered.

At the next red light, a convertible purred to a stop beside them, the driver an image of curated perfection. Designer sunglasses on her face, hair swept back in a flawless wave, and a glowing Aether band (gold, of course) hugged her neck like a trophy. Harper leaned toward the window, her eyes lighting up.

"That's like Mr. Kael!" she said, pointing.

"Mr. Kael?"

"Yeah," Harper said, nodding enthusiastically. "He runs the afterschool programs. He's always talking about how his Aether helps him stay focused. I bet she's, like, super important."

Elise looked again at the woman in the convertible, and for a brief moment, she wondered. Did the band really make a difference? Did it elevate people the way it promised, or was it just another luxurious cage?

The light turned green, and Harper turned to her with wide, hopeful eyes. "Mom, can we stop at Necessity Mart? It's right there, and they have Aether demos!"

Elise hesitated, gripping the wheel tighter. The glowing storefront ahead cast long beams of light onto the pavement, drawing customers like moths to a corporate lantern. She sighed and turned into the lot, the decision made as much for herself as for Harper.

"Alright," she said, pulling into a space.

Harper's usual pre-teen nonchalance evaporated. She bounced in her seat, her excitement spilling over as she scrambled to unbuckle her seatbelt. Elise, slower to exit, lingered by the car for a moment, taking one last look at the woman in the convertible as she sped away, her golden Aether catching the last rays of the sun.

The store glowed like a modern temple, its walls alive with endless scrolling screens. Harper ran ahead, drawn to the allure, while Elise hesitated near the entrance. There was something almost sacred about the space, an aura of devotion wrapped in commerce. Floating cases showcased Aether bands, their metallic finishes shimmering under the carefully designed lighting. Screens flickered with testimonials: radiant faces admiring the device's transformative power over careers, relationships, health.

"Mom, look at this one!" Harper yelled, pointing to a screen where a group of students smiled in front of their presentation. "See? Everyone's using them for group projects."

Elise started to respond, but the words never came out as a prickling sensation swept over her. She noticed a man standing near a display of bands. He wasn't browsing. His posture was too still. His eyes followed Harper's movements, lingering just a second too long before moving to Elise.

Her heart jumped. She turned back to Harper, brushing the feeling away. Paranoia, she thought. It's just another customer. Nothing more.

Before she could dwell, a sales associate appeared with a polished smile. Her azure Aether band glowed softly, matching the crisp blue of her uniform. "Welcome to Necessity Mart," she said warmly. "Are you two here to learn more about the Aether? Perhaps starting a mother-daughter journey to optimization?"

Elise forced a smile. "Something like that."

"Wonderful." The associate's name badge read *Sarah,* the letters shimmering in the light. "Let me show you to our interactive demo station."

Sarah led them to a row of smart mirrors embedded with augmented reality displays. She lifted a model from the floating case. "The Aether is designed to read your unique physical signature," she explained. "It optimizes posture, tracks wellness, and helps you focus in ways you didn't think possible."

She held it out to Elise. "Would you like to try it first?"

Elise hesitated, then took the band, slipping it around her neck. The soft hum pulsed against her skin, and almost immediately, her shoulders straightened. She caught her reflection in the mirror—a poised, confident version of herself, the kind of person she hadn't seen in years. Not since before James's death.

"It feels…" Elise searched for the word.

"Empowering?" Sarah suggested, her smile widening knowingly.

Harper's eyes lit up. "Can I try?"

"Of course!" Sarah handed her a student model, helping her fit it around her neck. "This version is optimized for academic performance and social coordination, perfect for someone in school."

Harper grinned as the band settled into place. On the mirror, the metrics appeared: focus, group participation, emotional balance. She turned to Elise, her excitement noticeable. "Everyone at school uses them! It'd be so good for our science fair groups."

Elise's stomach tightened. She peeked at the price tag. $899. It might as well have been $8,990. Sarah noticed the hesitation and intervened. "We offer financing options, of course. And don't forget to check if your employer has a wellness program."

Elise exhaled. "I'm familiar with that," she said. "Too familiar."

Her phone buzzed. She glanced at the screen. *Exclusive Offer. Transcend the Ordinary with Aether.*

Harper turned toward her, hope glowing in her eyes as brightly as the band on her neck. "Please, Mom?"

Sarah leaned in slightly, her voice dropping to a persuasive whisper. "The Aether isn't just a device, it's an investment. In yourself, in your family. Would you like to start your optimization journey together?"

Elise looked back at her reflection, then at Harper. She could almost hear Grayson's voice echoing. *Lead by example.* But all she felt was an ache of uncertainty, a quiet voice in her gut whispering that some investments cost more than money.

In the mirror, the numbers danced like fireflies. But behind her reflection, just past the glowing screens, she thought she saw the man again, watching. Her heart skipped, but when she turned, he was gone.

"Mom?" Harper's voice pulled her back.

"I'll think about it," Elise said softly, her words a flimsy raft in rising waters.

The store's doors sighed open as Elise and Harper stepped into the cool night air. The sensation of the glowing storefront seemed to cling to Elise's skin.. Harper bounced ahead, clutching the brochure like a prize, her words tumbling over each other as she excitedly listed the Aether band's features.

"It tracks focus! And group dynamics! And there's even this thing for emotional balance. Like, it can tell when you're stressed and helps you calm down. Isn't that cool, Mom?"

Elise nodded, her thoughts barely tethered to the moment. The day had left her mind raw and overexposed, each new piece of information piling on top of the last until everything blurred into static. She adjusted her bag on her shoulder, forcing herself to keep moving.

As they passed the store's massive windows, the glow of the screens and displays reflected their silhouettes drawing her attention. For a moment, she froze. In the glass, she saw herself and Harper, side by side, both wearing Aethers. The bands pulsed softly, perfectly synchronized, casting halos of light onto their necks. A knot formed in her throat, her chest tightening. It was like looking into a future she hadn't agreed to.

She blinked.

The reflection was normal again. The halos were gone, replaced by the harsh lights above and the muted amber glow of the parking lot. She let out a slow breath, her hand brushing against her throat as if to confirm its emptiness. She shook her head, trying to push away the lingering unease.

"I need to go to sleep," she mumbled.

"Did you say something, Mom?" Harper asked, already skipping ahead toward the car.

"Nothing," Elise replied, forcing a thin smile as she followed.

As they approached the car, Elise dug into her purse for her keys, her movements stiff. The sensation of being watched crept over her, subtle but insistent, like a shadow just outside of her field of vision. She stopped mid-step, scanning the lot.

And then she saw him.

Again.

Near the edge of the lot, in the shadows just outside of the flickering light of a dying streetlamp, stood the man from the store. He wasn't pretending to browse now. His posture was rigid, his eyes locked on them, unblinking. He didn't move. He didn't flinch. He simply stood there, watching.

"Harper, get in the car."

Harper had already opened the door and climbed into the passenger seat, oblivious to the tension strung tight in her mother's voice.

"Mom?" she called, impatient.

Elise hesitated, her hand gripping the door handle as she snuck one last look toward the man. But the space he had once stood was empty now. Just the noise of the streetlight remained, casting long, empty shadows over the asphalt.

"Mom?" Harper called again.

"Coming," Elise said, sliding into the driver's seat. Her hands trembled as she turned the key, the engine growling to life beneath her.

As they pulled out of the lot, she peeked in the rearview mirror, half-expecting to see the man standing there, watching them leave. The parking lot blurred into darkness, and there was nothing.

But the unease lingered.

As Harper resumed her chatter, Elise found herself gripping the steering wheel harder, her eyes moving between the road ahead and the shadows creeping behind them. She couldn't shake the feeling that something, or someone, was following.

∞∞∞∞∞

The house smelled like garlic and simmering tomatoes, but the warmth did nothing to settle Elise's nerves. She set the plates down, clinging to routine as if it could hold back the chaos.

Then doorbell rang, startling and unexpected. Elise barely had time to look up before Harper rushed to answer, excitement propelling her forward like a wind-up toy.

"Wait—" Elise started but the words evaporated as Harper flung the door open.

"Aunt Maggie!" Harper yelled. "Guess what? I might get an Aether. Mom says—"

"That's… great, sweetie." Maggie's voice was a weak echo of its usual strength. She bent down to hug Harper, the gesture stiff, as if her body were going through the motions while her mind was elsewhere. Her dark-circled eyes locked on Elise over Harper's shoulder, a mix of accusation and something more fragile… desperation.

"Why don't you start your homework?" Elise suggested. Harper, oblivious to the tension, skipped back to the living room, humming softly.

The kitchen felt colder as Maggie stepped inside. She looked worn. Her wrinkled cardigan was buttoned unevenly, and her hair was a mess. This wasn't the Maggie who commanded rooms at the Patchwork Society. This was someone unraveling.

Her eyes landed on the FutureReady Academy brochure sitting on the counter. She picked it up with trembling fingers, her lips tight with disapproval. "So, you're really doing this?"

Elise stiffened, her hand gripping the spoon she had been using to stir the pasta. "Don't," she said. She turned back to the stove, stirring with more force than necessary. "Not tonight, Maggie."

"I just…" Maggie's voice was hesitant as she sank into one of the kitchen chairs, her body folding on itself. "Daniel says I'm being unreasonable. That optimization is… inevitable."

"He hasn't come home for dinner in over a week. Always the same excuse. Says his Aether suggests optimal meal times that don't align with mine."

Elise stopped stirring as she turned to face her sister. "What do you mean?"

"Everything has to be perfect now. Optimized." Maggie's laugh was brittle. "Did you know they have compatibility scores for couples? Daniel's Aether keeps flagging me as a 'harmony disruption.' He actually said those words during our fight last night, like he wasn't even speaking for himself anymore."

"Jesus, Mags. Why didn't you tell me it was getting this bad?"

"Because I'm supposed to be the strong one, right?" Maggie's voice cracked. "The activist. The truth seeker. But yesterday…"

"Yesterday he said if I really loved him, I'd want to optimize our marriage. That my resistance was… selfish."

"That's not Daniel talking," Elise said gently, pulling out a chair and sitting across from her sister. "You know that's not him."

"Do I?" Maggie's fingers picked at a loose thread on her cardigan. "He tracks everything now. Sleep efficiency, conversation optimizations… Even our intimate moments have metrics. And when I object, his Aether pulses these warning colors. He says it's trying to help us achieve our best potential, but…" Her voice trailed off, her eyes staring off into nothingness.

"What are you going to do?" Elise asked, though she wasn't sure she wanted to hear the answer.

"What can I do?" Maggie's eyes filled with tears that she blinked away. "His company's making it mandatory. No Aether, no job. And now he's talking about our HOA implementing optimization requirements. We could lose everything if we don't play by their rules."

She looked up, her eyes wet. "I used to think standing against the machine was simple. Black and white. But now…"

"Now we're both compromising to protect the people we love," Elise finished quietly, her thoughts drifting to Harper.

Maggie reached across the table, gripping Elise's hands with a strength that surprised her. "Promise me something," she said. "Don't let it become your whole world, or Harper's. I see what it's doing to Daniel, how it's changing him, and I'm terrified that one day I'll wake up next to a stranger who only speaks in corporate language."

The silence that followed was heavy with fear and impossible choices. Finally, Maggie asked, "How did you do it, E? After James? How did you keep going when everything fell apart?"

Elise stared at their joined hands, her mind flashing through the sleepless nights, the hollow ache of loss, the countless moments she'd caught herself reaching for someone who wasn't there. Her voice was a whisper when she finally spoke. "Some days... I'm not sure I did."

From the living room, Harper's soft humming carried through the stillness, a fragile melody oblivious to the storm brewing in the kitchen. The sound filled the space between the sisters, gone as soon as Elise reached for it.

∞∞∞∞

Water filled the sink, suds swirling in spirals as Maggie scrubbed the plates, her motions almost hypnotic. Elise stood behind her, towel in hand, drying each plate, her thoughts looping endlessly, circling their conversation like a hawk unable to find a place to land.

Her phone buzzed on the counter, its vibration cutting through the domestic silence. Elise glanced at the screen. A text from Miles.

I've got something. Can you meet now.

Her stomach dropped. She sat down the dish towel, trying to force her voice to sound calm. "I have to run to the office."

Maggie turned from the sink, soap suds dripping from her hands. "At this hour?"

"One of my escalated claims was flagged for immediate review," Elise said, sliding on her shoes quickly, avoiding her sister's eyes. "If I don't handle it tonight, the client loses coverage tomorrow."

Maggie gripped the edge of the sink. "Can't someone else deal with it? You're always dropping everything for that job."

Elise picked up her bag, fighting the urge to argue. "It's my case. Besides, it'll be faster if I just handle it myself."

"And Harper?"

"I won't be long. An hour, tops."

Maggie sighed, turning back to the dishes. "Fine. But Elise?" She paused, her voice softening. "You can't keep doing this forever. Running yourself ragged for everyone else."

Elise hesitated, guilt twisting in her chest—not for the work excuse, but for the lie itself. "I know," she said quietly, heading for the door. She stopped briefly, her hand holding the doorknob. "Thanks, Mags."

The door closed, leaving Maggie alone in the kitchen.

∞∞∞∞

The parking lot stretched out in long slabs of asphalt, the overhead lights throwing uneven shadows between the rows of mostly empty spaces. Elise's hand gripped the wheel as the engine ticked down, her pulse matching its uneven rhythm. Two spaces over, Miles's sedan sat dark, his silhouette shifting against the glow of the BetterWay store sign.

She stepped out, pulling her coat tight against the crisp the night air.

"I thought you said this would take a couple of days?"

Miles walked with a slight limp and a black case tucked under his arm. His face was more worn in the artificial lights, deeper lines, colder eyes.

"Normally, it would've," he said. "Turns out I've got friends in low places. One of the officers on the case owed me a favor. Since the investigation's closed, they didn't mind sharing."

Elise crossed her arms. "And?"

Miles snapped the case open. Inside, James's phone rested on a bed of black foam.

"There are inconsistencies I can't shake."

Elise barely heard him. Her eyes locked on the phone, as if it might suddenly come to life.

Miles scanned the lot before continuing. "James's car was too clean for someone on a business trip. No personal items. Just his phone, his messenger bag, and a bottle of over-the-counter migraine pills."

Elise swallowed. "He got migraines sometimes, but—"

"But here's the thing… His bag was empty." Miles cut her off. "No papers, no files, nothing."

He shifted his stance, grimacing slightly. "They called it an accident. Single-vehicle crash, slick roads, maybe drowsy from the pills. But the phone—" He exhaled. "It wasn't on the dashboard. Wasn't in the console. It was carefully tucked under the driver's seat. Like it was hidden."

Elise gasped. "And nobody thought any of this was suspicious?"

"Not officially." Miles shook his head. "No foul play. Case closed."

He held the phone out to her, screen locked with a passcode prompt. "I couldn't get in. Any chance you know the code?"

Elise took the device, her fingers tingling. The passcode was burned into her memory. James used the same one for everything. Harper's birthday.

She hesitated, then typed in the numbers.

The lock screen dissolved.

"Let's see what we've got," Miles muttered, leaning in as they scrolled through the phone. His movements slowed, each flick of his fingers more deliberate. Elise's stomach twisted at the way the look on his face darkened.

Finally, he straightened, rubbing his jaw. "This isn't right."

Elise's throat tightened. "What?"

"The way this phone's been cleared."

"Someone didn't wipe everything. They were careful. Precise."

"Meaning?"

"Meaning someone went through it and decided what to leave behind." He turned abruptly, eyes scanning the lot. "We need to get somewhere more private. There's something you need to see."

A car door slammed in the distance.

They both froze.

Elise snatched the phone, her pulse hammering in her ears. The parking lot was mostly empty, but the sound had to come from somewhere. Too close.

Miles stepped toward his sedan. "Let's move."

Elise didn't argue. She just followed, gripping James's phone like it might answer all the questions clawing at her mind… or confirm her worst fears.

CHAPTER FOUR

Warranties Not Included

There are no solutions. There are only trade-offs.
– Thomas Sowell

Rain hammered against the roof, sealing them inside the car like a confession booth. The parking lot stretched empty beyond the wipers, their squeak the only sound between them. A dull glow from the dashboard lit James's phone where it sat on the center console, its presence heavier than the storm outside.

Miles hunched over, swiping through the remnants of its data, his frown deepening with every tap.

"This is interesting," he mumbled, his voice low, like the car might have ears.

Elise leaned in. "What?"

"When phones are wiped, it's usually all or nothing." He tapped the screen again. "This... was selective."

"Meaning?"

"Meaning they didn't wipe it clean... they picked what to leave."

Miles scrolled through the stripped-down contents. Texts, call logs, scattered fragments of a life. Then, he stopped.

A message about a coffee shop meeting.

A few calls.

And the last one. To Elise.

The memory punched through her, fast and merciless. James's voice, strained but steady. Complaints about his migraines getting worse. The strange, urgent *I love you* before the call cut out.

Then came the photo.

Grainy. A parking lot. A figure standing near a car, just a silhouette in the dark.

And then, the voice note.

James's voice filled the car, sounding rushed, breathless. *"If something happens... the key is—"*

The recording stopped.

Elise's grip tightened on the seat. The air inside the car felt suffocating.

Before she could speak, Miles hunched over in a coughing fit, his entire body shaking from the force. Elise instinctively reached for him.

He waved her off, but not before she caught the tremor in his fingers. Something was wrong with him. Really wrong. But the look he gave her stopped any questions before they even formed.

Instead, he straightened, exhaling. "Listen. That text. J.S. Coffee house. It's not much, but it's something. I've got a contact who can pull metadata from that photo. Maybe we can figure out where it was taken."

Elise swallowed, nodding.

"I'll start making calls in the morning. There can't be that many with those initials in the area James was working."

He tucked the phone into his jacket like an artifact. Outside, the rain thickened, turning the world beyond the windshield into a liquid blur. A distant security light flickered, just enough to catch their reflections in the glass.

Two figures, hunting for ghosts.

Elise stared at them for a long minute before whispering, "Whatever James found... someone wanted it buried."

Miles didn't answer.

Outside, the storm raged on. Somewhere across the city, Harper slept soundly, unaware that her father's last words might be the most important thing he ever said.

∞∞∞∞

Morning came like a slap.

Elise rubbed her eyes, last night's storm still rattling around inside her like a bad dream that wouldn't shake loose. The office coffee was burnt and useless. No time to sit in it. Work was waiting.

A fresh stack of claims dropped onto her desk just as she clicked *Submit* on Harper's scholarship application. The confirmation screen glowed back at her, but it didn't loosen the knot in her stomach. A necessary compromise, she told herself. If it helped Harper, if it made things easier... then it was worth it.

Her messenger pinged. Angie Mooney.

Hope you're having a good morning! Do you have a moment to chat? Just a quick wellness check-in :)

Elise felt her jaw stiffen. The smiley face felt like a knife wrapped in a ribbon.

Before she could type a response, Angie appeared at her desk, perching on the edge like a cat sizing up a mouse. Her silver Aether band pulsed softly, its light bouncing off her designer blazer.

"How are you holding up?" Her voice dipped into something meant to sound concerned, but Elise recognized the rehearsed edge. "Grayson mentioned you might be struggling with the transition."

"I'm fine, actually," Elise said, shifting files to make it look like she was busy. Through the glass walls of her cubicle, a sea of glowing Aether bands marked her coworkers like branded cattle.

"You know," Angie leaned in, lowering her voice. "An Aether would really help streamline your workflow."

Right on cue, her own band pulsed, casting a silver light across her manicured fingers.

Elise inhaled slowly. "I've reviewed the employee handbook. We can't be required to purchase technology as long as we meet performance metrics."

"Oh, honey." Angie's smile barely flickered.

"No one's *requiring* anything. We're just concerned about your ability to serve policyholders without firsthand experience. Especially in this new division."

The unspoken threat hung between them like barbed wire. Elise thought of the scholarship confirmation still glowing on her screen. Thought of Harper. Thought of the walls closing in.

She forced a smile. "It's something I'm considering. Just not in my budget right now."

"Well." Angie stood, smoothing an invisible wrinkle from her skirt. "Just remember, we all have to adapt to survive. The workload only gets heavier from here."

She paused. "I'd hate to see you fall behind."

And then she was gone, gliding away like she'd never been there at all.

Another batch of claims populated Elise's screen. A new message pinged. Amanda Singh asking to borrow a stapler.

Elise stood, stretching the tension in her shoulders. Walking over to Amanda's desk, when the disparity hit her, Amanda's stack of files was a fraction of Elise's. Manageable. *Reasonable.*

Amanda smiled as she took the stapler. Her Aether glowed warm against her skin. "Thanks. They must be easing me in slowly, new division and all," she said, catching Elise's gaze.

Her tone was casual, but there was something behind her eyes. Something knowing.

"How many cases are you handling now?" Amanda asked.

Elise swallowed. The number formed on her tongue, nearly double Amanda's workload. But she couldn't admit it out loud.

"Just keeping busy," she mumbled, sinking into her chair as another notification came to life, a silent metronome ticking toward inevitable surrender.

She let out a slow breath, fingers stiff over the keys. The screen swam— numbers, deadlines, pressure, all burning into one.

Five minutes. That's all she needed. A reset. A breath.

∞∞∞∞∞

Ness waved her over before she could think of an excuse to leave the breakroom.

"Elise! Grab a seat."

Elise hesitated, Angie's words still pressing at the edges of her thoughts. But Ness's grin was infectious, too warm, too normal in a world that no longer felt that way. She sat before she could talk herself out of it.

"You're just in time," Ness said, spinning her phone toward Elise. The Aether app glowed on the screen.

"I'm doing great on this week's Optimization Challenge. Check it out."

Elise barely heard her. Her attention drifted to the large display mounted on the wall, the *Optimization Leaderboard* she'd been trying to ignore all week.

Names scrolled past with corresponding tiers. Grayson Powell at the top with his Golden Glow, Angie right behind him.

Ness followed her eyes. "Oh, that?" She grinned. "Pretty motivating, right? They update the rankings every hour. I'm still stuck in Azure, but I'm getting there."

She swiped through her app. "See? I've been hitting 95% compliance on posture alone. That boosted my Harmony Score by three points."

A voice cut through the room.

Across the breakroom, Alan Pierce was on his phone, voice tight with barely contained frustration.

"No, you don't understand... my mother's coverage shouldn't be affected by my optimization score. The policy clearly states—"

He ran a hand through his hair. His shoulders tense.

"Can I speak to your supervisor?"

Elise watched as he ended the call, his posture slumping. He walked to the vending machine, swiped his card, hesitated, then selected a chocolate bar.

"So," Elise turned back to Ness, keeping her voice casual. "Alan eating that will hurt his score, right?"

"Oh, definitely." Ness nodded, glancing at him. "It'll register as a non-optimal choice. That affects his Harmony Score." She gestured to the leaderboard. "See? He's been stuck at Azure. He'll figure it out soon. He's smart."

Elise watched Alan unwrap the chocolate bar, his movements slow, unhurried. His Aether pulsed with a soft glow... *a warning?*

He didn't flinch. Just took a bite, chewing slowly, staring into space.

Something about it unsettled her.

"Hey, speaking of scores," Ness said, oblivious to the quiet unraveling happening at the other end of the room. "Have you looked into getting one yet?"

Elise barely heard her. Her eyes kept drifting back to Alan, to the way he sat alone, to the crumpled chocolate wrapper.

The room felt too bright. The air too thin. How had they all gotten here? When did this become normal?

"Elise?" Ness's voice pulled her back.

Elise's phone buzzed on the table. A notification flashed across the screen.

Congratulations! Harper Winters has been selected for the Horizon Scholars Program sponsored by Necessity Mart. Full tuition coverage will begin immediately upon completion of Aether device registration. Please visit the Student Services Office today between 2-5pm for device fitting and orientation.

Her stomach twisted.

"Everything okay?" Ness asked.

Elise shoved the phone into her pocket. "Yeah," she said. "Just need to leave early. School stuff for Harper."

"Oh, before you go," Ness called after her, "don't forget about the financing options! I can send you the links—"

But Elise was already gone, her footsteps echoing against the polished floor.

∞∞∞∞

Elise gripped the steering wheel, her knuckles white. The scholarship was a blessing, a chance to stabilize everything—work, Harper's education, their lives. *If Harper settles into the program, I'll finally be able to focus at work.* Saying it out loud made it feel more real, less like she was making a deal she didn't fully understand.

She pulled into the pickup loop at FutureReady Academy, scanning the thinning crowd of students. Harper stood alone by the flagpole, her backpack hanging off one shoulder, kicking at the pavement. Usually, she was laughing with friends, her voice one of the first Elise noticed. Today, she looked smaller. Quieter.

Elise parked and stepped out. "What's wrong, honey?"

Harper kept her eyes glued to the ground. "Where are your friends?"

"They're inside."

Elise crouched slightly, brushing a strand of hair from Harper's face. "Did something happen?"

Harper hesitated. Then sighed. "Some kids were teasing me in class. I got an answer wrong, and they said... they said it's because I don't have an Aether."

"What exactly did they say?"

Harper kicked her foot against the pavement. "They weren't loud or anything, but one of them said, 'No wonder she's so slow... she doesn't even have an Aether.' Then another laughed and said, 'Yeah, that explains why she's always the last one to get it.'"

Elise exhaled slowly, swallowing the words forming on her tongue. *Breathe. Don't make it worse for her.*

"I'm so sorry, sweetheart," she said. "That wasn't fair, and it isn't true. You don't need an Aether to keep up, you're already smart, already capable. Don't let them make you think otherwise."

Harper looked up at her, eyes hopeful. "Did you hear about the scholarship? Am I going to get one?"

Elise smiled, meeting her eyes. "I have good news," she said. "Your scholarship was approved. We're meeting with Dr. Delgado now to get everything sorted."

Harper's face lit up. The weight in her shoulders seemed to vanish. "Really? Does that mean I'll get the band today?"

Elise giggled, brushing imaginary dust from her pants. "It does. Let's go."

Harper practically skipped toward the school, flipping through the app on her phone, already immersing herself in the idea. *She'll fit in now,* Elise thought. *She won't feel left out anymore.*

The halls of FutureReady Academy were lined with posters of smiling students, each with an Aether band glowing at their necks. *Optimized Learning. Smarter*

Students. A Future Without Limits. The words floated there like plastic flowers in a garden.

Through the glass of Dr. Delgado's office, Elise caught a glimpse of another family inside, a young boy grinning as he fitted his Aether band around his neck, his mother nodding along as Dr. Delgado spoke.

"It's so cool!" the boy said, tilting his head to admire the glow.

Elise inhaled. *This is good for Harper. It has to be.*

Dr. Delgado stood as they entered, her smile warm as stage lights. "Congratulations, Harper!" she said, extending a hand. "You've officially been selected for the Horizon Scholars Program. We're thrilled to have you."

She turned to Elise. "And congratulations to you, Ms. Winters. All of Harper's tuition fees have been waived, effective immediately."

Elise let out a breath she didn't realize she was holding. "Thank you," she said, relieved. "This is… it's a huge help."

Dr. Delgado nodded, waving for them to sit. "Let's go over the program details."

Harper slid into the chair, practically vibrating with excitement. Delgado flipped open a folder, her tone shifting to something more structured. "The Aether will play a central role in Harper's success here. It will monitor her academic progress and integrate optimized meal plans based on her focus and energy levels."

Elise nodded, trying to focus. But something about the phrasing gnawed at her.

"It's important that Harper wears the Aether daily and follows all program guidelines," Delgado continued. "Non-compliance could affect her scholarship eligibility."

Elise's fingers twitched. "What happens if she struggles to meet the requirements?"

Dr. Delgado's smile stayed perfectly calibrated. "The Aether is designed to assist every step of the way. If Harper needs extra support, we'll work with her to ensure she stays on track."

She turned the case on her desk, flipping it open. Inside, a smaller, colorful version of the Aether band rested on a black cushion. Harper reached for it eagerly, her fingers tracing the cool, smooth surface.

"Wow," she whispered.

Dr. Delgado nodded approvingly. "Let's get this fitted."

Harper slid the band around her neck. It pulsed gently, adjusting to her posture. Her reflection in the office window showed the glow casting a soft halo against her collarbone.

Turning to Elise, Dr. Delgado handed her a tablet. "This will allow you to monitor Harper's progress in real-time," she explained. "You can track her focus, posture, and stress levels, as well as daily activity. You'll receive notifications about her weekly challenges and reminders for compliance."

Elise took the tablet, scrolling through the minimal interface. Something inside her resisted. The tracking, constant monitoring—it was almost too much. But then she looked at Harper's face, how excited she was, as she tapped through the settings.

Delgado smiled. "Harper's first assignment is simple: complete tonight's focus exercise and get a good night's sleep. The Aether will guide her."

Harper nodded eagerly. "I can't wait to try it."

As they left the office, Harper bounced ahead, turning her phone in her hands. The Aether glowed steadily against her skin. "Mom, did you see how it adjusted when I stood up straight? It's so cool!"

Elise forced a smile, trying to ignore the weight pressing in her chest. "I saw, sweetheart. You're going to do great with this."

Harper grinned, lost in the novelty, but as Elise saw her reflection in the hallway's glass, something made her stop.

For just a second.... Just a flicker. She swore she saw herself wearing an Aether, its glow matching Harper's.

She blinked.

The reflection was normal again.

Elise exhaled and shook off the moment. *Just tired. That's all.*

Harper laughed about something on her phone, oblivious to the way her mother's hands had started to tremble.

∞∞∞∞∞

By the time they got home, Elise still couldn't shake the moment.

She sat her purse on the counter, exhaling slowly as Harper tossed her backpack to the floor. Her daughter's hand went straight to the Aether band on her neck, fingers brushing its edges, like she was still trying to figure out where it ended, and she began.

"Mom," Harper said, her voice uncertain. "Can I show you something?"

Elise turned, catching the weight behind the question. "What is it?"

Harper hesitated, pulling out her phone. Her thumb hovered over the screen before she handed it over. "There's this video... Everyone at school's been talking about it."

Elise took the phone. On the screen, the caption flashed. *"Aether Glitch Goes Viral... Is Optimization Dangerous????"*

Her chest tightened as she pressed play. The footage was shaky, amateur. A busy shopping plaza, the kind of place that should have been unremarkable. Then the camera locked on a man in the middle of the frame.

He stood frozen, his Aether glowing celestial. The highest tier. But something was wrong. His movements were erratic, jerking like a puppet with tangled strings. His breathing cut through the grainy audio.

"What's wrong with him?" someone nervously asked off camera.

"Is he okay?"

The man stumbled forward, grabbing at a trash can for balance. Sweat poured down his face, soaking his shirt. His Aether flickered violently, cycling from celestial to green to an angry, pulsating red. A loud beep rang out, matching the man's growing panic.

Elise's grip tightened on the phone. She could feel Harper watching her reaction.

Onscreen, the man's hands flew to his neck, clawing at the band. His voice cracked as he screamed, "Get it off! Get it OFF!" His efforts left angry red welts, but the device didn't budge.

And then, over his cries, came the calm monotone sound of the Aether.

ERROR: DISCONNECTION ATTEMPT.

The video ended abruptly as the man collapsed.

Elise stared at the frozen frame. The phone felt heavy in her hands.

"Why didn't you show me this earlier?" she asked, her voice more aggressive than intended.

Harper shifted uncomfortably, her fingers brushing the edge of her own band. "I didn't want to scare you," she admitted. "And... I wanted to get the scholarship. I didn't want you to think it was a bad idea."

Elise lowered the phone, locking eyes with her daughter. Harper's face was a mix of guilt and calculation, like she'd weighed the risks and chosen the path that scared her the least. The maturity in it broke Elise's heart.

"Mom," Harper whispered. "Will this happen to me?"

Elise crouched, gripping Harper's shoulder gently. "No, sweetheart," she said. "That man... there must have been something else wrong. A health issue. Something we don't know."

"But what if—"

"Harper," Elise cut her off, pulling her into a hug. "You're fine. These devices... they wouldn't give them to kids if they weren't safe. Okay?"

Harper nodded, but her hands hovered near her band, her fingers tracing its edges as if testing it for cracks.

"Go start your homework," Elise said, releasing her. "I'll make dinner in a bit."

Harper nodded again, giving a small, uncertain smile before disappearing upstairs. The melodic chime of her Aether followed her footsteps.

Elise sat heavily on the couch, the phone still in her hand. The screen went dark, but the images from the video were seared into her mind. The man's desperation, his clawing hands, the band's unrelenting glow. She set the phone on the coffee table, leaning back and staring at the ceiling.

What the hell did I just sign her up for?

∞∞∞∞

Later, Elise sat at the kitchen counter, the low rumble of the refrigerator filling the silence. Her laptop screen glowed in the dim light, reflecting the lines of tension on her face. Upstairs, Harper's voice drifted down occasionally, accompanied by the sound of her Aether, syncing, guiding, optimizing.

Elise's hands hovered over the keyboard. Then she typed.

Aether malfunction viral video.

Search results flooded the screen—headlines, thumbnails, reaction videos. At the top of the page, Necessity Mart's official statement sat, its pristine branding unfazed. She clicked.

The message scrolled across the screen:

> Following yesterday's incident, we want to reassure our customers that this was an isolated, health-related event. Our thorough investigation has confirmed external contributing factors unrelated to Aether's performance. The system remains a safe, proven tool for optimization and wellbeing, helping individuals achieve their highest potential. Trust the data. Trust the process.
> Together, we thrive.

Elise rubbed her temples. The words blurred together, their calculated reassurance only fueling her unease. She scrolled the comments.

@FutureHarmony2025: *Glad to see Necessity Mart addressing this responsibly. The Aether is a tool. Its success depends on proper integration and user compliance. Optimization isn't just about technology, it's about trusting the process.*

@ResistOptimization: *Watch the video again. That band LOCKED onto him. No 'health condition' explains that.*

The comments spiraled into arguments, conspiracies, denials. Elise's eyes caught one buried deep in the chaos.

@DigitalLiberation: *How much longer until this happens to someone we know?*

She closed the laptop with more force than needed. Her hands trembled slightly as she gripped the edge of the counter. Upstairs, Harper's Aether chimed again, the sound soft but insistent, a reminder that the device was always there.

"What have I done?" Elise whispered. The kitchen, like the rest of the house, offered no answer.

CHAPTER FIVE

No Refunds

The cost of a thing is the amount of life which must be exchanged for it.
– Henry David Thoreau

The man's screams wouldn't leave her head. Elise saw him every time she blinked—clawing at his throat, his Aether flickering like a dying lightbulb, his voice raw and frantic. Even now, as she sat at her desk, her screen filled with claims and policy numbers, she felt his panic like a pulse beneath her skin.

Between every task, her fingers found themselves back to social media, searching for any mention of the video. Each time, she found less. Posts disappeared. Comments were buried under influencer endorsements, each eerily identical. Praise for Necessity Mart. Praise for Aether. As if someone was scrubbing the internet clean, sweeping the panic under a perfectly optimized rug.

Her phone buzzed. A message from Harper.

Mom! Got my Focus Streak badge! 12 hours of perfect concentration scores!

She stared at the words. Before she could type a response, another message popped up.

Ms. Bennet says I'm the fastest learner in class now. The Aether really helps.

Elise swallowed the lump in her throat and forced herself to reply.

That's great, sweetie. How are you feeling?

The response was instant.

Amazing! My neck was a little sore this morning... but the Aether adjusted itself and now it's better.

She was about to type another question when Amanda's voice cut through the office.

"I don't get these protestors," she said, leaning against the breakroom doorway, her Gold Aether glowing against her skin. "Did you hear they're planning some kind of protest at the downtown store?"

Elise shoved her phone into her pocket, turning her chair with a neutral expression. "No... I didn't."

"It's ridiculous," Ness added. "I was skeptical at first too, but I've had mine for ages now, and I've never felt better."

"Exactly," Amanda nodded. "That video going around is a total overreaction. The guy probably had some kind of condition. Necessity Mart's statement made that very clear."

The room moved like a single organism, voices overlapping in praise of the system, of progress, of the *vision*. Elise looked around, noticing how her coworkers' postures mirrored each other—backs straighter, heads higher, words flowing in a rhythm that felt too perfect.

Elise stood abruptly, grabbing her things.

The walls of the break room felt closer.

"I need to leave early" she said, her voice optimized for professional interaction.

Amanda looked up, her Aether flashing briefly. "Everything okay?"

"Harper's not feeling well," she said, the lie tasting like metallic on her tongue.

Amanda's voice softened. "Oh, of course. Has she tried the Wellness Protocol? It worked wonders for my daughters—"

But Elise was already moving, her legs eating up the carpet like a woman who knows what's chasing her isn't going to knock first.

She needed to see the protest. Needed to know if she was the only one who felt this creeping unease, or if there were others who could see the cracks forming in the illusion of harmony.

As the elevator doors slid shut, she took one last look at the office. A sea of glowing Aether bands, pulsing in perfect unison. Her own neck felt bare, exposed, as if the absence of that glow made her something *other*.

And in that moment, she wasn't sure she wanted to belong.

∞∞∞∞

The protest spilled across the plaza in front of Necessity Mart's downtown flagship store, its pristine glass windows reflecting the growing crowd outside. Elise lingered at the edge, stunned by the rage of the people who had gathered. Students waved hand-painted signs, their voices raw from chanting. Elderly couples stood hand in hand, their expressions somber, their necks bare. Parents hoisted children onto their shoulders, their small fists clutching banners that read:

"My Mind is Not for Sale."

"Optimization = Oppression."

"Think For Yourself (While You Still Can)."

From deeper in the crowd, angry voices rose in unison

"NO MORE CONTROL! NO MORE CONTROL!"

Elise's eyes caught a woman near the front, gripping a sign with shaking hands. The message was simple. "I Lost My Son to the Aether."

Their eyes met. Just for a second. But it was enough. Loss recognizes loss.

For the first time in weeks, the pressure in Elise's chest eased. *I'm not crazy. I'm not alone. Other people see it too.*

"Elise!"

She turned to see Paul from the Patchwork Society weaving through the crowd toward her. His face, weathered from years of protest, was lit with something between exhaustion and triumph. A few others followed, familiar faces from late night meetings, each one wearing the Society's signature patchwork armband.

"We got a tip about the protest," Paul said, raising his voice to be heard over the chanting. "Pulled everyone we could last minute. It's bigger than I expected. People are waking up."

Elise scanned the group, searching for one face in particular.

"Where's Maggie? This is exactly what she's been fighting against."

Paul hesitated, adjusting his armband with unnecessary focus. "She said she had… stuff to sort out with Daniel. Marriage things."

A lie. Or at least not the full truth. Elise knew it. Maggie missing *this*? It didn't add up.

Paul looked away, and before Elise could press him further, another member tugged at his sleeve, asking about the crowd's organization.

"Strange times," a quiet voice said beside her. Elise turned to see Tasha, another Society member, standing close. Her dark curls spilled wild and free around a face that had seen too much.

"Never thought I'd see Maggie step back from a fight," Tasha mumbled. "Especially not for Daniel. Have you talked to her lately?"

Elise shook her head. A bad feeling grew in her gut. Before she could answer, a ripple moved through the crowd.

Across the street, *they* appeared.

A dozen figures in pristine white clothing stepped forward, forming an unbroken line between the protestors and the store. Their Aether bands pulsed with a steady ethereal glow.

"The Ascension Order," Paul muttered, rejoining Elise. His tone was dark. "Necessity Mart's true believers. Watch yourself. They're not what they seem."

Elise studied them. The serene smiles. The unblinking stares. There was something unsettling about the way they stood… not rigid, not stiff, but *too* still. Their eyes were wrong. Glazed. Vacant, yet watchful.

A chant surged through the crowd.

WE WILL NOT BE OPTIMIZED! WE WILL NOT BE OPTIMIZED!

Elise joined in, but her attention was locked on the Order.

Then one of them stepped forward.

He was taller than the rest, his Aether burning brighter, its glow almost unnatural against his skin. He moved with an unsettling grace, hands folded in front of him as if addressing children.

"I see the chaos has drawn your attention," he said. His voice was smooth. Controlled.

Elise's skin crawled.

"Such confusion," he continued. "Such fear. You people misunderstand the gift you've been given."

The words left Elise's mouth before she could stop them. "What about the video?" she called, pushing forward. "The man in the mall. What happened to him?"

The leader turned to her. He smiled, but it didn't reach his eyes.

"An unfortunate case of resistance," he said. "When one refuses to fully embrace the system, they invite imbalance. But perfection is available to all who align."

He reached into his coat and extended a flyer toward her. Elise hesitated before taking it. The paper was heavy, expensive.

The text shimmered subtly.

The Ascension Order Invites you to explore the truth of perfection. Join us to learn how optimization frees us from the chains of chaos.

Below it, an address. And a time.

"I'm not sure I—" Elise started.

"Your hesitation is natural," the leader interrupted, his voice almost soothing. "Come, hear us out. We offer clarity."

Behind him, the protest grew louder. Someone was reading names over a loudspeaker, a list of people who had suffered 'optimization incidents.' Their voice cracked with grief.

Elise's fingers clenched around the flyer.

The meeting wasn't far. And the time—she could go. She *should* go. If Harper was going to keep wearing the Aether, Elise needed to understand exactly what they were up against.

"Welcome to your first step toward harmony," the leader said, as if he already knew her answer.

His Aether pulsed in perfect rhythm.

For a split second, the noise from the protest blurred.

Elise blinked, snapping back to reality.

The chants. The anger. The grief.

She stuffed the flyer into her pocket and turned away, her mind racing.

She didn't trust the order.

But she had to know what they were hiding.

∞∞∞∞

The protest was over.

The crowd had dispersed, voices swallowed by the city, but the energy lingered. Static in the air, a charge that hadn't found release. Elise's ears still rang with chants, her pulse still beat with the rhythm of defiance. The streets felt empty now, too quiet, the absence of bodies somehow louder than their presence had been.

She walked without thinking, cutting through side streets, the crumpled flyer still in her pocket. Each step felt heavier, her mind replaying the leader's voice, the eerie way the protest had seemed to dull when he spoke.

A café came into view, its warm glow spilling onto the sidewalk. She pushed inside. A handful of customers lingered at tables. Normalcy. Or something close to it.

She ordered a coffee, her voice coming out steadier than she felt. As she waited, she pulled out her phone, scrolling instinctively. The protest had already been reduced to clips, dissected in real time. Edited footage painted the crowd as unruly, misguided. A few accounts claimed agitators had turned violent.

Lies, all of it.

Her fingers hovered over the screen. She wanted to say something. Call it out. But what was the point? The truth didn't seem to stick anymore.

The barista called her name, and as she grabbed the cup, she felt it again.

That *feeling.*

Like being watched.

She turned, scanning the café. No one looked at her. No one seemed out of place. And yet, the unease curled in her stomach like a whisper she couldn't quite hear.

She took a slow sip of the coffee, then pulled the flyer from her pocket, smoothing it against the table. The address gleamed under the café lights.

The Ascension Order invites you to explore the truth of perfection.

She exhaled.

She needed answers.

And she knew exactly where to get them.

∞∞∞∞

Elise's phone buzzed just as she reached the address from the flyer.

A message from Maggie.

Just leaving the Necessity Mart protest. Going to pick up Harper. Can you come get her at the Patchwork Society?

Elise stopped cold.

The lie was so blatant, so careless, it might as well have been a slap. I was at the protest. I looked for you. Maggie hadn't been there. Not in the crowd, not on side streets, nowhere.

Her fingers hovered over the screen, heart hammering. She typed, *Sure, I'll head over soon. Wrapping up at work.* Lies stacked on lies. She wanted to call, demand the truth, but she didn't have time for confrontation. Not yet.

The Ascension Order meeting was about to begin. And Elise needed answers more than she needed an argument.

She pocketed her phone and looked up.

The building stood out in all the wrong ways.

Wedged between a high-rise and a vacant storefront, it shouldn't have felt imposing, but it did. It was too clean. Too untouched. A glass entrance reflected only by darkness, as if the city itself refused to acknowledge what was inside. The only marking was an ∞ symbol etched into the door.

She pushed inside.

The world shifted.

Everything about the space was designed to unnerve in ways you couldn't quite name. The lighting was soft but calculated. And the silence. It wasn't empty. It was expectant.

Elise moved down a hall that seemed longer than the building should allow, her footsteps swallowed by thick, seamless floors. The walls were too smooth, as if no one had ever touched them.

She wasn't alone.

Others walked ahead of her, their movements slow, no one rushed. They wore white, immaculate, unblemished, as if nothing in their lives had ever been out of place. Some had Aether bands already glowing, their lights pulsing in quiet synchronicity.

Others, newcomers, like her, walked with hesitation.

The hallway opened into a vast chamber. It had the bones of an old cathedral. Arched ceilings, grand architecture. But the soul had been sucked out. Rows of white chairs stood where pews should have been.

As she was taking it all in, he entered.

The leader from the protest.

In here, he was more unsettling than Elise had realized. Taller. Stretched, almost unnatural. As if he had been carved rather than born. His white robe shimmered in the light, shifting with every step. But it was his Aether that drew the eye. It didn't just glow, it radiated, casting an almost liquid sheen over his skin.

He raised his hands in welcome.

"The Algorithm knows you," he said. His voice was smooth, reverent. "True freedom lies in alignment."

The congregation responded in eerie unison, heads bowing, their Aethers pulsing together in slow, hypnotic waves.

Elise swallowed, trying to keep her expression neutral.

"The recent *glitch* some call an error..." the leader continued, "... was no mistake." He smiled as if sharing an inside joke. "It was justice. A system doing what it was designed to do. Rewarding harmony and punishing chaos."

A ripple of approval moved through the crowd, quiet and unquestioning.

Then came the confessions.

One by one, members stood, their voices trembling with shame. Not for sins, but for failing their Aether.

"I ignored my meal suggestions," a man admitted. "I paid for it with migraines."

"I questioned my sleep optimization," a young woman whispered, clutching her band. "I thought I knew better. But resistance only brings suffering. The Algorithm sees what we cannot."

Elise's skin prickled.

The ceremony followed. A symbolic act of submission.

One by one, the members deactivated their Aether bands. The room dimmed for a moment, a breath of darkness. Then, in perfect unison, they reactivated. A synchronized pulse of light filled the space, as though the system had breathed them back to life.

The leader smiled. "See how beautiful harmony can be?"

The air felt thicker.

This wasn't enlightenment. This wasn't peace. This was something else.

Elise got up, easing toward the exit. The room felt smaller, the walls pressing in.

The leader's voice followed her.

"Remember," he said, "resistance breeds the pain you fear. Surrender brings peace."

The words crawled under her skin.

She stepped back into the hallway, the cool air hitting her like a wake-up call. Her pulse slammed against her ribs as she walked faster, pushing through the front doors and back into the night.

Her phone buzzed.

Another message from Maggie.

Harper's asking for you. Everything okay?

Elise exhaled, gripping the phone so tight her knuckles ached.

She looked down at the crumpled flyer still clutched in her other hand. The shimmering text no longer looked elegant. It looked like a warning.

Those who couldn't be controlled by force might yet be seduced by the promise of perfect peace.

And Maggie, who once fought against everything the Ascension Order represented, was nowhere to be found today.

She quickened her pace, walking toward the one place she knew Maggie *should* have been. The people she should have been alongside.

She needed answers.

And she was done waiting for them.

∞∞∞∞

The Patchwork Society buzzed with post-protest energy, the air heavy with conversation, ink, and exhaustion. Voices bounced off the exposed brick walls, tangling with the scent of drying paint and permanent marker. Half-finished banners sprawled across the battered wooden tables, slogans written in bold, angry strokes. Near the community board, Paul pinned up polaroids from the demonstration, as others tossed out ideas with the urgency of people who had seen too much to stop now.

"Weekly protests," Michelle called from the back. "We need to keep the pressure on."

"Social media campaign," someone else said. "Show people what real resistance looks like."

Elise stood just inside the doorway, her pulse still offbeat from the Ascension Order meeting, from the unease that clung to her like a second skin. She spotted Harper across the room, oblivious to the storm brewing around them. The soft blue glow of her Aether pulsed against a pile of fabric squares, lighting up the unfinished quilts. Each pulse was like an accusation in a space built to fight everything it represented.

"Well."

Tasha's voice cut through the room like a blade. She sat by the window, silver needle catching the light as it wove through fabric. She looked at Harper, then back to Elise, the ghost of a smirk on her lips.

"Look who finally graced us with their presence."

The room quieted. Not completely, but enough.

Tasha gestured lazily with her needle toward Harper. "Bold move, bringing that thing in here while playing resistance. Hypocrite much?"

Across the room, Maggie stiffened.

Elise barely noticed. Her focus locked onto her sister, the weight of everything crashing down at once.

"The protest?"

"You were there?"

Elise's jaw clenched. "Funny you should ask, since you told me you were too." She crossed the room, keeping her voice low. "We need to talk. Outside. Now."

The alley was cold and quiet.

Before Elise could say a word, Maggie looked around then let out a shaky breath, staring at the cracked pavement like it held the answers. "I got an Aether."

Elise blinked. "You what?"

"Last week."

Her mind spun. Maggie. The same Maggie who had built the Patchwork Society from the ground up, who had stood against Necessity Mart at every turn, was wearing one of *their* devices?

Maggie wrapped her arms around herself. "Daniel thought—"

"Daniel thought?" Elise let out a humorless laugh. "The same Daniel who's been trying to kill everything you built here? That Daniel?"

"You don't understand. He threatened to leave me, Elise!"

"You weren't there for the fights, the silence, the way he looked at me like I was losing my mind."

Her fingers brushed her collarbone, an unconscious motion.

Elise felt sick to her stomach. "Maggie, tell me you're not wearing it right now."

Silence.

"Jesus Christ, Maggie."

"I would never wear it here," Maggie whispered.

She lifted her chin. "You compromised too."

"It's not the same."

"Isn't it? You let Harper wear one. You signed the papers. You stood by while they fitted it around her neck. And I get it... you did it for her future. But don't you dare act like you're standing on higher ground."

Elise shook her head. "You're lying to them." She pointed toward the building. "To us."

"Because I needed to figure this out on my own."

"And what exactly are you figuring out?" Elise demanded. "How to be a double agent?"

Maggie didn't answer.

A creak of footsteps cut through the tension.

Paul.

He stood at the alley entrance, his expression carefully neutral.

"Everything okay out here?"

Maggie's face was red. "Paul, how long have you been standing there?"

Paul took a slow step closer. "Long enough."

A suffocating silence stretched between them.

Finally, Paul exhaled. "Let's go inside. We have bigger things to focus on."

Back in the main room, Harper sat cross-legged in the children's corner, stitching a quilt square with careful concentration. Elise's stomach twisted as she watched her daughter's Aether pulse softly against the fabric. A glowing contrast to the resistance woven into every stitch.

Paul cleared his throat, cutting through the tension. "We need to discuss Project Harmony."

Heads turned. Eyes stopped blinking.

"Our sources indicate it's more than just a 'community wellness initiative.' We have reason to believe it's an extensive surveillance network, designed to monitor and control entire neighborhoods."

"They're already installing Hestia Hubs in the new developments," Tasha added, her needle never stopping. "Once they're in, they can track everything."

Elise felt like the air had been sucked from the room. Surveillance. She thought of Harper's school, her every movement logged, her sleep monitored. The Aether adjusting itself.

She turned back to Harper, who was standing now, clutching something to her chest. "Look what Aunt Maggie made for me!"

Elise forced a smile as Harper held up the quilt.

Mismatched squares stitched into something chaotic yet beautiful. A bird breaking free from a cage. A tree, its roots and branches stretching beyond the frame. Abstract swirls of movement, of resistance.

The border stitches were still fresh.

Maggie's stitches.

Elise knelt, running her fingers over the fabric.

"It's beautiful, sweetheart. Aunt Maggie really outdid herself."

Harper smiled.

Elise looked over Harper's shoulder, her eyes meeting Maggie's across the room.

Love. Guilt. Betrayal. Understanding.

It passed between them in an instant. A silent admission that neither of them knew how to win this fight anymore.

Elise stood, taking Harper's hand. "Let's get you home."

Harper held her quilt close, her Aether casting a soft glow across its defiant patterns.

The irony wasn't lost on Elise.

Even this symbol of rebellion had been tainted by the system it resisted.

Just like all of them.

∞∞∞∞

The front door latched shut behind them, the sound brittle and quiet. Elise watched Harper as she moved through the kitchen. Same place, same routine, but something was wrong. Her daughter moved with eerie precision, each motion crisp, automatic. Bag on the counter. Cabinet open. Glass filled. A sequence performed without thought. The soft blue glow of the Aether on her neck pulsed against the counter as she drank, her posture perfect, fingers curled in an unnervingly measured grip.

"Harper." Elise barely recognized her own voice. She softened, taking a breath. "Sweetie, take off the Aether for the night."

Harper froze mid-sip, water trembling against the glass. "Why?"

"Because this is our home," Elise said, stepping forward. "No scores. No optimization. Just us."

67

Harper held her ground. "I'm in the middle of my Evening Focus sequence. If I stop now, my sleep score—"

"I don't care about your sleep score." The words landed before Elise could filter them. She softened, but stayed firm. "I care about you. The real you. Not some optimized version."

Harper's face twisted. "This *is* me," she screamed, fingers brushing the band around her neck. "The Aether helps me. I was top of my class in science today. Even Jessica wants to work with me now."

"And what happens when you're not perfect?" Elise took a step closer. "What happens when you have to think for yourself?"

Harper jerked back, her hands flying to her Aether as Elise reached for it.

"Don't!" Her voice cracked. "If I take it off, my Harmony Score drops. I'll get moved to a lower group. Everyone will know."

Elise clenched her jaw. "Listen to yourself. You're twelve, Harper. You shouldn't even have a Harmony Score."

"When you were twelve, Mom," Harper replied, eyes glassy with tears, "you didn't have to beat perfect kids! You don't understand. The Aether makes everything easier. Why do you want to take that away?"

The band at her neck pulsed slightly. Harper's breathing calmed, regulated. A programmed response to emotional distress. Elise's stomach twisted.

"This isn't up for debate," she said. "While you're in this house, the Aether comes off. Period."

Harper stared at her. Then, with slow, burning rage, she ripped the band from her neck and stormed toward the door.

"Where are you going?" Elise demanded.

"Ethan's." Harper grabbed her jacket. "His mom understands optimization."

The door slammed hard enough to rattle the windows. Elise watched from behind the glass as her daughter disappeared into the Suarez's house. Hannah Suarez greeted her at the door, her own Aether casting a golden glow in the night.

Elise let her go.

The Suarez's house was visible from the kitchen window. Right now, she needed a minute. To breathe. To think. To remember the way Harper used to be, before every second of her life was scored, tracked, controlled.

She stared at the empty space where Harper had stood, where the glow of the Aether had reflected off the counter.

"What would you do, James?" she mumbled into the quiet.

He would've made a joke. He always knew how to reach Harper, even in her worst moods. But those days were gone. James was gone. And Harper... Elise wasn't sure who she was becoming.

Maybe the Aether wasn't just about school. Maybe it was something to hold onto. A system to replace the stability they lost when James died.

Elise shut her eyes.

The thought made her chest ache.

∞∞∞∞

Elise moved fast, the night closing in like a held breath. The Suarez house towered ahead, tall, rigid, untouched by time. Its sterile glow bled into the darkness, a cold divide from the comfortable chaos of her own home. The Hestia Hub emblem shimmered in the entryway, an ever-present reminder that inside, everything was monitored, measured, adjusted.

The door swung open before she even knocked. Hannah Suarez stood at the door, polished, as if expecting to be on a magazine cover. Her smile was a little too even, her eyes a little too bright. The house adjusted instantly to her presence, the lights shifting, temperature recalibrating, an invisible algorithm whispering what was optimal.

"Elise!" Hannah's voice gave off a curated warmth. "Come in, come in. The kids are in the den. Rob, honey, look who's here!"

Elise stepped inside, feeling the shift in the air. It was like walking into a staged set, every detail designed to project seamless harmony. Rob was at the kitchen island, scrolling his tablet, his golden Aether pulsing.

"Hey, Elise," he said without looking up. "Keeping up with those harmony scores?"

"Actually—" Hannah interrupted. "We just upgraded our Hub."

She swiped through the control panel on the wall. Barely able to contain her excitement. "Watch this."

She swiped again, and a gentle voice filled the space.

Dinner preparation mode initiated. Calming ambiance activated.

A soft chime followed, and the lighting shifted, washing the room in warm neutrals.

Rob sighed, setting his tablet down. "Honey, maybe Elise isn't here for a product demo—"

"Of course she is," Hannah interrupted again. "Who *isn't* interested in optimization?" She gestured around them like she was revealing a grand estate. "Our household harmony is at ninety-three percent."

Rob's laugh was tight. "Holding at eighty-seven for couples' harmony. The Hub says we could push it higher if someone stopped overriding the morning routine settings."

Hannah's smile disappeared.

"We don't talk about that week, dear. It wasn't... optimal."

The Hub chimed again.

Attention: Group tension detected. Initiating harmonic lighting sequence.

The lights dimmed. A chill ran through Elise.

In the den, Harper sat beside Ethan, surrounded by perfectly aligned school supplies. Her Aether was gone, her neck bare, and yet she sat unnaturally still, back straight, shoulders squared. She wouldn't meet Elise's eyes.

"We noticed Harper's not wearing her Aether," Hannah said lightly, the concern in her voice as artificial as the smart lighting. "Is everything alright? The Hub has been suggesting specialized study arrangements, but it works best when both kids are properly integrated."

Elise felt the pressure in her chest tighten.

"She's taking a break."

Rob chuckled, though there was no humor in it. "A break? That's like taking a break from running water." He looked at Hannah. "Remember when you tried that?"

Hannah's fingers twitched at her side. "We don't—"

"Talk about that week," Rob finished with a smirk.

Elise's patience snapped. "Harper," she called. "Time to go."

Harper hesitated. "Mom, we're in the middle of—"

"Now."

Harper exhaled loudly but stood, clearly annoyed.

As she grabbed her jacket, Hannah leaned in close. "We're hosting another optimization gathering next week. You should come. The neighborhood's so close to qualifying for Elite Unity status. With your buy-in..." She let the words hang, her meaning crystal clear.

"Thanks, but—"

The Hub chimed again.

Reminder: Couples' optimization session scheduled for 8 PM. Attendance is recommended for optimal harmony maintenance.

Hannah laughed, but the sound was weak, strained. "Always keeping us on track, isn't it? We haven't missed a session in months. Not since the... incident."

Something cold slithered down Elise's spine.

"We should go," she said, steering Harper toward the door.

As they stepped out, the Hub spoke again.

Farewell. Current household harmony: Eighty-nine percent. Decline noted. Adjusting parameters.

The door sealed behind them with quiet efficiency. Elise exhaled, gripping Harper's shoulder as they walked back into the night.

Her phone vibrated.

Miles.

Can't reach your secure line. Need to talk now. Parked down the block, running lights on. Important.

Elise's heart jumped. Miles wouldn't come here unless it was serious.

"Harper," she said carefully, scanning the street. "I need to make a quick work call. Head home and start your reading. I won't be long."

Harper hesitated. She peered back at the Suarez house, its soft, welcoming glow spilling onto the pavement, the promise of order and certainty lingering.

"But, Mom—"

"Not up for discussion."

Harper's shoulders dropped, but she turned, stomping toward their house. Elise waited until she was inside before heading toward Miles's idling car, her thoughts racing.

She slipped into the passenger seat, the cracked leather cool against her skin. The glow from Miles's phone lit his face, highlighting the exhaustion settling in the lines around his eyes.

"I found J.S. Coffee House," he said, voice rough. "Juniper & Sage. Riverside Heights. Matches the timeframe of James's last known movements." He coughed into his sleeve. "Took some convincing, but I got access to the security archives."

He handed her his phone. "Watch carefully. Tell me if you recognize her."

Elise pressed play.

The footage was grainy, but it was James. No mistaking him. She sucked in a breath as he sat at a window table, messenger bag closed, barely touching his coffee.

"There," Miles pointed. "12:30 PM."

A woman appeared. Dark coat. Knit hat. Purposeful steps. Her face was obscured, but something about the way she moved screamed of nervous control.

"Do you know her?"

Elise shook her head, gut twisting as James reached across the table, touching the woman's hand. A brief, intimate gesture. Then the exchange, an envelope from James, a folded note from her.

Miles fast-forwarded. "Now, watch him."

James alone. Agitated. Rubbing his temples. The same headaches. Then his abrupt departure, disoriented, unsteady.

"But that's not all," Miles muttered. He scrubbed the footage forward. "Look who shows up next."

A man in a baseball cap entered. Casual, but not too casual. Scanning the table James had abandoned. He checked beneath it, inspected the coffee cup, and snapped a photo before leaving.

"Professional," Miles said.

Elise's fingers went cold. "Miles... what is this?"

"James was into something bigger than patent law." Miles rubbed a hand down his face. "We need to find that woman. She's the key to all of this."

Something shifted in his expression. His eyes quickly moved to his rearview mirror.

"Miles?"

"Don't react," he said. "There's a car parked down the block. Dark sedan. No plates. Engine just turned on."

The air caught in Elise's throat.

"What do we do?"

"You get out. Walk home. Don't look back."

He hesitated, then added, "And Elise... be careful who you trust. That woman wasn't the only one being watched that day."

She pushed open the door, stepping out into the cold.

Somewhere behind her, a car door shut.

She turned, but Miles was already pulling away, leaving her alone on the sidewalk with the creeping certainty that someone... *something*... was watching.

CHAPTER SIX

Terms and Conditions

By signing this, you're essentially selling your
soul to the corporate machine.
– Unknown

Elise stepped into the communal space, and the office felt different. Charged. The air carried a low vibration, like a barely audible frequency worming its way into her bones.

OptimumCare had always been pristine—soft white walls, abstract art designed to be inoffensive, a scentless hum of air purification. But now, something had changed. The balance had tipped from clean to clinical, from welcoming to waiting.

Workers in Necessity Mart uniforms rushed around, installing what Elise could only describe as living technology. Metallic floor panels glowed, rippling as if they were breathing. Overhead, recessed lighting pulsed in perfect timing, an artificial heartbeat syncing with the floor below. It was all in rhythm, the room an organism, subtly dictating the movements of those inside it.

The Necessity Mart logo glowed in the ceiling's corner. Its tagline etched beneath in smooth, sterile letters. *Optimized Space—Recharge. Reset. Refocus.* Elise slowed her steps as she passed a technician fine-tuning a futuristic looking bench. Across the room, another worker adjusted a cube in the corner labeled *Hestia Integration Unit.* A holographic display hovered above it, scrolling through metrics. *Environmental Optimization. Device Charging Efficiency.*

"Impressive, isn't it?"

Elise turned to see a coworker holding a mug of tea, his Aether glowing softly at his throat. He nodded toward the Hestia. "That's an Ambient Charging Zone. Just sit there, and it powers your Aether automatically. No cords, no hassle."

"No plugs?" Elise asked skeptically.

"None," he said, sipping his drink with a smile. "See that?" He pointed toward the glowing cube. "That's the Hestia Hub. Syncs with everything... energy flow, environmental conditions, even us."

Elise forced a polite nod, but beneath it she felt sick. *Even us.*

She glanced toward the new benches, watching her coworkers settle in, their Aethers pulsing in harmony. The air itself felt different. Clinging to her skin like static before a lightning strike. A thought lodged itself in the back of her mind.

They're making it impossible to exist outside their reach.

At her desk, the weight in the office felt heavier. Conversations clustered near the charging zone. Quiet laughs exchanged over rising optimization scores.

Elise's eyes landed on Ness, standing confidently in the group. Her Silver Resonance flickered, a subtle flex that she'd leveled up.

Elise swallowed, an uneasy tightness spreading in her chest.

As she passed the group, their voices lowered, just enough that she knew the whispers were about her.

"How is she managing without one?"

"I don't think she's even trying."

"It's just... weird at this point, isn't it?"

Her bare neck burned. It wasn't just the lack of an Aether. It was what it meant. It was noncompliance.

Elise pushed into the breakroom, gripping her coffee mug.

Across the room, Ness now sat at a table, scrolling through her optimization dashboard. The glow of her Aether reflected on her face, casting delicate silver streaks along her cheekbones.

Elise leaned against the counter and gestured toward the charging zone.

"So, do we have to pay extra to breathe in here now, or is that included in the optimization package?"

Ness looked up. Her lips curved, but it was hardly a smile.

"You know, Elise," she said lightly. "Jokes like that? They're why I can't afford to hang around people who aren't optimized anymore. It tanks my alignment metrics."

Elise blinked. People who aren't optimized. Not coworkers. Not even friends. Just variables dragging down her score.

She forced a smile. "Come on, Ness, I'm just—"

Ness looked back at her screen. She tapped once, cutting Elise off mid-sentence. Then she stood and nodded toward the group by the charging zone.

"I'm going to sync with the team."

Ness pushed back her chair but didn't leave. Instead, she turned toward the coffee station, reaching for the pot of their usual blend.

Elise watched as Ness started to pour. Then stopped.

A low tone emitted from the Aether, barely audible, like a whispered warning. Her free hand twitched toward the device, hesitating just below the smooth band at her neck.

A second beep, more insistent. Ness stiffened.

Elise didn't move.

She watched as Ness slowly set the coffee pot back. Her movements were controlled now, too careful, like someone overriding their own instincts. She reached for something else instead.

A fresh bag.

OptiBlend: Harmony Roast—Perfect for Focus and Clarity.

The Necessity Mart packaging shined under the breakroom lights. She mechanically poured the pre-approved blend into her mug.

Then took a slow sip, and something in her shifted.

The tension in her body unraveled instantly. Her posture adjusted, her breathing evened out, like a reset program completing its cycle. The glow of her Aether returned to a soft, steady silver.

Elise felt something crack inside her.

The nausea that had been circling in her gut swelled.

Her eyes darted to the other employees. No one reacted. No one noticed.

Ness's trembling hands. The way her posture *snapped* back into place. The way the device regulated her.

They had seen it happen. They just didn't *see* it.

Elise's heartbeat ticked up. *Am I really the only one noticing this shit?*

She sat her coffee down and turned for the door, her heels clicking against the tile, louder than the quiet rhythm of the office.

Behind her, Ness returned to her desk, smiling, as if nothing had happened at all.

As if there had never been a moment of hesitation.

As if she had never doubted at all.

But Elise had seen it.

And now, she couldn't unsee it.

∞∞∞∞

The office swallowed sound at this hour. The glow of Elise's screen was the only light left in the communal space, casting sharp angles across the stacks of flagged Aether claims piling up on her desk. The numbers blurred as exhaustion gnawed at the edges of her focus, but she forced herself to keep going. There was something here. Something beneath the paperwork and corporate jargon. She just had to find it.

Then she heard it. A name, drifting low across the office.

Her name.

She blinked, shoulders tensing. Lifted her head.

Angie's glass-walled office was a stage, perfectly curated for dominance. It offered little privacy, but she wielded it like a throne, making sure everyone saw what they were supposed to see. Angie stood near her desk, speaking in hushed tones to another HR rep, one of those interchangeable, perfectly optimized employees who never seemed to blink too much or stand the wrong way. The colleague nodded, arms folded, as Angie waved her hands around.

Elise didn't mean to listen. Didn't want to. But then—

"Elise Winters."

Cold. Clipped. Irritated.

Elise forced herself to move, rising from her chair as if she were just stretching, just getting a refill. She made her way to the coffee station slowly, her hands light, her posture easy, every step calculated, as if trying to maintain invisibility.

"She's a liability." Angie's voice, stripped of its usual syrup. *"Still dragging her feet on optimization, and it's affecting morale. Grayson's noticing too."*

A hollow crack echoed through Elise's skull.

The coworker mumbled something in response.

Elise only caught the tail end.

"... You think she's going to make it?"

Angie sighed. A sound of irritation. *"We'll see. For now, she's on thin ice. Grayson's not going to keep cutting slack for someone who isn't a team player."*

The words slid under Elise's skin.

She kept her movements steady, adjusting the coffee machine like it was the most interesting thing in the world. But her hands wouldn't stop trembling. She turned away before they could see.

Back at her desk, the glass walls felt smaller, more like an exhibit than an office. No protection. No soundproofing. Just walls of transparency, eyes, and whispers pressing from every angle.

Elise clenched her jaw and forced the anger down. If they were watching her, she'd give them a reason to look closer.

She buried herself in flagged Aether claims, pushing through fatigue, combing through the data until patterns emerged. Denied claims, always marked with the same vague reason: *non-compliance.* But beneath the surface, another story. Users reporting the same symptoms—migraines, vertigo, neural instability. Their complaints were dismissed, buried.

One name kept appearing.

Jamal Beckford.

A former Necessity Mart employee. A problem they tried to erase. His repeated reports of severe side effects told a story the company didn't want to know. His claim had been denied without reason, and Elise knew, without a doubt, it was intentional.

The phrase from Angie's mouth looped in her head. *Liability. Thin Ice.*

Fine.

If they wanted to call her a liability, she'd become one.

∞∞∞∞

The office was a tomb now. The last whispers of life had drained out hours ago. Elise reached for her phone, keeping it low beneath her desk as she typed.

Mr. Beckford, I'm reviewing your claim at OptimumCare. There are things we need to discuss. Privately. Can we meet?

Her thumb hovered over the send button. This was it—the point of no return. She thought of Harper. Thought of Maggie. Thought of the man in the viral video, clawing at his own throat while the Aether refused to let go.

She pressed send.

The reply came right away.

Who is this? How did you get this number?

Elise typed quickly.

Someone who needs to know the truth about the Aether. I'm reviewing your claim at OptimumCare.

A long pause. Then—

I signed an NDA. I can't talk about that.

Elise felt her pulse against her ribs.

People are getting hurt. Like you did. I just need to understand what happened.

The typing dots appeared. Stopped. Appeared again.

They're watching.

She didn't hesitate. *I know. That's why I need your help.*

Another pause. Longer this time. The silence stretched so thin she almost wondered if he had disappeared.

Then...

I can't. I'm sorry. It's just not safe.

Her grip on the phone tightened. She swallowed, thinking of what to say.

My daughter has one now. At school. Please. I need to know what we're up against.

Minutes passed. Too long. She stared at the screen until her eyes burned. Then...

Public park by the library. Noon tomorrow. If I see anyone else, I'm gone.

She quickly typed, *Okay. I will be there.*

Elise deleted the thread and set her phone down, exhaling slowly. The office felt colder. Her reflection in the glass walls looked smaller, swallowed by the space around her.

She had crossed a line.

Now she had to see how far she could go before they pushed back.

∞∞∞∞

The drive home was quiet. Not the peaceful kind.

Harper sat in the passenger seat, her face bathed in the glow of the Aether wrapped around her neck, its pulsing light too steady, too calculated. She scrolled through something—metrics, probably. Scores she wouldn't have cared about months ago. Elise gripped the wheel, resisting the urge to say something. To break the silence. But she wasn't sure which version of her daughter would answer.

The takeout bag rustled beside her, the smell of greasy, perfectly charred beef filling the car. Harper's favorite. Well, before at least. Before every bite was measured. Before a machine told her what her body needed. Before she started looking at food like a formula instead of something she used to love.

Elise pulled into the driveway, the headlights sweeping across the porch. Harper didn't move right away. Just stared down at her screen, the Aether's glow catching her lashes. Then, as if on cue, she straightened, shoulders back, spine aligned, the way the device had trained her.

Elise killed the engine, the rumble cutting off mid-breath. She reached for the takeout, intentionally crinkling the bag, breaking the silence. "Brought your favorite," she said, keeping her tone light. "Double bacon cheeseburger. Extra fries."

Harper hesitated. Then, carefully, she unbuckled her seatbelt and opened the door without a word.

Elise watched her daughter walk up the steps, posture perfect, movements robotic. Like she was being graded.

The house felt too still when they stepped inside. Elise set the takeout on the kitchen counter, but Harper stood a few feet away, arms crossed.

"Aren't you hungry?" Elise asked, pulling the food out of the bag.

Harper's fingers grazed her Aether. "The ratios are off," she mumbled.

Elise's jaw tightened. *Here we go.*

"It's just a burger, Harper." She forced a smile, while unwrapping her own. "You used to love these."

Harped stared down at the food like it was something foreign. "I should be having grilled chicken." A pause. Then, quieter, like an echo of something she's been told. "The Aether says I need better macros."

Elise set her hands on the counter, slow and steady, like she was dealing with a wild animal she didn't want to spook. "You don't need a machine to tell you what you like, Harper."

Harper's face twitched. Some kind of war between recognition and resistance. But the Aether pulsed again, soft, insistent, a whispering metronome against her skin. She exhaled, then moved her attention to her phone.

Elise clenched her teeth.

Something was winning inside her daughter.

And it wasn't her.

"Anyway, you know the rule, Harper. You need to take that Aether off."

Elise didn't move, didn't breathe. The air between them had thickened. Harper's fingers hovered at her neck, reluctant, like she was peeling away a second skin.

"But Mom—"

"I'm not doing this with you."

"This is our time together. And you need a break."

Harper's expression twisted. Then, like something snapping inside her, she slammed her palms onto the table. "You don't understand."

Her breaths came quick, uneven.

"Sophie had a seizure today!"

Elise froze. The words hit with the weight of something irreversible

"What?"

"In math class," Harper's voice was shaky, the fight suddenly gone from her. "She was fine. And then she wasn't. Her Aether started making this weird sound, and she—" She swallowed, blinking fast. "She couldn't stop shaking. Dr. Delgado ran in, but—"

Elise set her food aside, appetite vanishing. "Did they call an ambulance?"

Harper shook her head. "No."

"These men in suits showed up first. They took Sophie to the nurse's office. Made everyone delete the videos from their phones."

The room felt colder.

"And Sophie?"

"They said she had a history of seizures. That it *wasn't* the Aether. That we have nothing to worry about." Harper stared down at the food like she couldn't remember why it was there. "But, Mom... she was fine before. She was always fine."

Elise's grip on the table tightened.

"Sweetheart, that's exactly why I want you to take a break." She tried to keep her voice gentle, but it was hard to breathe past the weight in her chest. "It's not healthy to—"

"What's not healthy is being the weird kid!" Harper's voice cracked. "And this meal isn't even optimized! The Aether says I need—"

"I don't care what the Aether says, Harper."

"It's not going to dictate every part of your life."

"I listen to the Aether because it knows better!"

Elise felt her pulse hammering now, but before she could respond, Harper's face crumpled.

"What if I end up like Sophie?

"What if I'm not optimized enough and something goes wrong?"

The anger bled from Elise's body all at once.

Harper's fingers trembled as they hovered at her throat. "Mom... can I please keep it on? Just for tonight?"

Elise stared at her daughter. The fear behind her eyes. The way her shoulders shook ever so slightly. She wasn't just afraid of being different.

She was afraid of what happened to people who were different.

Elise inhaled. "Eat your food."

Harper hesitated, then poked at her fries, not eating.

Elise let the silence sit between them. Let the weight of it sink in.

"Harper."

"Take off the Aether. Now."

Harper's lip quivered.

"That's not a request."

Reluctantly, Harper's finger brushed her neck.

The latch on the Aether released with a soft click. The glow flickered once, then died. Harper placed it on the table, but the thing didn't feel off—not really. It sat there, looking more like something watching than something waiting.

Harper let out a slow breath, rubbing her bare skin like the absence of it left an ache.

"My head hurts."

Elise was already moving. "How long?"

"I don't know. A while, maybe?" She pressed her fingers into her temples, squeezing her eyes shut. "It's like it's inside my skull."

Elise cupped the back of Harper's head, pressing a palm to her forehead. No fever, but there was something about how her skin felt. Clammy.

"I'm fine," Harper muttered, the words barely believable.

Elise wasn't convinced. She watched Harper grip the table's edge, fingertips going pale. A shiver ran through her, quick and involuntary.

"Elise."

She turned her head quickly, expecting... what? A voice from the hallway? A stranger in the window? But the kitchen was still, silent except for the quiet breath of the house.

Then her eyes dropped.

The Aether pulsed.

Just once. Barely noticeable. A blink of blue light, quick, like a heartbeat.

Elise snatched it off the table. The plastic casing was warm, warmer than it should have been, like it had been running too long, overheating beneath Harper's skin.

Her pulse pounded behind her eyes.

She turned back to Harper, who was blinking sluggishly, as if sleep was pulling at the edges of her mind.

"No more tonight. Let's get you some medicine. Then bed."

Harper nodded, slowly.

Elise guided her toward the stairs, one hand steadying her back. As they disappeared down the hall, the kitchen behind them remained frozen in perfect stillness.

The takeout sat untouched.

The Aether, clutched tight in Elise's grip, felt heavier than it should. She set it on the counter, far from Harper's reach.

And just before she flicked off the kitchen light, she swore she saw it pulse again.

Slow. Steady.

Like it was breathing.

∞∞∞∞

The next morning the house felt off. The silence was different now.

Not the heavy kind that comes with grief, but the tight-lipped hush of something else.

Elise stepped onto the porch, locking the door behind her. The click of the deadbolt didn't make her feel any safer. The house wasn't hers anymore, not since the break-in. Someone else had been there first, leaving their presence behind in rifled through drawers and papers that didn't belong to them. She could still see it, the ghost of their hands disturbing James's things, searching for something they hadn't found.

The air had a stillness, the kind after a storm, where nothing has quite settled yet. The scent of James's cologne still clung to the office like an echo.

She hovered in the doorway, watching the room.

A crime scene without tape.

You should have done this sooner.

The thought whispered through her as she stepped forward, brushing a hand over the surface of the desk. A thin layer of dust clung to her fingertips. The place felt frozen in time, as if James might walk in at any moment.

But James is dead. And someone else had been here instead.

The slow work began. Stacking books, aligning papers—just enough order to keep her hands from shaking. Then came the objects weighted with ghosts. Harper's Father's Day mug knocked over and cracked. Receipts James had stubbornly hoarded. His reading glasses, their case pristine amid the wreckage.

Something was off.

The drawer didn't slide back in quite right. Just a fraction misaligned. Elise frowned, pulling it open again, slower this time.

Her fingers traced the inside, feeling for what her eyes had missed. The wood was smooth… until it wasn't. A slight unevenness at the base. Barely noticeable, but there. She ran her fingers along the bottom edge, pressing lightly. A hollow sound. Not solid. Not meant to be found.

She swallowed her spit.

A trespasser in her own home, following the same steps as the intruder before her, but this time, she would find what they didn't.

82

She searched the wreckage until she found a paperclip. A poor excuse for a crowbar, but good enough. She jammed it into the seam and pried.

A small crack.

The false bottom gave way.

Elise leaned in, pulse hammering as her eyes landed on what laid inside. A business card from a Robert Blackwood. A partial receipt for a safety deposit box at Civic First Bank. And the note. James's handwriting, frantic.

"G.C. flagged discrepancies... need to confirm."

"Check lead reviewers link to Mercer Holdings. Too many coincidences."

"Meeting with E."

"Mrala."

"I can't ignore this anymore. They've taken more than I ever realized. E is the only one left I can trust. This has to stay buried... for their safety. It's the only way to prove what we started wasn't for nothing."

Elise sank into James's chair, the leather creaking beneath her.

The paper trembled in her hands.

This wasn't just paranoia. This was something real.

The room felt smaller.

She could hear it now, the same thing James must have heard before he died.

A warning... or a promise.

She reached for her phone to text miles. Then paused.

Who had been here first? Who had been looking? Who else already knew?

Before she involved anyone else, she needed to understand exactly what James had uncovered—

And why it had gotten him killed.

Elise's breaths were shallow, her grip tightening on the paper. The air in the office felt wrong—too still, like the house itself was holding its breath. She read the note again, the words vibrating in her skull.

"They've taken more than I ever realized."

James hadn't been paranoid. He had been right.

A buzzing shattered the silence. Elise flinched.

Her phone. A message.

Jamal.

We still meeting? I'm about to head that way.

For a second, she just stared, the letters swimming. She had almost forgotten. Almost let this slip through the cracks like everything else.

Her fingers moved before she could think.

83

Yes, I'm getting ready now. See you soon.

Ok. Meet me by the chess tables in Oakwood Park, next to the Maple Street Library. I don't have much time. And if I see anything weird, I'm gone. No offense.

Her hands worked on autopilot, gathering what James had hidden—Blackwood's card, the receipt, the note, each item slipping into her bag like a crime scene in reverse. Evidence, but of what?

The silence stretched. She swore she could hear her own pulse ticking like a second hand against the walls. She forced herself to move, stepping out of the office like she was stepping off a ledge.

The morning pressed against her skin as she crossed the street. The Suarez house stood like a showroom, its windows glowing too evenly, the automated ambiance too controlled.

She knocked. The door swung open, and Hannah filled the frame, perfect posture, perfect smile, her Aether casting an unnatural glow against her skin. Too polished. Like a mannequin in a luxury store.

"I need to run a quick errand," Elise said. "Harper okay to stay another hour?"

"Of course!"

From somewhere inside, Rob's voice snapped through the air, annoyed.

"The Hub says you're disrupting the harmony metrics again—"

"Not now, Rob!"

Hannah's expression never changed, her eyes locking onto Elise's like she hadn't just cut her husband off mid-sentence. "The kids are fine. Take your time."

Elise nodded, mumbled her thanks.

But as she turned back toward her car, she felt it again. That prickling sensation at the base of her skull, the kind animals get before a storm, before the first strike.

She didn't look back.

But she knew, she was being watched.

∞∞∞∞

Oakwood Park was too quiet. The wrong kind of quiet. No children laughing, no joggers passing by. Even the trees seemed to hesitate, their branches barely moving. A dog trotted by, its nails tapping the pavement, its owner gripping the leash tight, walking faster, as if sensing they'd lingered too long.

Elise scanned the park's entrance, then the chess tables. Only one was occupied. Far corner. Hoodie. Head down. Shoulders tight. A man trying to hold himself together but failing miserably.

She moved toward him cautiously. "Jamal?"

His head jerked up. His eyes were dark, jittery. He looked past her, scanning the path behind her like he expected someone else to be there. His knuckles gripping the edge of the table. For a moment, he looked ready to take off running.

"Anyone follow you?" He asked nervously.

"No," Elise said, but she checked anyway, glancing over her shoulder. "I was careful."

Jamal studied her for a second before exhaling, his grip loosening just slightly. "Good," he muttered. But his shoulders didn't relax.

A gust of wind kicked up dead leaves across the pavement. The sound made him flinch.

"I worked for Necessity Mart," he said, his voice flat, mechanical, like he'd rehearsed it. Like he needed to say it fast, before something stopped him.

"Three years. Rarely took a vacation. First in line for an Aether when they rolled them out." He let out a dry laugh. "Didn't need much convincing. We all wore them. We had to."

He dragged a hand down his face, fingers pressing hard into his temples, like he was trying to dig something out. Elise had seen that same motion in James. In Harper.

"Then the headaches started."

She leaned in. "What kind of headaches?"

Jamal hesitated, for a second. "Like nothing I've ever felt." He pounded his chest. "I was an athlete. I know my body. This... this was different." He exhaled through his nose, shaking his head. "They told me I was stressed. Overworked. But then my coworker started getting them too."

"And when you took it off?"

Jamal's whole body stiffened. His fingers curled into his palms. He didn't answer right away.

"It got worse," he said finally. "Way worse."

"Non-compliance," he muttered. "That's what they called it. I was flagged immediately. My metrics plummeted. I wasn't *'aligned with the culture'* anymore."

"Then one day I blacked out. Woke up in the hospital."

Elise felt her skin tighten.

"The doctors played dumb," he continued. "Didn't want to call it what it was. But I heard them talking. ODS. That's what they called it."

"They fired me after I filed a claim," Jamal went on. "Forced an NDA on me before I could even cash my last paycheck." His hands trembled. He shoved them under the table. "But I've been digging. I'm not the only one."

Elise's breath hitched. "Harper..." Her voice was barely there. "She's getting headaches."

"Then you have to get proof. Now." He leaned in, voice low. "Document everything. I need the medical records they buried. I need my file. You still have access at OptimumCare, right?"

Elise hesitated. That line—it wasn't just blurry, it was electric. Cross it, and she'd never be able to step back.

"I'll try," she said. "They're watching. I can feel it."

"They're always watching," he muttered.

Then his posture stiffened. His eyes locked onto something past her shoulder. Footsteps.

Slow. Steady.

Jamal stood immediately. "I have to go."

"Wait." Elise pushed off the bench as he left. "Jamal—"

Then he was gone. A shadow swallowed by the trees.

Elise stood there, heart hammering. Hands clenched at her sides. The chess table, the trees, the wind—all of it felt like something watching.

Footsteps, heavier now. Closer. She turned.

A man in a dark jacket walked the path, hands in his pockets, shoulders slightly hunched. Not toward her. Not away. Just there. Like he had nowhere to be.

Then... just for a second... his eyes met hers.

Not a glance. Not the passive, empty look of a random stranger.

Something else entirely.

Elise's pulse stuttered.

She turned away, but her mind cataloged everything. No phone. No earbuds. No watch. A man alone in a park where no one lingered. Just walking. Just watching.

Her fingers tightened on the strap of her bag. The note inside pressed against her ribs like a secret trying to escape.

She walked. Even steps. Controlled. Casual.

But the air had changed.

The trees felt taller. The space between them, smaller.

She told herself she wouldn't look back.

Didn't need to.

Because even as she crossed the parking lot, unlocked her car, slide inside.

The feeling came with her.

Like she hadn't left him behind at all.

ACT II

The Cost of Harmony

The nail that sticks out gets hammered down.
– Japanese Proverb

CHAPTER SEVEN
Optimization Denied

*The only way to deal with an unfree world is to become so
absolutely free that your very existence is an act of rebellion.*
– Albert Camus

Elise sat at the kitchen table, pen hovering over Harper's math worksheet. She tried to focus, but her mind kept circling back to James, to the hidden note, to the wrongness in everything lately.

Her phone buzzed.

Maggie.

She hesitated, then pressed the phone to her ear.

"Daniel's gone." Maggie's voice was broken. "And Tasha just called."

The pen slipped from Elise's fingers. "Gone?"

"We fought." Maggie's breaths were shaky. "He's been tracking everything. Every conversation, every interaction, every goddamn emotional response."

Elise pinched the bridge of her nose. "Tracking?"

"With his Aether," Maggie said. "At first, it was just work metrics. Then it was... us. Every conversation rated. Every argument flagged as a 'harmony disruption.' Do you know what it's like to have your marriage constantly measured?"

Elise didn't answer.

"He told me the data proved it."

"The numbers... said I'm the problem. Me!"

A long pause.

"He showed me the reports... My 'emotional alignment' kept dropping. My communication wasn't efficient enough. And those damn suggestions... 'enhance marital harmony.' 'Schedule recalibration time.'"

Her voice broke. "I finally snapped. Told him he couldn't even love me without an algorithm telling him how."

Elise's skin prickled. "What did he say?"

Maggie let out a bitter laugh. "That 'optimization enhances natural connection.' Like a goddamn robot."

Another long pause.

"So, I pushed harder. I told him there's nothing natural about scheduling when to care!"

"Then... his Aether started flashing."

"A red warning."

"He froze, Elise. His face went blank. Like the thing was rerouting him. Then he said, 'We should pause. My readings indicate—'" Her voice cracked. "I told him I don't care about your readings. I want my husband back."

Elise gripped the edge of the table. "And then?"

"The Aether chimed, 'Harmony disruption detected.'" Maggie's voice lost any color still left. "And then he just... walked out."

Elise shut her eyes.

"He said he needed to 'recalibrate in a more optimal environment.' Then he left. Like I was a failed experiment."

Elise exhaled slowly. "You tried calling him?"

"Every call went straight to voicemail. He put his phone on Do Not Disturb." Her voice dropped.

"Then Tasha called."

"What did she say?"

Maggie hesitated. "Daniel went to headquarters. Told them everything!"

Elise sat up straighter. "What do you mean, everything?"

"My secret Aether purchase. How long I'd been hiding it. Screenshots of my compliance scores. Even messages where I said optimization wasn't so bad."

"He reported me, Elise."

Elise pressed a hand to her chest.

"Tasha sounded... different," Maggie whispered. "Not like my friend. Like my handler. Like she knew. She said I'd compromised everything. That I was a liability."

"What did they do?"

The silence stretched.

"They exiled me. Suspended me from the Society. Locked me out of headquarters. My access codes are dead."

Another bitter silence. Then Maggie choked out, "Even Paul texted me. Paul! He said, 'I defended you for years, Maggie. Don't even know what to believe anymore.'"

Elise's head spun. "Maggie, I'm so sorry."

"Don't," Maggie interrupted. "Daniel did what he was programmed to do. He doesn't even realize what he's become."

Elise swallowed the lump in her throat. "Have you had headaches?"

"What?"

"Migraines. Sharp pains. Have you had them since wearing it?"

An awkward silence passed.

"Elise," Maggie said, annoyed. "My life just imploded, and you're talking about—"

"I think the Aether's dangerous," Elise pressed. "Harper's getting symptoms. A client whose case I've been working on had them too. And Sophie, Harper's classmate, she had a seizure."

"Oh my god," Maggie snapped. "Are you serious right now?"

"Maggie, listen to me—"

"God, Elise." Maggie's voice shook with something past anger. Betrayal. "For once, can you stop making this about Harper?"

"That's not what I'm—"

"I needed my sister tonight." Maggie's voice shook. "Not a conspiracy theory."

Elise's throat burned. "Maggie—"

"Call me when you actually want to help."

The line went dead.

Elise just stared at her phone, the silence ringing in her ears.

Movement in the doorway made her flinch. Harper.

She stood there, her Aether missing, swallowed by her oversized pajamas. Her eyes, usually bright with curiosity, looked dull. Like something had already been taken. Something more than the Aether.

"Mom?" Her voice was small. "Did I... do something wrong?"

Elise's hands curled into fists, ready to tell her no... of course not, when her phone buzzed again.

A new notification.

Her blood went cold.

NOTICE: OPTIMIZATION COMPLIANCE ALERT

Her vision blurred with anger as she read it.

> Our systems have detected extended periods of non-compliance with required optimization protocols. As outlined in the scholarship agreement, minimum thresholds must be maintained. Home use metrics are currently falling below acceptable parameters. Continued non-compliance may affect enrollment status.

Elise's fingers clenched so tight around the phone she felt her nails dig into her palm.

The timestamp seared into her brain.

9:47 PM.

They were tracking Harper, inside their own home.

A cold rage settled over her.

Tomorrow, she was going straight to Dr. Delgado.

No more polite conversations.

No more waiting.

It ended now.

∞∞∞∞

Elise gripped the steering wheel as she pulled into the school parking lot, her mind spiraling through rehearsed arguments. Each one felt brittle, ready to shatter the moment she opened her mouth. But that email, it was imprinted into her thoughts, lodged so deep it felt like part of her.

Monitoring her daughter, even in their own time.

They weren't just tracking her. They were enforcing.

Harper stood near the curb, Aether pulsing steady at her throat. The soft glow didn't look like a tool anymore. It looked like a tag. A claim. A reminder that Elise wasn't the only one making decisions about her daughter's future.

She rolled down the window.

"Stay for whatever afterschool program they have today," she said.

"I need to speak to Dr. Delgado."

Harper's hand went to her Aether, brushing it absently. "Am I in trouble?"

Elise forced herself to soften. "No, honey. I just need to talk to Dr. Delgado."

Harper hesitated, then slung her backpack over her shoulder and disappeared into the crowd. Elise watched the other students, their glowing bands pulsing in perfect rhythm. It made her feel sick.

She let out a deep breath and stepped out of the car.

The hallways smelled artificial. Like they wanted to scrub away anything human. FutureReady posters lined the walls, each one a smiling, optimized student looking down at her, promising success, compliance, perfection.

Elise didn't knock.

She pushed open the door.

"You're tracking my daughter at home?"

Dr. Delgado flinched. It was small, barely noticeable, but enough.

"Mrs. Winters, please, have a seat—"

"No."

Elise stepped forward.

"You sent that email at 9:47 PM. You're monitoring her in our house."

Dr. Delgado folded her hands on the desk, fingers clasped too tightly. Her Aether caught the overhead light, glinting like a blade.

"The scholarship program requires optimization standards."

"Continuous monitoring ensures student success."

Elise let out a dry laugh.

"Success?" she said. "You mean compliance?"

Dr. Delgado didn't blink.

"We've seen remarkable improvements in students enrolled in the program. Focus, academic performance, even emotional regulation—"

"And Sophie?" Elise interrupted.

The counselor hesitated.

"That incident was investigated," Dr. Delgado said carefully.

"By who? The same men who showed up to erase the footage? Who made my daughter's classmates delete their videos?"

The counselor froze. Then, for the first time, she looked toward the door.

Like she was checking for something. Someone.

Then she leaned in.

Lowered her voice.

"You're not the only parent who's noticed... changes."

Elise's heart hammered against her ribs.

Dr. Delgado sighed, the first sign of emotion slipping through the corporate veneer. "Necessity Mart controls more than you think. The school's funding. All of our technology. Even the staff—" she swallowed. "—even us. They monitor everything."

Elise stayed silent.

"We have compliance evaluations. Staff performance metrics. There are ways to remove... problematic elements."

Her fingers twitched toward her Aether.

"Without Necessity Mart's support, the school wouldn't survive. Without Aether compliance, the students wouldn't either."

Dr. Delgado's eyes met hers. "There's nothing we can do."

The silence stretched.

Elise stood abruptly, her chair scraping the floor.

"Then I'll take my chances."

"Mrs. Winters," Dr. Delgado said quickly. "Please understand—"

"No, you understand," Elise interrupted.

"If you actually cared about these kids, you wouldn't be hiding behind policies while they suffered."

Dr. Delgado opened her mouth, but Elise was already turning.

She stopped at the door.

Didn't look back.

"There are worse things than losing a scholarship." Elise paused, hand on the door. "Like looking in the mirror and not recognizing what's staring back."

She left Dr. Delgado in silence, fingers still brushing the Aether around her neck.

The hallway stretched ahead, unnervingly still. The kind of silence that felt programmed.

Elise moved toward Harper's classroom. Her heels clacking against the tile, a sound that should have echoed, but didn't.

She reached the door, looked through the window... and stopped.

Inside, the students sat in perfect rows. Backs straight. Movements precise. Their Aethers pulsed in unison, an eerie wave of light moving through the room.

The teacher's voice pierced the glass. Calm. Even. Rehearsed.

"Optimization isn't just about scores," he said.

Elise's hands clenched.

"True harmony comes from perfect alignment."

Her breath went shallow.

She searched for Harper. Found her. Near the front. Back straight. Eyes fixed forward.

Listening.

Elise reached the door handle, about to push inside—

And then the teacher turned.

Not gradually. Immediately.

His eyes locked on her like he'd felt her watching.

Recognition punched the air from her lungs.

The man from the Ascension Order. The leader. He saw her. And smiled.

It wasn't warm. It wasn't polite.

It was intentional.

He slowly gestured toward Harper, an elegant sweep of his hand.

Harper stood without hesitation, gathered her things, and walked toward the door.

94

Elise stepped back as her daughter slipped out, blinking up at her like nothing was wrong.

"Hey, Mom."

Inside the classroom, the teacher's voice resumed, the rhythm of his words unchanged. As if nothing had interrupted his train of thought.

As if Elise hadn't even been there.

Outside, the car ride was quiet. Elise kept her voice calm, kept the panic locked behind her teeth.

"New after school program?" she asked.

Harper lit up.

"Yeah! Mr. Kael says optimization is like a superpower. If we use it right, we can be perfect."

Elise felt her grip tighten.

"Perfect, huh?"

"Yeah," Harper said, oblivious. "He says surrender is the key. If we let the Aether guide us, it makes us our best selves. And if we align together, we get stronger."

Elise forced her jaw to relax. "Sounds like you've learned a lot."

"He used to teach normal classes. But now he helps kids understand their Aethers better. He says not everyone gets it yet, but we can show them."

Elise didn't respond.

She couldn't.

Her mind was already moving. Spinning. Calculating.

Necessity Mart owned the school.

The Ascension Order was in the classroom

They weren't just tracking her daughter.

They were teaching her how to surrender.

She looked in the rearview mirror, saw the glow of Harper's Aether pulsing.

A countdown.

How long did she have left before Harper was theirs?

∞∞∞∞

Elise paced the kitchen, her footsteps tracing frantic circles across the worn tile floor. The house was suffocating. Only the occasional groan of the settling wood broke the silence.

Her thoughts colliding, shattering, reforming. Jamal's warnings. Sophie's seizure. Kael's voice, tightening around Harper like a noose.

She squeezed her eyes shut. *Breathe. Keep breathing.*

It has to be now. Wait any longer, and the choice would slip from her hands. She turned toward the stairs.

"Harper," Elise called, her voice strained. "Come down. We need to talk."

The footsteps were hesitant, each one a pause, like Harper already knew the storm waiting below. She entered the kitchen, shoulders hunched, her eyes scanning Elise's face with growing suspicion.

"What's wrong?" Harper asked, her fingers brushing the Aether.

Elise took a deep breath. "We're taking it off. Tonight."

Harper froze. "What?"

"It's not safe." Elise forced the words through clenched teeth. "The headaches, the seizures… this thing is hurting people, and I'm not going to let it hurt you."

Harper's face crumpled, twisting between disbelief and rising panic. "You can't be serious."

"Harper—"

"No! Mom, I need it." Harper backed up a step, hands flying to her neck, shielding the band. "Everything's connected now! We work in teams! My science project depends on synced data. Ethan and I—" She stopped, tears filling her eyes.

Elise moved closer, hands raised in a useless attempt at reassurance. "Sweetheart, listen—"

"Do you know what it's like to be unoptimized?" Her voice broke. "They put those kids in the back of the classroom. No one talks to them. They can't keep up. They're…" She swallowed. "They're invisible."

Elise's heart twisted, but she stayed firm. "You are not invisible."

Harper paused. Her tears still fresh but her anger burning through. "You don't get it! You don't go to school every day. You don't have to explain why your mom is some anti-tech weirdo who thinks she knows better than everyone else!"

"That's not—"

"Do you know what it's like to sit there and feel like you're less than everyone else?"

"Because that's what you're asking me to do!"

Elise reached for the Aether. "This isn't up for discussion. I'm doing this because I love you, and I'm scared of what it's doing to you—"

"Dad would have understood."

The words knocked the breath out of her.

"He actually cared about my future. He wouldn't be trying to ruin my life just because he was scared of change."

Silence stretched, heavy, suffocating.

Harper wiped her face with the back of her sleeve. Then, without another word, she snatched the Aether off, threw it on the floor, and ran upstairs. The bedroom door slammed hard enough to shake the whole house.

Elise stood there, staring at the ground.

The Aether laid between her feet, still glowing.

The house felt impossibly quiet. Elise glanced over at the wall, to James's photo. His frozen smile, untouched by time, mocked the fractured family he left behind.

She sank into a chair, her head in her hands. The silence felt predatory, like it was waiting for her to break.

Her phone buzzed. A new notification lit up the screen, cutting through the dim kitchen.

FutureReady Academy.

NOTICE: Optimization Compliance Alert.

She didn't read the rest.

Her thumb hovered over the screen, then, with a long exhale, she deleted the message.

The Aether still sat on the floor, glowing like an unblinking eye.

Upstairs, Harper cried, the muffled sobs bleeding through the ceiling. Each one cut deeper than the last.

Elise leaned back in her chair, her eyes closing as the weight of the house settled over her like a black cloud.

∞∞∞∞∞

Hours after the fight, Elise laid in her bed, her body exhausted but her mind refusing to shut down. The darkness around her felt too vast, pressing in from all sides. Above her, the ceiling stretched endlessly, a black void where Harper's words echoed like ghosts.

Every time she closed her eyes, she saw it. Not through her own memories, but through Harper's. The scene played out in flashes, pieced together from her daughter's hushed retelling, from the tension in her voice, the way her hands shook when she described it.

Sophie collapsing. The thud of her body hitting the floor, limbs convulsing, eyes rolling back. The gasping. The panicked shuffle of desks scraping against the floor as students jumped back.

And then... the silence that followed. The way the suited men moved in, clinical and rehearsed, erasing the panic, rewriting the story in real time.

She let out a slow, heavy breath and rolled onto her side, reaching for her phone on the nightstand. Nothing. Maggie still hadn't called back. She stared at the screen, willing it to glow, to buzz, to break the silence pressing against her soul. Instead, it only reflected her own face—pale, drawn, eyes shadowed with exhaustion. A ghost staring back.

The loneliness wrapped around her like a snake. She swung her legs over the edge of the bed.

Downstairs, the kitchen was empty, the silence of an unraveling life. Elise didn't bother with the overhead light. She let the laptop's glow cut through the dark as she settled it on the table, fingers already moving.

Aether headaches children.

The screen filled instantly. Too fast, too polished. She clicked the first link.

"Why Your Child's Headaches Mean Optimization is Working!"

Her pulse ticked up. She clicked another.

"Adjustment Period: Supporting Your Child's Optimization Journey."

Another.

"Understanding Natural Adaptation to Aether Technology."

Her nails drummed against the table, the click-click-click of corporate doublespeak buzzing through her head. Every article read the same—careful, rehearsed, reassurance. Aether wasn't the problem. Your child was. Their resistance. Their unwillingness to align.

She deleted the search and tried again. *Aether withdrawal symptoms kids.*

More of the same. Sanitized language, glowing testimonials, parents smiling, praising the "transformative effects of optimization."

Page after page. Dead end after dead end.

She was ready to close the laptop when a buried link caught her eye. A single line among the clutter.

Parents Against Optimization.

She clicked.

The page was a mess—no branding, no modern UI, just raw, frantic conversation. A message board. Old-school. The kind of place built by people who couldn't afford polish, who just needed to be heard.

Threads spread in every direction.

"My daughter's migraines started just three days after getting Aether."

"School says it's normal, but my son isn't himself anymore."

"They're changing how our kids think, and nobody's talking about it."

Elise sat forward. This was real. The words weren't carefully curated. They were desperate.

She scrolled faster.

Then, near the bottom of a thread, a comment got her attention, anonymous, buried beneath a tangle of replies.

"This is from the Necessity Mart CEO before Necessity Mart. This tells you what they're really up to."

Beneath it, a link.

Consciousness and Optimization:

A Framework for a Perfect Society, by A.R.

Her pulse pounded as she clicked

The article was dense, academic. Writing with the kind of calculated detachment that made her skin crawl. But the message beneath the jargon sent something cold slithering up her spine.

"Free will, while heralded as a cornerstone of human identity, is ultimately a source of inefficiency and societal discord."

Her fingers curled into fists against the table.

"Personal desires and emotions introduce unnecessary variables into decision-making processes."

Her eyes moved down the page.

"The chaotic nature of human autonomy can be corrected through predictive algorithms and behavioral modifications."

She highlighted passage after passage.

"Optimization is not about removing freedom but about perfecting the human experience."

"A world free from error-prone decision-making is not a dystopia but the pinnacle of human progress."

The words sat in her chest like a brick.

Elise slammed the laptop closed. The room plunged back into darkness.

She sat still, letting it sink in.

Somewhere upstairs, Harper was sleeping. No Aether. No optimization nudges. No silent, glowing corrections adjusting her breath, her posture, her thoughts.

Tomorrow would be the first day without it. The first real test.

Elise wasn't sure how hard Harper would fight her. Wasn't sure how much damage had already been done.

But she was sure of one thing.

There was no turning back.

She stood, moving to the stove, hands steady as she set the kettle to boil. The click of the burner was loud in the quiet.

In the reflection of the kitchen window, she caught a glimpse of herself. Tired. Haunted. But beneath the exhaustion, something else.

A hint of certainty.

She would fight.

∞∞∞∞∞

Elise sat at her desk, staring through the computer screen, the text blurring into meaningless blocks of data. Her eyes ached from a night without sleep. The buzzing office lights drilled into her skull, amplifying the sound of keyboards clacking, coffee cups settling on desks, the shallow, synchronized breaths of a workforce in perfect rhythm.

Her inbox overflowed, a mess of flagged claims and automated reminders, each one a demand, a weight pressing heavier against her ribs. She ignored them. Her focus was on the phone sitting beside her keyboard, motionless, silent.

She'd called Maggie that morning. No answer. Sent another text. No response.

Her fingers drummed against the desk, restless, waiting. The pressure behind her eyes built, the exhaustion morphing into something else.

Then, the phone rang.

The sound shot through her, a lightning bolt cracking through her haze. She snatched it up, barely registering the caller ID. *FutureReady Academy.*

A fist clenched around her ribs.

"This is Elise Winters."

A voice, urgent. "Mrs. Winters, this is Nurse Callahan from FutureReady Academy. Harper fainted during PE. We've already contacted an ambulance. She's en route to Metropolitan General."

Elise's grip on the phone tightened. The air around her warped, muffled.

"Is she... was it serious?"

"She regained consciousness quickly, but we thought it best to have her checked. The paramedics will assess her on arrival."

Harper. In an ambulance.

Elise's chair scraped against the floor as she shoved it back, standing too fast. The room tilted.

She grabbed her bag with numb fingers, barely aware of Gerald's voice cutting through the fog. "Everything okay?"

"Harper fainted. I need to go."

Gerald's expression changed. "Go. I'll tell Grayson it's a family emergency. Don't worry about it."

She barely managed a nod before pushing through the rows of cubicles, feet moving faster, pulse hammering in her throat.

By the time she reached the elevator, her breath was shallow, hands shaking. She jabbed the button, willing the doors to open faster.

The moment they did, she was inside, the walls closing in as the weight of what had happened crashed down on her.

Harper. The Aether. The words from the message board.

She squeezed her eyes shut. *Not now.* Just get to the hospital.

The doors slid shut, sealing her inside.

∞∞◌◌∞

The hospital parking lot was busy with movement. Cars sliding in, doors slamming shut, engines purring as they pulled away. Elise maneuvered into a spot near the entrance, cutting the ignition with shaking hands.

Her eyes caught a black sedan idling at the far end of the lot. Tinted windows. No visible driver. It didn't move. She stepped out, heart racing. The moment her feet hit the pavement, the sedan eased forward then disappeared onto the main road.

She gulped. Just a coincidence.

Inside, the ER pulsed with quiet urgency, a rhythm dictated by necessity more than panic. Patients shuffled into designated lines based on wristband colors.

Elise rushed straight to the intake desk.

"I'm here for Harper Winters," she said, breathless, her palms damp against the counter.

The receptionist, a woman with the eyes of someone who had seen it all, typed quickly.

"She's being evaluated in Room 4A."

"A nurse will update you shortly."

"Is she okay?" Elise pressed, the words clawing their way out of her throat.

101

"She's stable. A doctor will speak with you soon."

Elise nodded, retreating to the waiting area. The chaos in her chest didn't match the controlled movements of the hospital. Every chair, every patient, every second felt unbearable. She sank into a seat, gripping her phone so tight her knuckles ached.

A nurse entered the waiting area, scanning the room.

"Elise Winters?"

Elise jumped to her feet, legs feeling like lead as she followed the nurse down the corridor. The waiting was over. Now came answers.

The examination room was too bright. The paper on the exam table crinkled as Harper shifted, her shoulders hunched, her small hands pale and clammy.

Elise sat beside her, fists pressed against her knees to keep herself still

The door opened. A doctor stepped inside, tall and fluid in his movements. Dr. Rivera. His Aether band glowed, a soft golden pulse that cast soft reflections against his coat.

"Mrs. Winters," he greeted, a polite nod before his focus shifted. "And you must be Harper."

He moved to the wall-mounted tablet, fingers skimming through data.

Elise caught the pause, the tension in his face as it stopped on a gap in the records.

Then, a calculated shift. Professional.

"These symptoms… lightheadedness, fainting… they're increasingly common in adolescents," he said, turning back toward Harper with a reassuring smile. "Could be dehydration, low blood sugar, anxiety."

"Have you been drinking enough water?" He looked at Harper.

Harper gave a small shrug. "I guess."

"With school activities, the pressure to keep up, it's easy to miss the basics," he continued.

Elise leaned forward. "Could it be ODS?"

The air in the room changed.

Dr. Rivera's hand stopped mid-motion. His posture straightened, just slightly.

"ODS?" he asked, carefully.

"I've read about it," Elise said, heart hammering. "The headaches. The fainting. It matches Harper's symptoms."

Dr. Rivera adjusted the clipboard, angling it away from the Hub's line of sight. His expression didn't change, but when he spoke, his voice lost its rehearsed quality.

"I see."

"For the record," he continued. "This appears to be a stress response. Dehydration, compounded by physical activity. Not uncommon."

But his eyes lingered on Elise's… just a fraction too long. A silent acknowledgement. *A warning.*

"There are treatment options," Dr. Rivera mumbled.

Elise barely breathed.

"A temporary course of medication can help manage symptoms while addressing the underlying stressors," he continued, turning to the counter and writing a prescription.

"This," he said, "is a standard anxiety medication."

But when he handed her the slip, his fingers pressed briefly against hers. A barely perceptible nod.

Elise looked down.

"These symptoms should improve within forty-eight hours," Dr. Rivera said, his voice returning to full volume.

"If they don't, follow up with me during my next shift. I'll make time for you."

Harper sat still on the exam table.

Dr. Rivera crouched slightly. "You're going to be okay," he said.

"But rest. Don't push yourself too hard."

Harper nodded.

Dr. Rivera stood, turning back to Elise. "For now, the official diagnosis is stress-induced fainting. If symptoms persist, we'll reevaluate."

His hand moved quickly, barely noticeable, as he slipped a small card into her palm.

A private number. Handwritten.

"Call me if you have any follow up questions," he said.

"Take care," he said quietly, as they stepped into the hall.

Elise led Harper toward the exit, her grip firm in her daughter's hand. Her other hand, curled in her pocket, pressed against the crumpled prescription.

Behind them, the hospital carried on. The patients. The wristbands. The seamless efficiency.

But Elise knew better.

Somewhere, beneath the polished order, the system was cracking.

And whatever Harper had just gone through, whatever had caused her to collapse, was only the beginning.

∞∞∞∞

The house sat still, holding its breath. Shadows gathered in the corners of the darkened living room. The only light came from above the kitchen sink. Two prescription bottles stood beside an empty glass.

Elise curled in the armchair, her legs drawn up, thumb flicking at the edge of James's old lighter. She hadn't smoked in years, but the weight of it in her hand relaxed her. Upstairs, Harper slept, her breathing crackling through the baby monitor Elise hadn't used since she was a toddler. The static wove in and out, a quiet reminder that her daughter was still here. Still breathing.

A knock shattered the stillness.

Elise flinched, the lighter snapping shut in her hand. She was on her feet before she realized, her pulse racing as she moved to the kitchen drawer and yanked it open. The gun Miles had given her sat inside, heavier than it should have been. She flicked the safety off, the cold metal pressing against her palm as she moved toward the door.

Another knock.

She lifted the gun slightly, held it low. Checked the peephole.

Miles.

His face was drawn, shadowed by exhaustion. His collar loose like he'd been pulling at it.

Elise exhaled, tension bleeding out—but not completely. She cracked the door open just enough to let him in.

He stepped inside and let the door click shut behind him.

"What's wrong?" she asked, setting the gun on the counter.

Miles looked at the gun, then back to her.

"You expecting someone else?"

"No," she said. "But I don't take chances anymore."

His shoulders carried a new kind of tension, something different from the usual exhaustion.

"We need to talk."

The moment the words left his mouth, her composure broke. The fear, anger, the unbearable uncertainty—it all clawed its way out.

"Harper collapsed at school today." The words fell from her mouth. She paced the kitchen, hands clenched. "Fainted during PE. The doctor said stress, dehydration, but you should've seen him, Miles. The way he talked around it, like he couldn't say what he wanted to."

104

Miles didn't interrupt. His hands stayed buried in his jacket pockets.

"And then there's the withdrawal." Her voice rose, unsteady. "Harper's upstairs right now, drugged just to handle the pain. I keep thinking about James... how distracted he was before the accident. The headaches, the dizziness. What if—"

She stopped short, pressing her fingers to her temples.

"What if he was wearing one, Miles?"

"What if he was trying to break free?"

There was a long silence between them.

"What if that's why he crashed?"

Miles exhaled. He pulled a small plastic organizer from his pocket, popped open a compartment, and dry-swallowed two pills.

"Sometimes the hardest part of an investigation is sitting with uncertainty," he said.

No sympathy. No empty reassurances.

Elise breathed through her nose, trying to steady her nerves.

She reached into her bag and pulled out the crumpled papers and the business card. Smoothing them against the counter.

"James left this," she said. "It's not much, but— 'G.C. flagged discrepancies.' 'Mrala.' A business card, and this bank receipt."

Miles leaned in, the exhaustion momentarily pushed aside. He picked up the paper, flipping the card in his fingers.

"G.C.," he muttered. "Could be regulatory staff from that period. Maybe an internal review."

His jaw tightened.

"This could be something. If we can figure out who G.C. is, it might explain why we've hit dead ends with the café woman."

Elise nodded, the pressure in her chest easing just slightly.

"What do we do next?"

"I'll look into the safety deposit box," Miles said, tucking the items into his jacket. "Cross-reference agencies with those initials. Try to track down this Blackwood character. You focus on documenting everything at work." His voice dropped. "But be careful. You're already on their radar."

The warning settled in her bones.

Miles turned toward the door but stopped, coughing into his fist. His body shook with the effort.

Elise frowned. "Miles, are you—"

"I'm fine," he muttered. But his face was pale.

His phone buzzed. He looked at the screen. Froze.

"What is it?" Elise stepped closer.

Miles exhaled and shoved the phone back into his pocket.

"Someone else is looking into James's accident."

A cold wave crawled up her spine.

"Who?"

"NovaShield hired a private investigator."

Her throat went dry. "Why?"

"They're building a case to deny your claim."

The words barely registered. "What?"

"They're saying James staged his own disappearance."

Elise felt the breath leave her lungs.

Miles sighed, dragging a hand over his face. "I'll look into it. See who they hired, what angle they're working." He was already moving, grabbing his keys from the counter. "I'll call you when I have something."

Then he was gone. Leaving the house impossibly quiet.

Elise stood there, his words circling like vultures.

James. Staging his own disappearance.

It didn't fit. Not the man she knew. Not unless—

Her pulse ticked faster as the threads wove together. The migraines. The dizziness. The way he'd grown restless, distracted, pulling away. What if he had been trying to break free? What if he'd seen something, something big enough that NovaShield was sweeping under the rug?

Her hands found the edge of the counter, gripping it hard.

A knock at the door sent a shock through her.

Miles.

Maybe he'd forgotten something. A final thought before heading out.

She moved without thinking. No hesitation. No reaching for the gun this time.

Elise yanked the door open. Nothing.

The porch stretched out before her, empty. The street eerily quiet.

No sign of Miles. No sign of anyone.

A chill licked the back of her neck.

Then she saw it. A box.

Small. Black. Sitting on her doormat, waiting.

The Aether logo glowed under the porch light.

Elise's breath slowed. Her skin tightened.

She stepped onto the porch, eyes sweeping the street, the hedges, the dark spaces between parked cars. No figures. No footsteps. Just trees shifting in the wind.

She crouched, hesitating before reaching out. The box was flawless—no scuffs, no dents, as if it had been placed with careful intention.

A folded slip of paper sat beneath the lid. White. Crisp. The text printed in a smooth, impersonal font.

Consider this a courtesy.

Her fingers clenched around the note.

A feeling of unease twisted through her ribs.

This wasn't a gift.

It was a warning.

CHAPTER EIGHT

Restricted Access

*None are more hopelessly enslaved than those who
falsely believe they are free.*
– Johann Wolfgang von Goethe

The office vibrated with a quiet energy. The sound of conversations, the clattering of keyboards, the occasional sigh of frustration. Rows of identical desks stretched in every direction, each occupied by figures bathed in the cold glow of their monitors. Elise sat at her terminal, her fingers moving quickly over the keyboard as she toggled between tabs: flagged claims, emails, and the ever-distracting check of her phone. Harper's silence since the hospital visit gnawed at her, but there wasn't time to dwell on it now.

She needed answers.

Jamal Beckford's case sat open on her screen; a bold red flag slashed across the top.

OPTIMIZATION NON-COMPLIANCE – DENIED.

She exhaled through her nose. The file was bloated, thick with medical reports, appeals, back-and-forth's between Jamal and Necessity Mart, and the final, clinical rejection. Case closed. No Further review.

Elise clicked Export. The file saved to her computer without protest. That was the easy part.

Next, she forwarded it to her personal email under the subject line: *Case Study Reference.* A flimsy excuse, but enough to slip past the system's automated filters. If anyone checked, she could pass it off as research.

Across the room, someone shifted abruptly in their chair. Aether pulsing against their neck, a corrective nudge. Elise stared at the Ambient Charging Zone, where employees lingered, their devices glowing softly, feeding.

She turned back to her screen, opening the internal database. The sterile interface flickered to life. Under the guise of researching Wellness Program Policies, she typed her real query.

Aether Side Effects. ODS.

At first, nothing useful. Walls of corporate jargon. Reports so redacted they were unreadable.

Then she saw it.

ODS: Internal Reports.

The file sat there, harmless on the surface, but something in the metadata sent a prickle down her spine. Recently updated. Recently hidden.

Her heart hammered.

Weeks ago, during a mind-numbing compliance seminar, Alan from IT had demonstrated a backdoor tool meant for department heads, just a little workaround for minor access restrictions, he'd said. Elise wasn't a department head. But she'd quietly stored away the knowledge, unsure if she'd ever need it.

Until now.

She activated the tool, fingers steady despite the weight pressing against her chest. The screen blinked once, then loaded. A warning flashed at the top.

Unauthorized Access Detected.

She swallowed. Routine verification, she told herself. Keep moving.

The file cracked open, revealing incident reports tied to Aether usage.

Optimization Dependency Syndrome (ODS): Symptoms include migraines, cognitive decline, dizziness, and withdrawal-related neurological distress.

Elise's skin went cold.

The next section was worse.

User Suppression Protocols

A familiar name jumped out at her. Grayson Powell. Internal Reviewer.

A lump formed in her throat.

Suppression strategies implemented to mitigate non-compliance trends. Ensure alignment of flagged users with corporate standards through targeted interventions.

Her cursor hovered over the text.

Then... her screen froze.

The document vanished, replaced by a black alert:

Unauthorized Access Detected. Your session has been terminated. Report to Grayson Powell for assistance.

She felt sick.

Across the office, everything remained normal. People worked. Conversations continued. No one looked at her.

But then, she heard it. Heels clicking against the tile.

Angie.

Elise didn't turn. Didn't need to. The voice reached her before the woman did.

"Oh, Elise! Looks like you hit a little snag. No worries. Grayson asked me to come get you so we can sort this out together."

Elise swallowed the lump in her throat and stood. Angie's smile stayed plastered on her face, but something else was behind her eyes. Something darker.

"This won't take long," she promised, leading Elise down the hallway.

Each step like tightening a noose.

The room felt engineered for discomfort. The kind of place that made people shrink without realizing it. A long, glass table stretched before Elise, empty except for the tablet at the center, its dark screen waiting like an executioner's block.

On the far wall, a projection came to life, her login timestamps. Each attempt to access restricted files glowing in a damning red.

Grayson Powell sat at the head of the table, suit crisp, expression unreadable. A man who never needed to raise his voice to make himself heard.

To his left stood a security officer—broad-shouldered, blank faced. Not needed, but present. A reminder.

The door clicked shut behind her. Angie's voice followed.

"Grayson, I've brought her as you requested."

Grayson didn't look up. "Thank you, Angie."

"That'll be all."

Then it was just Elise, the security officer, and Grayson dissecting her from across the table.

"Please, have a seat." He gestured to the chair.

Elise sat slowly, keeping her hands on the armrests instead of the table. Her pulse drummed in her wrists, but she kept her face neutral.

Grayson let the silence stretch, before he leaned forward, threading his fingers together like this was just another performance review.

"Elise," he said, calmly. "We've noticed some concerning behavior."

The projection behind him flickered, her unauthorized logins stacking like tally marks.

"Specifically, repeated attempts to access files beyond your clearance level." He tilted his head slightly, studying her. "Would you care to explain?"

Elise tried to keep her breathing steady. "I was verifying details related to compliance cases. It's my job to ensure accuracy, especially with flagged claims."

Grayson exhaled, almost amused. "Accuracy," he repeated. He pointed toward the projection. "And yet, the files in question were clearly restricted. Proprietary information. Surely you understand the importance of confidentiality."

"Of course."

"But given the circumstances, I thought—"

Grayson held up a hand.

"It's not about what you *thought*. The system decides, not you. And the system has safeguards for a reason."

The officer beside him remained still, but Elise felt the weight of his presence. A silent threat in a company-issued suit.

Grayson leaned back, drumming his fingers on the table. "This isn't about punishment," he continued. "It's about ensuring alignment. Effective immediately, you'll be placed under a performance evaluation period."

Elise's fingers curled around the chair's armrests. "What does that mean?"

"For the next three months, we'll closely monitor your work output, adherence to policies, and, of course, compliance with our optimization initiative."

He looked at her neck—the bare skin where the Aether band should be.

A calculated pause.

Elise felt a slow burn creep up her spine, but she didn't move.

"And if I meet those expectations?"

"Then you'll be restored to full status." He folded his hands. "But until then, your access will be limited."

Elise's jaw locked. "You're tying my hands. How am I supposed to do my job?"

Grayson's smile was polite. "We trust you'll adapt. After all, adaptability is a key value here at OptimumCare." He leaned in slightly. "Think of it as an opportunity to refocus on the basics. Prove yourself, and we'll reevaluate."

The meeting was over before she could argue further.

Back at her desk, Angie hovered just long enough to offer a hollow *"let me know if you need anything"* before vanishing, her Aether band pulsing with an unbothered efficiency.

Elise sat, flexing her fingers before setting them on her keyboard.

She tried pulling up a flagged claim.

ACCESS DENIED. CLEARANCE REQUIRED.

She tried an internal reference document.

UNAUTHORIZED ACTION DETECTED. CONTACT ADMINISTRATOR.

Her email inbox had shrunk, restricted correspondence only with her direct manager and team. No way to loop in a colleague with higher access. No way to bypass the walls closing around her.

The Ambient Charging Zone glowed in her periphery, its soft light reflecting off the bands around her coworkers' necks. Aether users chatted, laughed, leaned into the system's embrace.

Elise sat in the eye of it, an island in the current.

She opened her personal email. The message she'd sent earlier was still there, the attachment intact. A small victory.

She closed it quickly.

They were watching.

Elise moved through the office like a ghost, her body on autopilot while her mind ran in circles. Every blocked access, every denied request, every quiet look from coworkers felt like walls closing in, air running out. Grayson thought she would break under pressure.

Let him think that.

She grabbed her coat, her bag, and walked out without looking back.

∞∞∞∞

The drive to Maggie's house was quiet. No music, no calls. Just the distant sound of the engine and the clicking of the turn signal

Maggie's street unfolded before her, identical houses standing in neat, complacent rows. But Maggie's wasn't like the others. It sagged under the weight of something unseen. Newspapers cluttered the porch, some caught in the wind, spread across the lawn like abandoned messages. The driveway was empty where Daniel's car should've been.

Elise pulled to the curb, cutting the engine. She sat there, fingers curled tight around the wheel. The street felt *off.* No kids on bikes, no evening walkers, no TVs spilling into the streets. Just the slow rustle of dry leaves scraping the pavement.

She stepped out.

The porch creaked beneath her weight, and the house—Maggie's house, once warm, once *hers*—felt like an empty shell.

Elise knocked.

Once.

Twice.

No answer.

She cupped her hands around her eyes, pressing her face to the glass. The living room was quiet, furniture crouching in the shadows, untouched. Most curtains drawn tightly closed.

She knocked again, harder.

"Maggie?"

Silence.

A ripple of unease crawled up her spine.

Elise crouched by the front steps, her fingers searching through the brittle weeds until she found it—the fake rock, still in place. Her hand gripped the key. Cold metal tingled against her palm.

She hesitated.

This had always been their rule. No locked doors, no questions. A key meant trust. It also meant permission.

But standing there, with the street too empty and the house too quiet, it felt like she was intruding.

The lock clicked, and the door swung open.

The air inside was stagnant.

The house was wrong.

Not trashed, not ransacked—just off.

A stack of unopened mail sat on the table, gathering dust. The kitchen sink overflowed with dishes, water spots crusted along the edges.

And the photos.

Face down on the living room floor.

Elise crouched, flipping one over.

A wedding photo. Maggie and Daniel, frozen mid-laugh, champagne flutes raised. The glass had cracked down the center, a scar between them.

Her pulse ticked faster.

She turned toward the hallway.

Soft shuffling. A rustle of paper.

Elise stepped forward, past the mess, past the silence.

Maggie sat cross-legged on the floor, surrounded by old magazines, slowly stacking them into careful piles. Her movements were slow, as if handling something delicate.

"Maggie?" Elise kept her voice low, not to startle her.

Maggie looked up.

"Oh, hi." Her tone was nonchalant, as if Elise had just popped by for a coffee. Her eyes, though... off. Just like the rest of the house. A little too distant.

Elise moved closer. "I've been calling. You weren't answering."

Maggie smiled, absently smoothing the edges of a magazine. "Oh, you know how it is. Just got caught up with everything."

Elise crouched, searching her sister's face. "Where's Daniel?"

Maggie's hands didn't stop moving. "Gone."

"Gone?"

"It's for the best. Things are... *simpler* now."

The way she said it made something cold settle in Elise's ribs. She hadn't noticed before, the way Maggie's collar sat high, slightly stiff. But now, as her sister shifted, she saw it. The glow beneath the fabric. The pulsing light.

Elise's mouth went dry.

"Maggie," she whispered, "you're still wearing that?"

Maggie tilted her head, her smile softening a bit. "It's not a big deal. I've just been using it more. It helps me stay balanced." She exhaled. "I don't think I realized how much I needed it."

A ripple of nausea twisted through Elise.

"This isn't you."

"Maybe you don't know who I am anymore."

Elise gritted her teeth, forcing herself forward. "Harper collapsed yesterday. At school." Her voice cracked. "She's struggling, and I don't know how to help her. And you—"

Tears filled her eyes.

"Maybe this is all part of the process," Maggie mumbled.

Elise shook her head. "You can't seriously believe that."

"Sometimes," she said softly, "surrender is the best thing we can do."

Elise stood abruptly, backing away, the room suddenly smaller, suffocating.

"What about Patchwork? Everything you've been fighting for?"

Maggie shrugged.

"Stepping back has been a relief," she said simply. "You wouldn't understand. Not yet."

The floor felt unsteady beneath Elise's feet.

"Maggie—"

Her sister was already standing, already turning away. "I'll visit Harper soon," she said, sounding detached. "We'll talk more then."

Elise wanted to shake her, to scream, to pull the damn thing off her neck. Instead, she just left.

The evening pressed in as she climbed into her car, her hands gripping the wheel too hard. She forced herself to breathe, staring at the house from the driver's side window.

Maggie's shadow moved behind the curtains.

Not watching.

Not waiting.

Just existing in that dim, controlled glow.

Elise turned the key, the engine rumbling to life.

Maggie thought surrender made things simpler.

She had no idea what was coming.

Maggie's house disappeared in the rearview mirror, dark and silent, its warmth long since hollowed out. She wanted to march back inside, shake her sister, drag her out of that perfect, empty glow, but Maggie was already gone, swallowed whole by the system she once swore to fight.

Elise forced herself to drive.

By the time she reached her own street, the exhaustion had settled deep in her bones. But the moment she pulled into the driveway, her fatigue splintered into something else.

The house was too bright. Every window blazed, curtains yanked back, like eyes pried open.

She killed the engine and stepped out, the cold biting at her skin. But beneath the chills, sweat prickled along her spine.

The front door was unlocked.

It swung open with barely a push.

Inside, the house was loud in disorder. A mess that didn't belong.

Textbooks spread across the dining table, pages torn wide like open wounds. Crumpled papers littered the floor, ink scratches bleeding through.

Elise took a step forward. Something crunched beneath her shoe. She looked down.

A pencil, snapped in half.

From upstairs, a chair scraped violently across the floor.

She dropped her bag and moved, heart hammering as she climbed the stairs. Her palms sweaty against the handrail.

Harper's bedroom door was open.

Elise stepped inside.

Harper sat hunched over her desk, a storm of paper swallowing her whole. Pages were scattered across the bed, the floor—some crumpled, others clawed through with half-erased words, discarded before they even had the chance to become something.

Her laptop screen glowed, a battlefield of overlapping tabs, flashing reminders, missed deadlines, all screaming for attention.

Harper gripped her pencil with force, wrote something, then slashed through it with an angry X. Moments later, she tore the page from her notebook and threw it to the floor. It landed among the wreckage, joining the rest of the casualties.

Elise took a careful step forward.

"Harper."

Harper's head snapped up, eyes wild, face flushed.

"No," she spat. "No, I'm not okay."

Elise kept her voice steady. "Talk to me."

"I can't do this." Harper slammed the pencil down, the wood rattling against the desk. "I can't think. I can't breathe."

Elise's eyes glanced at her laptop. A chat window blinked with new messages from Ethan.

You there? Need your half of the data.

Below it, a flood of unread notifications.

Missed optimization check-ins. Homework deadlines. Project updates.

"It's the science fair," Harper said, voice shaking. "We have to present next week, and I... I can't focus without my Aether. Ethan's going to think I'm an idiot, and then I'll fail, and then I'll get a bad grade, and then I'll get kicked out of school, and it'll all be your fault!"

"Harper, I know this is hard, but—"

"No, you don't!" She jumped to her feet, knocking the chair over. Her breathing was too fast, too shallow. "You don't understand anything."

Elise took another step closer. "I—"

"You're ruining everything, Mom!"

"You don't care about me. You just care about proving you're right!"

"That's not—"

"Do you even know what it's like to sit in class and feel nothing?" Harper screamed. "To have everyone look at you like you're a loser? Like you don't exist without the Aether?"

Elise felt the words hit like a slap she hadn't braced for.

Harper's breathing was erratic. And then, her face twisted, something ugly breaking free.

"Maybe if you were better at anything, Dad wouldn't have had to work so hard and get himself killed!"

The air drained from the room.

Elise heard the words, felt them sink in deep, but for a moment, she couldn't move, couldn't breathe.

Harper's chest heaved, her hands clenched to fists at her sides.

Then the rage cracked, leaving only something small and shaking in its place.

Her voice was quieter.

"I just want to be normal." Tears filled her eyes.

"I just want to stop feeling like this."

The pencil slipped from her fingers, rolling off the desk with a soft clack.

Elise exhaled and moved toward her, reaching out.

"Sweetheart, I know this is difficult. I know it feels impossible right now, but—"

Harper flinched away.

"I don't want to hear it." She turned, burying her head in her arms. "You don't understand."

Elise stopped.

Her hands shaking at her sides.

She wanted to say something, anything that would fix this. But Harper had already closed her off, shut her out.

Instead, she took a step back.

Then another.

She turned, walked out, and closed the door softly behind her.

In the hallway, Elise pressed her back against the wall, covering her face with shaking hands.

Harper's sobs carried through the wood, muffled.

The frantic rustle of papers, and typing of keys resumed.

The chaos inside Harper's room raged on.

But outside, Elise stood in stillness, drowning in the weight of everything she couldn't fix.

∞∞∞

Morning came without mercy.

Elise sat at her desk, fingers hovering uselessly over the keyboard. The screen pulsed with rows of numbers, but they may have well been static. Just a meaningless blur of approvals, denials, cold calculations that had nothing to do with real people.

Her mind was stuck on the night before.

Harper standing there, voice cracking under the weight of something too big for her to carry.

Elise had barely slept. She'd closed her eyes, but the words had stayed awake, curling in the corners of the room, slipping beneath the blankets, whispering in the hollow space behind her ribs.

118

By the morning, they had settled in. Not just words anymore. A presence. Something with claws, clinging to her every breath.

The office was quieter than usual, but it wasn't the comfortable kind of quiet. It was silence before the storm. The kind that made your skin prickle because you knew something was coming—you just didn't know what.

A shift in movement caught her eye.

Two men in tailored suits strode through the far end of the office, their presence slicing through the stillness. One of them wore a Necessity Mart badge clipped to his lapel, the other carried a leather briefcase stamped with OptimumCare's logo. They didn't stop to chat, didn't even look at the rows of desks as they passed. Just walked straight to Grayson Powell's office and disappeared inside. The door clicked shut behind them.

Elise exhaled slowly.

This wasn't routine.

She stood, grabbing a random folder from her desk—an excuse to move. Her steps were careful, as she wove through the maze of desks toward Powell's office. But then something made her stop.

Alan Pierce's desk.

He was hunched over his keyboard, typing fast, fingers stabbing at the keys. His screen glowed with a back-end interface, lines of data shifting too quickly to be standard work.

Then she saw it.

Manual Adjustment Log.

Her throat tightened.

Alan must have felt her presence. His hand jerked, the mouse moving quickly toward the tab, closing it instantly. When he turned to her, his face was blank—almost too blank.

"Elise," he said, the word tight in his throat.

"Everything okay?"

She tilted her head. "Just stretching my legs."

Alan nodded stiffly. His eyes moved back to his screen, his typing slower now, calmer. But she could feel the tension rolling off him, thick as fog.

She lingered for a while before turning away.

Powell's door was ahead. Voices, muffled but distinct, filtered through the wood.

"... *system integrity is critical...*"

A low voice.

"... *monitoring certain individuals...*"

Rougher. More familiar.

"... *avoid unnecessary attention...*"

The words settled into her bones, heavy and cold.

Elise took a step closer, tilting her head, but before she could make out more—

"Looking for something?"

She jumped.

Angie Mooney stood behind her, her pastel cardigan wrapped tight, her smile stretched too thin.

Elise's mind scrambled for an excuse.

"Just... taking a breather," she said, forcing a casual shrug.

Angie looked at Powell's door, then back to Elise.

"Don't forget those claims," she said, her tone chipper, but the warning underneath cut like glass.

"We're all about staying on top of things."

Elise nodded, retreating under Angie's watchful eyes. But inside, her mind was already spinning.

That timing was too perfect.

Too deliberate.

She veered back toward Alan's office, slowing as she passed. He didn't notice her this time, too focused on whatever he was doing.

She leaned against the doorframe, her voice light, but piercing.

"So, what are you working on?"

Alan flinched, his shoulders stiffening.

"What?" His laugh was forced, his fingers curling into the edge of his desk.

"Just fixing some bugs. You know how these systems are... glitchy as hell."

Elise saw his desk. A half-eaten bag of chips and a crumpled candy wrapper sat in plain view, clear violations of the optimization diet protocols. She tilted her head, her smile slow and knowing.

"Not worried about your score?"

Alan chuckled nervously, his face barely masking the panic.

"Oh, just stress eating. The score dip's temporary." He waved a hand, dismissively. "Anyway, they're focused on the bigger fish right now."

"Bigger fish?"

Alan shrugged, too casual.

"You know, the suits. Internal review. Checking how the new programs are rolling out."

Elise let the silence stretch until it was unbearable.

Alan finally met her eyes. His jaw tensed.

"It's nothing. Routine stuff."

"Right. Routine."

As she walked back to her desk, she felt his eyes on her. Wary. Watchful.

She sat down, her thoughts racing.

The candy wrappers. His strange calm about the suits. The Manual Adjustment Log.

Alan Pierce was hiding something.

The office thinned out by seven. One by one, the rows of desks emptied, leaving behind only the hum of idle screens and abandoned chairs.

Elise kept her head down, waiting. Watching.

Alan hadn't left.

She stood, smoothing the wrinkles from her blouse, and crossed the room with unhurried steps.

Alan looked up before she reached his door, eyes darting toward his screen, his expression shifting—guilt flashing like a neon sign before he could mask it.

She stopped beside his desk.

"Alan," she said.

"We need to talk."

His mouth pressed into a thin line. He straightened slightly, forcing a grin.

"Uh, sure, Elise. What's this about?"

She leaned in, just enough to make him nervous.

"It's about some inconsistencies. And I think you can help clear them up."

Alan blinked.

"Inconsistencies?" He let out a weak chuckle, rubbing the back of his neck. "Not sure what you mean."

Elise crossed her arms.

"Don't play dumb. You're near the bottom of every performance metric, but somehow, you're still here. Still covered. That doesn't add up."

The grin vanished. His shoulders went tight.

"Elise, if this is about my work, I'm doing what I can. We all are—"

"Cut the act." She leaned closer, her shadow stretching across his keyboard.

"I know what you're doing. You're manipulating the system. Probably for your mom. Noble, maybe. But it's still fraud."

His hands curled into fists.

"You don't know what you're talking about."

"Oh, don't I?"

"I've seen the internal logs. OptimumCare's good at burying things. But some things slip through."

She shifted her weight, voice dropping to a dangerous calm.

"Tell me what's being covered up. And while you're at it, you're going to help me access the files I need."

Alan stiffened. His eyes darted around the empty office.

"Elise, you know I can't do that. Even if I wanted to, it's against policy. You're asking me to put my job, my life, on the line."

"You think you're the only one with something to lose?"

Alan swallowed the lump in his throat.

"If I go to Powell with what I found, what do you think happens to you?"

The blood drained from his face.

"You wouldn't."

"I would."

Elise let the silence stretch. Let him feel the weight of it.

Alan hesitated. His fingers twitched near the keyboard.

Elise watched him, waiting for the inevitable.

He was going to break.

It was just a matter of time.

Elise folded her arms.

"Every flagged entry tied to internal investigations. I want timestamps, names—anything that proves OptimumCare is hiding something."

Alan's fingers twitched. He looked ready to run, but the weight of what she'd already uncovered kept him chained. Finally, he exhaled through his nose, turning back to his screen.

"This could get us both in trouble," he muttered.

"Only if you drag your feet."

With a resigned shake of his head, Alan typed a series of commands, his breaths coming short and fast. A second later, the screen blinked red. He cursed under his breath.

"We can't do it here. Server room B3. No cameras."

Elise raised an eyebrow. "Why B3?"

"Legacy systems," Alan said, shoving away from his desk. "It's the only place we can do this without setting off flags."

He stood, gathering his things with jerky movements, like a man marching toward his own execution. Elise followed as he led her through the quiet corridors, passed the glass offices, their emptiness making them feel hollow. The deeper they went, the more the building changed. The polished efficiency turning to exposed pipes and walls without the corporate glamour meant for show.

"Why this way?" Elise asked.

Alan didn't slow down. "Fewer cameras. No one watches this section unless something goes wrong."

At a rusted door labeled SUBBASEMENT ACCESS, Alan swiped his badge. His hand trembled slightly. The lock released with a reluctant click.

The air beyond was colder, with the scent of old wiring and the static of machinery left running too long.

Alan unhooked his Aether, shoving it deep into his bag. "If you're wearing one, they track you. Even here."

"How long do we have?"

Alan checked his watch. "Twenty-two minutes before the next security sweep."

The server room was ahead—B3.

Inside, rows of machines stood like silent monoliths, blinking in synchronized patterns. Wires sprawled across the floor like veins, feeding data into the humming beasts. A deep, mechanical pulse filled the space, masking their footsteps.

Alan went straight to an old terminal in the corner, a relic tucked between the towering servers. He gestured to the rickety chair beside it.

"This is the last direct connection to OptimumCare's original systems. Everything else runs through Necessity Mart now."

Elise swept the room. Shadows flickered across steel panels, making the space feel alive.

Alan cracked his knuckles, fingers flying over the keys. "I can mask this as routine maintenance, but we've got maybe fifteen minutes before the system flags it. After that..." He gave her a look. "You know what they do to whistleblowers."

"Just get me in," Elise said, eyes locked on the monitor.

He worked fast, entering temporary admin credentials. The terminal chirped, and the database came to life before them. A long list of case files, reference numbers, dates. Alan scrolled quickly.

"Here, optimization compliance incidents. Withdrawal cases. It's all tagged under ODS."

A file popped open: *Case 7865 - Jamal Beckford. Status: Closed.*

Elise scanned the text. "Symptoms consistent with withdrawal. Claim denied due to non-compliance."

More cases followed. Same symptoms. Same denials. Same silence.

"They're tracking this," Alan mumbled. His voice had turned hoarse. "Tagging anyone who removes the devices. It's not just denial—it's containment."

His scrolling stopped abruptly.

"What the hell?"

Buried deep in the data, a routing code. *Status: Contained.*

And a Necessity Mart case number.

Elise leaned in. "Pull it up."

Alan hesitated, then clicked.

A new file opened. Clinical documentation. Necessity Mart's logo stamped on the header.

Three words jumped out at them like a knife in a horror movie.

Overstimulated Cognitive Collapse (OCC).

Alan's face went pale. "This… this is the final stage of withdrawal." His voice shook. "It's why they push compliance so hard. Once someone reaches this point—" He stopped, swallowing.

The document was a death sentence in medical jargon.

Synaptic degeneration. Catastrophic neural breakdown. Terminal outcomes.

A case flagged under OCC had a single red notation: Facility Transfer Approved.

Alan's breath hitched.

"My mom," he whispered. His hands clenched into fists. "She's in their care facility. Serenity Springs."

He turned to Elise, eyes wide, voice cracking.

"This is what they're hiding."

A loud beep sliced through the room. Elise's head jerked toward the badge scanner by the main corridor.

Someone was outside.

"Shit," Alan said, yanking the portable drive from his pocket and jamming it into the terminal.

"I'll copy what I can. It's not everything, but it's enough."

Seconds dragged. The drive's progress bar crawled forward. Elise's pulse thundered in her ears.

The scanner beeped again.

Red light.

Whoever was outside wasn't just passing by. They were trying to get in.

Alan ripped the drive free the moment it clicked done and shoved it into Elise's hand.

"Take this. Don't access it through any main network. They're watching everything now."

He spun back to the terminal, typing furiously, filling the logs with fake maintenance reports. The words scrolled like a frantic prayer.

"This'll cover our tracks, but not for long."

Elise shoved the drive into her pocket, her mind a wildfire of next steps. "Where do we go?"

Alan's fingers never stopped moving. "Separate exits."

A final keystroke. He pushed back from the chair, breathing fast.

"And whatever you do..." His eyes locked onto hers, deadly serious.

"Don't trust anyone who asks about this."

Elise turned for the back door to the server room.

Her hands were steady, but inside, she felt the walls closing in.

She stepped out, slipping into the shadows of the corridor.

Behind her, the red light on the scanner blinked again.

And then, the lock clicked open.

She moved.

Not too fast. Not too slow. Just another late worker, ending a long night. She kept her pace even, her breathing controlled, though every nerve in her body screamed at her to run.

Her mind worked ahead, mapping the path back to the elevators. She couldn't go through the main hall. Too Open. Too many cameras. She needed a side route.

The subbasement area was a maze of industrial corridors, metal panels and exposed piping giving it a forgotten feel—like a part of the building that didn't exist on paper. Up ahead, a stairwell sign hung above the door. Emergency Exit – Level 1 Access Only.

She grabbed the handle. Locked.

Damn it.

Footsteps echoed from behind, fast and heavy. Security.

Elise pivoted, darting into another corridor. The walls pressed tighter here, the air heavier. Ahead, a Maintenance Access door sat slightly cracked.

She ducked inside.

The space was small, cluttered with supply shelves and electrical panels. She pressed her back against the cold metal of a storage rack, her breath coming quick and shallow. Through the cracked door, she saw them.

Two security officers.

Both in OptimumCare uniforms, but their posture was different tonight. Stiffer. More alert.

"Necessity Mart's orders." One of them muttered. "They're tightening protocols."

The second officer nodded. "I know... Lotta eyes on us now."

Elise's pulse pounded as they passed. The first officer's radio crackled.

Unidentified access in B3. Still unaccounted for. Sweep all exit points.

Her saliva caught in her throat. She had minutes. Maybe seconds. Before they locked this place down entirely. Her exit was the elevator. It was the only way back up. But that meant going through the main hall. Past security.

She forced herself to move.

The front desk was lit like a stage, bright and clinical against the dimness of the empty office beyond. A single security officer sat behind the desk, arms crossed, bored, but the moment he saw her approaching, his expression changed.

Elise adjusted her bag, keeping her grip as loose as her hands would allow. She walked toward him with the exhaustion of someone who had spent way too much time on a late shift.

She was almost past him when he spoke.

"You're here late."

Elise stopped. Forcing a tired smile. "Yeah, lost track of time."

The guard didn't smile back. He stood, stepping around the desk.

"There's a new policy," he said. "They're implementing stricter security protocols for late shifts. More checks, less free movement."

Her heartbeat spiked.

"Didn't hear about that," she said casually.

"Just rolled out," he replied. He nodded at her bag. "Need to check that."

Elise stiffened.

Inside, the drive burned against her side, heavier than it should have been.

She forced a breath through her nose. "Seriously? I've worked here for years."

The guard shrugged. "Not my call."

Elise forced her hands to stay still. "What are you looking for?"

The guard just stared. "Compliance."

She didn't move.

This was it.

He reached for the bag.

Then. A *crash.*

126

The sound of something slamming into the floor, followed by a muffled curse from a back hallway. The guard turned.

"What the hell was that?"

Elise's pulse jumped.

The radio at his hip crackled. *Security needed—main office corridor. Possible breach.*

The guard hesitated.

Elise's heart pounded.

Then the emergency lights blinked—a power surge flickered through the overhead systems. Just for a second. Just long enough.

Alan.

The guard hesitated for a fraction of a second too long, then jogged toward the disturbance.

Elise moved fast, striding past the checkpoint with purpose, her bag slung over her shoulder like there was nothing inside worth questioning.

She was through.

The doors slid open, and cold air slapped her in the face.

The city outside was quiet.

She walked quickly, not looking back.

Her mind raced.

Alan had saved her. He had done something, triggered an alert, caused a distraction, maybe even tampered with the lights.

But that meant they would know someone was helping her.

And that means Alan was a target now too.

Elise turned the corner, ducking into the shadows of the side alley. She pulled the drive from her bag, gripping it tight.

She had what she needed.

But she wasn't safe. Not yet.

This was only the beginning.

∞∞∞∞∞

Elise sat in her car, staring at the diner's lights from a few blocks away, its neon sign buzzing in the dark night. The drive sat in the passenger seat, now buried inside an empty gum wrapper. She had copied the files, backed them up, but that didn't ease the weight in her chest. The OCC reports, the rerouted claims, the

127

systemic cover-ups. This wasn't just negligence. It was something colder. Deliberate.

If OptimumCare wanted to punish her for knowing the truth, she'd make damn sure they burned with her.

She tapped her phone on her thigh, restless energy building like static under her skin. The moment she'd left the building, she called Jamal.

"We need to meet. Tonight."

He didn't argue.

Now, she was here, and something felt *wrong.*

She pocketed the drive and stepped out into the night.

The diner was the kind of place that clung to another decade. Through the window, she spotted Jamal slouched in a corner booth, hospital paperwork scattered in front of him. Bandages around his wrists, a plastic monitoring bracelet still clinging to his arm like a restraint.

Elise stepped inside.

The bell above the door jangled, too loud. Jamal looked up, quickly gathering his papers.

"Elise," he said as she slid into the seat across from him. "I wasn't sure you'd—"

"Cut the small talk." She kept her voice low, scanning the room.

A waitress topped off coffee at a nearby booth. An old man flipped through a newspaper. A couple in the far corner ate in silence. Normal.

She leaned in.

"What's the latest from your lawyer?"

Jamal exhaled, rubbing his temples. "They're documenting my symptoms— migraines, tremors, spasms. But I can't mention the Aether."

His voice tightened.

"They keep coding it as 'psychosomatic.' I'm sick, but legally, I can't say why."

"They know," Elise said. "They've always known."

"What are you talking about?"

She reached into her bag, pulled out the gum pack, and slid it across the table.

"This is everything I found. They've been tracking cases like yours for a while."

Jamal hesitated, fingers hovering over it like the package might be wired to explode. Finally, he picked it up, his hands shaking.

"This could… this could change everything."

"It should help your case," Elise said. "Shows they know exactly what's happening to people like you."

Jamal nodded, but something about his reaction set her teeth on edge. He pocketed the drive, glancing at his phone before looking back at her.

"There's more," Elise said. "I found files about something called Overstimulated Cognitive Collapse."

Jamal froze.

"It's the final stage of withdrawal," she continued. "Catastrophic neural degeneration, irreversible synaptic failure. They're labeling it 'contained' in their systems and rerouting every case."

Jamal rubbed his wrist, his leg bouncing under the table.

"OCC," he mumbled. "They used to call it something different."

"A couple of us knew people who..." He gulped, shaking his head.

"Who what?" Elise pressed.

Jamal hesitated, then sighed. "Randy. He worked in logistics. Same symptoms. When it got bad, he checked into a clinic. Last I heard, they called it an 'unexplained neurological event.' He's been in a coma ever since."

Elise felt the words slam into her, heavy.

"And they don't know why?"

Jamal laughed bitterly.

"Of course they know. They just don't want to admit it."

A cold certainty settled over Elise as she thought of Harper. The restless sleep, the distant look in her eyes, the small things she had ignored.

"What about treatment?" she asked.

Jamal stiffened. "There are... places. Facilities. Official channels. But you don't want to go down that road."

"Why not?"

Jamal didn't answer.

Outside, a black SUV pulled up to the curb.

The headlights flared against the diner's window, cutting into the booth's dim glow.

Elise's heart jumped.

Jamal's phone buzzed. He looked at it and his face drained of color.

"You need to leave," he said suddenly. "Now."

"What?"

Jamal wouldn't meet her eyes. He stood, cramming his papers into his bag.

"Just go. Trust me."

Elise grabbed his arm before he could take off. "Jamal, if you're not telling me everything, I can't help you."

Jamal pulled free, his voice urgent. "You don't get it. They don't care what you know. They care what you do with it."

The bell above the door jingled.

Elise turned.

Two men in dark suits entered, their posture too straight, too controlled.

Jamal was already slipping away, moving toward the back.

"Shit." Elise said under her breath. She stuffed her bag under her arm and moved fast, cutting through the diner. She looked once at the SUV outside. Couldn't see who was inside. Didn't need to.

The message was clear.

She pushed through the kitchen doors, the heat and smell of grease slamming into her. A dishwasher barely glanced at her before going back to his work.

The back door led into the alley.

Elise stepped outside.

The air was cold, damp with the lingering stench of garbage and old fryer oil. She hesitated, listening.

The door clicked shut behind her.

Silence.

Then. Footsteps.

Not rushed. Measured.

Coming from the alley's entrance.

She moved.

Elise cut between dumpsters, her breath quick. The alley stretched toward a side street, mostly dark. She took another step—

She forced herself to walk. The alley stretched ahead, the pavement cracked and uneven beneath her feet.

She glanced quickly over her shoulder.

No one.

Not yet.

Turning the corner onto a quieter street, she moved faster, her pulse hammering behind her ribs. Her car was close. Two blocks away, parked intentionally out of sight from the diner. Now it felt like miles.

Passing a darkened storefront, she caught a flash of movement in the window's reflection. A shape. A figure turning the corner behind her.

Following.

Her heart was in her throat.

She picked up her pace, careful not to break into a full run. If she ran, it meant she knew. And if they knew she knew, she was as good as dead.

Another turn. A quick cut through the parking lot.

Then—her car.

Relief flooded through her as she fumbled for her keys to put them into the lock. She yanked the door open, ducking inside, slamming the door shut, locking it in one swift motion.

For a second, she just sat there, gripping the wheel, forcing her breathing to slow.

The silence in the car was suffocating.

Then she felt it.

The wrongness.

The way the car sat too low.

Elise's gut twisted.

No. No, no, no.

She grabbed her phone and switched on the flashlight, angling it toward the window. The beam swept across the pavement, glimpsing shredded rubber.

Her tires.

All four of them.

Slashed.

Panic shot through her.

She jerked her head up, her eyes darting across the street. The sidewalk was empty. The alley behind her was still. The only sound was the distant rush of traffic, and the occasional honk of a horn on the main road.

Then. A low rumble.

Headlights.

The black SUV crept around the corner, like a shark circling wounded prey.

Elise's hand clenched around the wheel. She had seconds, maybe.

The SUV inched closer, the tinted windows concealing whoever was inside.

She reached for the glove compartment, feeling blindly for something, *anything.* A weapon, a tool, a miracle.

The SUV stopped.

Another set of headlights cut through the dark.

A second car.

Moving fast.

Brighter. Closer.

Tires screeched as the sedan tore around the corner, barreling straight toward her.

The SUV hesitated.

Elise's phone vibrated in her lap.

"Get in. Now."

The sedan skidded to a halt in front of her, passenger door popping open.

Behind the wheel—

Alan.

Elise didn't think.

She moved.

Elise barely had the door shut before Alan slammed on the gas, the tires screeching as they peeled away from the curb. The seat belt snapped tight against her chest as the car jerked forward, cutting onto a side street.

"How did you—" she started, her pulse still hammering.

Alan's knuckles were gripped tightly around the wheel, his eyes glancing between the rearview and the road ahead. "I followed you," he said. "Figured if you got caught, that meant I'd be caught too."

Elise turned, glancing over her shoulder. The SUV hesitated at the intersection before slowly turning onto their street.

It was following.

"What the hell were you thinking?" Alan snapped. "What are you doing with the drive?"

Elise's pulse pounded in her ears. "I gave it to someone."

Alan's head whipped toward her, his face going pale. "You *what?*"

"I had to. It's no good if it's just sitting in my bag, Alan."

Panic flashed across his face. "Who? Who did you give it to?"

Elise clenched her jaw, refusing to answer.

Alan cursed under his breath. "You don't get it. If they know you had it, they know you gave it away. And if they know, that means whoever has it is already a target."

Elise felt like she was about to throw up.

Alan swerved onto another road, cutting through a residential block. The SUV was still behind them, unhurried, patient.

Watching.

Hunting.

Alan gritted his teeth, gripping the wheel tighter.

"We need to lose them now."

Elise kept her eyes locked on the side mirror, watching the SUV as it trailed them. A cat playing with a cornered mouse.

"They don't have proof," she said, forcing herself to sound calm.

Alan let out a bitter laugh. "Proof? They don't *need* proof. They'll burn everything down just to make sure. You think they don't have contingencies for this? You think they won't make us disappear if it keeps the system clean?"

Elise turned aggressively.

"Then why the hell did you follow me if you were just gonna panic?"

Alen clenched his jaw, his grip so tight on the wheel she thought he might rip the leather apart. "Because if you go down, I go down. I don't have a choice anymore."

The SUV gained on them.

"Fuck!" Alan yelled, yanking the wheel to the left, cutting down a narrow street. Garbage bins blurred past. Houses sat dark and quiet.

A right turn. Then another.

He killed the headlights, coasting into an alley, breath coming in ragged gasps. Elise pressed herself back into the seat, pulse hammering in her throat. The SUV rolled past the intersection ahead, still creeping, still searching.

They didn't stop.

They were gone.

For now.

Alan exhaled, gripping the steering wheel like it was the only thing keeping him together.

"We're dead," he muttered, shaking his head.

Elise straightened. "No, we're not."

Alan turned to her, eyes wide, frantic. "You don't get it. This isn't some corporate scandal, Elise. This is *them*. They don't do lawsuits. They don't do PR cleanups. They make problems disappear."

His voice cracked on the last word, and for the first time, Elise saw it—the real fear. The knowledge that this wasn't just about exposing the truth.

It was about surviving it.

Elise swallowed. "Then we make sure it's too late for them to clean this up."

Alan gave her a wild, disbelieving stare, then looked away, running a shaking hand through his hair.

Elise barely remembered the rest of the drive. Her nerves were stretched too thin, her thoughts racing through every possibility. Had she made the right call? Had she just put someone else in danger?

The moment they turned onto her street, she saw it.

Her front door was open.

Not wide. Just enough. A sliver of darkness.

Elise's fingers curled around the doorknob before she even realized she'd reached for it.

Then, movement.

She turned abruptly, her breath catching as a figure stepped out of the shadows. Rob Suarez.

He raised his hands in a calming gesture, his expression tight with something she wasn't used to seeing on him. Fear.

"Elise." His voice was low. "We have Harper."

The ground tilted.

"What?" Elise's voice barely made it out of her throat.

Rob looked at the open door, his body shifting slightly, like he was ready to block her if she ran inside. "I saw some guys hanging around your house. Didn't like the look of them. They weren't from the neighborhood."

Elise felt the anxiety wrapping around her.

"Where's Harper?"

"She's with us. At our place. She's safe."

Elise's legs nearly gave out.

Rob stepped closer. "Elise, what the hell is going on?"

She didn't answer. Couldn't.

Because if she did, she might have to admit that she had no idea how to keep them safe anymore.

Elise gripped the burner phone so tight it dug into her palm. The line clicked once, then rang.

Miles answered on the second ring.

"What happened?" He said, without pleasantries.

"My car's useless," she said. "Tires slashed. An SUV trailed me." She pressed a hand to her forehead, exhaling. "Somebody was at my house, Miles. Rob scared them off, but Harper—"

She glanced toward the living room. Where Harper now sat curled on the couch.

"She's safe," Elise finished. "For now."

A pause. Then, Miles cursed under his breath. "You're not staying there. It's not safe. I'm coming to get you."

Elise turned away, pacing. "Where are we going?"

"Safe house," Miles said. "I'll take you somewhere secure."

Elise gripped the phone tighter. "Where?"

"A place no one's looking." His voice left no room for argument.

She exhaled, dragging a hand through her hair. "How long?"

"Thirty minutes." A pause. "Be ready."

The line went dead.

Elise shoved the phone into her pocket, then turned toward Harper. "We're leaving."

Harper didn't move.

"We just got here," she mumbled. "Now we have to run again?"

Elise crouched in front of her. "It's not safe here."

Harper lifted her head. "When is it ever safe?"

Elise's breath caught. She had nothing to give her—no reassurance, no promises she could keep.

So, she did what she had to.

She stood, grabbed their bags, and started moving.

Harper followed, silent and shaking.

Outside, the night stretched wide and waiting. Somewhere down the road, a car engine rumbled low, patient.

Watching.

Waiting.

Elise clenched her jaw.

Thirty minutes.

They just had to make it thirty minutes.

∞∞∞∞∞

By the time they made it to the safe house, Elise's nerves were shot.

The drive had been too quiet. Every headlight in the rearview mirror felt like a hunter's eyes. Harper hadn't spoken since they left.

The stairs up to the safehouse were exposed to the alleyway, the metal railing cold beneath Elise's fingers. Harper trudged ahead, shoulders hunched, gripping her backpack like a life preserver.

Miles pushed open the door without hesitation. No wasted movement. He wasn't there to make them comfortable, he was there to keep them safe.

The apartment smelled of dust, stale detergent, and memories that didn't belong to them. A single bedroom, a cramped living space with a fold-out couch, and a kitchen barely big enough for two people to stand in at the same time.

Harper dropped her bag on the floor.

"How long are we staying here?" she demanded.

Elise looked at Miles, but he was already at the table, spreading out files, printed maps, a laptop balanced dangerously close to the edge. He wasn't going to intervene.

"We don't know yet," Elise admitted.

Harper scoffed, shaking her head. "You don't even have a plan."

"We do," Elise snapped, then softened. "I do... But I need time to figure things out. I need you to trust me."

"Trust you? Like how you trusted that keeping me out of optimization would make my life better? Like how you trusted we'd be okay without Dad?" Her voice cracked on the last word, and she turned away, arms crossed tight over her chest.

Elise's breath hitched, but before she could respond, Miles cut in.

"Enough," he said, not raising his voice, but the weight behind it was enough to silence them both. "We don't have time for this. Elise, sit. Harper... cool off in the other room if you need to, but don't go far."

Harper huffed but stomped toward the bedroom, slamming the door.

Elise pressed her hands against the table, grounding herself.

Miles didn't sit. Instead, he pulled out a thick folder and spread its contents across the table.

"What the hell happened?" He asked. "You sounded ready to come unglued on the phone."

Elise sighed, rubbing a hand over her face. "What didn't happen?" she muttered, shaking her head. "Someone was following me. I left the diner, tried to get to my car, but—" she let out a bitter laugh. "All four tires. Slashed. Just sitting there."

Miles, who had been flipping through documents, stopped.

"Who picked you up?"

Elise hesitated. "Alan."

Miles sat the folder down, slowly. "Alan Pierce? From IT?"

She nodded.

Miles dragged a hand down his face, letting out a slow breath. "Jesus, Elise."

"He was already following me," she said, defensive now.

"He knew I was in trouble, and—"

"He knew you were in trouble because you were in trouble," Miles interrupted. His voice wasn't angry, but there was an edge to it.

"Elise, do you realize how many people have vanished for less than what you're doing? You're not just poking the bear anymore... you're climbing into its damn den."

"You think I don't know that? But I didn't have a choice. I had to act. At work, I—"

"What did you do?" Miles's voice dropped, suddenly more serious.

She hesitated.

"I got into the internal database," she admitted. "Not just the standard reports. I found everything... flagged claims, rejected appeals, system override logs." She swallowed. "Alan helped me access restricted files. That's how I found the OCC cases. They're tracking people who try to remove their Aether bands, marking them as 'non-compliant.' It's not just denials. They're containing them."

Miles muttered something under his breath, standing up and pacing the small apartment. "Jesus, Elise."

She continued. "And it's worse. The system isn't just tracking withdrawals, it's predicting them. Using their own optimization scores to flag people before they even try to opt out."

Miles stopped pacing. "And what did you do with that information?"

Elise hesitated again. "I gave it to Jamal."

Miles let out a slow breath, his eyes locking onto hers. The silence between them felt suffocating.

"Elise, you're in deeper than I thought. We need to move fast."

"I need answers. I need to figure out who's watching me, what's happening to Harper, and why my job is part of all this."

Miles nodded slowly. "And you think you're going to tackle all that in one night?"

"I don't have time to wait!" she snapped, planting her palms on the table, staring him down. "I have a kid in the next room who was hospitalized because of this system. My husband's dead, and I still don't know why. Every time I get close to the truth, something, or someone, blocks me. So no, I'm not waiting."

Miles let her words hang in the air before responding.

"Fighting is good," he said. "But you need to fight smart. And right now, you're flailing."

Elise glared at him, but before she could respond, he reached for one of the documents on the table. He flipped it around and slid it toward her.

"Let's start with this," he said. "Grace Collins."

Elise looked over the paper, her eyes narrowing as she took in the details. A photo of a woman in her late forties was clipped to the corner—gray streaking her tightly pulled-back hair, a tiredness etched into her features.

"Who is she?" Elise asked.

"Former FDA compliance officer," Miles said, pulling out another document. "She's the G.C. person from your husband's note."

"She oversaw the approval process for a company called Synapse Dynamics who I believe James was working with. She was the lead reviewer... until she wasn't."

"What happened?"

Miles leaned on the back of the chair, his fingers tapping the edge of the table. "She was reassigned. Suddenly. From a lead role to some desk job in the regional office. Two months later, she resigned. No explanation."

"And you think she found something?"

"I don't think... I know. After she left, she did consulting work for smaller biotech firms... until every one of them mysteriously dropped her. She applied for a PI license in another state about a year ago. That's where her trail goes cold."

Elise stared at the papers, her mind racing. "You think she's still alive?"

Miles shrugged. "If she is, she's keeping her head low. But I have her last known address. She's about five hours away, in Port Lawrence."

"Then we find her," Elise said immediately. "She's the link."

Miles held up a hand, interrupting her. "There's more."

He flipped open another folder and pulled out a map. Several locations were marked in red circles, most clustered in the same region.

"These are old medical facilities," Miles explained. "Former psychiatric hospitals, rehab centers, small clinics... most of them shut down years ago. But here's the thing... Necessity Mart owns every one of them. Through shell companies."

Elise leaned over the map. "Why?"

"That's the question," Miles said. "There's no public record of what they're doing with these properties. But I checked the utilities. The power usage in these 'abandoned' buildings is off the charts. Whatever's going on in these places, it's big, and it's likely not legal."

Elise's eyes locked onto his. "And you're just now telling me this?"

"You think this is easy? I've been piecing this together while trying not to get us both killed."

Elise stared at the files on the table, the threads of information tangling in her mind. Grace Collins. Synapse Dynamics. The clinics. Harper's hospitalization. James's death. Every piece felt connected, but the picture was still incomplete.

"We need to go to Grace's last address," Elise said, pacing the room now. "If she's alive, she can help us."

Miles folded his arms. "You don't even know what you're walking into."

"Neither do you. But sitting here isn't an option."

As she spoke, her phone buzzed on the table. She grabbed it, her stomach dropping when she saw the message.

Alan.

They know. Entire system locked down. Don't come in tomorrow.

Elise felt the blood drain from her face. She handed the phone to Miles without a word.

He read the message, his expression darkening. "Looks like they're moving faster than I thought."

"What exactly does that mean?" Elise asked.

"It means... We don't have time to play catch up anymore. Whatever you thought you had at OptimumCare? It's probably gone. They're covering their tracks."

Elise clenched her fists. "Then we hit them where it hurts."

Miles's eyes met hers. "You better be ready for this. Once you step into the fire, there's no getting out."

Elise's lips tightened. "I was ready the day James died."

The room fell silent.

From the other side of the thin bedroom wall, Harper's muffled voice whispered something to herself, too low to make out. Elise swallowed. She had to end this before Harper was pulled any deeper.

Because next time Necessity Mart came for them, Elise wouldn't be running.

She'd be ready to fight.

CHAPTER NINE

Customer Retention

If you want to keep a secret, you must also hide it from yourself.
– George Orwell

The old sedan groaned beneath Elise's grip, its suspension wheezing over every crack in the asphalt. Miles had lent her the car until they could get hers running again, and it felt every bit of its years. Steering loose, engine rattling just enough to put her on edge. The heater barely worked, its weak gusts doing little to cut through the damp chill clinging to the morning air.

The silence inside the car felt unnatural. The radio played low, static between stations crackling under her nerves. She peered in the rearview mirror.

Harper sat slumped in the backseat, head resting against the window, a smudge of condensation forming where her breath touched the glass. Her backpack was crumpled beside her, straps tangled, books hanging out like they'd been thrown in without care. Harper never tossed her things.

"Hey," she said carefully. "You okay back there?"

Harper blinked slowly, like pulling herself out of something deep. "Huh?"

"I said, are you okay?" Elise tried again.

Harper shifted, rubbing at her face with stiff fingers. "I'm fine," she muttered. "Just tired."

It wasn't just tired.

Elise hesitated before she spoke again. "I get it. Long night. I'm sorry about everything. About… Miles, the apartment, this old car."

"What apartment?"

Elise blinked. "Last night. The apartment. Remember?"

Harper just stared, eyes wide but unfocused, like she was trying to place a face in a crowd. "We stayed at an apartment?" she said slowly.

"We weren't at home?"

"No," Elise said quickly. "We weren't. We left. Harper, we—" She stopped, taking a deep breath. "You really don't remember?"

Harper frowned, rubbing her temples. "I don't know. I guess? I was tired. Why are you making a big deal out of this?"

Elise's grip tightened on the wheel. "It's not a big deal."

"I just... I want to make sure you're okay. You didn't sleep well last night, that's all."

Harper crossed her arms. "Can we not do this right now?

Elise exhaled, staring at the road. The conversation scraped against something raw inside her, setting her on edge. She was imagining things. Harper was exhausted. The move, the fear, the constant uncertainty—it was too much for her.

"It's okay," she said quickly. "Don't worry about it. You're probably just tired."

Harper's hands sat on her bag. She didn't look up. "Yeah," she said. "Tired."

Elise watched her in the mirror. This wasn't just exhaustion. It was something deeper, something wrong.

Harper had forgotten an entire night.

Elise pressed a hand against her chest, trying to steady her breathing.

Could it be ODS... or even worse, OCC?

The thought slid into her mind like a blade.

No. No, it wasn't that. It couldn't be.

Maybe it was the meds. But what if it wasn't?

What if Harper's Aether was doing this?

Elise swallowed back the nausea rising in her throat. "Harper... you'd tell me if something felt off, wouldn't you?"

"I'm fine, Mom. Really."

Elise nodded.

The rest of the drive passed in silence.

By the time they reached the school, Elise's nerves were raw. She pulled into the drop-off lane and stopped the car, but Harper didn't move right away. She gripped the door handle, then hesitated, looking back at Elise.

"Are you mad at me?"

Elise blinked. "What? No. Why would you think that?"

Harper shrugged. "I don't know. You just seem... upset."

"I'm not upset. I'm just worried. If something's bothering you, I need you to tell me. Okay?"

Harper nodded, but it was automatic, empty. "Okay."

She climbed out of the car, moving slower than usual.

Elise sat there, gripping the wheel, watching her daughter disappear through the doors.

A tap on the window shattered her thoughts.

Elise jumped, turning her head to the source. A man stood just outside the driver's side window, leaning in too close. His face was calm. Dressed in a charcoal-gray coat, collar turned up against the cold.

She cracked the window an inch. "Can I help you?"

The man smiled, but there was nothing warm about it.

"You had quite a night," he said.

The man glanced toward the school doors, where Harper had just disappeared. "Busy morning, too. Must be exhausting, keeping up."

"I don't know what you're talking about."

The man tilted his head. "Sure you do."

"I'd be careful. People in your position tend to make... mistakes."

Elise didn't respond. Couldn't.

He smiled again, stepping back from the car like they'd just had a polite conversation about the weather. Then, just as suddenly as he appeared, he turned and walked off, disappearing into the shifting crowd of parents and students.

She slammed the car into gear and peeled away from the curb.

∞∞∞∞

By the time Elise pulled into the OptimumCare parking lot, her grip on the wheel was iron tight. The shadow of the school drop-off lingered in her mind. She wanted to turn around, to drive Harper back home, to demand someone, anyone, fix this. But she didn't. Instead, she was here, the car idling in a space farther from the entrance than usual, where the cameras wouldn't catch the exhaustion on her face.

For a long moment, she considered leaving. Just backing out, disappearing before anyone saw her. Showing up might look suspicious. Not showing up might look worse. The internal tug-of-war was pointless. Her decision had already been made the moment she parked.

She stepped out into the cold. Her breath fogged as she moved toward the glass entrance, her heart pounding like a war drum. Inside, the lobby was still and sterile, the usual morning bustle muted. Something felt... off.

As she passed through the maze of glass-walled offices, movement caught her eye.

Alan.

He sat in one of the smaller conference rooms, two men in suits across from him. One was typing on a tablet, the motion of his fingers slow and calculated. The

143

other leaned back in his chair, his body language relaxed but his eyes were predatory. Alan's posture was hunched, his head in his lap, his shoulders caved inward as though trying to fold himself into nothingness.

Elise stopped mid-step, her pulse spiking.

Alan didn't look up. He wouldn't meet her eyes.

The door opened, and a security officer stepped inside, his presence menacing. Alan stood, slow and mechanical, and followed him out. His eyes stayed glued to the floor as they walked past Elise. She caught a glimpse of his face—pale, damp with sweat, his lips pressed into a thin, bloodless line.

"Alan," she said softly, more reflex than intention.

He flinched but didn't stop. Security led him to his office, where IT staff were already at work, pulling cables and emptying drawers. Alan watched helplessly, his hands twitching at his sides, before he was ushered toward the elevators.

He never looked back.

Elise barely had time to process Alan's departure before she felt a presence at her side. Grayson Powell, stood too close, his immaculate suit barely wrinkling as he gestured toward the hallway.

"Join us in Conference Room B," he said.

Her stomach dropped, but she tried to keep her face neutral. She didn't ask questions. She just followed.

The conference room was small, its walls frosted glass that only partially obscured the view of the busy office beyond. Inside, a man sat at the end of the table, a black tablet resting in front of him. He stood as they entered, extending a hand with a calculated smile.

"Ms. Winters," he said, his voice pleasant but cold.

"I'm Harrison. From Necessity Mart."

Elise didn't shake his hand. She slid into a chair across from him, her back stiff, her jaw tight. Harrison didn't seem fazed. He sat back down, tapping something on his tablet before folding his hands neatly in his lap.

Grayson sat beside her, offering no explanation. No reassurance. Just silence.

"Let's start with something simple," Harrison began.

"How long have you known Alan Pierce?"

Elise tilted her head, forcing her expression into one of confusion.

"Why?"

Harrison smiled, the kind that didn't reach his eyes.

"We're reviewing some discrepancies in our system access logs. It's standard procedure. How long have you worked together?"

"Five years," Elise said. "But we're not close. Different departments."

Harrison nodded, making a note on his tablet.

"Did Alan ever discuss system access protocols with you?"

"No." The answer came out faster than intended, but she didn't backtrack. Instead, she leaned forward slightly. "Is Alan in some kind of trouble?"

Harrison didn't answer.

"Have you noticed any unusual behavior recently? Late nights, closed-door meetings, anything of that nature?"

Elise's fingers twitched against the edge of the table, but she kept her face blank.

"No. Alan keeps to himself."

Harrison tilted his head, studying her like a specimen under glass.

"You're sure? Because we've noticed some... unusual login patterns. Accessing areas of the system outside his clearance. I'm sure you understand how serious this is."

"I do," Elise said, her voice tight. "But like I said, I wouldn't know."

Harrison paused, his fingers hovering over the tablet.

"It's important we understand the scope of this issue, Ms. Winters. If there's anything you've seen or heard, anything at all, now would be the time to tell us."

Elise met his gaze.

"I don't know anything."

The tension in the room thickened, but Harrison didn't press further. Instead, he typed something else into his tablet.

"Well," he said finally, standing.

"Thank you for your time, Ms. Winters. We may need to follow up."

Elise didn't move as Grayson stood beside her, his hand brushing her shoulder briefly—an unspoken warning... or reassurance, she couldn't tell.

She waited until they'd left the room before letting herself breathe.

Elise returned to her desk, her pulse still racing. She sat down, logging into her computer out of habit. The screen blinked once, then froze.

Aether verification required.

Her stomach twisted. She clicked again, but the message didn't change. A second later, an email pinged on her phone.

From: IT Department
Subject: Enhanced Security Protocols
Message: Due to recent updates, all workstations require Aether integration. Please visit HR to collect your device.

Before she could process the implications, Angie Mooney appeared at her side, smiling too wide.

"Perfect timing!" she said, holding up a black box.

"We've got your new Aether device ready. Fully covered by the company. It's all about making this transition easy for you."

Elise stared at the box, her blood running cold. Angie placed it on the desk with a gentle pat, her eyes lingering too long before she straightened.

"Let me know if you need any help setting it up. We're all so excited to see you thrive."

Elise didn't respond. She waited until Angie walked away before touching the box, her fingers trembling as she lifted the lid. The device inside shined under the office lights, a reminder of everything she was fighting against.

This wasn't just a tool. It was a leash. And now, it was hers.

Her phone buzzed, breaking through her thoughts.

Air caught in her throat. Dr. Delgado.

The school counselor never called directly. Her communications were always through official channels—email or portal messages. Elise hesitated, her thumb hovering over the screen, before swiping to answer.

"Dr. Delgado," she said impatiently, "this isn't the best time."

"I know," Dr. Delgado replied, her tone strained.

"But this couldn't wait."

Elise froze, the tension in Dr. Delgado's voice was unlike anything she'd heard before. Normally, the counselor's words were calm. Now, they were hurried, borderline panicked.

"What's going on?" Elise demanded.

There was a pause, the sound of papers shuffling on the other end.

"I need to preface this by saying, I'm breaking protocol by making this call."

"Our new policies require that any concerns about students be reported through Necessity Mart's channels. But I thought you deserved to hear this first. Unofficially."

Elise's grip tightened on the phone.

"Why? What's wrong with Harper?"

Dr. Delgado hesitated again, then took a deep breath.

"Her English teacher, Mrs. Bennet, flagged some... disturbing behavior."

Elise's heart raced as Dr. Delgado continued, her words tumbling out.

"Harper has been... withdrawn. More than usual. She's staring blankly at her desk, missing entire chunks of class discussions. Mrs. Bennet says it's like she's physically present but mentally elsewhere."

"She's tired," Elise said, the words sounding hollow even to her. "It's been a tough week."

"I understand that," Dr. Delgado said.

"But it's more than that. She's showing signs of confusion... like she doesn't realize time is passing. When Mrs. Bennet asked her about material they'd just covered, Harper responded as if days had gone by instead of minutes."

"That doesn't make any sense," Elise said, her voice shaking. "She's... she's just adjusting. She was just in the hospital, remember?"

"There's more," Dr. Delgado said gently but firmly.

"Mrs. Bennet mentioned an incident in class today. Harper turned in an essay, but three paragraphs in, she repeated the same one verbatim. When Mrs. Bennet pointed it out, Harper had no memory of writing it. She became distressed. Almost panicked when she couldn't explain why."

Elise's throat tightened. She sank into her chair, the Aether box still looming in her peripheral vision.

"She's a kid," she said, trying to keep her voice steady. "Kids mess up their work all the time."

Dr. Delgado hesitated again, the silence unbearable.

"It's not just her schoolwork, Mrs. Winters. She's withdrawn socially too. She's stopped participating in group discussions. She sits alone at lunch. And... she doesn't seem to register when her classmates speak to her directly."

The words landed like punches, each heavier than the last. Elise squeezed her eyes shut, gripping the edge of the desk.

"What are you saying?"

Dr. Delgado's voice lowered.

"I'm saying it's serious enough that the school administration wants to escalate this. They're pushing for a cognitive evaluation, likely through Necessity Mart's post-optimization support program."

Elise's head snapped up, anger cutting through her feat.

"She's not optimized."

"I know that. But the administration sees it differently. Harper's recent hospitalization is on file, and they're framing these symptoms as post-optimization adjustments. If they document this officially, it will trigger a mandatory intervention."

Elise's hands were shaking now.

"You're telling me they're going to use a condition that she doesn't even have to take control of her?"

"I'm telling you to document everything," Dr. Delgado said firmly. "Her memory gaps, her behavior... keep a record. You may need it."

"Why are you calling me like this?" Elise asked, frantic.

"Why not use the system?"

Dr. Delgado let out a shaky breath.

"Because if I report this officially, I lose control of it. Everything goes straight to Necessity Mart, and I can't protect her... or you."

Elise's heart sank. "Protect her from what?"

"Just... keep an eye on her memory gaps, Mrs. Winters. And watch for anything unusual. Don't let them pressure you into signing anything."

The line went silent for a moment before Dr. Delgado added, almost in a whisper. "Someone's coming. I have to go."

The call ended abruptly, leaving Elise staring at her phone, her thoughts spinning. Her hands were still trembling when a chime alerted her to a new email. She opened it, dread already curling in her gut.

From: FutureReady Academy Administration
Subject: Post-Optimization Support Services
Message: We've scheduled a meeting to discuss the next steps for Harper's cognitive evaluation. Please check your portal for details.

Elise swiped the email away, her jaw tightening. Another ping followed—an automated request for a meeting with the Student Wellness Team.

Her eyes drifted back to the Aether box on her desk. It just sat there, as if mocking her. She felt the weight of every choice pressing down on her. Her daughter's health. Her job. The truth about Necessity Mart. Every path was a trap, but she couldn't stop moving forward.

She was out of time.

∞∞∞∞∞

Elise stood at the kitchen sink of the apartment, staring out the window into the street below. The neighborhood was dark and still. Her eyes flicked to every movement. A stray cat jumping into a bush, the ripple of leaves caught in the breeze. She told herself she wasn't looking for the black SUV, but her heart jumped at every shadow that lingered too long.

She turned from the window and moved to the drawer beside the stove, opening it just wide enough to see the small handgun tucked beneath a stack of dish towels. She'd checked twice already tonight, but her fingers brushed over it again, the cool metal steadying her nerves.

Satisfied, she shut the drawer softly and turned to the living room.

Harper was sprawled on the sofa, her quilt pulled halfway over her legs, her eyes glued to the tv.

"Harper," Elise said, leaning against the kitchen wall.

"Can we talk for a minute?"

Harper didn't respond immediately, her eyes fixed on the flickering images. After a moment, she blinked and turned, her expression distant.

"What?"

Elise hesitated, choosing her words carefully.

"I talked to Dr. Delgado today."

Harper's eyebrows raised slightly, but she didn't say anything.

"She told me you've been... having a hard time at school. Forgetting things. Getting confused."

Harper frowned, sitting up a little straighter.

"I'm not confused."

"Sweetheart, your teacher said you wrote the same thing three times in your essay."

Harper shrugged, pulling the quilt tighter around her.

"It was just a mistake."

"It's not just that," Elise pressed gently, stepping closer.

"They said you've been zoning out, forgetting what day it is."

Harper's face tightened.

"I said it's fine, Mom. Can we not do this right now?"

"I just want to help you. If something's wrong—"

"Nothing's wrong!" Harper snapped, her voice cracking. Her eyes filled with sudden tears, and she turned away, her shoulders hunching. "I'm just tired, okay?"

Elise swallowed, her chest tightening. Before she could respond, Harper wiped her eyes roughly and muttered, "Can I go to bed?"

Elise hesitated, then nodded.

"Of course. I'll clean up here."

Harper stood, the quilt slipping to the floor, and shuffled toward the room. Her steps were slow and unsteady, her body slumping as if the effort of standing was too much. Elise watched her walk down the hallway, her heart sinking deeper with every step.

The apartment was silent except for the sound of the refrigerator. Elise leaned against the counter, staring at the dark hallway Harper had just disappeared down, when her phone buzzed on the table. She grabbed it without thinking, her breath catching when she saw the name. Jamal.

She swiped to answer.

"What the hell happened with you?" she demanded.

"And why are you calling me now?"

Jamal's voice crackled through the line, tense and hurried.

"I didn't have time to explain before, okay? They were there. Watching us. I couldn't risk it."

Elise's jaw tightened. "And now you think it's safe?"

"I need to talk to you," Jamal said urgently.

"In person."

"Why? What is this about?"

There was a pause, just long enough to make her stomach twist.

"It's about Harper."

Elise froze. "What do you mean?"

"I've been digging into OCC," Jamal said, his voice dropping to a near whisper. "The symptoms. The stages. Elise... she might be at risk."

Her grip on the phone tightened.

"How do you know that?"

"I don't want to get into it over the phone," Jamal said quickly. "But I have some information that might help. I just... I need you to trust me."

Elise's pulse thundered in her ears.

"You didn't answer my question."

"Look," Jamal said, desperate. "If I wanted to screw you over, I'd have done it already. Can you meet me at Pete's Sandwiches in an hour?"

Elise hesitated, her thoughts racing.

"Fine," she said finally. "But you better have answers."

She ended the call and immediately dialed Miles.

Miles answered on the second ring.

"What now?"

"Jamal called me," Elise said, pacing the small kitchen. "He says he has information about Harper. He wants to meet."

"And you believe him?"

"I don't know. But if he has something that can help her, I have to find out."

Miles let out a bitter laugh.

"You think this guys trustworthy? He's been dancing around the edges of this thing since the beginning."

"Do you have a better idea? Because right now, I'm out of options."

"You're walking into a trap. I don't like this, Elise."

"You don't have to like it. But I'm going."

There was a long silence. Finally, Miles sighed.

"Where?"

"Pete's Sandwiches. One hour."

"I'll meet you there," he said grimly.

Elise knocked softly on the bedroom door, cracking it open. Her daughter was curled up on the bed, her breathing slow and steady. The sight filled Elise with equal parts relief and guilt.

"Hey," she said softly. "Let's go get some ice cream. You deserve it."

Harper turned over, blinking groggily.

"Huh?"

Elise forced a smile. "Come on."

Harper groaned but got up, pulling on her hoodie without much enthusiasm. Elise waited by the front door, checking the locks twice before they left. The drive was quiet, Harper staring blankly out the window as Elise gripped the wheel, her nerves fraying.

Pete's Sandwiches was a run-down corner shop with flickering neon lights and a faded awning. Elise parked across the street, her eyes scanning the lot for any sign of Jamal... or anyone else. Harper leaned her head against the window, half-asleep.

Elise's phone buzzed. It was Miles.

I'm here. I'll be in the alley in case anything goes wrong.

She let out a breath, typing back.

Can Harper wait in the car with you?

A pause.

Yeah, just hurry up.

Her fingers brushed against the handgun in her bag.

She turned to Harper. "Miles is meeting us here. You're going with him."

Harper frowned, finally peeling her eyes away from the window.

151

"Why? Can't I just wait here?"

"No," Elise said, too fast. "You go with Miles."

The moment Miles pulled up alongside them, Elise wasted no time. She climbed out and opened the door for Harper.

"Go," she said, softer now. "Just stay with him until I'm done."

Harper rolled her eyes but got out, tugging her hoodie tighter around herself. Miles leaned over to unlock the passenger side door. He didn't ask questions, just gave Elise a knowing look before Harper slid inside.

Elise shut the door and stepped back. Miles drove off without a word.

Now, she could focus.

She turned toward the sandwich shop, pulse thundering. The few patrons lingering at the outdoor tables look like they'd been there for hours. Older men sipping coffee, young couples with greasy sandwich wrappers spread between them. Elise's eyes moved to every shadow, every subtle movement, as she approached the patio. Her heart beat a steady drumline against her ribs, dread settling in her chest.

Jamal sat at a corner table, his body hunched over a steaming coffee cup. The metal chair beneath him scraped against the concrete as he shifted nervously, his leg bouncing uncontrollably. A cheap smartphone sat face-up beside his cup, its screen lighting up every few seconds with notifications. His eyes jerked up as she approached, and Elise could see the sweat beading on his temple despite the cold breeze.

"You said you had information about Harper?" Elise said, her voice low and urgent as she took the seat across from him. "Start talking."

Jamal's hands trembled slightly as he reached for his cup, then pulled back. He swallowed hard, avoiding her eyes.

"The drive you gave me..." His voice cracked, and he cleared his throat, glancing toward the street before continuing. "There's more to it than just ODS cases. The way they're handling claims... tracking people..." He finally looked at her, his eyes wide and bloodshot.

"It's deliberate, Elise. They're letting it happen."

"I already know this, Jamal. What does this have to do with my daughter?"

Jamal hesitated, rubbing a hand over his jaw. "I showed the drive to someone—"

"You did what?"

"I didn't know who else to go to," he said quickly, his words tumbling over each other.

"This person, they know things, Elise. About everything. About James."

Elise stiffened. Her hand rested on the edge of the table.

"What about James? What does James have to do with this?"

Jamal swallowed again, his fingers drumming against his cup.

"My friend said he was looking into Necessity Mart before... before his accident. They mentioned something specific. A safety deposit box."

Her blood ran cold.

"What do you know about that box?" she demanded, her voice trembling now.

Jamal's composure shattered. His hands shook as he grabbed his phone, glancing at the screen again.

"I'm sorry, Elise. I'm so sorry."

The words barely registered before she saw it—the black SUV creeping down the street, moving too slow to be casual. Its windows were dark, engine purring low as it passed.

A punch of déjà vu hit her square in the chest.

They were watching. Again.

"You know who's in that SUV, don't you?"

Jamal's eyes darted between her and the street. His mouth opened, then shut again, as if he was trying to decide between the truth and whatever lie might keep him breathing.

Elise didn't have time for his hesitation.

Her fingers slid beneath the table, wrapping around the grip of the gun in her bag. "I'm going to stand up and walk to the bathroom," she said, her voice deadly calm. "You will not alert them. Understand?"

Jamal nodded, gripping the edge of the table like it was the only thing keeping him upright.

Elise rose slowly. She couldn't rush this. Rush meant panic. Panic gets you killed. She crossed the patio, pushing through the glass door into the sandwich shop.

The moment she stepped inside, she caught it—a brief reflection in the door's glass.

Two men in dark suits emerging from the SUV.

Her pulse jumped, but she didn't stop.

She moved toward the counter, picking up her pace. The shop smelled of onions and grease. Too bright, too small, nowhere to disappear.

A wooden swinging door marked *Employees Only* was ahead. She quickly walked toward it.

Her knee hit the door harder than intended. BANG. Sending it slamming against the counter behind.

"Hey, you can't—" a worker started, but Elise was already through.

The kitchen was a mess of stainless-steel bins, half-prepped sandwiches, and the clatter of knives against cutting boards. Elise barreled through, knocking over a container of shredded lettuce. It scattered across the floor like confetti.

"Seriously, you can't be back here!" someone yelled.

She didn't stop.

She shoved past a stack of bread trays, slipping into the back hallway. An Exit sign glowed above a door. The push bar was cold and slick under her sweaty palms as she shoved it open.

The alley air was cold, damp, and smelled like trash.

Her head jerked left. Then Right.

Miles.

His sedan idled at the far end of the alley, half-hidden in the shadows. His arms were crossed, like he'd been waiting for this exact moment. Harper's silhouette was barely visible in the backseat, hunched low.

Elise sprinted toward the car, yanking open the passenger door and diving inside, reclining the seat all the way back.

"Go!"

Miles didn't hesitate. The engine roared, tires screeching against the pavement as he slammed the car into gear.

Through the rear window, Elise saw them—the men in suits, dragging Jamal toward the SUV. His arms flailed, his shouts muffled by distance, but it didn't matter.

He wasn't getting away.

"They're taking him," Elise said, her voice hollow.

Miles looked in the mirror, his jaw locked. "He's not useful to them anymore."

Elise closed her eyes. The SUV disappeared from view, but the image of Jamal's terrified face lingered.

"Mom?" Harper's voice was small, scared. "What's happening?"

Elise reached back, fingers brushing Harper's knee in an attempt at reassurance.

"It's okay, sweetheart," she said softly, though her voice felt like it belonged to someone else. "Everything's going to be okay."

But as the silence thickened, Elise knew she was lying.

Miles pulled the car behind the laundromat, cutting the engine. The alley was quiet except for the ticking of the cooling motor. He gripped the wheel, exhaling through clenched teeth.

"They know where you live. You can't go back there."

Elise's hands tightened on the door handle.

"The car—"

"Give me the keys."

She turned, met his eyes. They were steady.

"I'll have someone bring it here tonight," Miles said.

"What matters is keeping you two safe."

Elise reached into her bag, her hand still shaking slightly as she pulled out the keys.

"Thank you," she mumbled. "For everything."

Miles snatched them and shoved them into his pocket.

"The safety deposit box," Elise pressed. "You've looked into it?"

"Civic First Bank," Miles said, rubbing a hand over his face. He coughed, the sound deep and rattling.

"I confirmed it exists, but without a key…" He shrugged. "Whatever James left in there, he made damn sure only the right person could access it."

Elise's heart pounded through her shirt.

The box. James died for it. Now, they knew she knew.

"Mom," Harper mumbled.

"I need my school things."

Elise swallowed. "We'll figure it out sweetheart."

Miles opened his door.

"Be careful, Elise," he said. "They're done playing games."

She watched his taillights fade, then turned toward the narrow stairwell leading to the safe house. But the thin barrier between them and the outside world felt laughably useless.

Harper dropped onto the couch without a word, curling into the cushions, her face buried against the armrest. Elise moved to the window, peering through the curtain.

Empty. For now.

Her fingers brushed against the curtain's edge, lingering as her thoughts spun.

The safety deposit box. Whatever is in there, they killed James to keep it buried.

She stepped away, crossed to the kitchen. Pulled open the drawer. The gun. Cold metal beneath her fingertips. She slid it under some dish towels, just in reach.

"Mom?"

"What is it, sweetheart?"

Harper's face was pale, her eyes glassy as she looked up from the couch.

"Do we... have school tomorrow?"

Elise knelt beside her, brushing a strand of hair from her face.

"No," she said gently. "Not tomorrow."

"Okay. I just... I don't know if I did my homework."

"You don't have to worry about that right now."

Harper nodded, already fading, exhaustion pulling her under.

"Can I go to bed now?"

Elise helped her up, guiding her to the bedroom. Tucked the quilt over her, smoothing it over her small body.

She stayed a moment longer, watching Harper's breathing slow, her face soft and innocent in sleep—like nothing in the world was hunting them.

If only that were true.

She backed out of the room, closing the door without a sound.

The second she returned to the living room, the weight of everything slammed into her. She dropped onto the couch, pressing the heels of her palms into her eyes, but there was no blocking out reality. No escaping the fact that they were losing ground.

Her phone buzzed.

She flinched, the vibration rattling against her leg. She pulled it from her pocket, her heart hammering against her ribs.

The screen glowed in the dim room.

Unknown Number.

A cold knot tightened in her stomach.

She answered. "Hello?"

Silence. A long, suffocating pause.

Then, a low, distorted voice crackled through the line.

"You're running out of time, Mrs. Winters."

Then the line went dead.

Elise didn't move.

For a second, the only sound was the blood roaring in her ears. She inhaled, forcing the chaos inside her into something she could hold. Control. Weaponize.

She turned to the window, peering through the curtain, scanning the alley below again.

Dark. Still.

But the stillness meant nothing. It never did.

Elise let the curtain drop.

They were closing in.

She wasn't waiting for them.

This time, she'd make the first move.

CHAPTER TEN
Loyalty Program

*The surest way to corrupt a youth is to teach him to hold in
higher esteem those who think alike than those who think differently.*
—Friedrich Nietzsche

The white government vehicle sat at the curb like a vulture perched on a dying branch, an unwelcome intrusion on the quiet suburb. Sunlight bounced off its windshield in blinding flashes as Elise turned onto her street. Two women in dark blazers stood at her front door, their posture stiff, one holding a tablet. The letters *CPS* imprinted across a vest caught her eye. The letters blurred as dread crashed into her.

"Stay in the car, Harper," Elise said

Harper, slouched in the passenger seat, barely looked up. "Why? What's happening?"

"Just stay here."

She pulled into the driveway, her engine idling as she stepped out. Her knees felt weak, but she forced herself to move.

As she approached the front yard, she spotted a uniformed officer leaning casually against the government vehicle. Her stomach clenched when he began walking toward her car, his eyes locked on Harper's window.

"Excuse me," Elise called. "How can I help you?"

The taller of the two women turned, "Elise Winters?"

Elise nodded, her mouth dry.

"I'm Sandra Morris with Child Protective Services." She extended a hand Elise didn't take. "We're following up on reports regarding Harper's wellbeing."

"What reports?"

The second woman, shorter with a hawkish stare, tapped at her tablet. "A recent hospital visit. Reports of cognitive decline. Concerns from school staff about her memory and focus."

Elise's thoughts tangled. *How do they know all of this?*

"She's had some challenges," she managed. "But she's fine. We're handling it."

Sandra's voice dipped to something softer, something almost too gentle. "Mrs. Winters, we also have concerns about erratic behavior on your part. Incidents at work. Unusual visitors at your home."

Elise's jaw locked. "Who called you?"

"We're required to investigate any credible report of a child at risk."

Behind her, the officer had moved closer to the car. Elise's stomach twisted as she saw him speaking softly to Harper through the cracked window.

Sandra adjusted her stance. "Given the circumstances, we need to take Harper for a standard 48-hour evaluation."

"No." The word came out of Elise's mouth before she could stop it. "Absolutely not. You can't just take my daughter."

"Sure we can, Mrs. Winters."

"Mom?" Harper's voice was muffled by glass. "What's happening?"

Elise took a step toward the car. "Harper, stay—"

Sandra blocked her path.

"This will be easier if you cooperate. The evaluation is standard protocol for cases involving potential OD—" She stopped, lips tightening. "Cognitive concerns."

The world tilted. "What did you just say?"

Sandra's face smoothed. "It's for Harper's wellbeing. Please don't make this harder than it needs to be."

Movement on the periphery caught Elise's attention. Hannah and Rob Suarez appeared on their porch, their Aethers glowing like halos at their necks. Across the street, other neighbors started to emerge, drawn by the commotion. Their stares were heavy with judgement.

"You're not taking her," Elise said, her voice low, dangerous.

She pushed past Sandra, heading for the car.

"Harper, stay—"

Too late.

The officer already had a hand on Harper's elbow. She stepped out, sluggish, blinking like she was waking up from a dream.

"Mom?" she mumbled, her voice confused. "I don't... I don't feel right."

Panic punched through Elise's chest. She lunged forward, but the shorter woman cut her off.

"It's just for 48 hours," Sandra repeated, firm now. "Don't make this more difficult."

"Harper!" Elise shouted, her desperation spilling over. She tried to push past the woman, but the officer was already guiding Harper toward the government vehicle.

"Mom!" Harper twisted, reaching for her, tears streaking down her face. "I don't want to go!"

Elise shoved against Sandra's grip, nearly breaking free, but the officer was faster. The car door slammed shut, locking Harper inside.

Her terrified face pressed against the window.

"If you resist," Sandra muttered close to her ear, her grip tight around Elise's arm, "we'll be forced to extend the evaluation period. Is that what you want?"

Elise froze, her entire body trembling with anger.

The car pulled away, disappearing around the corner.

The air turned thick, suffocating. Elise stood frozen on the lawn, her fists clenched, her breath coming in ragged gasps. The Suarez's approached.

"Oh, Elise," Hannah said, her voice dripping with artificial sympathy.

"This is for the best. You'll see."

Elise barely heard her. Her phone buzzed in her pocket, shaking her back to reality. She yanked it out. A message from Miles.

Don't try to follow. They're waiting for you to do something rash. I'm looking into it. Stay calm.

Stay calm?

Her daughter had just been taken.

And whatever this was... it was personal.

They were going to regret it.

The house felt hollow without Harper's presence, every room an empty echo of what it had been mere days ago. Elise moved through it like a ghost, grabbing clothes from drawers and tossing them into a duffel bag. The weight of her thoughts weighed down on her, each one more suffocating than the last.

Was it Jamal? Dr. Delgado? She stuffed Harper's favorite hoodie into the bag, her mind spiraling. *The Suarez's? Maggie?*

She stopped in the middle of Harper's room, the bag hanging limply in her hand. Maggie's face flashed in her mind, the strange detachment in her sister's voice the last time they'd spoken. Maggie had been acting odd, distant, almost rehearsed. But even Maggie didn't know all the details.

Elise shook her head, gripping the edge of Harper's desk to steady herself. *How did CPS know everything? How would the school know about my work incidents?*

Nothing made sense.

Her pulse spiked with a sudden burst of anger, and before she could stop herself, she pulled out her phone and dialed Maggie's number. Her hand trembled as it rang, the sound loud in the silence of the house. She almost hung up, doubting Maggie would even answer after how strained things had become between them.

But on the second ring, Maggie picked up.

"Elise," Maggie said, her tone neutral.

Elise's breath caught, a mix of relief and suspicion.

"They took Harper," she said, her voice cracking.

"CPS just showed up and—"

"I know," Maggie interrupted. Her voice was distant, eerily calm.

Elise froze.

"You... you know? How could you possibly—"

"Everything that's been happening is necessary, Elise."

"For Harper's safety. For everyone's safety."

Elise's grip tightened on the phone.

"What are you talking about? Maggie, they took my daughter."

"Your resistance is hurting her," Maggie said, as if reciting something rehearsed.

"I see that now. How our chaos damages those around us. Harper deserves the chance to achieve true Harmony."

Elise's knees nearly buckled. She sank onto the edge of Harper's bed, clutching the phone.

"Listen to yourself! This isn't you—"

"I've never been more myself," Maggie said firmly.

There was a pause, and when she spoke again, her voice was softer, almost pitying.

"The path to perfection requires sacrifice, Elise. Some of us must lose everything to find truth."

"Maggie, please," Elise begged, her voice breaking.

"Whatever you're involved in, this isn't right. Harper is my daughter. She belongs with me."

"When you're ready to accept the truth, you'll understand," Maggie said.

There was another pause, longer this time, the silence pressing down on Elise like a boulder.

"Until then, Harper is safer with them."

The line went dead. Elise pulled the phone away from her ear, staring at the screen as if it might bring Maggie back. Her sister's words settled like ice in her stomach.

Elise stood, the duffel bag forgotten on the floor. Her heart pounded, her breath coming in shallow gasps. Maggie had chosen a side, and it wasn't hers. But Dr. Delgado? Delgado might still have answers.

Her phone buzzed again. A text from Miles.

Stay put. Let me handle this.

Elise ignored it. She grabbed the bag, slinging it over her shoulder, and stormed toward the door. She was done waiting, done reacting. Whatever was happening to Harper, whatever web Necessity Mart had spun around her family, she was going to tear it apart thread by thread.

As she stepped outside, the morning light felt harsh, the world too bright for the storm forming inside her. She climbed into her car, her hands gripping the wheel so tightly her fingers ached.

She needed to see Dr. Delgado. Now.

∞∞∞∞∞

Elise pushed open the door to Dr. Delgado's office and was met with an alarming stillness. The smell of coffee lingered in the air, but the room felt abandoned. Her eyes swept over the desk, where an Aether band laid gleaming under the overhead light. Its polished surface caught her eyes like a trap waiting to spring. She stepped closer, her heart pounding, every instinct screaming that something wasn't right.

The band's placement was too staged. Why would Delgado leave it here? Elise's pulse ticked up as her phone buzzed in her pocket. She fumbled to pull it out, her breath catching when she saw the message.

Loading dock behind the gym. Five minutes.

Elise glanced back at the Aether one last time before tucking her phone away and leaving the office. She moved through the halls of the school, her footsteps echoing in the empty corridor. By the time she reached the gym's loading dock, the sun had dipped lower, bathing the pavement in a fading glow.

Distant noise from the schoolyard drifted through the heavy silence, doing little to settle the tension gripping her chest.

"Elise."

Dr. Delgado's voice made her jump. She stepped out from between the bleacher supports, her jacket pulled tightly around her as if shielding herself from more than the cool air. Her movements were cautious.

"Dr. Delgado!" Elise hissed, closing the distance between them.

163

"They took Harper—"

"I know," Dr. Delgado interrupted, her voice low.

She looked over her shoulder, the shadows around them stretching longer as the sun dipped further.

"Word travels fast here. Too fast."

Elise's eyes narrowed.

"Your Aether," she said, pointing to Delgado's neck.

"Why isn't it with you?"

Dr. Delgado stiffened.

"I don't trust it anymore," she said.

"I think it records conversations. More than it's supposed to. Most of the staff don't realize it yet, but..." She paused, running a hand through her hair. "There are things I've been hearing, Elise. Patterns I can't ignore."

"What patterns?" Elise demanded, stepping closer.

Her throat felt tight, her desperation bleeding through her words.

Delgado hesitated, her hand gripping the edge of a metal support. "It's not just Harper," she said finally. "Three students this month, bright, excelling kids, suddenly flagged for 'cognitive irregularities.' Removed for 'evaluation.' Some, never seen again. And every time I ask questions, I'm told it's confidential... between the principal, CPS, and the families."

She met Elise's eyes, her voice a whisper. "It doesn't feel right."

"Did you report us?"

Dr. Delgado grew defensive.

"No. But someone did. Someone with access to Harper's records... her hospital visits, her school evaluation. Someone who knew everything." She stepped closer.

"Elise, have you done anything recently? Anything that might've drawn attention to your family?"

Before Elise could answer, the sound of gravel crunching underfoot made them both freeze. A man emerged from the shadows near the gym wall, his face hollow, his clothes hanging loosely like they hadn't been washed in weeks.

"Mrs. Winters," he rasped. "I saw you two... talking."

Dr. Delgado stiffened, her hands folding tightly against her chest.

"Mr. Ramirez—"

"It's okay," he cut her off. There was no warmth in his tone.

"I'm Sophie's father. David Ramirez."

Elise's breath caught. Sophie. The girl Harper had mentioned... the seizure.

"They told me it was a pre-existing condition," David said, his voice breaking slightly.

"But she never had seizures before the Aether. Now, she's in a coma, and they won't even let me see her."

He stared at Dr. Delgado.

"Be careful who you trust, Mrs. Winters. Some people here... they're not what they seem."

Dr. Delgado's face paled, her hands shaky as she took a step back.

"I... I have a meeting. I should go."

"Tell her about the other parents, Delgado. The ones who asked questions and lost their kids."

Dr. Delgado's eyes widened, her lips parting as if to respond, but no words came out. Instead, she turned on her heel and retreated toward the school.

Elise watched Dr. Delgado disappear into the distance, her thoughts spiraling into a chaotic mess of doubt and fear. David stepped closer, his presence tense. He pulled a worn business card from his pocket and pressed it into her hand.

"There's a group of us," he said quietly, his voice rough with exhaustion.

"Parents, teachers who've quit... we meet in secret. Call me when you're ready."

Elise stared at the card, its edges fraying beneath her trembling fingers.

David's eyes lingered in the direction Dr. Delgado had gone.

"But Mrs. Winters?" He paused, his voice lowering. "Watch your back. She's not telling you everything. No one here is."

Elise stumbled back to her car, her mind buzzing with conflicting thoughts. She sat behind the wheel, gripping the business card, the edges digging into her palm. Her phone buzzed in the cup holder, shaking her from her thoughts. She picked it up, her chest tightening when she saw the name.

"Miles," she answered, her voice unsteady.

"I found something," he said, his voice urgent.

"About the CPS visit. And it's worse than we thought. A lot worse."

Elise's blood ran cold. "What did you find?"

"Not over the phone," Miles said quickly.

"Get back to the safe house. Now."

Elise ended the call. Her mind raced as she stared out the windshield, the pieces of the puzzle scattering further apart with every step she took. Whatever was happening, it was closing in on her faster than she could keep up.

And Harper's time was running out.

∞∞∞∞∞

Evening crept into the small apartment like an intruder. The table chaotic—scattered papers, coffee-stained notepads, and a laptop fan that struggled in the oppressive silence.

Elise sat at the cramped kitchen table, shoulders hunched, eyes scanning line after line of text on the screen. The clack of her fingers on the keys was the only sound, except for the occasional rustle of paper as she cross-referenced notes. Her focus was manic, her exhaustion evident by the dark bags under her eyes.

The documents spread across the table told a story, but the pieces didn't fit. Not yet. Elise scribbled something in the margins of a crumpled printout, pausing to look back at a photo clipped to the edge of her notebook. James's face stared back. He'd left behind just enough for her to chase, but not enough for her to catch.

The sound of the stairwell buzzer shook her from her thoughts. Her hand instinctively moved to the small handgun hidden in her jacket on the table's edge. She waited, her breath held, until she heard the knock they'd agreed on: three quick taps, followed by a pause, then two more.

Elise exhaled shakily and crossed to the door, peering through the peephole. Miles stood outside, hunched over the cold evening air, clutching a paper bag. She unlocked the door, glancing up and down the alleyway before pulling him inside.

"Chinese food," Miles announced, setting the bag on the counter. His voice was gruff. He dropped heavily into the nearest chair, wheezing slightly as he adjusted the thin scarf wrapped around his neck.

Elise frowned, her eyes lingering on his shallow breaths.

"Should you even be eating that?" she asked.

Miles waved her off, pulling out a carton of noodles and a pair of chopsticks.

"It's fuel," he muttered. "Not like I've got time to worry about cholesterol."

His dismissive tone didn't mask the tremor in his hand as he pulled the chopsticks apart. Elise opened her mouth to say something else but stopped, watching as he steadied himself and ate in silence.

"I found something," he said, after a moment.

He set the carton down and reached into his jacket, pulling out a thin folder.

"CPS paperwork on Harper. Got it from a contact in the courthouse."

Elise grabbed the folder, her heart racing. The pages felt heavier than they should as she flipped through them. Her eyes darted over the stamped approvals, the signatures.

"This... this was filed before the school even contacted them. How—"

166

"It wasn't reactive," Miles interrupted. "It was planned."

He leaned forward.

"The judge who signed off... tied to OptimumCare. And there's a pattern. Other kids flagged for 'post-optimization cognitive decline.' Same CPS officers, same 'evaluation facility.' And all roads lead back to Necessity Mart."

Elise stared at the papers, her stomach twisting.

"And the timing... This happened right after I accessed the restricted files at work."

"Yeah." Miles leaned back, rubbing a hand over his face.

"They're watching you, Elise. Every step."

Her mind spun, images of Harper's tear-streaked face flashing behind her eyes.

"I need to get her back," she said, her voice cracking. "Miles, I—"

A violent coughing fit interrupted her. Miles hunched over, his hand clutching his chest as he struggled for breath.

"Miles!" Elise rushed to his side, gripping his arm.

"What's wrong? What's happening?"

He waved her off weakly, his other hand fumbling for the pill organizer in his pocket.

"Congestive heart failure," he said between shallow breaths.

"Not exactly news."

"You knew about this? And you didn't tell me?"

"I didn't think it mattered," Miles said, his voice rough but steadying as he swallowed a pill.

Their eyes met, he looked tired but defiant. "I'm on borrowed time, Elise. Figured I might as well do something with what I've got left."

The words hit her, their finality making the room feel colder.

"Grace Collins," Miles mumbled.

"She might have answers about James... About Harper."

Elise hesitated, her mind racing.

"She's five hours away," he said.

Miles pushed himself up from the chair, wincing as he did.

"Whatever's happening to Harper, Grace might know why."

Elise nodded, determination settling over. She gathered the scattered papers, shoving them into her bag alongside her laptop. Miles checked his medication and stuffed the pill organizer into his jacket before grabbing the car keys.

"You drive," he said, tossing them to Elise. "I need to rest."

The weight of his words hung between them as they climbed into the car. Elise looked back at the apartment, she had a gnawing sensation she wouldn't be seeing it again.

The clock on the dashboard read 8:47 PM. As the car pulled away, Elise gripped the wheel tighter, her willpower hardening with every mile between her and the life she was leaving behind.

∞∞∞∞

By the time they reached Port Lawrence, the sky had softened to a bruised shade of early morning. 8:07 AM. The city wasn't completely awake yet, but neither was Elise. At least not fully.

She hadn't realized how often Miles had to stop and piss until now. His body was failing him in ways he refused to acknowledge, but the man still drove like a ghost with unfinished business.

The last stop was just outside of the city. After that, he made it the rest of the way. Elise dozed off, head against the window, and woke to a rough tap on her shoulder.

"Wake up."

Her vision focused just in time to see Grace Collins stepping out of a car. Her figure unmistakable despite the years. Her hair was shorter now, her posture more defensive. Her eyes moved up and down the street before she headed toward the door of her building.

"She's careful," Miles said, watching her with a hunter's focus.

"Not careful enough, though."

"What now?" Elise asked.

"Now... we wait."

Near the building's entrance, three kids played soccer in a small concrete courtyard. The ball rolled toward Grace, and she stopped it with her foot. The children laughed, and one of the boys called out.

"Ms. Grace, did you bring us anything today?"

Grace smiled.

"Not today. Maybe tomorrow."

Then Grace disappeared into the building.

Elise's hand moved instinctively to the car door.

"Don't even think about it," Miles growled.

Elise hesitated.

She clenched her jaw. "We can't just sit here."

Miles wheezed, coughing as he struggled to get the words out.

"Listen, Elise... I've done this long enough. You don't go charging in unless you're sure the ground's solid under your feet."

Her hand tightened on the door handle.

Miles's voice softened, though his tone still carried weight.

"These kids... They're not part of this. Whatever you're about to drag them into, think twice."

Elise stepped out of the car before Miles could continue. She crossed the street, her heart pounding as she approached the kids. The soccer ball bounced between them, echoing against the building walls. The two boys were around ten. The younger girl, maybe seven, hung back, clutching a stuffed bear.

Elise forced a smile, summoning her best "mom voice."

"Hi there. I'm looking for my Aunt Grace. She forgot her medication, and I need to bring it to her."

The girl's eyes narrowed, suspicious.

"Ms. Grace doesn't have family."

One of the boys stepped up.

"She lives in 4C. She gives us candy sometimes."

"Yeah, when she remembers," the other boy added.

Elise fumbled in her pocket, pulling out a crumpled twenty-dollar bill.

She crouched slightly, meeting their eyes.

"Would you help me surprise her? I'd really appreciate it."

The boys exchanged looks, their excitement barely contained.

The younger girl hesitated, her grip tightening on her bear.

"Why do you need us to help?"

Elise hesitated for a second.

"Because I want it to be a fun surprise. Don't you like surprises?"

The girl didn't look convinced, but the boys were already debating who would get to knock. The girl sighed and joined them.

Elise waved Miles over from the car. He trudged reluctantly toward her.

"This is reckless," he muttered as they followed the children into the building.

"We won't get another shot if this goes sideways."

"Then we'll make it count," Elise said.

The stairwell smelled of mildew and cheap cleaning supplies. A section of the handrail was missing, forcing Miles to steady himself against the wall as they climbed. His breaths were shallow, but he pushed on without complaint.

The kids ran ahead, their laughter echoing. By the time they reached the fourth floor, they were arguing over who would knock first.

Apartment 4C looked as worn as the rest of the building, its door weighed down by a series of mismatched locks. The older boy won the argument and pounded on the door.

"Ms. Grace! Ms. Grace!" he yelled.

Elise and Miles pressed themselves against the wall, breathing slow, just outside the peephole's reach. Elise listened, heart pounding, as footsteps shuffled on the other side. A pause. Then the scrape of metal as one deadbolt slid free. Another. A third.

The door cracked open slightly, just enough for Grace's face to appear.

"What are you doing here?" she asked, her voice low but warm.

The younger girl held up the twenty-dollar bill.

"Your niece says you forgot your medicine."

Grace's face froze.

Her eyes moved to the shadows where Elise and Miles were hidden.

"Please, she said, her voice trembling as she tried to slam the door.

"I told them everything. I have nothing left to give—"

Miles's boots wedged against the doorframe just in time.

"We're not with them," Elise said. "James Winters sent us."

Grace paused.

"James?" she whispered in disbelief.

"But he... he stopped contacting me months ago."

Elise stepped forward. "He's dead. And now they have my daughter."

Grace's eyes flickered, something maternal breaking through the fear. Her shoulders stiffened. She looked once more down the hallway, then back at Elise.

She stepped aside. "Inside. Now."

The apartment was dirty and cluttered. Someone who had stopped caring. Grace shut the door, twisting the locks back into place.

Layers of yellowed newspapers covered the windows. The floor was covered in stacked magazines, old takeout containers, and towers of folders labeled in uneven handwriting.

"Don't touch anything," Grace muttered, leading them toward a small kitchen table.

She moved with purpose, her hands trembling as she reached behind a leaning bookshelf, fingertips brushing along the wood until she found what she was looking for. A loose panel. A hidden compartment.

She pulled out a thick stack of papers and spread them across the table, her fingers twitching as though she were exposing an old wound.

"I was assigned to review SnyapticEase," she said. "Routine FDA compliance check. Synapse Dynamics was like any other startup... ambitious, promising, maybe a little overeager. But then... the patterns started."

Elise leaned in. "What patterns?"

Grace sifted through the papers, pulling out a heavily redacted FDA document. "Delays. Vanished paperwork. Anomalies in trial data. And every time I pushed for answers, I got pressure from higher-ups to reject them outright. Quietly."

She tapped a page stamped with the name Mercer Holdings.

"Then James showed me what they were really doing."

Miles, silent but watching closely, nodded for her to continue.

Grace swallowed, her voice quieter now. "James wasn't just looking at Synapse Dynamics. He was following the money... shell companies, forged safety reports, fabricated approvals. Mercer Holdings was everywhere, moving through fake subsidiaries like a goddamn shell game. By the time he had enough to expose it, Synapse was out of options. They had to sell."

Her hands curled into fists. "Then the system turned on me. Reassignments. Emails ignored. Colleagues started avoiding me, like I was infected with something contagious. And then... accidents started happening."

Elise's breath caught. "And James?"

Grace hesitated.

"He was getting too close. He knew it was only a matter of time."

She leaned forward, pressing her palms flat against the table. "They don't come for you all at once. They chip away... your credibility, your connections, your sanity. By the time you realize you're trapped, there's nothing left of you to fight back."

She looked at Miles. "And you... you know what they do to people like us."

Miles said nothing. His jaw flexed. He didn't need to answer.

Grace reached for another stack of papers. She hesitated, then slid them forward.

"This is just the tip of the iceberg."

Three hard knocks cut her off.

Elise jerked in her seat. Miles, still slouched, went stiff. Grace's entire body turned to stone.

Then... more knocks. Harder this time.

A voice seeped through the door. "Ms. Collins."

A second voice followed, deeper. Somehow worse. "Open up."

Grace moved fast. She grabbed the stack of papers, shoving them back into their hiding place, and turned, eyes burning into Elise and Miles.

"Closed. Now." She hissed, pulling open a narrow hallway closet.

Elise didn't hesitate, practically shoving Miles in first. It reeked of mothballs and old fabric. They pressed against each other, the walls pressing back, the space barely enough for both. Coats hung limp around them, absorbing the sound of their breathing.

Through the sliver of light between the door, Elise watched Grace take a long breath before unlatching the first lock. Then the second. Then the third.

The door creaked open.

The first man stepped inside like he owned the place. Late forties. Neatly pressed slacks, gray jacket, gloves he didn't bother removing. The younger one followed. Bigger, broader, looking like he'd rather be breaking down doors than knocking on them.

The older man smiled. "It's been a while, Ms. Collins."

"Not long enough," she replied.

He took a slow step inside, his eyes looking over the walls.

"You always did have a way of making yourself comfortable," he mumbled.

Grace didn't move from the door. "What do you want?"

"We're looking for someone," the older man said. "A woman. Been causing some... issues."

"You wouldn't know anything about that, would you?"

"You think I still talk to people? Since you destroyed my career. My reputation? My entire goddamn life? I haven't spoken to anyone."

The older man took another step. His shoes barely made a sound against the rug. "We heard reports. Woman matching a certain description. Traveling with an older man. Her grandfather, maybe?"

Miles muttered under his breath. "Grandfather? Seriously? That's the best they could come up with?"

Elise didn't answer. She barely breathed.

"I don't know anything," Grace said.

The man's voice dropped, almost to a whisper. "See, what I'm worried about is that you're lying. And I'd hate to see another accident ruin your week."

"I have nothing," Grace said. "No career. No friends. No family. You already took everything from me. So tell me... what exactly do you think I have left to lose?"

The man studied her. The silence stretched. Then without a word, he turned.

The younger man hesitated, he didn't want to leave. His eyes scoured the room again, lingering on the narrow hallway, on the closet where Elise and Miles held their breath.

Then he followed.

At the door, the older man looked back. "If you do see her... do yourself a favor." He stepped into the doorway, adjusting his gloves. "Look the other way."

Then the door clicked behind them.

Elise and Miles didn't move until they heard the locks snap back into place.

Grace braced her hands on the table, head bowed, breaths coming in shallow bursts.

Elise pushed open the closet door, stepping into the dimly lit apartment. "Grace—"

Grace held up a shaking hand. "Go."

Miles peeled back a yellowed newspaper covering the window.

"They're leaving. But they will come back," he mumbled.

"I know," Grace snapped. "They'll be watching me now. They'll be watching everything."

She looked at Miles.

"And you should stop looking like you're about to drop dead."

Miles smirked. "Been hearing that a lot lately."

Grace exhaled. "Get out of here."

Elise took one last look at the apartment.

Then she turned and stepped into the hallway.

Behind them, the locks slid back into place.

Outside, Elise finally let out a breath she'd been holding.

Somewhere in the city, those men were still looking for her.

And she was running out of places to hide.

∞∞∞∞

The sedan cut through the deserted highway, tires drumming against the pavement. The only other sound was Miles coughing in the passenger seat, hunched over his laptop. His phone was sitting on the console, his mobile hotspot barely clinging to life.

Elise gripped the wheel, her eyes forward. Grace's revelations sat heavy in the car, a phantom in the back seat. The clock dash read 5:47 PM. Every minute that passed was another taken from Harper.

"Anything?" she asked, breaking the silence.

Miles didn't look up. "Scrubbed. Synapse Dynamics is a ghost online. Every link is dead. Corporate cleanup."

He muttered under his breath, fingers moving faster.

"Wait... cached version of an old article. Let's see if they missed a spot." His eyes glossing across the screen. "Six years ago."

Elise looked over. "What's it say?"

"Puff piece. Synapse Dynamics was a biotech darling... four researchers, big buzzwords about 'revolutionary trauma therapy.' They were developing something called the SynapticEase for PTSD patients."

He skimmed further, then frowned. "Four names. Dr. Thomas Reed, behavioral psychology. Dr. Nadine Carter, implementation specialist. Dr. Marcus Wills, neural interface design. And the lead, Dr. Elena Santos."

"Do they mean anything to you?"

Elise shook her head. "Not yet. What about them?"

Miles's typed faster. "Let's see who's still standing."

A tense minute passed. Then, his voice became more urgent. "Dr. Reed—suicide, three years ago. Found in his home. Stress-related breakdown, they said."

Elise's heart jumped. "Convenient."

"Dr. Wills... car accident. Same year. Skidded on ice. But get this. His car had just been serviced for brake issues." Miles turned, his eyebrow raised. "Sound familiar?"

"James," she whispered.

Miles sighed, scrolling faster. "Dr. Carer? Gone. No trail, no record. And Dr. Santos? Same. Vanished after Synapse folded."

"All of them?"

Miles leaned back, fingers drumming on the laptop. "Yeah. That's not a coincidence. That's a cleanup."

"James knew, didn't he? He was digging into this."

Miles shut the laptop. "And now, it's your daughter paying the price."

The silence lingered between them. Outside, the night stretched endless.

Miles cleared his throat. "We're close. But I'm not sure how much time we got."

They pulled into the alley behind the laundromat. The building was dark, cracked brick and rusted fire escape barely visible in the glow of a single streetlamp. Elise cut the engine, the sudden quiet amplifying the pounding in her ears.

Miles groaned as he climbed out of the car, stretching stiff limbs. Elise grabbed the files from the back.

"We'll dig into this tomorrow," Miles said. "I'll call some people. Maybe we can find something on Carter or Santos."

Elise nodded, but her mind was already moving ahead. As they walked up the stairwell, Miles's cough echoed, a loud, rattling sound. She looked at him.

"You should sleep," she said.

Miles waved her off. "I'll sleep when this is over."

At the top of the stairs, he hesitated, gripping the railing. "Tomorrow," he mumbled, almost to himself. "We follow the scientists."

Inside the safe house, Elise set the files on the kitchen table, pulling out her phone. Her stomach was in knots. No messages. Harper's evaluation window was down to twenty-four hours.

She dropped the phone, placing her hands on the table. Miles slumped into a chair, head tilted back, breathing shallow.

"Get some sleep," he grumbled.

The bedroom door shut behind her. The weight of everything settled in her chest. And in the suffocating quiet, she knew, the morning wouldn't come gently.

∞∞∞∞∞

The TV played in the corner, its anchors forcing hollow cheer as they rattled off the morning's headlines. The markets were up. A new tech innovation promised to "revolutionize human potential." A local charity gala raised record funds.

Elise didn't hear any of it.

She sat hunched at the kitchen table, Grace's documents spread across it like pieces of a puzzle with missing edges. Redactions cut through the paragraphs. Notes written in the margins formed frantic, disconnected thoughts. The timelines refused to align. She shuffled the pages, stacking them in patterns only she understood, her mind clawing for something solid.

The phone rang. Elise flinched.

Dr. Delgado.

Her stomach dropped.

She swiped to answer. "Hello?"

The voice on the other end was different. It was stripped from its usual polish.

"Mrs. Winters... I'm calling about Harper."

The air in Elise's lungs turned to ice. "What about her?"

A pause. Too long. Too unnatural.

"The school board reviewed Harper's... cognitive episode," Dr. Delgado said finally. "Her performance metrics. They flagged a pattern of dissociative behavior in class."

Elise gripped the counter with her free hand.

"What are you talking about?" she demanded.

Dr. Delgado sighed.

"They claim it's a liability concern for the school's insurance. Officially, they've determined she requires specialized cognitive support beyond what we can provide."

Elise's vision blurred.

"This is about CPS, isn't it?" She got louder. "About the Aether. This is all connected."

"I don't know," Dr. Delgado admitted. "The school says it's standard protocol, but something about this feels..."

She stopped, leaving the thought unfinished.

When she spoke again, her tone had become more bureaucratic.

"The recommendation is to transfer Harper to a partner institution better equipped for her unique situation. You'll receive the official paperwork tomorrow."

Elise's mind raced.

A long exhale from the other end. Then, apologetically, "I should have said something sooner. About Sophie. About all of it."

Silence.

"And the others," Dr. Delgado admitted. "There's a pattern, Mrs. Winters. I—"

A knock in the background.

Dr. Delgado's voice shifted immediately, back into its professional mask.

"I have to go. Someone's here."

"Wait!"

"The transfer paperwork will arrive tomorrow," Dr. Delgado said, like she was reading from a script. Then, after a hesitation, so low it almost wasn't there.

"Just... be careful."

The line went dead.

Elise stood in the kitchen, unable to move, the weight of the phone pressing into her palm. The TV continued its empty monologue.

She turned to the counter. Ramirez's card sat next to the gun.

The patterns were clearer now. Sophie's seizure, Harper's dissociative episodes, the quiet disappearances of children marked as *liabilities.* It was a pipeline. A polished, corporate system of containment designed to slip by unnoticed.

But what was the goal?

She grabbed the phone again. No hesitation this time. She dialed.

The line rang twice before a gruff voice answered.

"Ramirez."

"This is Elise Winters. Harper's mom. We met at the loading dock at FutureReady."

Silence. Then, hesitantly. "I remember. What's this about?"

"They're trying to remove my daughter. Same language you mentioned. Liability concerns, specialized support, partner institutions. I need to know what's happening."

Ramirez sighed, and it was the sound of exhaustion carved into a man's bones.

"It's a script," he said. "They've used it on dozens of families. My Sophie. The Johnson's boy. A girl named Avery. Same story every time. 'Cognitive episodes.' 'Behavioral concerns.' And always tied to the Aether."

Elise gripped the phone. "How's Sophie?"

"Still in a coma."

The silence stretched.

"We're meeting tomorrow," he said finally. "Families like us. People who've lost kids to this. Six p.m., old community center on Cedar Street. No cameras, no optimization zones. Just the truth."

Elise scribbled the address onto the business card with shaky hands.

"I'll be there."

Her phone buzzed again. Another message.

Paul from the Patchwork Society.

Ramirez's voice turned urgent.

"Be careful, Mrs. Winters. They take everything."

Elise barely heard him.

Her pulse pounded as she opened the text thread.

Maggie's posts are getting worse. She's not herself.

Below, Paul had attached screenshots from Maggie's social media.

True freedom comes from perfect alignment.

Individual choice is the prison we build ourselves.

The Algorithm knows what's best for us all.

Optimization isn't control... it's liberation.

The words weren't hers. They were cultish.

Paul's next message landed like a fist to the ribs.

I checked on her today. No answer at the door. Mail piling up. Looked through the window... rooms are partially empty. Neighbors haven't seen her in days.

Elise's breath came too fast. She typed back.

Did you go inside?

No. Something about the house feels... wrong. Empty, but not abandoned.

Then another.

She's talking like them now. The ones who believe in total surrender. The Ascension Order is always recruiting people like Maggie. People who feel like they've lost everything.

Elise's hands trembled.

Thank you, Paul. I will see what I can find out.

She dialed Maggie.

Straight to voicemail.

She tried again. Same result.

The room suddenly felt smaller. The world, emptier. Harper was slipping. Maggie was slipping. And if Elise didn't move fast, they'd both be gone.

She placed the phone on the table and exhaled slowly.

Tomorrow couldn't come soon enough.

∞∞∞∞

The drive to Maggie's was a blur.

Elise didn't even park... she abandoned the car, tires grinding against the curb. The engine cut off, but the pounding in her chest didn't. Her fingers clenched the wheel, stiff, locked in place, as if letting go meant everything would unravel. For a moment, she just sat there, breath shallow, the house towering ahead like a waiting trap.

She swallowed the knot in her throat, forcing herself to move.

Maggie wasn't just *gone*, she had disappeared herself. Wiped away every trace. It wasn't like her. Not this calculated precision. Not this type of emptiness.

Elise moved back through the house, faster this time.

The coffee table was bare except for a single coaster. The couch cushions sat undisturbed, perfectly arranged. Maggie never lived like this. She existed in a flurry

178

of motion, stacks of books, half-written notes, a sweater draped over the armrest where she had last abandoned it.

This wasn't a home anymore. It was a shell.

Elise's fingers tightened around a note on the counter, its creases cutting into her skin.

They showed me the path to perfect peace.

She felt sick.

She turned toward the stairs, walking up them two at a time.

The second floor was dark and still. The bathroom door slightly cracked, and Elise caught a glimpse of a perfectly folded towel, the toothbrush missing from its holder. Another detail erased. Another piece removed.

Then Maggie's office.

Elise hesitated before pushing the door open.

The desk was cleared except for a single notebook. Elise flipped through it quickly, scanning for something, *anything,* that felt real. But it was nothing like Maggie's usual frantic scribbles. The pages were full of calculated diagrams, alignment charts, and phrases that sent a cold chill through her.

Surrender is the path to clarity.

Through unity, we transcend the burden of choice.

The Algorithm provides. The Algorithm knows.

Elise could feel her pulse pounding in her ears.

She backed out, turning to Maggie's bedroom.

The bed looked untouched, perfectly made. Maggie didn't make her bed. Not like this. Not with hospital corners and a smoothing so precise the fabric barely wrinkled. A crystal pendant glinted on the blanket, coiled like a snake waiting to strike.

Elise's fingers hovered over the pamphlet sitting next to it.

Embracing Unity Through Surrender.

She forced herself to breathe.

Then a piece of paper with coordinates, and a time.

She grabbed the scrap of paper, her grip tightening as she looked at numbers. Whatever Maggie had been pulled into, it wasn't just about optimization anymore.

It was something deeper.

And Elise wasn't letting her go without a fight.

She turned quickly, moving back through the house, each step faster, more determined. The emptiness was no longer just a warning—it was a declaration.

This wasn't just a disappearance.

It was a conversion.

∞∞∞∞∞

The basketball game flickered on the muted TV, a blur of movement against the heavy stillness of the safe house. An open pizza box sat on the coffee table, its last few slices abandoned.

Miles slumped in the armchair, labored breathing cutting through the quiet. Empty pill bottles lined the table beside him, a silent testament to his stubbornness.

Elise couldn't sit. She paced, the edge of Maggie's note crumpling in her restless fingers. The words burned into her mind. The meticulously arranged house, the pamphlet, the coordinates. Numbers that could lead to anywhere. Or nowhere.

"I went to Maggie's house," she said abruptly.

"It wasn't empty, but it might as well have been."

Miles looked up from his laptop, exhaustion covering his face, but not his eyes. They were sharp. Always sharp.

"What do you mean?"

She slid the note across the table. "Read this."

Miles raised his eyebrows as he scanned the writing. His jaw tightened.

The algorithm knows best.

He set the note down slowly.

"That's not Maggie," he mumbled.

"No," Elise agreed. "It's not."

She reached into her pocket, pulling out another slip of paper. "This was next to a pamphlet on her bed." She placed it beside the note. "Coordinates."

Miles leaned forward, fingers brushing the keyboard as he entered the numbers into his laptop. The screen refreshed dropping a pin over a location on the outskirts of town.

Elise shivered, the image of the Ascension Order members from the protest flashing through her mind. Their unnatural smiles.

"Paul said she's talking like them now," she muttered. "Like the Ascension Order."

Miles marked the location with a pin, his voice low.

"We'll check it out. But first..."

He turned back to his screen, fingers moving carefully. Before he could continue, a coughing fit overcame him, his whole body convulsing. He braced himself against the chair, hacking into his fist.

Elise stepped toward him, worried. "Maybe we should get you something other than pizza." She nudged the box aside.

Miles waved her off between coughs, voice hoarse but defiant. "Pizza might be my last joy in life. Let me have this."

Elise shook her head. "You won't be much use if you—"

She stopped herself.

"I'll worry about that later," he mumbled, grabbing a napkin, dabbing at his mouth. He straightened, eyes focusing on the screen. "You need to hear this."

He tapped a few keys, pulling up a sparse timeline.

"Dr. Nadine Carer? Trail goes cold in 2019. No credit cards, no social media, no utility records. Like she was erased, not just missing."

"And Dr. Santos?"

"She left traces," Miles said. "Research papers, grant applications. Then nothing. Last known address was a clinic in Brookfield Heights."

"That's not too far. Could she still be there?"

"Maybe," Miles said. "But that's not all."

He opened another tab, with a series of documents.

"Mercer Holdings. A shell company, just like we thought. But when I traced its formation, I found ties to early Necessity Mart filings. Everything loops back to them."

Elise clenched her fists.

"Whoever is running this knows how to hide their tracks. But they're not perfect."

Miles clicked an archived newspaper article. The headline was unremarkable, but the accompanying photo made Elise lean in. A young Adrien Rey Zhao, no older than nineteen, staring blankly at the camera.

"Zhao?" Elise frowned. "Who is he?"

"The puppet master before he got his strings." Miles tapped the screen. "The CEO of Necessity Mart. Before he was just A.R., he was Adrien Rey Zhao."

The article was from years ago. Before Necessity Mart. Before the empire.

"This was before he disappeared for nearly a decade," Miles continued. "His mother had a psychotic break... killed the rest of the family. Adrien was the only survivor. He was trapped in the basement for three days. Heard everything."

"He heard them die?" Elise asked, nearly whispering.

"Not just die." Miles clicked to another article, showing Zhao years later. "His mother believed individual consciousness was suffering. She thought she was setting them free."

Miles sat back, rubbing his temple. "After that, Zhao vanished. Resurfaced with Necessity Mart. No public appearances. No interviews. Even board meetings are virtual."

Elise exhaled slowly.

Miles was about to continue when something on his screen stopped him. "Wait..."

Elise leaned in further. "What?"

Miles enlarged the cafe footage. The last recorded meeting of James Winters.

He rewound, played it again. Froze the frame.

The woman across from James.

Miles stared at her. "The way she touches his hand. It's calm, almost clinical."

"Okay, and?"

Miles didn't answer. He was already pulling up another image. A grainy group photo from a Synapse Dynamics research article. His cursor hovered over one of the faces.

Dr. Elena Santos.

"She's aged," Miles mumbled, zooming in as far as the computer would allow.

"But look at her posture. The way she holds herself."

It was her.

The woman James met before he died.

Elise's mind spun. "What did James give her? What did she give him?"

"She might know what's in that safety deposit box," Miles said.

The realization hit them both.

Miles leaned back. Elise stared at the frozen frame on the screen.

The pieces were finally coming together.

And someone was going to a lot of trouble to keep them apart.

CHAPTER ELEVEN

Out of Stock

We don't see things as they are, we see them as we are.
– Anaïs Nin

Elise's house didn't feel like a home anymore. The silence was too aware, like the walls were listening. She had been pacing the living room since dawn, her bare feet tracing a restless circuit across the worn rug. The gun sat on the kitchen counter, within reach. She hadn't even realized she'd been keeping it out. Not for protection or comfort, but as a warning.

The call came at 8:30 AM.

A woman's voice. "We'll be returning Harper within the hour."

Elise didn't thank her. She didn't ask questions. She just hung up and stared at the phone until the screen locked.

Miles had texted just after sunrise.

Stationed at the end of the block. Eyes open.

Another layer of reassurance. Yet none of it filled the gnawing emptiness inside her. Harper was coming back. That was supposed to mean something, wasn't it?

At 9:07 AM, the car rolled in, its engine quiet as a whisper. Plain white, government issue. Elise stood at the window watching as the doors opened.

Sandra Morris stepped out first, the same unreadable expression she wore last time she was there, posture as rigid as ever. Behind her, another woman followed, clipboard in hand, exuding the same brand of suffocating officiousness. A uniformed officer stayed in the driver's seat.

And then, Harper.

She sat in the back, still as a doll. Too still.

Elise's throat tightened. The gun on the counter was suddenly too visible. She moved fast, snatching it up, sliding it into the drawer beside the sink. She left it cracked open. Today wasn't a day for loose ends.

A knock. Loud like a gavel hitting wood.

Elise counted to three before opening the door, keeping her face blank.

Sandra's smile was thin. "Mrs. Winters, thank you for your cooperation during Harper's evaluation."

Cooperation. Elise held back a laugh.

"Our assessment revealed some patterns in the home environment that we found... concerning."

The clipboard woman flipped a page, her voice rehearsed. "Erratic behavior, paranoid tendencies... those terms came up more than once in our interviews."

Elise bit at her nails. "Interviews with who?"

The woman smiled, the kind that wasn't meant to be reassuring. "These findings were part of a broader analysis. They don't reflect judgement, merely observations."

Sandra leaned in slightly, not enough to be aggressive, just enough to make her point. "Further investigation could be warranted if certain... activities were to persist. I trust that won't be necessary."

The message was clear. *Keep digging and we'll bury you.*

The officer opened the back door.

Harper stepped out.

She moved carefully, like someone testing the ground after a fall. Her legs stiff, her arms hanging limp at her sides. Her skin was pale, her eyes unfocused, pupils too wide.

She didn't run to Elise. She didn't cry, didn't smile. She just stood there, staring at the house like it was wrong.

Elise forced herself to breathe. "Sweetie, you're home."

Harper nodded. But didn't respond.

Inside, Harper sat at the edge of the couch like a guest in someone else's home. Elise knelt in front of her.

"How are you feeling? Are you hungry?"

Harper blinked slowly. "I'm... tired. Can I go lie down?"

Something in her voice. It wasn't monotone, not exactly. But it carried no weight, no texture.

"Of course," Elise said.

Harper stood, hesitated at the bottom of the stairs.

"Do you need help?"

Harped frowned, as if the question itself didn't make sense. "No. I just... forgot which way."

Elise's stomach twisted.

She followed Harper up, watching every step. Her daughter moved like she was walking through a place she'd only seen in pictures.

In her room, Harper sat on the bed, staring at the wall. Elise sat beside her. "Can you tell me what happened? Where did they take you?"

Harper didn't look at her. "I don't know... everything's fuzzy."

"Fuzzy how?"

"I don't know," Harper whispered, voice breaking. She turned, eyes wide, something close to panic flickering behind them. "Please don't make me talk about it. I don't want to go back."

Elise forced herself to nod. "You won't," she said. "I promise."

"We need to pack some clothes," Elise said. "We can't stay here."

Harper looked up, frustration across her face.

"Why can't things just be normal?"

Elise placed a hand on her shoulder. "I know this is hard. But we'll figure it out. I just need you to trust me."

Harper nodded, reluctant, the fight draining from her. She started packing, her movements slow.

At one point, she stopped and looked up.

"Mom? Why can't I remember yesterday?"

Elise's chest tightened.

She sent a text to miles.

Coming now. They did something to Harper. Something is wrong.

This wasn't just disorientation.

This was theft.

∞◦◦◦◦∞

The safe house was small, worn, barely held together. Takeout containers cluttered the table, the smell of soy sauce clinging to the air. A radio muttered music that was more static, the melody buried beneath the white noise.

Harper sat across from Elise, picking at her fried rice with indifference. She was more here than before, eyes more focused, but still moving like she was running on half-speed. Elise hadn't touched her food. She was too busy watching, waiting for something. Anything.

Miles sat at the head of the table, pushing a piece of broccoli with his chopsticks. Then, a cough hit. Hard and sudden. His whole body shook, tearing through his chest.

Elise flinched.

The chopsticks fell to the floor. Miles barely caught himself, hand flying to his mouth.

"Miles," Elise screamed, grabbing a napkin.

He waved her off, but she caught the stain before he crumpled it. Red. Not much. But enough.

Across the table, Harper stared. Silent.

"I'm fine," Miles croaked.

"You're not." Elise's eyes cut through him. She crouched beside him.

"How bad is it?"

Miles didn't answer right away. He leaned back, breath slowing, the color draining from his face.

"Not much time left," he admitted. "Days. Maybe weeks."

"I need to finish this while I still can," Miles said, determined despite the fragility of his body.

Harper shifted. "Mom?"

Elise turned.

"What about my history project?"

Her words were clearer. More her.

Elise and Miles exchanged a look.

"You're not going back to FutureReady," Elise said carefully.

Harper blinked, confusion turning into anger. "What? Why not?"

"It's not safe."

Harper pushed back from the table, her movements unsteady but powered by frustration. "You're ruining everything!" Her voice cracked, the words spilling out with force she hadn't seemed capable of earlier.

"Sweetie, it's not like that—" Elise started.

"Then what is it like?" Harper interrupted. She stumbled as she tried to stand, bracing herself against the edge of the table. "What about my friends? The science fair? Ethan and I were supposed to finish our project."

Her voice rose with each sentence, the force of her anger pulling her further out of the fog.

"Harper, I'm trying to protect you," Elise said.

"I don't need protection!" Harper yelled.

"I just want things to be normal for once!"

She stormed toward the bedroom. The door slammed shut behind her.

"This isn't sustainable," Elise muttered, more to herself than to Miles.

Miles exhaled, looking up from his laptop. "We'll figure it out. One thing at a time."

Elise ran a hand through her hair. "I need to go to the support group soon. Ramirez said I have to see what they're not telling us."

Miles nodded, but his focus had already shifted back to the screen. "I've been looking into Robert Blackwood. Turns out, he handled James's investigation into Mercer Holdings. He might know what James found."

"Do you think he'll talk?"

Miles shrugged. "He's spooked, but everyone has a breaking point. If we get to him fast, maybe he'll still feel safe enough to give us something."

Elise folded her arms, staring toward the hall. "What about Harper? I can't leave her alone here."

"It's just for an hour or two," Miles said. "She'll be fine. She's not going anywhere in her condition."

The words sat heavy in the space between them.

Elise finally pushed herself up. "I'll check on her."

She knocked lightly on the bedroom door. "Harper?" She waited. No response.

Elise hesitated, then tried the knob. It turned easily, but when she pushed, the door didn't budge. Locked.

"Sweetheart? I just want to make sure you're okay."

A long pause. Then, muffled through the wood. "I'm fine."

Elise stepped back, not willing to push further.

Back in the kitchen, Miles was dry-swallowing his evening medication, each pill another silent acknowledgement of time running out.

Elise leaned against the counter, arms crossed. "We'll keep it short."

Miles nodded, but neither of them voiced the thoughts pressing at the edges of the room.

Leaving Harper alone might be the biggest mistake they'd make.

∞∞∞∞

The community center room had a tangible tiredness to it, like a space that had seen too many battles without ever being a battlefield. Folding chairs clattered into place as latecomers shuffled in, avoiding eye contact while taking their seats. David Ramirez hovered by the door, nodding to each new arrival with a look that said he wished he didn't have to see them there.

187

Elise stayed near the back, watching as people settled into the uneven circle. There was something about the faces, each carrying a weight they couldn't put down, that made her throat tighten. She hated that she recognized them, not individually but in what they shared. That sense of something stolen from them, and worse, the knowledge that it had been taken by people they'd trusted.

Adrienne Chen stood at the center, her presence quiet but commanding. Her natural authority wasn't a force of volume or physicality but of focus. She gave the impression that every piece of information in the room had already been cataloged in her mind.

"We're not here to fight the system," Adrienne said, addressing the group. "We're here to help each other survive it."

When the stories started, they came hesitantly, like dipping a toe into freezing water. A teacher spoke first, about how one of her brightest students had changed practically overnight after removing her Aether. "She stopped asking questions. Stopped smiling. It's like the spark was just... gone."

One by one, the group added their pieces. A tech worker talked about strange accidents at her office, all involving people recently unoptimized. "They said it was human error," she said bitterly, "but those weren't accidents. They were symptoms."

Every story carried echoes of Elise's own experiences, and with each one, the room felt heavier, the stakes clearer.

When it was her turn to speak, Elise's voice was calm, as she explained what she'd found. "It's called Optimization Dependency Syndrome," she said, holding the room's attention with a quiet intensity. "It's in internal documents from OptimumCare. It's not just something that happens... they know about it. They've classified it. And they're still doing it anyway."

The silence that followed held the room.

A woman in the corner leaned forward, her pen moving furiously across a notepad. A man in a hoodie rubbed his face, muttering something too low to hear. Adrienne's expression didn't change, but her fingers tapped lightly on the armrest of her chair.

"What exactly does it say?" Adrienne asked.

Elise described the symptoms: withdrawal-like effects, neural instability, memory lapses. She detailed the language used in the documents, their cold precision disguising the horror underneath.

A teacher in the circle exhaled, her voice trembling as she said, "That's why my student had seizures."

Another parent, sitting stiffly with their arms crossed, nodded slowly. "That's what happened to my son... it's exactly what happened."

The room shifted, a collective realization settling over the group. It wasn't paranoia. It wasn't coincidence. It was a system.

As the conversations died down, one of the younger members of the group spoke hesitantly. "Has anyone... has anyone heard of The Sunder?"

Adrienne's head tilted slightly, her interest piqued. "Go on."

"They're this... underground group," he continued, his hands fidgeting nervously. "Not like us, though. They're advanced. Organized. They help people remove their Aethers safely and deal with the fallout afterward. I've only heard whispers, but apparently, they know things. Things about how the devices actually work."

Adrienne leaned back. "And no one here has had contact with them?"

Heads shook around the room.

"It's just rumors," someone muttered.

"Maybe," Adrienne said. "But if they're real, they might have answers we don't." She made a note on her pad, her pen moving quickly. "We'll keep an ear out."

Elise filed the name away in her mind, something about it digging into her.

The conversations inevitably turned to theories.

"They're using the devices to control behavior," one man argued. "Think about it... half the people in this room described personality changes."

"No, it's about data," a woman responded. "Everything we do on those devices is tracked. This is about surveillance, not mind control."

A third voice jumped in. "It's both. They're building profiles, testing how far they can push people. This is a lab, and we're the rats."

Adrienne held up a hand, silencing the rising tension. "Theories are fine," she said. "But they won't help our loved ones. Action will. Let's keep this focused."

As the meeting wrapped up, Adrienne approached Elise directly, her eyes scanning her face as though memorizing every detail. "What you've brought tonight is important," she said. "If we can connect more cases, it could change everything. But we have to be careful. This isn't about taking them down. It's about helping others understand what's happening."

She gestured to a clipboard on the table. "There are more groups forming. Quiet, but they are there. If we spread this information the right way, it'll reach the people who need it the most."

Elise nodded, feeling the weight of Adrienne's words settle alongside her own burden.

Adrienne exhaled, rubbing the back of her neck. "I used to be a journalist," she said. "Spent years chasing the next big story, thinking if I could just expose the truth, everything would change. But stories don't save people. Action does."

Her eyes met Elise's. "Now, I care more about helping people than headlines."

Elise hesitated for only a second before slipping a flash drive from her pocket. It was small, but heavy in her palm. "Maybe you can do more with this than I can," she said quietly. "Just in case."

Adrienne took it, her fingers brushing Elise's briefly. She turned it over in her hand. "What's on it?"

"Files from OptimumCare. Patient records, internal reports. Things that don't add up." Elise swallowed. "I pulled what I could before I had to leave."

Adrienne's grip tightened around the drive. "This could be dangerous to hold onto."

"I know," Elise said. "But I think it's too late for me to worry about that."

Adrienne studied her for a moment, then slid the drive into the inside pocket of her coat. "I'll keep it safe."

The words felt like a promise, but Elise knew better than to believe in safety anymore.

As the group thinned out, Ramirez caught Elise by the elbow, pulling her toward the door. His grip was firm but quick, like he didn't want to linger in plain sight. He pressed a worn folder into her hands.

"Sophie's records." He said quietly. "Everything in here matches what you described—ODS, OCC. I didn't see it before, but now…"

Elise flipped through the pages, her pulse climbing with every line. The patterns weren't just similar. They were identical. The same flagged behaviors, the same cognitive deterioration, the same quiet erasure of a child's individuality.

Ramirez sighed, staring out the window. "If you find anything else, use this."

He slipped a folded piece of paper into her palm. A phone number, handwritten.

"Not the one on my card."

Elise didn't ask why. She just nodded, tucking it deep into her bag.

By the time she stepped outside, the name *The Sunder* lingered in her mind, tangled with too many other things—Harper's blank stare, Maggie's hollow house, the untouched note in James's handwriting she still hadn't deciphered.

The system was vast, but all connected somehow.

For the first time, she saw the faintest thread to pull.

∞∞∞∞

The frozen yogurt bag swung lightly in Elise's grip as she climbed the stairs, its bottom damp from condensation. She hadn't even noticed the heat until the plastic stretched under the weight of the container inside. Salted caramel with crushed cookies on top. Harper's favorite. The thought of it melting before she could hand it to her added a strange sense of urgency to her steps.

Her keys jingled as she unlocked the door, already rehearsing the apology for being late.

"Harper?"

Her voice cut through the apartment's stillness. No response.

Elise stepped inside, flicking on the light. Everything was exactly where she had left it. The folded quilt on the couch, the takeout containers on the table. The only thing out of place was the silence itself.

She set the yogurt down, forcing herself to sound casual. "I got your favorite."

Nothing.

A ripple of unease crawled up her spine. She looked toward the hallway, the bedroom door was slightly cracked. That wasn't right. Harper usually kept it closed. Her privacy a sacred ritual.

Elise called again, louder this time. "Harper?"

Still nothing.

The hallway stretched longer than it should have, each step sending a whisper of dread through her veins. The bedroom door creaked open under her touch.

The bed was still made. Untouched.

Elise turned, checked the bathroom. Empty.

Back in the bedroom, her eyes swept the space, scanning for something wrong. That's when she saw it.

Harper's phone, lying in the center of the bed.

Harper never left her phone behind. Not willingly.

Elise's breath came shorter now. She yanked open the dresser drawers—clothes missing, pulled hastily from their neat stacks. Her backpack, usually slumped in the corner, was gone too.

She reached for her own phone, her fingers clumsy with panic. Before she could check for messages, the front door opened.

She heard Miles's voice before she saw him, full of urgency that didn't match his exhaustion.

"Elise! Blackwood came through with—"

191

He stopped mid-sentence. Took one look at her face.

"What's wrong?"

Elise swallowed, forcing the words out. "She's gone."

Miles stepped inside, scanning the room. The phone, the missing backpack, the half-opened drawers. His hands settled on his laptop, his expression dark.

"Did she say anything earlier? Give you any clue she was planning this?

Elise shook her head. "No. She was upset, but this—" She gestured to the empty room. "This doesn't make sense."

"We need to call the police—" Elise started.

"No," Miles interrupted. Then he softened. "Think about how this looks, Elise. Your daughter disappears the same day CPS brings her back?"

The logic hit her like a fist to the ribs.

"They'll say you're unfit. That you did something. It'll play right into their hands."

She opened her mouth to argue, but he shook his head.

"They're already building a case against you," Miles continued. "This is exactly what they want. CPS won't investigate. They'll just take her permanently next time."

Elise clenched her fists, her mind spinning.

"We need to handle this ourselves," Miles said, leaning against the wall. "Quietly. Can't risk losing her for good."

Elise exhaled, shaking off the panic. "She was upset about school."

Miles nodded. "That's a start. If she reached out to anyone, we need to know."

His hand settled on her shoulder, shaking slightly.

Elise moved through the apartment, sweeping every surface. She checked the windows for signs of forced entry, yanked open the drawers and closets, even looked under the bed. But there was nothing. No struggle. No note. No obvious sign of how or when she'd left.

Miles stood in the doorway, watching her.

"Elise," he said after a moment. "I'm going to make a call."

She barely registered his words, too focused on finding anything that would tell her where Harper had gone.

Through the window, she caught a glimpse of Miles outside, hunched over his phone. His voice was low, urgent, though the sound of traffic from the street drowned out his words.

Elise sat on the bed, staring at the cracked phone in her hands.

She unlocked it.

Scrolled.

The last message sent appeared immediately.

I can't let them take me back there.

A lump formed in Elise's throat.

The timestamp was forty minutes ago.

Below, three unread answers from Ethan.

What do you mean? Where are you going?

Harper... Please answer me.

Harper.

Elise's grip tightened around the phone.

In the kitchen, the frozen yogurt sat forgotten, spilling onto the counter in a slow, melting puddle.

Miles's voice muffled somewhere outside.

Elise stared at the screen, at the unanswered texts, at Harper's last words.

A hollow, sinking dread settled deep in her chest.

This wasn't just Harper running.

This was Harper running from something.

And Elise was already too late.

∞∞∞∞

The gym sat at the edge of the block, its neon sign flickering weakly. Thuds of fists against heavy bags rattled through the night, mixing with the sound of weights and the screaming commands of the trainers. Elise parked a few spaces down, fingers fidgeting with her steering wheel before she exhaled and stepped into the thick evening air.

Miles was already out, leaning against the car door, arms crossed. "Don't let the smell of sweat and testosterone scare you off."

"Charming," Elise muttered, nerves winding tighter as they approached the entrance.

Inside, the gym was humid. Boxers weaved in the ring, gloves clapping against each other. A row of people pounded heavy bags. The whole place buzzed with effort, with aggression, with something just short of violence.

She stepped carefully around a pile of hand wraps, taking it all in. The slam of lockers, the old motivational posters, the smell of stale sweat in the air. This wasn't the fancy, corporate type of gym. This was where people came to fight for something.

A short man approached—Eddie. A beret sat on his head, gray hair peeking from beneath it. His smile was wide, but there was no warmth in it.

"Whitaker." His voice was rough, years of cigarettes and shouting over gym noise. "Thought you disappeared."

Miles shrugged. "Not yet. We're here to see Shanti."

Eddie tilted his head. "Her cave. Same as always."

Elise frowned. "Cave?"

Miles smirked. "Her office."

Eddie chuckled, nodding toward the back of the gym where a door marked PRIVATE was slightly cracked.

"Don't knock her papers over. She hates that."

They wove through the gym, dodging jump ropes snapping too close to their ankles and sidestepping sparring matches that moved too close to the main walkway.

Miles knocked once and pushed it open without waiting.

The office was small, cluttered. A cork board took up most of the far wall, covered in photos, maps, and tangled red strings that looked less like an investigation and more like the inside of someone's unraveling mind. Papers spilled across the desk, among them a coffee mug that read: WORLD'S OKAYEST DETECTIVE.

Behind the desk, Shanti Brown barely looked up, pen tapping against her notebook. She wore jeans and a hoodie, a leather jacket draped over the back of her chair. Reading glasses sat on her nose, making her look like a professor, though everything about her screamed cop.

"Unless you've got a lead or a warrant, I'm not interested."

Miles grinned. "Good thing I've got both."

She looked up curiously. "Whitaker. Didn't expect you so soon."

"Still kicking," Miles said, dropping into the chair across from her.

Shanti looked at Elise, scanning, assessing. "This the one you mentioned?"

Elise stepped forward. "Elise Winters. My daughter's missing."

Shanti's demeanor shifted. Still focused, still guarded, but something softer settled beneath it. "Missing? How long?"

"Less than a day," Elise said. "But CPS was probably involved. There's more to it."

Shanti motioned to the chair in front of the desk, her voice lowering slightly. "Start from the beginning."

Elise did. She laid it all out—the CPS visit, the cryptic warnings from Harper's school, the way her daughter had come back *wrong*. The empty stare, the slow movements, the text messages before she vanished. Miles filled the gaps, detailing what they'd uncovered about Necessity Mart, the patterns they were starting to piece together.

Shanti listened, pen tapping in a slow, methodical rhythm. When Elise finished, Shanti turned to the cork board, her eyes moving across the red strings.

"You think Necessity Mart is involved?" she asked finally.

Miles's voice was steady. "We don't think. We know."

Shanti pulled a few photos from the board, laying them on the desk. The faces of young adults, their expressions frozen in time.

"I've been tracking disappearances for months," she said. "At first, they seemed random. No connections. But Necessity Mart?" She shook her head. "I didn't think they were part of it. Until now."

Her eyes settled on Elise. "You ever heard of the Ascension Order?"

Elise stiffened. The words like a trigger pulled in her brain. "I... I went to one of their meetings."

Shanti's pen stopped mid-tap. "You did what?"

Elise adjusted in her seat. "It was after a protest. A man approached me— charismatic, intense. His name was... Kael, I think."

Shanti's jaw tightened. "Kael Zenith?"

Elise nodded. "That sounds right. Why?"

Shanti sighed, leaning back in her chair. "Kael's been on my radar for months. He runs the Ascension Order. They say they're about enlightenment, self-improvement. But it's a cult. They find vulnerable people, pull them in, break them down."

Elise's stomach knotted. She thought back to Maggie's house.

"If Kael's involved..." she swallowed. "This is worse than I thought."

Shanti leaned forward. "If your daughter's connected to the Ascension Order, we don't have time to waste. Kael moves fast. And when people disappear around him, they don't come back."

Before Elise could respond, Shanti's phone buzzed on the desk. She looked at the screen, and gritted her teeth.

"What is it?" Elise asked.

Shanti tossed the phone onto the desk, the screen still glowing. "Another missing person. Young woman. Same pattern."

The weight settled over them.

"That makes four this month."

Elise's breathing became shallow. Her fingers curled into fists. "So, what do we do?"

Shanti pulled a file from a stack, flipping through it until she found what she was looking for. A photo. A girl. No older than seventeen, her eyes too familiar.

"These aren't random," Shanti mumbled. "They're collecting people, Elise."

She slid the photo across the desk. Elise's blood ran cold.

The girl looked eerily similar to Harper.

"If I'm right, we don't have much time."

Elise stared at the picture. The girl's face was too young, too familiar. Her vision blurred as one terrible realization took root.

Harper wasn't just missing.

She was next.

ACT III

The Echo of Control

A system cannot fail those it was never designed to protect.
– W.E.B. Du Bois

CHAPTER TWELVE

Inventory Check

A man is no less a slave because he is allowed to choose a new master once in a term of years.
– Lysander Spooner

The safe house was a wreck.

Clothes draped over chair backs, a lone sock peeking out from under the coffee table like it was trying to escape. Last night's Chinese takeout fossilizing on the counter. Soy sauce packets spilled like tiny crime scenes. The TV flickered in the corner, its glow cutting through the mess. Morning show hosts grinning at an invisible audience. Their voices mechanical, their cheer so forced it made Elise's teeth ache.

She sat at the kitchen table, staring at Harper's phone like it might suddenly give up its secrets. She unlocked it again. Thumb moving straight to the message thread with Ethan.

Still nothing.

Three unanswered texts. She checked the call log, then the search history, then the gallery… again. As if sheer repetition might unearth something she'd missed.

It didn't.

Her clothes felt wrong. The blouse too crisp, the slacks stiff against her legs. Dressing for work was slipping into another woman's skin—someone who cared about meetings and deadlines and office chatter. That woman was gone, buried under the weight of Harper's absence, under everything.

The TV hosts shifted to their next segment, smiles stretching wider, like they'd practiced in the mirror. "Today, we're diving into the world of self-optimization programs," the man announced.

"And how they're shaping the next generation," the woman continued.

A graphic flashed on the screen: *Self-Optimization in Schools: A Growing Trend.* The words brushed against Elise's thoughts. Something about them itched at her, but her focus was elsewhere—on the silence in the apartment, on the empty bedroom where Harper should be.

The hosts kept talking. Cheerful voices, bright promises. *Optimization in education.* A segment about corporate partnerships in schools, tracking student "Harmony Scores." Each word dug deeper, picking at her unease.

Then her phone buzzed.

Miles's name lit up the screen. She swiped to answer before the second ring. "Miles?"

His voice cut through with static, rough and wet, like he was speaking through clenched teeth. "Elise."

Her grip tightened. "Are you okay?"

"I'm hanging in," Miles rasped. A cough rattled through the speaker, harsh and dry. "But listen. I know Harper's your priority right now, I get it. But we need to talk about Blackwood."

"Go on."

His voice steadied, but the hoarseness lingered. "Blackwood dug into Dr. Thomas Reed's finances. Turns out, Reed was compromised. Bad. Offshore payments, shell companies... all roads lead back to Necessity Mart."

Elise frowned. "How compromised are we talking?"

"One of the payments went to a trust account in his wife's name," Miles said. "James suspected as much, but this confirms it."

Elise exhaled. "And?"

"Blackwood thinks Reed's family might still have something." Paper shuffled on the other end of the line. "Margaret Reed. 316 Tidespring Avenue, Willowbend."

Willowbend. An hour away. A lead she couldn't ignore. But Harper—

"Blackwood said James believed this was critical," Miles pressed. "The financial ties between Reed and Necessity Mart... this could be the linchpin. The reason Synapse Dynamics collapsed. The reason James—" He stopped, letting the weight of the words hang between them.

Elise closed her eyes. The puzzle pieces were too heavy now.

"Did Blackwood say anything else?" she asked.

"Yeah." Miles hesitated. "He said to be careful. If Reed's family has something, we're not the only ones looking for it."

A cold pit opened in her stomach.

"You're not well, Miles," she said finally. "Maybe you should sit this one out."

He laughed, dry and brittle. "Not a chance. I'm not wasting my time sitting around."

Her thoughts hardened into something grim but determined. "Fine. I'll go tomorrow."

"Good." A pause. "We'll meet after. Figure out the next steps."

As she hung up, the TV hosts' voices shifted, their bright chatter turning urgent.

A *Breaking News* banner slashed across the screen.

"A local high school student has been reported missing," the anchor announced. "Authorities are asking for any information regarding her disappearance."

Elise froze.

The girl's photo filled the screen. Dark hair, kind eyes, a smile that still belonged to the world.

The puzzle pieces weren't just heavy anymore.

They were crushing.

She shut the TV off.

Harper's phone sat on the table, screen dark now, but the unanswered texts glowed in her mind. No more circling, no more waiting for the next clue to fall into her lap.

If James believed Reed's family had something, she'd tear it out the shadows herself. She grabbed her coat, shoved Harper's phone into her bag, and headed for the door.

Tomorrow, she'd get her answers.

∞∞∞∞

The office felt alien the moment Elise stepped inside. The sound of synchronized Aether bands, once just background noise, now rang accusatory. The air felt colder, sterile, inhuman. The desks were still neatly arranged in their endless rows, but the space felt hollow.

The glances came first. Quick looks from coworkers who immediately snapped back to their screens when she caught them. Then the whispers—thin currents of sound barely reaching her ears.

"She's back?"

"Thought she was done?"

Her steps felt heavier as she moved through the maze of desks, each one a reminder of the years she'd spent here. The people behind them were motionless, locked into their work, faces calm in that eerie, optimized way. No one stopped typing, but their presence felt like a wall, an unspoken *you don't belong here.*

Then she reached her desk.

Or what used to be her desk.

It was empty. Stripped bare. No photos, no coffee mug, no neat stack of labeled files. The monitor sat unplugged, the chair pushed aside like an afterthought.

For a moment, she just stood there. The emptiness of the space screamed louder than the whispers.

"Oh, Elise."

The voice sliced through her thoughts.

Angie Mooney approached, her smile thin, her posture carrying the kind of power that made people stand up straighter. Elise saw it then—the look in her eye, the predatory confidence of someone who had already won.

"Back from your little... vacation?" Angie said, drawing out the last word like it was dipped in poison. "I was beginning to wonder if you'd just disappeared."

Elise opened her mouth, but Angie didn't give her a chance. She gestured toward the hallway.

"Come with me, dear. Greg will be joining us."

Greg. Broad shoulders. Security. Standing just a few feet away, arms crossed, face blank.

Elise clenched her teeth. *So this was it.*

The conference room was too bright, the table too long. Elise sat on one side. Angie on the other, hands folded neatly, her expression a careful mask of sympathy. An HR rep sat beside her, shuffling papers they didn't really need to read.

"First," Angie began, "let me just say how much we've all appreciated your contributions to OptimumCare."

Elise didn't respond. She knew what was coming.

"Unfortunately, we've come across some... troubling information. Alan, bless him, came forward and shared some concerns."

Elise forced herself to breathe. *Alan.*

"What concerns?" she asked.

Angie tilted her head, her Aether band pulsing softly. "Breaching protocol. Violating employee trust. Compromising sensitive company data. All of which, of course, are clear violations of our Ethics Guidelines."

The HR rep slid a folder across the table, the weight heavier than it should have been. Elise didn't open it.

"After much consideration," Angie continued, her voice smooth, final, "we've decided to terminate your employment with OptimumCare. Effective immediately."

She placed a hand over her heart, the gesture so fake Elise almost laughed. "I do hope you understand... This wasn't an easy decision. You've been such a... unique presence here."

She wanted to climb over the table and slap Angie right then and there.

But instead, she leaned forward. "Alan told you? Told you what, exactly?"

Angie's eyes sparked with something gleeful beneath her mask of regret. "Oh, you know Alan. He's so... thorough. Always paying attention. He told us you had been accessing files outside your purview. That you've been... distracted."

Elise didn't flinch.

Alan was gone. Fired. And she knew damn well he hadn't said a word. But they knew.

Which meant someone else had told them. Or they had been watching all along.

Angie leaned in slightly, savoring it. "Poor thing hated coming forward, but integrity is everything, isn't it?"

Elise kept her expression neutral, her fingers flexing slightly against the table. There was no point in arguing. No point asking how they knew.

This wasn't an accusation. It was a sentence.

Greg stepped forward, making his presence known. Angie stood, brushing imaginary dust from her skirt.

"You'll be receiving your final paycheck and COBRA information soon," she said. "Best of luck, Elise. Really."

Her desk was already someone else's.

Her coworkers snuck glances but kept their heads down. Greg lingered nearby, silent but close, while she gathered the last of her things. Her photos, mug, and a single notebook.

The walk to the elevator felt like a death march. The sound of Aether bands filled the air, blending with the soft clicks of keyboards. The soundtrack of an efficient, soulless machine. Conversations stuttered to a halt when she passed. Whispers evaporated into nothing.

Elise stopped on the sidewalk, staring at the polished glass door she'd walked through every day for years. Her reflection stared back at her, unfamiliar, fractured, furious.

They think they've won.

Her thoughts were already turning. If they thought firing her would stop her, they didn't understand what they'd just unleashed.

∞∞∞∞

The Patchwork Society building stood as it always had, a place of warmth in an otherwise cold world. The glow spilling from its windows and the sound of conversation inside were as inviting as the smell of lavender and fresh bread drifting through the cracks in the door. It was a place meant for comfort, a haven for the displaced and disillusioned. But for Elise, it felt like a museum exhibit, a glimpse into a life she could no longer reach.

She hesitated just outside the entrance, her fingers grazing the edge of the doorframe. Inside, she could see people sewing at long tables, organizing stacks of flyers, discussing upcoming rallies and actions with a quiet intensity. There was so much life here, so much purpose, and yet Elise couldn't shake the weight pressing on her.

Her hand tightened on the strap of her bag, her body urging her forward even as her mind resisted. She pushed the door open.

"Elise."

Paul's voice drew her attention immediately. He was already approaching her, his smile warm but lined with something deeper—concern, maybe even grief. He placed a hand on her shoulder.

"It's been a while since we've seen you in these parts," he said. "I was starting to wonder if we lost you too."

The words hit her harder than he probably intended. Elise felt her throat tighten as she struggled to find a response. Instead, she blurted out what she'd been holding in.

"Harper's gone," she said. "And Maggie... she's gone too. I don't know how it happened. I don't know how to fix it."

Her voice cracked, the admission raw and unpolished. "I'd do anything to bring them back. Anything."

Paul's smile faded as he took in her words. His hand stayed on her shoulder, grounding her as he nodded slowly. "We've been seeing more of this," he said. "People disappearing, neighborhoods hollowing out. We don't know what's going on yet, but..." He trailed off, choosing his next words carefully. "Whatever it is, it's picking up speed."

He hesitated, as if weighing whether to say more. "This could be the kind of thing we rally around. If you're ready, we could—"

"No," Elise interrupted, shaking her head. "Not like this. I need to keep this quiet, Paul. I already have people looking into it, and... it has to stay discreet."

Paul's frown deepened, but he respected her decision. "Harper's a smart girl, Elise. And Maggie, despite everything she's been through, she's a fighter. You'll get them back. I know it."

He squeezed her shoulder again before stepping away to check on a meeting. Elise's eyes followed him for a moment before she turned to see Tasha walking towards her, a partially finished quilt draped over her arm.

"You look like you could use a distraction," Tasha said, holding up the quilt.

Elise stared at the colorful patches, her fingers brushing the fabric. It was uneven, some pieces fraying at the edges, but the colors blended beautifully—deep blues, warm yellows, soft grays.

"I don't know how to knit," Elise admitted.

Tasha grinned, pulling a needle from her pocket and handing it to her. "Perfect. You'll learn. Sit with us."

The long table was crowded with people stitching quietly. Elise hesitated before sliding into a chair, the fabric was cool against her hands. She fumbled at first, pricking her fingers and pulling the thread too tightly, but the rhythm came quickly. Her thoughts, racing just moments ago, began to slow.

As they worked, the conversation shifted naturally to Project Harmony. A woman to Elise's left spoke first. "My community center lost its funding last week. They said it was underperforming, but the truth is, we didn't meet their metrics."

A man across the table nodded. "They've already started designating neighborhoods as non-optimized zones. Once you're labeled, it's over. Schools lose resources, housing subsidies disappear. They're forcing people out."

"It's by design," Tasha added, her needle moving through the fabric. "Divide people, make them feel like they can't survive without their systems. That's how they tighten their grip."

Elise's hands paused as their words settled over her. Everything they described felt connected, another fragment of the puzzle she was clawing to solve. Harper, Maggie, Project Harmony... it was all part of the same machine.

Paul returned after a while, placing a cup of tea beside her. He sat across the table, his expression soft. "You're doing what you can, Elise. That's all anyone can ask. And no matter what happens, you're not alone in this."

Elise nodded, her eyes drifting to the quilt in her lap. The patches felt symbolic. Messy, uneven, but stitched together into something that held. Something stronger.

As she gathered her things, Paul walked her to the door. His tone was firm but supportive. "Elise, if you hear from Maggie, tell her to reach out. We want to reconsider her place here. She belongs, no matter what's happened."

Elise nodded, her heart heavy with the weight of everything she'd learned. But Paul's words kept her from sinking entirely.

The car door shut behind her. She took a deep breath, her hands gripping the wheel. She could still feel the fabric of the quilt against her fingers, a small anchor in the chaos

The next stop was the boxing gym and Shanti. Recharged by her time at the Patchwork Society, Elise promised to keep pushing. She might not see the full picture yet, but she'd keep pulling at the threads until it unraveled.

She sat in her car, engine off, fingers wrapped around the steering wheel like it was the only thing holding her together. The weight of the day pressed down, a vise tightening around her ribs—Harper, Maggie, Project Harmony, Shanti's warnings. Threads tangled, knots she couldn't pry apart. She let her forehead drop against the wheel, inhaling slowly, forcing the tension into some dark corner of her mind.

Her phone buzzed in the cupholder. The vibration shook her out of her haze. The screen lit up.

Unknown Number

She watched it ring. *Not again.*

Her fingers hesitated before snatching the phone. She answered without thinking, expecting static, a thinly veiled threat, another dead end.

Instead, a cold, automated voice filled the car.

This call is from an inmate at Clearwater Facility. If you wish to accept this call, press 1. If not, hang up.

Elise's thumb hovered over the screen, heart hammering. *Clearwater?*

She exhaled and pressed 1.

A rough voice rasped through the speaker.

"Elise."

One word. Thick with something she didn't want to name—guilt, desperation, the sour aftertaste of unfinished business.

Her grip on the phone tightened. "Jamal." His name was a blade in her mouth. "I told you not to contact me again."

Silence, then a breath. "I know. I'm sorry. For everything." His voice was shaky. "I didn't want to drag you into this, but Necessity Mart—"

Elise felt the unease creeping up her stomach and into her throat.

"What about them?"

"They threatened my family." His words tumbled out, fast and erratic. "If I didn't cooperate, they were going to hurt them. Do things. I didn't have a choice, Elise."

She let the silence stretch. "And now you're calling me why, Jamal? To confess? To clear your conscience?"

A pause. Then his voice calmed. "I'm calling because I can help you."

He told her how they'd come for him. How he tried to take the evidence to the police. "I thought—" A breath. "I thought I could blow the whistle, make it public. But they knew. Before I even walked into the station, they knew. I was arrested for tampering with proprietary data, violating NDAs. They made sure the case was airtight."

His laugh was bitter. "I'm not getting out of here, Elise. At least not anytime soon. But that's not the point. That's not why I'm calling."

"It's even in here," he continued, whispering now. "OCC."

Elise sat up straighter.

"They take off your Aether when you get booked. Standard procedure. But some guys... some guys just drop. Seizures, paranoia, full-body tremors. Some don't wake up." His voice got dark. "It's like their bodies don't know how to work without it."

Elise's breathing became shallow. *It's real. And it's everywhere.*

"I want to make this right," Jamal said. "I know I failed you before. But there's someone who can help. Someone who can make sense of all of this."

Elise was hesitant. "And why should I trust you?"

"Because he knows. His name is Malik Jefferson. He worked for Necessity Mart, built the damn algorithms they use. He spoke out once, and they buried his stories. But he knows how they think, how they operate. If anyone can help you, it's him."

Elise's mind raced. "And where do I find him?"

"Unplugged Minds," Jamal said. "It's a forum. He's got a profile there. ResistorNode. Message him. Tell him about the *Butterfly Effect*. He'll know. Tell him what's happening."

Elise didn't respond. Her brain was already breaking it down. wWhat she'd need to do, how she'd reach him, what this could mean.

"But Elise," Jamal's voice cut through her thoughts. "Be careful. If they knew about me, they know about you."

A click. The line went dead.

Elise stared at the phone, Jamal's words rattling inside her skull. Malik Jefferson. Another thread to follow. Another door to open.

She clenched the steering wheel. Harper's face flashed in her mind. Then Maggie's. Their images blurred together, a single, gnawing ache.

"One more lead," she muttered.

She turned the key. The engine roared to life, swallowing everything else.

∞∞∞∞

The gym hit her like a wall. But something was off.

Gloves cracked against bags, but the sound felt distant. Trainers shouted, but their voices seemed drowned out by something heavier. Jump ropes hissed through the air, but even that was off, like an orchestra missing its conductor. The sweat, the rubber, the metallic smell of dried blood... it should've been grounding. Instead, it put Elise on edge.

She scanned the room, searching for something, someone, to anchor her. Eddie stood near the ring, tightening the gloves of a young fighter, but his usual easygoing demeanor was missing. He barely looked up when Elise approached.

"Shanti here?" she asked.

Eddie exhaled through his nose, nodding toward the back. "She's in her office." His tone was quiet, too quiet. "You should go in."

Elise hesitated. "Eddie, what—"

But he had already turned back to his fighter, pulling at the laces with a little too much force.

The door creaked as she pushed it open. The office felt smaller tonight. The cork board on the far wall, normally an organized chaos of photos and connections, looked more like a crime scene.

Shanti sat at her desk, shoulders hunched, hands resting on the surface. The dim glow of the desk lamp cast shadows over her face, deepening the bags beneath her eyes.

"Shanti?" Elise stepped inside, shutting the door behind her. "What's wrong?"

Shanti didn't answer right away. She just stared. When she finally spoke, her voice was brittle.

"You haven't heard, have you?"

Elise's unease grew.

208

Shanti reached for the small TV in the corner, her fingers trembling slightly as she grabbed for the remote. The screen came to life, bathing the room in cold, blue light.

A news anchor sat stiff behind her desk, her voice the kind of somber that was detached just enough to still feel rehearsed.

"Breaking news this evening: an unidentified man was found dead in his home earlier today. Police were called to the residence after neighbors reported concerning noises coming from the property. Authorities have yet to release the man's identity, but initial reports suggest there were no signs of entry or foul play. Investigators are currently treating the death as natural causes, pending further examination."

Elise felt a lump form in her throat as the footage cut to the outside of a small house. Yellow crime scene tape fluttered in the wind. Two officers stood on the porch, their faces blank as a stretcher rolled past them, the body covered in a white sheet.

The anchor's voice continued.

"Neighbors described the man as quiet, largely keeping to himself. This is a developing story, and we will provide updates as more information becomes available."

Shanti muted the TV. She turned back to Elise, her eyes darker now.

"It's Miles," she said simply. "He's gone."

The words hit hard. Elise staggered, gripping the desk to keep herself upright.

"No," she whispered. The denial was automatic, a reflex, but it felt useless the moment it left her lips.

Shanti didn't fill the silence. She just let it sit there.

"No," Elise said again, shaking her head violently. "That's not possible. I just... I just talked to him this morning."

Her mind scrambled backward, replaying their last conversation, grasping for something that would make sense of this.

"He sounded tired, but... he wasn't... he didn't."

"They found him this afternoon," Shanti said. "No signs of forced entry. No struggle. No obvious foul play... They're calling it natural causes."

Elise sank into her chair, her hands clenched so tight her nails dug into her palms.

"He was sick," she mumbled. "I know that. But after everything? After all we've been through? Now?"

Shanti sighed, leaning back in her chair, arms crossing over her chest. Her expression turned to stone, but her eyes... just for a second, showed a softer side of her.

"Maybe it was natural," she said. "Maybe... But you know as well as I do, the timing's too perfect."

"No," Elise shook her head. "It had to be his condition. You don't know how bad it was. He could barely get through our calls without coughing."

Shanti's eyes locked onto hers. "Convenient, isn't it?" she said. "A man already dying. No questions. No investigation. Just another case closed."

Elise dropped her head into her hands. Her vision spinning, replaying that last call. Miles, coughing, exhausted. But not afraid.

"He didn't sound scared," she whispered. "He sounded weak, but he didn't think it was the end."

Shanti leaned forward. "Think about it, Elise. He had information. Connections. Things people wouldn't want getting out. Did he say anything to you? Anything that seemed off?"

Elise squeezed her eyes shut. Replaying it in her head. The words. The pauses. The weight between sentences.

"No," she said finally. "He didn't say anything out of the ordinary." She hesitated. "But... he did sound weaker."

Shanti sighed, rubbing a hand down her face. "Weak enough to make it sound natural," she muttered.

The weight of it all collapsed onto Elise's chest, crushing her. The tears came fast, sudden, choking. She didn't try to stop them.

Shanti stood and walked around her desk, resting a hand on Elise's shoulder.

"We'll figure this out," she said. "But we have to be careful. If this was a message, it's not just Miles they're after."

Elise wiped her face, forcing herself to breathe.

"He didn't deserve this," she whispered.

Shanti's jaw locked. "No," she agreed. "But this doesn't end here."

Something changed inside Elise. The grief didn't leave, but it turned into something else, anger, determination.

For Miles. For Harper. For Maggie.

She sat up straighter, wiping the last of the tears from her face.

"This isn't over."

Shanti nodded, eyes flashing with the same fire.

"Damn right it isn't."

CHAPTER THIRTEEN

Backroom Deal

Power is not a means; it is an end.
—George Orwell, 1984

The bathroom light flickered, buzzing like an old power line about to snap. Elise braced herself against the sink, her fingers pressing into the porcelain as if she could steady something inside her that had already broken. Her reflection in the mirror looked back at her, ghostly and unfamiliar. Hollow eyes, skin stretched too thin, grief carving deep shadows where sleep should have been.

Miles was still there, rattling around in her skull. His voice looped like a song with no ending. She could hear the weight in it, the way he said her name like an apology, like he'd already given up but hadn't found the words to tell her yet.

Elise swallowed, but the ache stayed lodged in her throat. She closed her eyes. It didn't help. Miles was still there, and she was still here, staring at a stranger in the mirror, trying to remember what it felt like to be whole.

Her phone buzzed on the counter. She didn't move. It rattled twice more before her eyes slid toward it. The screen glowed with a message from Shanti.

Bringing coffee. We'll need it.

Elise exhaled and reached into her jacket pocket, pulling out the scrap of paper Maggie had left behind. The coordinates scrawled in ink were smudged from days of handling, but they were still readable. A code she had yet to crack, a destination that felt less like salvation and more like a curse.

The paper crinkled in her hand as she slowly folded it anyway, as though her hesitation could change the gravity of what was ahead.

The crisp pre-dawn air bit at her cheeks as she stepped outside, pulling her coat tightly around her. A dark sedan sat at the curb, its headlights dimmed to avoid drawing attention. As she opened the passenger door, the aroma of coffee mixed with the smell of gasoline caught in her nostrils. Shanti sat behind the wheel, her face covered in exhaustion but still focused, like a blade that had cut too much and still wasn't done.

"You look like hell," Shanti said, passing a steaming cup over the center console.

"Thanks." Elise cupped the coffee in her hands, letting the heat soak into her frozen fingers.

The engine rumbled as they pulled away from the curb. Neither of them spoke. The city was a maze of flickering streetlights and concrete ghosts.

"Miles would've had backups," Shanti said finally, her fingers drumming against the steering wheel. "Hell, he'd probably have backups for his backups."

Elise kept her eyes on the road. "Yeah. But he's not here."

His absence was heavy. Elise tightened her grip on the coffee cup, letting the heat burn her fingers. It was something to hold onto.

The city thinned around them, the streetlights faded into the mist, absorbed by tall trees and the kind of quiet that felt unnatural. Shanti's shoulders stiffened slightly, just for a second, before glancing in the rearview mirror.

"Ascension Order's been buying up properties for months," she said casually. "Churches, community centers, abandoned buildings. Anything they can get their hands on, really."

Elise turned her head, watching the darkened streets slip past. "You think Maggie's caught up in this? That they have Harper?"

"I don't know," Shanti admitted. "But people get desperate. And they change."

"Maggie isn't some mindless follower. And Harper..." The words stuck to her throat. "She's just a kid."

Shanti exhaled. "Yeah. And kids don't get to stay kids in a world like this."

The road curved, pulling them deeper into the dark. Shanti eased off the gas a quarter mile out, letting the car roll to a stop beneath the gnarled limbs of an old oak.

She popped open the glove compartment, pulling out a map and a pair of binoculars. "We park here," she said, handing Elise the map. "Stick close. We'll take the long way around."

Elise looked at the map, but her mind was elsewhere, her pulse thundering in her ears as they stepped out of the car and into the darkness of the trees. The air was damp. The leaves rustled overhead in a slow whisper.

Through the brush, the compound appeared. A massive shadow against the deep gray of pre-dawn. The windows were blacked out, the walls covered in graffiti. There was a dirt lot in front, littered with parked cars.

Figures moved between them, gliding like ghosts, their white robes catching the faint glow of the distant lights. Even from this distance, Elise could see it—the soft, unnatural pulse of Aether bands.

Shanti raised the binoculars, adjusting the focus. "They're all wearing them," she muttered. "Kids too."

Elise took the binoculars, unease growing as she scanned the area. A taller figure emerged from the entrance, his posture poised, confident. Zenith Kael. His Aether glowed like a crown, brighter than the others.

Shanti nudged her. "Look again. Near the door."

Elise adjusted the focus, gasping as another figure stepped into view.

Maggie.

She was standing beside Kael, a stack of papers in her hands. Her face was calm, composed... too composed. Like she belonged there.

Elise's grip tightened around the binoculars. "Tell me I'm not seeing this."

"You're seeing it."

For a moment, nothing moved. Then, one by one, the white-robed figures filed inside the building, their movements like rehearsed choreography. The door shut behind them, sealing the night in silence.

Elise exhaled, her breath clouding in the cold air. "We have to—"

Headlights cut through the dark. Three white vans rumbled up the dirt lot, slowing to a stop. Doors slid open.

Elise swallowed the knot in her throat as people exited the building, moving in quiet, orderly lines.

Then she saw it. Maggie stepping forward.

Elise expected hesitation. A pause. A look over her shoulder. Anything to signal that she wasn't completely lost. Instead, Maggie lingered by the open van door, exchanging quiet words with a man in all white. Then without another word, she climbed inside.

Elise's fingers dug into the binoculars. "No," she muttered. "No, no, no, what the hell is she—"

Shanti grabbed her shoulder. "We can't move yet."

The vans filled quickly and disappeared into the early morning.

Most of the remaining members trickled back into the building. A few lingered, standing near the last couple of cars in quiet conversation. Too quiet to hear from this distance. But it wasn't long before they, too, disappeared, their taillights vanishing one by one.

Then, the lot was still.

And from the dark behind the building, Zenith Kael emerged.

Alone.

The glow of his Aether made him seem untouchable, a cold halo cutting through the dim light. He moved with the certainty of a man who owned everything around him. After a pause, he raised his phone to his ear, slowly pacing the back lot.

Elise could barely breathe.

"Why the hell is he out there by himself?" Shanti whispered.

Elise swallowed, her heart a hammer in her chest.

"I don't care," she said. "We need to hear what he is saying."

Shanti reached for her again, urgent now. "Elise, wait—"

But Elise was already moving, ducking through the trees.

Shanti swore under her breath, gripping the small knife tucked inside her jacket. Elise's focus locked on Kael like a hunter closing in on prey.

The wind shifted, curling around the empty lot like it had a mind of its own. It carried fragments of Kael's voice. Elise and Shanti crouched behind a stack of old crates, their edges warped from years of rain.

Then another gust whipped, harder this time, kicking up dirt and debris. A piece of paper peeled away from the ground, tumbling in the air before catching on the toe of Elise's boot. One of *their* papers. The ones they'd been handing out like scripture.

Elise reached down, fingers brushing the damp edges. She flipped it over, and squinted to read under the faint glow of the security lights.

"*YOU HAVE BEEN CHOSEN.*"

The words crawled up her back like a cold hand.

"*Beyond optimization lies transcendence.*

A place exists where limits dissolve, and clarity reigns.

Where every question finds its answer.

You are invited to explore the next step on your journey.

To experience the alignment of mind, body, and purpose.

This opportunity is exclusive, personal, and rare.

We ask only that you bring an open mind and leave your doubt at the door.

THE FUTURE AWAITS."

Elise's grip tightened, crumpling the edges.

Beyond the crates, Kael's voice slithered through the darkness.

"... the next batch is en route to transcendence," he said, his tone like silk stretched over a sharp blade. "All is prepared for their arrival..."

"Yes, my master... no deviations."

Elise's fingers dug into the crate, splinters penetrating her skin. She felt the flyer burning in her palm now, its empty promises twisting into something with teeth. Not a metaphor. Not a spiritual awakening. A place. A process. A destination.

"This is it," she whispered, her breaths short. "This is where they took Maggie."

Shanti placed a hand on her shoulder, her grip tight. "Stay calm," she muttered. "We don't know how many of them are nearby."

Elise swallowed, staring at the words THE FUTURE AWAITS one last time before stuffing the flyer into her pocket. The wind picked up again, but this time, it wasn't carrying scraps of paper.

It was carrying Kael's laughter.

Kael's voice continued, low and melodic, as if delivering a sermon. "The harvest aligns with the system's design. Perfection is within reach."

Elise's nails dug into her palms. The ease in his tone, the certainty in his words. *Harvest.* He was talking about Maggie, about all of them, like they were grain waiting to be cut down. The rage hit her fast, burning in her chest, leaving her breath shaky.

"He's alone," she whispered. "This is our chance."

"And what, Elise? You think we just walk up to him? No plan, no backup? You don't know what he's capable of."

Elise didn't answer. Her hand disappeared into her bag, pulling out a small handgun. It felt too light, too unnatural in her grip, but she held it steady.

Shanti's breath caught. "Where the hell did you get that?"

"Miles," Elise said. "And I'll use it if I have to."

"Elise—"

Too late.

Elise stepped forward, rising from the shadows like something pulled from a bad dream.

Kael paused, lowering his phone with the unhurried grace of a man who expected her. His expression didn't change… just the same slight, knowing smile, with a flicker of amusement behind his eyes.

"Ah," he said, almost warmly. "A seeker arrives."

Elise raised the gun. Her hands trembled, but her arm didn't. "Where's Maggie? She demanded. "Where are you taking her?"

Kael studied her like she was an insect pinned to glass. "Maggie has found her purpose," he said. "She's free now, untethered from the chaos you cling to."

Shanti stepped into view, her voice slicing through the quiet. "Cut the bullshit. What's this 'path' you keep pushing people down?"

215

Kael turned to her, his smile widening. "You misunderstand," he said gently. "The path isn't something I control. It's the natural alignment of those willing to see the truth."

Rhetoric. Doctrine. More layers of control.

Elise had enough.

"Enough with the riddles," she snapped. She stepped closer, the gun never wavering. "Where is she?"

For the first time, the mask cracked. A brief look of irritation passed over Kael's face, there and gone in an instant. He spread his hands, offering peace. "She is where she was meant to be," he said calmly. "Transcendence awaits her."

Elise's frustration erupted. She didn't think. Didn't hesitate. She just swung.

The butt of the gun connected with his jaw, the impact sharp and satisfying.

Kael stumbled, a hiss of breath escaping through his teeth. Blood formed in the corner of his mouth.

Shanti was already on him, grabbing his collar and slamming him against the wall. "Enough games. You're going to start talking."

Kael blinked, dazed, then let out a slow sigh. "You're trying to force understanding," he mumbled, blood smearing his teeth. "But you can't fight the system. Everything aligns as it must."

Shanti's grip tightened. "Who's pulling the strings?" she demanded. "Necessity Mart? What's the endgame?"

"The endgame?" he repeated softly. "It's already begun."

A sound behind them.

Shanti spun, her knife flashing in the dim light.

Elise turned, her stomach plunging. Shadows in the tree line. Members stepping forward, unhurried. Their Aether bands pulsed in eerie unison, halos of cold light cutting through the dark.

Kael chuckled.

"You see?" he said, wiping the blood from his mouth. "Resistance only invites chaos. But surrender..." He exhaled, his smile stretching wide, teeth still stained red. "Surrender is harmony."

Elise's grip tightened around the gun.

"They're coming this way," she whispered.

The cult members paused, heads tilting in unison. Then, like a switch had been flipped, they moved.

The illusion shattered. The calm, the grace, the serenity. Gone.

What rushed toward them wasn't human anymore.

Elise barely had time to process before Shanti's fingers dug into her wrist, yanking hard.

"That's our cue. Move."

Elise hesitated, just for a second.

Shanti didn't wait. She pulled her back, her voice frantic.

"Run!"

The moment they turned, the cultist unraveled.

The mask of control ripped away. They were hunting.

"They're not supposed to be this fast!" Elise gasped, her lungs burning as she pushed harder, branches whipping at her arms.

"Just run!" Shanti yelled.

The Aether bands flickered through the trees, glowing like predatory eyes. Elise and Shanti burst through the tree line, the clearing in sight. The car was where they left it... too far.

Shanti reached it first, snatching open the passenger door and shoving Elise inside before diving over her into the driver's seat. Her hands fumbled with the keys, breaths coming too fast.

The cultists broke from the woods. Glowing bands emerging from the darkness.

"Go! Go!" Elise shouted.

Shanti twisted the key.

Tires spun, spitting gravel, the car fishtailing as Shanti swerved onto the dirt road. The headlights cut through the mist, but behind them—

The cultists didn't stop.

Elise twisted in her seat, expecting them to disappear into the trees, but they kept coming. Not even slowing as the care tore away. They ran after it.

Then... headlights.

Elise's stomach dropped.

A single white van pulled onto the road from a hidden side path. Then another. And another.

Engines roaring behind them.

"So much for peaceful transcendence!" Elise shouted, gripping the dashboard.

"I'm starting to think they skipped that lesson," Shanti replied, her focus locked on the road.

One of the vans pulled alongside them. The window rolled down.

Muzzle flashes.

Glass shattered. Elise ducked instinctively as the side mirror exploded.

"They're shooting at us?!" Shanti shouted, jerking the wheel. "What kind of enlightened bullshit is this?"

Another shot ricocheted off the trunk.

"They're trying to kill us!" Elise cried, pressing herself low against the seat.

Shanti gritted her teeth, swerving as another van sped passed them, cutting them off. The road twisted into darkness, but the cult didn't hesitate. They knew the area. Another sharp turn, tires screeching—

Then... silence.

The engines behind them faded.

Shanti glanced in the rearview mirror.

"They're gone," she muttered, confused.

Elise twisted to look. The vans. The headlights. The relentless pursuit. Had vanished. The road behind them was empty, like nothing had ever been there.

"Where did they go?" Elise gasped.

Shanti slowed the car, pulling off onto the shoulder, hands still tight on the wheel. The scent of burning rubber clung to the air.

"They just... stopped," Shanti said.

Elise stared at the empty road, dread curling in her gut.

"They don't have to chase us," she mumbled. The crumpled flyer in her lap caught the glow of the dashboard lights, the words almost mocking.

YOU HAVE BEEN CHOSEN.

"They already know where we're going."

Shanti's fingers slammed against the steering wheel. "That wasn't just a cult," she said. "That was organized. That was... something else."

Elise gripped the flyer, its promises twisting like a knife in her ribs.

"They're connected to Necessity Mart," she said. "They have to be."

Shanti's eyes stayed on the road, mind racing. "We just blew any chance of going back quietly."

Elise sat up. "Good," she said. "Let's make some noise."

∞∞∞∞∞

The car rolled into the narrow alley, the neon sign of the laundromat flickering weakly above them. Early morning creeped over the cracked pavement, dull and washed out.

Shanti cut the engine.

The silence that followed felt different.

218

Neither of them spoke, adrenaline still pulsing in their veins. Shanti let her head drop back against the seat, staring at the cracked windshield, chest rising and falling. A faint, almost amused covered her face.

"You know," she said finally. "I should be pissed."

Elise turned to her, unsure where this was going.

"Months of work," Shanti continued. "All of it gone... up in smoke because someone couldn't keep their cool."

Elise's jaw locked. "Shanti, I—"

"But," Shanti interrupted, her smile widening.

"It's been a long time since I've felt this damn alive."

Elise blinked.

The department wasn't going to do anything. They'd file this away as bad intel and move on. Now? Now we've got something real."

She pulled out her phone. "I need to get to the precinct. If someone killed Miles, I'm going to find out who."

Elise nodded, still holding the flyer.

"There's something else I need to find," Elise said. "A guy who worked for Necessity Mart. Malik Jefferson. He might know where they took Maggie."

Shanti studied her. Then nodded. "Do it. But don't go in blind. Not again."

She unlocked the door. A silent cue for Elise to move. As Elise climbed out, Shanti leaned forward.

"Stay safe, Elise. And don't do anything stupid until I'm back."

Elise didn't answer.

Because stupid wasn't off the table.

As Shanti disappeared into the city's early morning haze, Elise stood in the alley, gripping the crumpled flyer like a fuse waiting to be lit. Her breath clouded in the cold air, her pulse still racing from the chase. The streets ahead felt endless, but one thing was certain.

This wasn't over. Not by a long shot.

The safe house swallowed her in silence. The air was stale, and she could still feel Miles's presence lingering. She sank into the battered couch, head to the ceiling, listening to the low rumble of the fridge.

The noise was too loud. An oppressive sound in the dead quiet.

Tea.

That's what James would have made her. His fix for everything. Panic attacks, sleepless nights, bad dreams. *You need something warm, E, something to hold onto.*

The thought of him sharpened the ache in her chest, but she forced herself up, shuffling toward the tiny kitchen. The safe house wasn't home. It wasn't even close. But she needed something familiar.

She reached for a mug, fingers grazing the ceramic handle, when something behind them caught her eye.

A bottle. Small. Plastic. Hidden.

Elise froze. It had been wedged behind the neat row of mugs like it didn't belong. She pulled it out, rubbing dust from the faded label.

WHITAKER, SARAH - DOCETAXEL 20MG - For chemotherapy treatment.

She choked on her breath.

The date. Seven years ago.

She stared at the name. Miles never talked about his sister. He never let his past touch the present, not in any way that mattered. But here it was. A tangible piece of a story he'd kept locked away.

Her hand trembled as she turned the bottle over in her fingers. It was empty now... long empty. But it still felt heavy.

"Miles," she mumbled. "You never said..."

The kettle whistled, shattering the moment. Elise exhaled, blinking herself back into the present, but her eyes drifted.

The old entertainment center.

It had been just another piece of mismatched furniture when she arrived. But now she noticed the dusty frame tucked among the clutter.

A photo.

Elise's feet moved before she could stop them. She reached out, lifted the frame with careful hands.

Miles. Years younger, lighter, freer. Standing beside a hospital bed with his arm around a woman. Sarah.

Her head was bald, her face pale, but her smile was radiant. She was carrying something heavier than anyone could imagine and still refused to let it crush her.

But Miles.

He was different. A version of him Elise had never seen. His face lacked the weight he carried right before he died. He looked like a man who still believed things could be fixed.

Elise set the frame down, unable to look any longer.

The bottle was still in her hand, and now the sight of it sickened her.

She turned, walking back to the couch, her legs suddenly heavy. The bottle pressed into her palm, the thoughts tangled in a thousand questions.

Miles's relentless drive to help her, his refusal to quit, even when he could barely breathe. It hadn't been just stubbornness. It had been guilt.

He couldn't save Sarah.

That's why he couldn't stop. Why he threw himself into her fight, why he risked everything. He saw a chance to do for Elise and Harper what he couldn't do for his sister.

And now he was gone.

Leaving nothing but fragments of a story she'd never fully know.

The kettle sat untouched on the stove, forgotten. Elise leaned back on the couch, fingers clenched around the empty bottle, letting the silence consume her.

She looked at the chair across from her.

Miles should have been there. Hunched over his notepad, muttering theories under his breath, piecing things together like it was the only thing keeping him alive.

The ache was unbearable.

On the coffee table, Harper's phone sat where she'd left it. Elise hesitated before picking it up, swiping across the screen. The glow illuminated her face as she scrolled through Harper's messages.

She needed answers.

Malik Jefferson.

Elise set Harper's phone down, her hands shaking as she pulled her laptop from her bag.

Her fingers hovered over the keyboard before typing the site Jamal told her about, Unplugged Minds.

A digital wasteland of conspiracy theories, anti-corporate rants, and whispers about things most people were too afraid to say out loud.

If there were answers, they were buried here.

And Elise was about to dig.

The front page was a tangled mess of paranoia... and truth.

"Optimization Dependency Syndrome: The Truth They Won't Tell You."

"The Aether's Grip on Society."

"Whistleblower Exposé - Hidden Harm."

The kind of headlines that made people scoff until it was too late. Elise's eyes scanned the chaos, hunting for a single name buried in the wreckage.

ResistorNode

There. Posts scattered across months, breadcrumbs buried in the noise. Malik had been careful, speaking in riddles, dropping cryptic warnings about Necessity Mart's systems while avoiding outright confession. Smart.

He knew they were watching.

Her heartbeat picked up when she saw it. Online.

She clicked *message* and began typing, keeping her words short.

ThreadSeeker88: *I need information about ODS and Necessity Mart. Jamal B. said to contact you. Urgent.*

The cursor blinked. One second. Two. Five.

ResistorNode: *No direct names.*

Elise exhaled. He wasn't trusting. This is good. Neither was she.

ThreadSeeker88: *Met J at OptimumCare after his incident. Said you were systems eng, left after finding something in backend. My daughter is showing withdrawal symptoms after taking off device. Trying to understand what's happening.*

ResistorNode: *Proof?*

Elise hesitated. Malik wasn't going to make this easy. She typed.

ThreadSeeker88: *J said you were the one who found the "butterfly effect" in the code.*

The pause stretched for too long.

ResistorNode: *Link expires in 3 minutes [encrypted link attached]*

Elise clicked. The screen flashed, then displayed a brief message.

Blue Door Diner. 1 hour. Far booth. Order black coffee. If anyone is in a blue jacket, walk out. No devices. No cards. Cash only. Reply "understood" in chat if you can make it.

Her fingers hovered. Once she hit send, there was no undoing this.

ThreadSeeker88: *Understood.*

ResistorNode: *Deleting thread. Don't reply.*

The chat vanished, leaving nothing but a blank screen.

Elise set Harper's phone on the couch, staring at it as if she could will it to buzz with reassurance. It didn't.

She stood, moving to the mirror. Her reflection stared back, exhausted and sleepless. She reached for the gun, tucking it into her waistband. The weight was still foreign but comforting.

Miles's voice surfaced in her mind, *"concealed but accessible. Always."*

She turned off her phone and left it behind. It felt like cutting an oxygen line, but Malik had made it clear. She checked her purse, counting cash. No cards. No trace.

Her fingers brushed against something else. A folded printout of Harper's school photo. She paused. A reminder of what was at stake.

Then, she grabbed her keys and walked out the door.

The drive to Blue Door Diner wound through an industrial graveyard—crumbling warehouses, old chain-link fences, trash everywhere. The kind of place that used to be something. Now it was just leftovers.

She pulled into the lot, parking at the far edge, sweeping the area. A couple of trucks. A delivery van. No blue jackets. Yet.

She took a deep breath, checked the gun one last time, and stepped out.

The bell above the door chimed softly as she entered.

The diner was old. A place that had seen better days and hadn't cared. Vinyl booths split at the seams, and the air smelled like burnt grease and something sweeter... pie maybe.

A waitress briefly looked up from her crossword but said nothing as Elise slid into the furthest booth, back to the wall.

When the waitress finally made her way over.

Elise exhaled slowly. "Coffee. Black."

Her voice was calm. Calmer than she felt.

Minutes crawled by, stretching too thin. Every time the bell rang, her shoulders tensed.

She scanned the dinner. No blue jackets.

Then the door opened.

A man stepped inside.

He was mid-thirties. He had a jittery, nervous energy hidden under a faded hoodie. He scanned the dinner.

Then he saw her.

He hesitated just long enough for Elise to know he was deciding whether to trust this meeting at all. But then, he walked toward her.

"You ThreadSeeker?" His voice was low.

Elise nodded, gripping her coffee cup. "Malik?"

He tilted his head slightly, studying her.

His eyes swept the diner one more time.

"No phones?"

"I left it at home," Elise said, slightly irritated.

"No cards?"

"Cash only," she said, flipping her pockets inside out to prove a point. "You want to frisk me too?"

Malik smirked. "Relax." He slid into the booth across from her, angling his body toward the exit. "I have to be sure."

"You sure now?" Elise asked.

"For now." He waved the waitress over without breaking eye contact.

"Coffee, black. No sugar."

The waitress barely acknowledged him as she jotted it down and walked away. Malik leaned forward, elbows resting on the table, fingers interlocked. Around them, the diner was typical.

Finally, he spoke. "Alright. Start talking. What do you know?"

Elise thought carefully before speaking, deciding where to start. "My sister, Maggie," she said. "She was recruited by a group called the Ascension Order. It's a cult, but I think it's more than that. I think it's connected to Necessity Mart."

Something changed in Malik's expression.

He knew something.

"They may have taken my daughter too," Elise continued. "I don't know if they're in the same place, but they're both gone."

"Ascension Order," Malik said. "Never heard of them."

"You're lying."

Malik's lip twitched. "I don't lie. I omit. There's a difference."

Elise let out a long breath. "They're linked. Maggie was pulled in after she started using the Aether. It's like the Order is tied to the same system Necessity Mart uses to... to control people."

That caught his attention.

"They're controlling more than you think," she pressed. "My husband, James... he was a patent lawyer. He worked with scientists at Synapse Dynamics. He got in over his head. I think he knew something."

Malik gripped his cup tighter. "Synapse Dynamics?" He was focused now.

"What do you know about them?"

Elise leaned forward. "Not enough. But James' last known meeting was with Dr. Elena Santos. Do you know her?"

Malik lowered his cup, his eyes locking onto hers with a new weight.

"Elena Santos," he mumbled. "Yeah. I know her."

"Do you know where she is?"

Malik shook his head. "Not exactly. But if you find her, she's the key. She knew more than the rest of us put together."

"We?" Elise raised an eyebrow.

Malik sighed. "I was inside before I got burned. Worked with the Synapse team early on. Helping them integrate their tech into the first Aether models. Back then, it was all above board. Or at least, we thought it was."

He looked away for a moment, as if considering how much to tell her. Then, finally, he leaned in.

"Before they fired me, I started hearing whispers. A project they never put in the official documentation. They called it 'The Happiness Factory.' Some hidden facility where they're running experiments. It's not about optimizing lives." He met her eyes with a seriousness in his voice. "It's about controlling them."

"Controlling them how?"

"Consciousness," Malik said. "Merging them, modifying them... hell, I don't know all the details. But A.R. took Synapse's tech and twisted it into something else. Something worse."

"Where is it? Where is the factory?"

Malik shook his head. "I don't know. But it's remote. Hidden. Somewhere in the forest, from what I've heard. If you're sisters in the Ascension Order, she's probably there. And if your daughter's gone missing..." He exhaled, rubbing his face. "Then yeah, maybe she is too."

Elise studied him. "I've told you everything I know. What about you? What aren't you saying?"

Malik leaned back, rubbing a hand over his chin. "You think I'm holding out? Fine. Here's the truth. I asked too many questions—about ODS, about the system's side effects, about what they were really doing. And they kicked me out before I could get real answers."

He dropped his voice lower.

"People are dying, Elise. Withdrawal symptoms. Neural damage. Worse. Whatever this next phase is, it's not just about profit anymore. It's bigger."

Before Malik could stand, Elise blurted, "What do you know about The Sunder?"

Malik froze.

"Why do you care about them?"

"I heard they help people dealing with optimization side effects. I'm worried about my daughter."

"The Sunder isn't a resistance group." His voice was quiet. "They're survivalists. Paranoids. They don't trust anyone. And they have good reasons for it."

"So how do I find them?" Elise pressed.

Malik hesitated. "They'll find you if they think you're worth their time. But don't expect a warm welcome."

Malik finished his coffee, checking the clock. "That's all I've got. Use the forum."

225

"That's it? That's all you're giving me?"

Malik smirked as he stood. "It's more than you had an hour ago."

He paused at the booth, before looking back one more time.

"One more thing," he said. "If you go after them, don't expect to win by playing fair. They don't."

And with that, he stepped into the morning air, disappearing before Elise could even breathe.

She sat there, staring at the cold coffee, at the weight of everything that had just changed.

And for the first time, she felt like the fight was just beginning.

CHAPTER FOURTEEN

Final Inspection

The most successful totalitarian state is one where the slaves
do not even realize they are enslaved.
– Aldous Huxley

Elise paced the narrow confines of the safe house restlessly, like motion alone could untangle the knot of the thoughts taking over her mind. Papers covered the coffee table—Miles's last work, a maddening collection of clues and dead ends. She'd sorted through them a hundred times since last night, and they still refused to give her anything solid. The neatness of his handwriting grated against her nerves. How could someone so meticulous leave so much unanswered?

Malik's words also clawed at her. *The Happiness Factory.* The name sounded ridiculous, like some dystopian theme park, but the weight behind it was anything but. She couldn't stop imagining what they were doing to people there. How they were taking bodies, minds, lives, and twisting them into whatever "transcendence" meant to Zenith Kael.

And Harper. Every time Elise's mind circled back to her daughter, it hit like a hammer to the chest. Harper was not at Suarez home. Ethan's frantic texts had shattered that thin layer of denial. Somewhere, Harper was slipping further away, into a world Elise didn't understand but couldn't stop herself from chasing.

She stopped pacing, her hand brushing against the edge of her jacket. Something crinkled. She reached in and pulled out a slip of paper, crumpled and damp at the edges. The writing was rushed, uneven, but undoubtedly hers.

From her final conversation with Miles.

Margaret Reed
316 Tidespring Ave
Willowbend

She stared at it, the memory resurfacing. Miles's voice, hoarse but insistent. *If James believed Reed left something behind, it matters. It's not random.*

Miles hadn't been the kind of man to waste words, especially not in the final stretch. Whatever he thought was there, it had been urgent enough for him to prioritize it over everything else. Elise looked at the paper again. Willowbend was hours away. It didn't matter. She had to go.

A tether to whatever slim hope was left. Elise moved with purpose now, pulling the gun from its hiding spot in the kitchen drawer and tucking it into her waistband. The weight of it was grounding, not reassuring, but necessary.

She grabbed what little cash she had left, stuffing it into her jacket pocket alongside Harper's school photo. Miles's notes went into her bag, a messy pile of theories and half-formed connections that might mean everything or nothing.

She let out a breath she didn't realize she was holding. No time to wait for Shanti. No time to second-guess. Margaret Reed might be the last chance she had to make sense of this nightmare.

She locked the door behind her, the metal bolt sliding into place with a finality that echoed in her chest. The street outside was quiet, but Elise's eyes swept over every shadow, every parked car, every possible hiding place for someone who might be watching. She couldn't shake the feeling that someone, or something, was always watching.

Her car sat at the curb, battered but reliable. She slid into the driver's seat, uncrumpled the address from Miles in her hand one last time, then tucked it into the sun visor. The engine roared to life, and she looked at the map on the dashboard, tracing the route to Willowbend with her finger. It felt absurdly ordinary, plotting directions to a place that might hold the key to saving Harper... or to unraveling everything.

She pulled onto the road, her mind set. There was no going back now. Whatever Dr. Reed had left behind, she would find it. She had to.

The drive to Willowbend was a slow descent into nowhere, the kind of empty highway that unraveled thoughts like loose thread. Elise had spent the entire trip wrestling her mind into submission, refusing to let it circle the drain of second-guessing. But the road had a way of pulling you under, stretching time, making every decision feel like a mistake waiting to be realized.

When she finally arrived the driveway was long, a downhill slope, stretching longer than it should have been. The house was surrounded by towering oaks that swayed like they knew something she didn't.

A single car sat untouched beneath the carport. A faded blue Volvo, its windshield covered in dust. Nothing moved. No sign of life. Just the wind blowing through the trees, whispering secrets she wasn't sure she wanted to hear.

Now, standing in front of Margaret Reed's house, she forced herself to breathe. Margaret was in there. And if Elise was lucky, so were answers.

If she wasn't...

She shoved the thought aside and knocked.

The response came slow. Three careful footsteps, each one louder than Elise expected, like someone making a point of being heard.

The door cracked open, revealing Margaret Reed.

She was older than Elise had pictured. Early sixties, maybe, but still mentally there. Not soft in the way some people got with time, but worn thin, like paper folded one too many times. The tiredness in her eyes didn't dull the suspicion behind them. She was dressed neatly, a pressed blouse and slacks that didn't match the quiet decay of her surroundings.

And her neck was bare. No Aether.

Margaret didn't speak right away. She studied Elise.

"Can I help you?" Her tone was polite, but hesitant. Probably from too many knocks on the door that led to nothing good.

Elise gripped the strap on her bag tighter. "I'm sorry to show up unannounced," she began, the words feeling clumsy in her mouth. "But I knew your husband. He worked with mine, James Winters. They were trying to finish something together."

Margaret's posture shifted. Not much. But enough.

"I don't know anything about Tom's work," she said. "That part of his life was... complicated. I've tried to move on."

Elise stepped forward slightly, careful not to push too hard. "I understand," she said softly, letting her own grief seep into her voice. "I lost James a few months ago. And it's been—" She exhaled. "Overwhelming."

"I know what it's like to want to leave it all behind. But I've found things. Notes, clues. It's like James was trying to tell me something, even after he was gone."

Margaret looked over Elise's face. Her shoulders stayed stiff, but the hardness in her voice started to wear.

Elise pressed on.

"James always said your husband was one of the good ones. That he was caught in something bigger than himself. He wanted to help." She hesitated. "If I could just see anything. His notes, his papers... It might help me figure out what they were trying to protect."

Margaret turned her head slightly, looking past Elise, somewhere far away.

"Tom," she muttered. "He was under so much stress. He started keeping notebooks, but I never read them."

Her voice dropped to a whisper. "I didn't want to know."

Elise held her breath. She could feel Margaret start to crack, the hesitation before a door is either shut forever or thrown wide open.

"I'm not asking you to relive any of it," Elise said gently. "I just... I need to know if there's something that can help me. Help all of us. Please."

The war playing out in Margaret's head was visible on her face. The instinct to protect herself. The lingering love for a man who had been drowning in something she could never pull him from.

Then, finally, she nodded and stepped aside.

"Come in."

∞∞∞∞

The living room seemed like a skeleton of what it once was.

Empty hooks covered the walls where pictures had once hung. Gaps on the shelves, the absence of books or trinkets that had been packed away or sold.

But on the mantel, one thing remained—a wedding photo.

Tom Reed was younger. Margaret stood next him, glowing, her smile belonging to another version of herself. One that hadn't known what was coming.

Margaret disappeared briefly and returned with a cardboard box, setting it on the dining room table.

"After he died, I couldn't keep his things around," she said. "It was too much. But everything's in here."

Elise moved closer as Margaret opened the box. Folders filled with medical papers, trial reports, pens, photographs, an old watch.

But Elise's eyes landed on the black leather-bound notebook at the bottom.

Margaret saw her expression and gave a small nod.

"That's his journal," she said quietly. "I couldn't bring myself to read it."

Elise reached in, lifting the notebook. The leather was cool, smooth. The moment she opened it, she knew—this was what she came for.

She flipped through the pages of hurried, desperate handwriting. Some entries were barely legible, written in moments of fear or frustration. She skimmed until something stopped her.

A heavily underlined entry.

She read.

Elena was right. The delays weren't coincidence. They were manufactured... designed to squeeze us until we had no choice. A.R. played us like pawns, creating chaos while presenting himself as the savior. And I... I fell for it.

Elena almost blew everything open today. She walked into the board meeting with evidence. Real, damning evidence of altered trial data. I sat there, silent, as they shredded her credibility. And yet... she stood her ground. Watching her fight for what's right while I cower in the shadows... it's unbearable.

Every 'optimization milestone' they celebrate is another betrayal of SynapticEase's purpose. We designed it to heal trauma, to free people from their pain... not tether them to a corporate leash. They call it progress. I call it perversion.

Elena told me she's moving her original research to Brookfield Clinic. She said she'd destroy it all before letting them corrupt it further. I don't blame her. She's the only one who still believes we can undo this.

Then, one final entry.

Margaret, my love, forgive me. I hope one day you can remember the man I was before all of this. Before I failed you.

Elise's pulse pounded in her ears.
Brookfield Clinic. Miles had mentioned it.
It was a lead. Maybe the only one she had left.
A sound shook her out of her thoughts. A ringing phone.
Margaret turned to answer, her steps slow.
Elise shut the journal, her heart hammering.
"Hello?" Margaret's voice was polite.
Then a pause, her eyebrows raised. "Yes, this is she."
She glanced at Elise. "Oh, the sweet girl? Yes, she's here now."
Ice licked up Elise's spine.
Margaret turned slightly, covering the receiver. "Dear, what's your name again?"
Elise forced a smile. "Ashley."
Margaret nodded, returning to the call. "Yes, Ashley. She said James was her husband."

Elise's blood ran cold.

She slipped the journal into her bag and grabbed her coat, forcing herself to stay calm. She needed to leave. Now.

Margaret turned, phone still pressed to her ear. "Ashley, they'd like to speak to you. Something about James. They said it's important."

Elise smiled again. "I'd love to, but I really need to get going. Thank you for everything."

"But—"

Elise didn't wait.

She stepped outside, the cold biting her skin as she rushed to her car. Margaret's silhouette was in the window, phone still pressed to her ear.

Elise gripped the steering wheel, breaths coming in quick, ragged gasps.

They knew she was here.

They knew.

Her focus locked on one thing.

Brookfield Clinic. Dr. Elena Santos.

The truth was waiting.

∞∞∞∞∞

The car rolled in the far corner of a gas station parking lot, away from the pumps and the brightly lit storefront. Elise killed the engine, the tick of the cooling motor filling the silence. She stared out the windshield at nothing in particular, the sound of the streetlights blending into the static of her thoughts.

Her hands moved on autopilot, pulling the journal from the passenger seat and flipping it open to the same underlined page she'd read at Margaret Reed's house. The words stared at her... *Brookfield Clinic.* She traced the name with her finger, as if the act might anchor her.

The phone screen lit up as she typed the address into the maps app. The route populated, winding through backroads and small towns, the estimated time being just over two hours. Two hours to the next step, the next question, the next risk. The thin, glowing line on the map felt fragile, pulling her toward something she couldn't see clearly but couldn't turn away from either.

Elise leaned back against the seat, the journal open on her lap, and let out a long breath. The truth felt heavier than the weight of the book. The files, Elise Santos, the possibility of answers. It was all there, but going alone felt like standing at the edge of a cliff and daring gravity to do its worst.

232

Her thumb hovered over the phone, scrolling to Shanti's number. For a second, she hesitated. She already knew the answer, already heard the "no" in her head. But she couldn't afford silence. Not tonight.

She pressed call.

The line clicked after the second ring.

"Brown."

"It's me," Elise said.

A pause. Then, a sigh.

"Elise, this really isn't a good time."

"I know you're busy," Elise said quickly, shoving past the dismissal before Shanti could shut her down completely. "But I need your help. I found something... something big. It's connected to James, to Necessity Mart. There's an old clinic... Brookfield Heights. I think someone hid important files there."

Shanti didn't answer right away. Elise pictured her on the other end, pinching the bridge of her nose, weighing whether she even wanted to get involved.

"Brookfield Heights?" Shanti's voice was more serious now. "Elise, that's hours away. What exactly is your plan? Just walk in and hope classified documents are sitting in a filing cabinet? Do you even understand how dangerous this is?"

"That's why I'm calling you! I need someone with experience. Someone I trust. You've dealt with this kind of thing before—"

"Elise."

Shanti's tone flattened, and that single word carried more weight than the rest of the conversation combined.

"I'm dealing with something right now. A missing kid from Sterling Ridge. Teenager. The family's barely holding it together, and I'm burning the candle at both ends. I can't just drop everything for a wild lead."

Elise swallowed. She didn't expect this.

"Shanti, this isn't just a lead," she said, her voice quieter, but no less desperate. "It connects everything. I'm not asking you to drop the case... Just give me something. Advice. Anything."

The line went quiet.

When Shanti finally spoke, her voice had softened, but there was still a wall between them.

"Elise, I get it. I do. But this case is a time bomb. If I don't stay on it, it all falls apart, and that kid might not see their family again. You need to think carefully about what you're doing. This isn't some amateur detective game. If Necessity Mart is involved, you're stepping into a hornet's nest."

Elise closed her eyes, gripping the phone tighter. "I don't have a choice. If I don't go, who will?"

More silence. Then another sigh.

Shanti's voice was lower now, a mix of frustration and reluctant understanding.

"Listen to me. Be smart. Don't go alone if you can help it. And if anything feels wrong, you get out. Immediately. Understand?"

"I understand."

"Good luck, Elise. Call me when you're back."

The line went dead.

Elise stared at the phone in her hand, the screen dark now. The parking lot pressed in around her, too big, too empty, too silent. The weight of Shanti's words settled over her, but it didn't change what she had to do.

She set the phone down, and looked at the glowing map on the dashboard.

The route to Brookfield Heights Clinic was still there, a thin, fragile thread pulling her toward something she couldn't fully see. The journal sat open in the passenger seat, its pages fanned out like a dare.

Elise turned the key in the ignition.

The engine rumbled to life.

Ahead, the thin line on the map glowed like a promise... or a warning. Elise didn't care which. She was already moving.

∞∞∞∞

The road unraveled before her, a thin, gray scar carved into the desolation. Elise slowed the car to a crawl, her fingers tight on the wheel as the blue dot on her phone crept toward its destination. The air felt heavier here, dense with everything left unsaid, undone.

She pulled onto the shoulder, cut the engine. Silence swallowed her whole, so thick it made the distant chorus of cicadas' sound deafening. The building stood in front of her, its skeletal remains blackened and peeling, as if something had burned away its skin but left the bones behind. A chain-link fence wrapped around it with rusted warnings that no longer mattered.

Elise stepped out, pulling her coat tighter against the cold wind. The place felt wrong. Not just abandoned—emptied. The kind of space where the past had been scraped clean but never quite erased.

She moved along the perimeter, her phone's flashlight casting a weak, flickering beam. Then she saw it. A section of the fence cut and curled back. Wide enough to crawl through.

She crouched and slid through. A snag in the wire caught her coat, tearing the fabric. She freed herself and straightened, pulling out her phone again.

The light swept across warped metal and broken glass, catching the gaping entrance ahead. She stepped forward, her boots crunching over scattered debris.

The door groaned as she pushed it open, the sound too loud.

She hesitated, eyes adjusting to the dark. The place had been gutted. The walls blackened, the floor littered with the brittle remnants of something that once mattered.

A desk sat against one wall, warped by heat but still standing. A rusted nameplate clung stubbornly to its surface, its letters barely legible. Papers were scattered, curling at the edges, most of them too far gone to make any sense of.

Elise crouched, sifting through the wreckage. Patient intake forms, supply orders—scraps of a life reduced to ash.

A rustle.

She froze.

The sound came again.

Louder, closer. A shuffle, the clink of something being moved.

Elise stood slowly, her hand drifting to the gun tucked at her waist. The flashlight shook as she lifted it, the beam slicing through the gloom.

"Who's there?"

Silence.

She took a step forward.

Then, a blur. A person jumping from behind an overturned desk.

A flash of ripped fabric, a dirty backpack. A face of panic.

Elise's grip tightened on the gun, but she hesitated. The man ran, footsteps pounding toward an exit. She could stop him. She should stop him. But something in her didn't, and by the time she raised the weapon, he was gone.

The silence rushed back in, thicker than before.

Elise exhaled, lowering the gun. *Get it together,* she mumbled.

She turned back to the wreckage, forcing herself to focus. The desk. The scattered papers. Something here mattered. She could feel it.

Then she saw it.

A collapsed shelf, half-buried. Beneath it, shielded from the worst of the fire, a cluster of papers. Elise crouched, brushing away the ash.

Most of it was useless.

But one sheet caught her eye.

A letter, edges singed, the handwriting frantic.

Dr. Carter, I'm relocating to my private facility in Pine Valley. Please forward any remaining records to the address below. Destroy duplicates immediately. They're watching.

A name at the bottom.

Elena Santos.

Elise's breath caught in her throat.

Beneath it, written in rushed letters: 728 Bird Hollow Road, Pine Valley.

She folded the note carefully, sliding it into her bag. This was it. Elena Santos wasn't here, but this address... it was the next step. A crack in the wall.

She retraced her steps, moving back through the ruined halls, past the ghosts and echoes. Ducking through the fence, the tear in her coat snagged again, as if the place didn't want to let her go.

The night air was crisp.

The car sat where she left it, waiting, quietly in the dark.

Inside, she locked the doors. The note burned in her bag, the address carved into her thoughts.

728 Bird Hollow Road, Pine Valley.

She started the engine.

The ruins disappeared in the rearview mirror, sinking into the dark.

CHAPTER FIFTEEN

Out for Delivery

*The limits of tyrants are prescribed by the endurance
of those whom they oppress.*
– Frederick Douglass

The diner hunched by the roadside, the kind of place that felt like it had been there before the highway was anything but dirt and wagons. The smell of fried bacon and grease that had seeped too deep to ever wash out. It clung to the walls, the floors, the cracked vinyl booths. Two truckers sat at the counter, their conversation slow, the kind of talk that didn't need to be rushed. A jukebox struggled in the corner, playing oldies.

Elise sat alone at a corner booth, back against the sticky vinyl. Her breakfast had gone cold, grease pooling in the dim morning light fighting through smudged windows. She hadn't touched it.

Harper's phone was in her hands, the glow of the screen casting her face in blue light as she scrolled through the galley.

One photo after another. A life that barely felt like hers anymore.

Harper laughing, Christmas morning, standing in a tornado of wrapping paper. James sunburned and grinning, his laughter frozen in time.

Then the last one.

Elise stopped scrolling.

A photo taken just a week before James died. Blurry, like the universe didn't want to capture it clearly. He had his arm around Harper, their heads tilted together, the kind of trust you didn't think about until it was gone.

Elise stared until the lines blurred. The life they had before his death felt like a mirage. No Aether bands. No optimization scores. No corporation breathing into the cracks of everyday life, whispering about efficiency.

Her voice barely broke the silence. "We didn't know how good we had it."

She sat the phone down and reached for the leather journal. The cover was cool under her fingers. She flipped through the pages, stopping on an entry she had skimmed but never really read.

The date was old. Years before everything fell apart. The handwriting was steady, untouched by the frantic, uneven mess of Dr. Reed's later entries.

We've done it. The prototype works. SynapticEase can heal trauma. Truly heal it. This isn't a theory anymore. It's real.

The words carried excitement, the high of a breakthrough. But beneath the optimism, the cracks had already started to show.

But how do we take it to the masses? The cost is astronomical, and we're burning through funding. The board is pushing for quick returns. They want a product yesterday. Elena says we need more time, but investors don't care about time. I can feel the fractures forming. Too many visions, not enough cohesion. Elena wants perfection. Marcus wants speed. I'm just somewhere in the middle, trying to hold it all together.

A margin in the note caught her eye, sloppily written.

Early interest from a retail giant. This could solve the funding problem.

Another, smaller, almost an afterthought.

Potential conflict. Their vision doesn't align with ours. Do we even have a choice?

Elise traced the words with her fingertip, imagining Dr. Reed at his desk, hopeful, naive. He'd seen it coming. Maybe not all of it, but enough to know the ground was moving beneath him.

A crash of plates from the kitchen shook her back to the diner. She looked up.

The waitress, middle-aged, silver Aether glowing under the diner's flickering lights. For a moment, she thought he was looking at her, but his focus was on the muted TV mounted above, the morning news cycling through its normal segments.

Elise shook off the unease and turned back to the journal.

Her coffee had gone cold, but she drank it anyway, the bitterness keeping her focused.

Harper's phone vibrated softly, a message lighting up the screen. Ethan. Again. Elise scrolled through the unanswered texts.

She locked the screen instead, tucking the phone into her pocket.

The waitress returned, check in hand. His smile was polite, but distant. Elise left a few bills on the table, gathered her things, and hopped out of the booth.

The journal went back into her bag, its weight heavy against her side as she stepped into the crisp morning air.

The air was cold, the windshield fogged. Elise sat there a moment before turning the key in the ignition. The journal rested in her bag on the passenger seat, the words Pine Valley seared into her mind.

The diner shrank in the rearview mirror, fading into the landscape.

She let out a slow breath, hands steady on the wheel.

"This started with James," she mumbled. "It ends with me."

The tires rolled against the asphalt, carrying her toward whatever waited at the end of the road.

The dirt road stretched on, cutting through fields of dying grass. Each bump and pothole made the car rattle, but Elise barely noticed. Her grip on the wheel was loose, her focus split between the road ahead and the pulsing blue dot on her phone, counting down the final miles. The horizon bled out the last breath of day before the dark took over.

Then she saw it. The house.

Elise eased off the gas, heart ticking faster. It sat alone in the field, slouched and silent, the kind of place that knew better than to draw attention. A single porch light flickered weakly, more of a dying signal than a warm welcome. To its side, a shed leaned at a dangerous angle, half collapsed, like it had spent years fighting the wind and finally lost.

She pulled off the road, gliding the car into the cover of a few bare trees at the top of the hill. From here, she could see the driveway. A sedan sat parked, its windshield streaked with dirt, its presence answering the one question that mattered.

Someone was inside.

Elise killed the engine. The quiet slammed down around her. She slid out of the car, bag slung over her shoulder, boots crunching softly over the frozen grass. The wind had a knife's edge, cutting straight through her coat, but she ignored it.

Keeping low, she moved down the hill, weaving through the tall grass that shifted in strange, restless patterns. The shed caught her attention first. The padlock on the door was rusted, cobwebs hung across the hinges. It hadn't been opened in a while. She moved on.

The basement window was buried under dirt and dead leaves. Elise crouched. Nothing but black. Further along, an open window near the back of the house. The wood frame had splintered, cracked inward like something forced its way through. Big enough to slip inside, but not without making a racket. Not worth the risk.

Then... movement.

Elise froze, holding her breath. Inside. A chair scraped against the floor. A shape passing too close to the curtain, sending shadows sprawling across the fabric. The flickering light pulsed again, and for the first time, it felt... unnatural. Like the heartbeat of something waiting.

No. She shook off the thought. Just a trick of the dark.

She took a deep breath then climbed the porch steps, keeping her movements steady. The wood groaned under her boots, the sound absorbed by the cold wind.

She hesitated at the door. Then three quick knocks, louder than she intended in the silence.

She held her breath.

Nothing.

She knocked again, softer this time. Her knuckles barely brushed the wood when—

Pain.

A bright, shattering explosion at the back of her skull. The world spun, tilted sideways. Her knees buckled. A rush of cold against her cheek, the taste of copper filling her mouth.

From somewhere above, a voice, low and unimpressed.

"Amateur."

Then everything went black.

∞∞∞∞

Consciousness returned in fragments. A dull, pounding throb radiated from the back of her skull. Her mouth was dry, like it had been stuffed with cotton balls. The air was damp, heavy with the stale rot of old wood. Somewhere close, a small space heater rattled, its noise barely breaking the suffocating silence.

Elise tried to move, but the ropes bit back. Her wrists were bound behind the back of a wooden chair, ankles tied together, tight enough that it had started digging into her skin. A blindfold was pressed against her face, a layer of darkness that made the space around her feel endless, and the danger immediate.

Then the footsteps. Slow. Methodical.

"Don't bother," a voice said.

"You're not going anywhere."

Elise swallowed, but there was no saliva left. The voice was female, calm but intense, with the kind of control that made her skin prickle.

"Who sent you?" The voice moved slightly, circling.

"Was it A.R.? Or one of his puppets?"

Her throat ached as she tried to speak. The ropes dug deeper as she adjusted, every breath slow, choppy, trying to find footing in the disorienting dark.

"No one sent me," she finally let out.

"My name is Elise. I came here because of James Winters."

Silence. Too long.

Then the quiet sound of movement, something heavy dropping onto a nearby table.

"James Winters?" The disbelief in her captor's voice was heavy. "You expect me to believe that? You have no idea what kind of game you're playing."

Elise grit her teeth, pushing past the pain, forcing her voice to stay steady.

"I know exactly what I'm doing. James was my husband. He died because of Necessity Mart. I'm trying to find the truth... just like you were."

Another long silence, then a loud slap—a book hitting a table.

"And this?" the voice snapped. "How did you get this?"

Dr. Reed's journal. Elise could almost feel it sitting there, open, exposed.

"It... it was left behind," she said quickly. "Margaret Reed had it. I thought it would help me understand what they were doing... what they're still doing."

A loud sigh, like the answer wasn't good enough. "Margaret had this? That doesn't explain how it ended up in your hands. What are you really after?"

Elise's jaw locked, knowing hesitation would only make things worse. "I'm trying to find my daughter. Harper. She disappeared a week ago. I think somebody took her. The same people that killed James."

The words felt enormous in the silence. But no response came, no breath, nothing. Elise pushed forward, desperately.

"...And my sister, Maggie," she continued. "She didn't vanish like Harper, not exactly, but I know Necessity Mart has her. I just want them back. That's all I want."

The tension in the air stretched, thinner and thinner.

Then, finally, the voice spoke. Quieter now.

"You really have no idea what this is, do you?" It was almost a whisper, something spoken to herself more than Elise. "What it means."

"I know enough," Elise said quietly.

"Enough to know it's all connected... Harper, Maggie, James. They're all trapped in this... machine. And I'm the only one left to pull them out."

Another pause, then the rough scrape of rope. The knot at the back of her head loosened, and the blindfold fell away. The dim light made her eyes water, as the shapes came into focus.

A woman stood in front of her, slender, her face covered in exhaustion. She looked older than Elise had imagined. Hair streaked with gray, sharp eyes dulled by many sleepless nights. But there was something still burning in them. Something that hadn't gone out.

Dr. Elena Santos.

"You think you can pull them out," Santos said, studying her. "That's almost admirable. But this isn't about your family, Elise. This is bigger than you."

Elise met her gaze. "Then help me. Don't let it take me under."

Santos didn't respond right away. She let out a long breath through her nose, before finally stepping forward and loosening the ropes at Elise's wrists.

"You're reckless," she muttered.

"I'm starting to understand why James didn't tell you everything."

The last knot fell away, and Elise flexed her fingers, blood rushing painfully back to her hands. She rubbed her wrists, watching Santos carefully.

"Don't make me regret this," Santos warned.

"Wouldn't dream of it," Elise muttered back.

Santos nodded toward the stairs. "Come on. If you're going to keep asking questions, I'd rather not stand here all night."

Elise stood slowly, her legs stiff, shoulders aching. She followed Santos up the wooden steps, the damp, stale air of the basement replaced by something warmer, electric.

The living room wasn't a living room. It was a war room disguised as one.

Elise took it all in—the walls lined with maps, pinned notes, names she recognized and ones she didn't. A stack of printed files sat on a desk, pages spread open like a corpse on an autopsy table.

Whatever Santos had been running from, whatever she'd been preparing for— she wasn't just surviving. She was still fighting.

Elise exhaled, pulse still hammering from the ropes, from the blindfold, from the way the night had tilted sideways.

She looked at Santos. "Where do we start?"

Santos looked at the journal on the table, then back at Elise.

"By not getting killed. After that... we'll see."

The room was suffocating under the weight of information. In one corner, laptops and monitors blinked quietly, their screens frozen on lines of dense code and grainy surveillance images Elise couldn't make sense of.

"This is... a lot," Elise mumbled.

Elena didn't turn around. She moved through the chaos like it was an extension of herself, flipping through pages without looking. "This is survival," she said. "Every scrap of truth I've managed to keep from them. Every lead I've chased. Every dead end I've hit. It's all here."

Elise stepped toward a table near the center of the room, looking at the documents. Then her breath caught. James Winters. Dr. Reed. Synapse Dynamics.

Photographs. Some places she didn't recognize, others of charred ruins she'd stood in herself.

Her hand hovered over a file, fingers stiff, her voice tightening.

"Do you know what they've done with my sister? Or Harper?"

Elena paused. The question lingered too long. She shuffled through a pile of papers on the couch. When she finally spoke, her voice was like broken glass.

"That depends. If what's in that box is what I think it is... they could both be dead."

Elise's chest tightened, her breath coming too fast.

She barely registered the cluttered room anymore. Harper. Maggie. The thought of them alone, trapped, or worse, sent a wave of panic surging through her. But there was something else beneath the fear, tangled and pressing against the edges of her thoughts.

The box.

She forced herself to focus, to push through the panic.

"You know about the box?" The words fell out quicker than she intended, somewhere between demand and disbelief.

Elena let out a humorless laugh. "Do I?"

It wasn't just the words. It was how she said them. Like Elise had just stumbled into something much bigger than she realized.

"How?"

"James told me about it."

"When?"

"The last time I saw him."

The room suddenly felt smaller. Elise stared at Elena, trying to read between the lines, searching for some kind of answer hidden behind her eyes.

"He wouldn't tell me what was in it," Elena admitted, folding her arms. "Only that it was important. That it had to stay hidden."

"Did he say why?"

Elena shook her head. "No. And I pushed him on it. He kept saying it was too dangerous. That he needed more time."

"We were supposed to meet again. He said he'd tell me everything then."

"And then what happened?"

Elena clenched her jaw. "I never heard from him again."

A long, unbearable silence stretched between them.

Then, Elena reached into her shirt, revealing a string around her neck, with a small, worn key attached to it. It caught the dim light, a secret she'd carried against her skin.

"I still have the key," Elena whispered.

James had kept his secrets. But this one, whatever was locked away in that box, was something worth dying for.

"They don't stop. Not for children, not for family. I've watched everyone I worked with disappear. One by one. James. Carter. Wills. Reed. Gone."

She paused, gripping the edge of the table. "And they didn't just erase them. They erased their work. Their research. Their lives. They tried to do the same to me."

Elise forced her voice through the knot in her throat. "Then why keep going? Why risk everything?"

Elena's eyes met hers, tired but relentless. "Because I can't stop. Not now. Not when there's even the smallest chance of making it right."

Elise swallowed. "What happened to your clinic?"

Elena sighed. She moved to the kitchen, filling a glass of water. The tap ran too long, like she needed an excuse not to answer.

"They burned it," she said finally, the words short, emotionless. "Everything we built. Every record. Every piece of research. Gone in one night."

She leaned against the counter, turning the glass in her hands. "And that was just the start. They hacked my files, planted fake data to ruin my credibility. Followed me. Broke into my home. They wanted to make me paranoid. Then they sent someone to kill me."

Elise felt the floor tilt beneath her. "They tried—"

"A bullet missed my head by inches," Elena said, her voice detached, like she was describing the weather. "They sent professionals. I got lucky."

Elise clenched her fists, her palms sweaty. But Elena continued.

"And yet, here I am," she said. "Because I've got nothing left to lose."

The room felt colder. Elise shifted her weight, trying to ground herself.

"What do you know about the Happiness Factory?"

Elena froze.

The glass stopped halfway to her lips. Her voice was different now.

"What do you know about it?"

"Not much, but I know it's where my family might be. That's all I have to go on."

Elena set the glass down, carefully. Like the weight of the conversation had become too heavy.

"The Happiness Factory is A.R.'s masterpiece," she said after a long pause. "I don't know everything, but I know enough. It's a nightmare wrapped in a promise."

She let out a bitter laugh. "He always believed free will was messy. That people didn't want freedom. They wanted order. Structure. Control."

"He used to say he was finishing what his mother started. That's all it's ever been to him... a continuation of some twisted family legacy."

Elise shook her head. "And the other scientists? They just... went along with it?"

"Not at first. But A.R. doesn't force you. He doesn't need to. He plants seeds. Doubt. Temptation. The illusion of choice. And by the time you realize what's happening, you're already tangled in his web."

She looked at the wall, where dozens of faces stared back. Some crossed out. Some circled.

"And by then, it's too late."

Elise swallowed the nausea rising in her throat.

"Do you know where it is?" Her voice barely sounded like her own.

Elena locked eyes with her. For a long moment, she said nothing.

Then... she nodded.

"Blackbriar Forest," she said. "They built it deep in the woods, surrounded by miles of nothing. But 'factory' is the wrong word. It's a fortress."

"Then tell me how to get in," Elise said, stepping forward.

"You don't understand. No one gets in unless they want you there. It's suicide."

"I don't have a choice! My daughter, my sister... They might be in there. I have to find them."

Elena studied her for a moment.

"And what if they're not?" she asked. "What if all you find is a trap?"

"Then I'll deal with it."

Elena exhaled through her nose, unimpressed. "You don't get it, do you?" she said. "This isn't a movie. You don't walk into that place and fight your way out. You don't walk out at all."

Their eyes stayed locked onto each other. "I know the risks," Elise said finally.

She swallowed the knot forming in her throat.

She couldn't afford fear right now.

"If you help me get into the Happiness Factory," she said, "I'll give you what's in the box."

245

Elena stopped moving.

"What did you say?"

"You heard me. You help me, and the box is yours."

Elena's fingers twitched, and Elise could almost see the gears turning in her head. The hesitation. The hunger.

"And how do you plan to do that?"

"I know where it is."

Elena narrowed her eyes suspiciously. "Convenient."

"I'm not lying."

Another pause. The tension rising, a wire pulled so tight it was about to snap.

Then, finally, Elena sighed.

A long, exhausted breath.

"Fine." Her voice was quiet. "I will help you get in. But get this straight... I'm not stepping foot in Blackbriar. I'm not going anywhere near that place."

Elise nodded.

"We'll go to HavenBrook first. Gather supplies. Information. Pull together a plan. But don't think for a second this will be easy."

She moved quickly, sweeping up papers, hard drives, notebooks, stuffing them into a worn messenger bag. She moved like someone who had done this before.

Many times.

"We'll find a motel in the city," Elena said, not looking at Elise.

"Something quiet, out of the way. If we draw attention, we're dead."

Elise nodded, her eyes lingering on the mess of papers left behind.

Elena slung the bag over her shoulder, pausing for just a moment.

"Let's hope you're ready for what comes next."

Then, without another word, she moved toward the door.

Elise followed, her determination burning low, but still burning.

∞∞∞∞

The road stretched ahead, a thin ribbon of asphalt cutting through the black void of the countryside. The sound of the tires was steady, the only noise in the car. But it did nothing to calm Elise's thoughts. The distant glow of HavenBrook slowly came into few, a barely visible haze in the dark night, growing brighter with each passing mile.

In the passenger seat, Elena Santos sat motionless, arms crossed, staring straight ahead. The air between them was heavy with everything left unsaid, words neither of them seemed willing to give life to.

Finally, Elise broke the silence.

"What do you think is in the box?"

Santos kept looking straight.

"Whatever it is, it was important enough to get James killed. And it's the only reason you're still breathing."

"What do you mean?"

"If they thought you had nothing, you'd already be dead."

Elise gripped the wheel tighter. The weight of it all settled on her, a pressure so heavy it felt like her ribs might crack under it.

Gravel crunched beneath the tires as she turned into the motel parking lot. The place was a relic of better days. A flickering neon VACANCY sign buzzed above the office.

A man leaned against the wall near the entrance, a cigarette burning between his lips. His hood was pulled low, covering most of his face, but there was a stillness to him that made Elise uncomfortable.

Further down the row of doors, a couple stepped outside. The man waved his hands wildly, clearly agitated. The woman ducked her head and hurried in front of him, shoulders slouched.

Santos unbuckled her seatbelt. "Stay here. I'll get us a room."

Elise nodded, gripping her bag tightly as she watched the older woman step out. The way Santos moved, her posture relaxed but her eyes scanning, always scanning.

Alone in the car, Elise pulled out her phone. Her fingers moved quickly, typing out a message.

Made it to HavenBrook. Will update when I have more.

She hesitated, staring at the screen, then exhaled and hit send. She glanced toward the office where Santos was speaking with the clerk through the grimy window.

A few minutes later, Santos returned, a key dangling from a cheap plastic tag in her hand. She tossed it onto the dashboard. "Come on."

Elise followed her across the lot, keeping her head low. The place had the same sketchy energy as every run-down motel. Low voices behind thin doors, distant sounds of TVs, and the occasional jerk of the curtains as someone looked out, just to make sure they were alone.

Above them, two men leaned against the second floor railing, speaking low. One was shirtless, his chest covered in faded tattoos. He smirked as they walked by, his eyes lingering just a second too long.

Elise's hand tightened around the strap of her bag.

Santos unlocked the door and pushed it open. A dull, yellow light flickered to life overhead, buzzing through the silence. The room was small, the air stale. Two thin beds sat in the center, their faded comforters sunken in the middle. A tiny television sat on a scratched dresser beside a lamp missing its shade.

"Home sweet home," Santos muttered, tossing her bag onto the dresser.

Elise stepped inside, letting the door shut behind her. The lock was flimsy.

Santos was already unpacking, spreading papers across the small table by the window, stacking them in neat piles. She didn't look up. "I'll sort through this in the morning. For now, we rest."

Elise sat on the edge of her bed, her muscles aching, her thoughts a mess. James. Harper. Maggie. The box. The Happiness Factory. Every answer led to another question, another door she wasn't sure she was ready to open.

Santos disappeared into the bathroom, and Elise reached into her bag, pulling out Harper's phone. She swiped through the messages again.

The weight of loss was heavy. Too big. Too crushing.

The bathroom door creaked open, and Santos stepped out, hair damp, face unreadable. She climbed into the bed closest to the door, flipping open a notebook.

Elise slid the phone back into her bag and laid back on the lumpy mattress, staring up at the cracked ceiling.

Outside, the neon light buzzed, its electric glow piercing through the thin curtains.

The weight of exhaustion dragged under her, but sleep didn't come easy.

Nothing ever did anymore.

∞∞∞∞∞

The first sound Elise registered was the shower, a low steady rhythm that pulled her from uneasy sleep. Her eyes blinked open to the weak morning light bleeding through the thin motel curtains. The scent of mildew and cheap disinfectant clung to her nostrils, the kind of smell that never really went away, no matter how many times the room had been scrubbed down before them.

Santos's bed was empty, the comforter smoothed into place, the pillow barely dented. Her bag still sat on the dresser, half-zipped, overflowing with papers. Elise stretched, trying to shake the stiffness in her shoulders, the lumpy mattress doing her no favors.

She stood, rubbing the sleep from her eyes, and spotted a small pile of papers on the table between their beds. Notes written in neat handwriting. Maps of Blackbriar Forest, layered with annotations.

Perimeter breach points.

Biometric overrides.

Surveillance chokeholds.

The words sank hooks into her.

The bathroom door swung open, and Santos stepped out, drying her hair. Her movements were calculated, the kind of control that never fully relaxed, especially in moments like this.

"We need to eat before we plan," she said, tossing the towel onto the chair. "Anywhere decent around here?"

Elise grabbed her coat, forcing her voice to sound casual.

"Yeah. The Blue Door Diner. Their food's decent."

Santos raised an eyebrow, unconvinced.

"Fine. But if the coffee's shit, you owe me."

The car ride was slow and silent. Elise kept both hands on the wheel, her grip a little too firm. Santos stared out the window, scanning the passing streets. But every now and then, she looked at Elise—calculating, waiting.

The diner came into view, its blue door standing out against the weathered siding. Elise pulled into the back of the lot. The place hadn't changed. The neon OPEN sign buzzed in the window.

Inside, the air was the same. An old diner. Fresh coffee and pancakes lofting through the air. Low conversations filled the space, interrupted by the occasional clatter of plates. Elise led Santos to a booth in the back, the same one she'd sat in days earlier.

Santos slid in first, planting herself against the wall, eyes sweeping the room before settling on Elise.

"We focus on the perimeter first," she said, getting straight to business. She pulled out a small notebook, flipping it open to a rough sketch of the Happiness Factory's layout. "If there's a weak spot, it'll be there."

Her pen tapped on the page. "I still have access codes, but they're old. Not sure what will work and what won't."

Elise leaned in, scanning the lines and notes. "What about the checkpoints?"

Santos exhaled through her nose. "That's the hard part. Their biometric systems flag non-registered personnel immediately. We'd need a way to bypass—"

The door swung open.

Santos stopped mid-sentence. Her eyes locked on the entrance.

Elise turned, her chest tightening.

Malik.

He stepped inside, shaking off the cold. His movements were purposeful this time, but his posture was stiff—like he was expecting a fight before he even walked in. His eyes swept the diner, landing on their booth.

His expression slightly flickered—first surprise, then something closer to regret.

"He's here," Elise said quietly.

Santos's head jerked toward her, anger flashing behind her eyes.

"You set this up?"

"No," Elise said quickly, her voice steady.

"I told him to meet me here. We need him."

Malik hesitated, then sighed, and crossed the diner. As he approached, his pace slowed, like he was considering whether to turn around.

"Elena," he said.

Santos leaned back, arms crossing over her chest. The tension in her body obvious.

"You've got some nerve showing up here after everything," she said.

Malik's shoulder sagged slightly, deep lines carving into his face.

"I didn't know you'd be here," he said.

"Good," Santos replied. "You shouldn't have come."

Elise's patience thinned. "Enough." Her voice cut through the tension.

"Both of you. We don't have time for this."

Malik looked at her, jaw tight. Then back at Santos.

"I know how things ended," he said.

"I know I should've done more. But if you know where the factory is—"

"You're assuming I'm going to work with you?" Santos interrupted.

The weight in her voice made it clear. She wasn't convinced. Not yet.

Elise looked around the diner. A waitress lingered at the counter, her eyes glancing toward the booth every few seconds. A couple in the next booth had gone quiet. Too quiet.

They were drawing attention.

"We shouldn't talk here," Elise muttered, lowering her voice.

Santos caught onto the growing interest around them. After a quick moment, she sighed. "Fine. Back to the motel. But I'm not agreeing to anything until I know exactly what he wants."

Malik nodded once. "Fair enough."

The three of them rose from the booth, stiff with tension. Santos walked ahead, posture rigid, steps heavy.

Malik exhaled, rubbing the back of his neck before following.

Elise walked beside him.

"This isn't going to be easy," she mumbled.

Malik let out a dry laugh. "Nothing ever is."

Outside, the cold air was crisp as they crossed the lot. The distant bark of a dog echoed in the quiet, the neon diner sign buzzing behind them.

Whatever fragile peace they'd manage to hold together was already threatening to crack.

∞∞∞∞

The hotel room had felt cramped before, but now it was suffocating. The table at the center of the room was buried in paper. Maps of Blackbriar forest, schematics of the Happiness Factory, handwritten notes.

Malik leaned back in one of the rickety chairs, arms crossed over his chest, his eyes locked on Santos. She sat stiffly across from him, her fingers tapping the table in an absent, repetitive rhythm—controlled, but barely. Elise sat at the edge of her bed, eyes moving between them like a bystander in a fight she knew was coming.

"The perimeter," Santos said, jabbing her pen at the map, "is where their surveillance is weakest. If we can find a gap, we slip through."

Malik shook his head. "That might've worked five years ago. You don't get it. They've upgraded everything. No gaps. No blind spots."

Santos stared at him. "And you'd know, wouldn't you?"

"Since you were so eager to work for them while the rest of us were suffering in the fallout."

Malik didn't flinch. He leaned forward, keeping his voice calm. "I wasn't eager to do anything, Elena. I was trying to survive. You think you're the only one who lost people? I lost everything because of Necessity Mart. The difference is, I learned how they operate. And you didn't."

Elise raised a hand, cutting through the charged air.

"Enough. If either of you has a way to get me inside, now's the time."

Malik sighed, rubbing a hand over his face. Then he tapped the map. "All of their facilities run on biometric access. Every guard, every scanner, every door. But there's one thing they don't micromanage… their supply chain."

Santos's posture stiffened. She sat back slightly, arms still crossed.

"Deliveries," Malik continued. "Medical supplies, food shipments. Those come through third-party vendors. Less scrutiny. Fewer questions."

Santos narrowed her eyes. "And you think they'll just let her waltz in on a delivery truck?"

"No," Malik said. "But their system isn't perfect. The manifests are routed through vendors. The guards don't care who's driving, as long as the paperwork checks out."

He leaned in, tracing a line along the perimeter of the map. "I can forge a manifest. Get us an approved shipment… medical supplies, most likely. It's routine. The guards won't look twice."

Santos studied him, skepticism still etched across her face. "And the driver's badge?" she asked. "They'll still check ID."

Malik nodded. "We'll need a stolen or forged contractor badge. It has to match the vendor handling the day's shipment."

Santos was quiet for a long moment, considering the plan. Then, finally, she tapped the map again. Her voice was lower now, the fight in her dimming just slightly.

"Once you're inside, they don't track people… The facility is designed to funnel personnel into specific zones. I can help you navigate, but you'll need to move fast."

"It's doable," Malik agreed. "But we need one last thing. A delivery van."

Silence.

Elise watched him carefully. His expression had darkened slightly, like he was holding something back.

Then he exhaled. "And there's one more problem," he hesitated.

"Every driver is required to wear an Aether. It's policy."

The room froze.

Elise's chest went tight. Her fingers curled into her palms as she stared at him.

"Aethers?" she repeated, whispering.

Malik nodded. "Yes."

He leaned back in his chair, arms crossed again. "I can get one."

Elise's stomach twisted. "You're saying I have to wear one?"

252

Malik's eyes met hers. "There's no other way. The Aether verifies your credentials, tracks your location, and monitors deliveries. It's how they keep control."

Santos's voice became quieter, bitter. "This is how they do it. They don't just kill you. They consume you. They make you part of their system. And then they own you."

Malik barely looked at her. "We don't have time for a philosophy lesson, Elena."

Santos's jaw locked but she didn't argue.

Elise's pulse pounded in her ears.

"Isn't there another way?" She asked, desperately. "Another route?"

Malik's eyes softened, but his voice didn't. "You think I haven't looked for one? You don't just walk into that factory without an Aether. Even their janitors wear them."

Elise dropped her head into her hands, her mind spinning.

Harper's face flashed through her mind. Her Aether pulsing at her neck, her voice light and unknowing as she told Elise about how it helped her focus. James's voice, tense whenever Necessity Mart came up, always holding something back.

"That's how it starts," Santos mumbled. "One step. One compromise. Then another. Before you know it, you're trapped."

Elise lifted her head, eyes burning. "You think I don't know that?" she snapped. "I've spent too long trying to keep my family out of this. And now it's my only way to save them."

Malik pushed back from the table and stood up.

"I'll handle it tonight," he said. "You'll leave in the morning."

He looked at them both, eyes lingering on Elise.

"Get some rest. You're going to need it."

Then he turned and walked out, the door clicking shut behind him.

The silence left in his absence felt suffocating.

Elise sat there, staring at the stained carpet, the weight of the decision pressing into her like a slow, tightening vice.

Finally, Santos broke the silence.

"You think you're ready for this?"

Elise's voice came hollow. "No."

Then she lifted her chin. "But I don't have a choice."

Santos studied her, her eyes piercing. "It's not just about wearing an Aether," she said. "You step into their world, and you don't come back the same."

Elise met her eyes. "Then I'll come back different." She swallowed. "As long as I come back with Harper and Maggie, nothing else matters."

Santos didn't argue. She just leaned back, exhaling through her nose, then turned back to the map, pen scratching across the paper again.

Elise laid back on the bed, staring at the cracked ceiling as the weight of the night settled over her.

The heater buzzed softly. The world outside crept closer.

Santos exhaled. "You look like you're about to crack."

Elise didn't answer.

"There's a bar up the road," Santos said. "What do you say?"

Elise hesitated. Then nodded. "I could use a drink."

Santos grabbed her coat. "Good. Let's go before I change my mind."

∞∞∞∞

The Rusty Lantern sat at the edge of a dirt lot, its warped wooden siding holding years of smoke, weather, and regret. The faded sign creaked on rusted chains barely clinging to the last breath of wind. A neon OPEN flickered in the window, buzzing like a dying insect, its glow barely strong enough to fight back the creeping dark.

Inside, the air smelled like stale beer, must, and the quiet weight of people who had nowhere else to be. The kind of place where time moves slower, not because anyone wanted it to, but because the past had settled into the wood and refused to leave.

Santos led the way, not looking back as she moved through the room with the kind of presence that made people instinctively get out of her way. Elise followed, scanning the room... worn faces, hollow eyes, men hunched over drinks like prayers.

At the counter, a grizzled bartender looked up from polishing a glass, his face lined with the kind of exhaustion that no amount of sleep could fix.

He'd seen too many nights like this.

"Two whiskeys. Neat," Santos said.

Elise raised an eyebrow but said nothing.

They took a small table in the back, away from the stragglers nursing their drinks. The bartender moved fast, sliding two glasses across the wood. Elise took a sip and made a face as it burned its way down her throat. Santos barely reacted.

254

For a moment, neither of them spoke. The silence wasn't comfortable, it wasn't forced either. Just a quiet truce in a room full of ghosts.

Santos leaned back, studying Elise over the rim of her glass.

"James never told you much, did he?"

Elise traced the edge of her drink with her fingertip. "Not enough," she admitted. "He thought he was protecting me. I didn't even know about the safety deposit box until after he died. I didn't know about any of this."

Santos's eyes flickered, something behind them.

"James had a good heart." She exhaled through her nose, shaking her head. "He believed in what we were doing, even when the rest of us started losing faith."

Elise looked down at her drink, swirling the liquid. "He never stopped fighting for what he believed in," she said softly. "I just wish I'd seen it sooner."

Santos took another sip, then set her glass down. "He fought hard," she said. "But he didn't fight smart. That's why we're here now... cleaning up the mess he didn't live long enough to finish."

The words hit Elise hard, but she didn't say anything.

Santos leaned forward.

"We need to get to the safety deposit box before you go into the factory."

Elise raised an eyebrow. "Why?"

"Because what if you don't make it out?"

Elise stiffened, the weight of the words dropping like a stone in her gut.

Santos didn't let up. "Whatever's in that box, James thought it was important enough to hide. If we don't get it first, and you go marching into Blackbriar and never come back, then what? What's left?"

Elise sat back, gripping the glass. "I will make it back," she said.

Santos studied her, quietly. Waiting for doubt to show itself.

Elise didn't give her the satisfaction.

"We'll go to the safety deposit box after," she said.

Santos sighed, unconvinced, but after a long moment, she gave a small nod.

The silence stretched between them again, heavier now. Elise stared into her drink, her reflection barely visible in the dark whiskey. Harper. Maggie. James. The factory. The box. The storm waiting for her on the other side of this night.

Santos's voice came quieter now, but no less intense.

"This isn't a redemption story, Elise."

"Whatever you think you're going to find out there..." she continued, "it might not fix anything."

"I'm not trying to fix anything," Elise said. "I just want my family back."

Santos held her gaze, then nodded again, slower this time.

More to herself than anything.

She lifted her glass. "Then finish your drink. Tomorrow's going to be hell."

Elise drank the rest of the whiskey, the burn cutting through the knot in her chest. The glass clinked softly against the wood as she set it down, steady hands revealing none of the doubt building inside of her.

They stood, neither speaking as they stepped toward the door.

Elise took one last look at the near-empty bar, its patrons lost in their own regrets. The world outside waited, cold and indifferent. She stepped into it without hesitation.

CHAPTER SIXTEEN
Happiness Guarantee

A world of unseen dictatorship is preferable
to one of overt violence.
– Aldous Huxley

The knock cracked through the silence, dragging Elise out of a shallow, restless sleep. She sat up too fast, her pulse hammering, the room snapping into focus in hazy pieces. The thin curtains struggling to hold back the weak morning light, the stale air of the motel, the distant rumble of a truck passing on the highway.

Her neck ached from sleeping wrong, but she ignored it, already looking toward the door.

At the table, Santos was already awake, sitting at the edge of the rickety chair, a notebook in one hand and a pen in the other. She hadn't even flinched at the knock.

"That's your guy," she muttered, not looking up. The pen kept moving, writing notes in casual strokes.

Elise swung her legs over the side of the bed, her muscles stiff with exhaustion she hadn't let herself feel until now. She crossed to the window, careful to stay out of sight as she peeled back the curtain.

Malik stood outside, impatiently. In one hand, he held a badge on a lanyard.

In the other, a box balanced against his hip.

Elise pulled the curtain shut and unlocked the door.

The moment she opened it, Malik stepped inside without hesitation, bringing the crisp, cold morning air with him.

"Morning," he said, already moving toward the table. He dropped the box down, then placed a stack of documents and the badge beside it.

"Let's get to it." Malik pulled a second bag from over his shoulder and set it on the floor. "Blackbriar is about an hour out. If their protocols haven't changed, deliveries are expected by noon. No later."

He reached into the bag and pulled out a folded uniform. Without looking, he tossed it toward Elise. She barely caught it before it hit the floor.

"See if that fits," he said, already opening the box.

Elise unfolded the uniform. A plain black shirt and cargo pants, standard issue for corporate delivery personnel. It was slightly oversized, but functional. No one asked where Malik had gotten it. The room carried the tension of unspoken questions, but no one wasted breath on the obvious.

Malik pulled an Aether from the box, the sound of its activation soft and surgical, filling the room like an insect's wings. He flipped it over in his hands, testing the weight, then set it on the table like a loaded gun.

"We don't have to put it on you yet," Malik said. "But it has to be fitted and synced with this manifest." He tapped the stack of papers beside it.

Elise's stomach twisted.

She'd seen plenty of Aethers. Around Harper's neck, around co-workers, wrapped around the throats of strangers who no longer thought twice about wearing them.

But this one was hers.

Her pulse pounded.

"I can't..." she started. The words barely made it past her lips.

Malik didn't hesitate. "You can... And you will."

Elise looked up, but the look on Malik's face didn't change.

"If you want to get into that factory," he said, "there's no other way."

Elise swallowed, forcing the thought down.

She straightened, gripping the uniform like it was the only solid thing left in the world. "What about the van?"

Malik smirked, gesturing his thumb toward the window.

"It's outside. Told you I'd take care of it."

Elise moved to the curtain, pulling it open.

A plain white delivery van sat parked near the entrance, clean but unmistakable, the kind of vehicle people glanced at without really seeing.

"Cell service near Blackbriar is nonexistent. Once you're close, you'll lose signal completely. We won't be able to communicate."

Elise nodded numbly, her fingers brushing the edge of the table.

Malik unfolded a map, spreading it across the bed. He pointed to a clearing just off the main road, a few miles from the facility.

"Drop me off here," he said. "I'll wait outside until you're out. If something goes wrong, you find me. Got it?"

Elise nodded again, her mind already racing ahead.

Santos hadn't moved.

She leaned back in her chair, arms crossed. Then, she finally spoke.

"I'm not going anywhere near that place." Her voice was calm, but final.

Elise turned, frowning. "Nobody asked you to."

Santos didn't blink. Instead, she reached into her bag and pulled out a handgun, checking the chamber with quick movements.

"Good." She snapped the magazine back in place. "Just make sure you get out in one piece. We still have business to handle."

Malik clapped his hands together once, breaking the tension.

"Alright. Let's get moving."

Elise's eyes locked on the Aether still sitting on the table.

She hated it.

Hated everything it stood for. Hated that it was part of the plan now.

But she reached for the uniform without a word.

The three of them stepped outside.

The air cut through Elise's clothes, colder than before. The van sat in the lot, waiting. Silent. Final.

Santos stopped near the door, her expression slightly softening.

"Don't do anything stupid." Her voice was almost reluctant.

Elise didn't answer.

She looked back at the motel door one last time, as if leaving it meant stepping over an invisible line she could never cross back.

Malik started the engine.

Then she climbed into the van.

The door shut behind her with an echo.

Elise stared out the window, watching her reflection in the glass, her face warped and unfamiliar.

Her jaw locked.

Her hands curled into fists.

Her voice was quiet. "Let's finish this."

The van rumbled over the gravel lot, its tires grinding against loose stone as they pulled onto the road. The engine was steady, a heartbeat beneath the tension settling inside the cabin. Blackbriar waited ahead, a shadow on the horizon, and whatever was beyond its gates was no longer a question... it was inevitable.

The forest thickened around them, towering pines stretching up in what seemed like forever, their branches allowing only tiny, fractured light through. Elise gripped the wheel, her hands steady but stiff, the pressure of every bump in the road traveling up her arms.

Malik sat beside her, unnervingly still. Not relaxed. His face was carefully neutral, but the way his jaw clenched, the way his fingers tapped against his knee, showed an anxiety beneath the surface.

The silence between them was heavy. The sound of the tires became a lifeline, something to cling to before they reached the clearing.

Elise finally broke the silence.

"You never told me why you left Necessity Mart."

She kept her eyes on the road. "...The real story."

Malik sighed, leaning back, his eyes locked forward.

When he spoke, his voice was calm but distant.

"I was one of the lead engineers in their Behavioral Analytics Division," he said. "Back then, I thought we were helping people. The algorithms we designed were supposed to optimize lives, help users make better decisions."

He paused. "But that was a lie."

Elise glanced over at him. He wasn't just remembering. He was reliving.

"Optimization wasn't about helping people. It was about control. Every update, every 'milestone' we hit, just made users more dependent on the system. And they knew it."

"And you stayed?"

"At first." Malik's shoulder slumped slightly. "I told myself it was just business, that the good outweighed the bad. But then..." He hesitated.

"Then they started targeting kids."

Elise held her breath.

"They wanted to shape behavior from the ground up," Malik continued. "Start with students, build habits, make sure they grow into compliant adults. It was sick."

Elise didn't say anything.

"I pushed back," Malik said, his voice strained. "I asked the wrong questions, raised too many flags. And that's when the threats started. Reassignments. People I worked with just... disappeared."

He ran a hand through his hair, his face clouded in regret. "By the time I left, I wasn't sure if I was running away or trying to make amends. But I knew I couldn't keep building something that was eating people alive."

Elise stared ahead, her jaw tightening.

"And now?"

Malik let out a slow breath. "Now I'm just trying to make it right." He shook his head. "But every step feels like it's too little, too late."

The silence that followed was different now.

Then, Malik straightened, his focus returning. The time for ghosts was over.

"Alright, listen up." His voice was all business now. "When you get to the gate, stay calm. This is routine for them, and it needs to feel routine for you."

Elise nodded, her throat dry. "What if they start asking questions?"

"Act like you're in a rush," Malik said. "Like you're annoyed. Guards are used to drivers just trying to get in and get out. If they push, point to the manifest and say, 'it's all there, I don't have time for this.'"

"And if they don't buy it?"

"Then you smile, apologize, and tell them it's your first week." He shrugged. "Play dumb. They'll roll their eyes and let you through."

The trees grew denser, the road narrowing into a single lane.

Malik pointed toward a break in the foliage ahead.

"There. Past that bend. Pull off into the clearing."

Elise eased off the gas, guiding the van onto a dirt shoulder. The clearing was barely large enough to park without being seen from the road

Malik reached down, lifting the box containing the Aether onto his lap. He flipped the lid open, revealing the device inside.

"Here," he said, holding it out to her.

Elise stared at it, anxiously.

She reached out slowly, taking it from him like it might burn her.

The clasp clicked into place as she raised it to her neck.

The sound grew louder.

Elise froze.

She felt it. Not just against her skin, but beneath it. A subtle shift, like a pressure just beneath her thoughts, smoothing over the edges, dulling the fight before it could even start.

Malik watched her carefully.

"It's synced with the manifest," he said quietly. "You're good to go."

He opened the passenger door and stepped into the clearing. Before closing it, he leaned back, his face unreadable.

"You've got this."

Elise's fingers brushed against the Aether at her throat.

Testing it. Feeling the weight of it.

She forced herself to nod.

"I'll see you on the other side."

Malik nodded, closing the door behind him.

He stepped back, and the van pulled onto the road, disappearing into the trees.

∞∞∞∞

Inside the van, Elise adjusted her grip on the steering wheel, but it didn't feel the same.

The Aether's hum was no longer just a sound, it was inside her now. A subtle vibration moving through her skin. She glanced at the rearview mirror, and there it was... the faint, traitorous glow reflecting back at her.

She should have felt sick.

Instead, she felt... lighter.

Her posture had shifted without her realizing it. Back straighter, shoulders squared. As if someone had reached inside her and realigned the parts of her that had been breaking down for years. Even her breathing had changed. The usual tightness in her chest, the familiar ache of stress and exhaustion, was just... gone.

Her fingers drifted, tracing the smooth, glassy surface of the Aether.

And the thought came, quiet.

Is this how they get you?

Make you feel like this...

Like you need it?

Her stomach twisted. No. She gritted her teeth and shoved the thought away, clenching the wheel as if gripping something real could drown out the feeling of everything else slipping.

The forest thickened ahead, the trees crowding closer. The road narrowed.

Elise exhaled slowly. Whatever was ahead, she was already in it now.

Then her phone vibrated on the dashboard.

The sudden noise shattered the stillness, moving through Elise like an electric current. She flinched. For a second, she just stared at the screen.

Shanti.

Elise snatched the phone, swiping to answer.

"Shanti?" Her voice was tight with tension.

Static swallowed the other end, turning Shanti's voice into fragments, scratchy and broken.

"Elise... you told me... after the clinic—"

Elise's stomach knotted. "I can barely hear you," she said, pressing the phone harder to her ear. "I'm in the forest... bad reception. What is it?"

The static cracked, then Shanti's voice came through, faint but urgent.

"It's about Harper."

Elise held her breath.

The world tilted slightly, the trees blurring.

Her hands clenched the wheel, her knuckles bloodless.

"What about Harper," she demanded.

Silence.

Then a burst of static. A half-formed sentence breaking apart.

"Another detective... someone... fits her description... near the train station."

Elise's heart slammed against her ribs.

"Near where? Shanti, I can't hear you. Say that again."

More interference, another brief cut of clarity—

"Someone called... young girl... lost, confused—"

Elise's vision blurred. Her thoughts spiraled. A girl. Lost. Confused. Harper.

Then... the line went dead.

The phone screen flashed CALL FAILED.

Elise stared at it, the weight of those last words crushing against her ribs. The world outside the windshield seemed unreal, the road stretching forward, but her mind was miles away—at a train station, searching the crowd, Harper's face somewhere in the sea of strangers.

Her hands loosened on the wheel. The van drifted slightly toward the shoulder.

A soft beep.

The Aether pulsed gently against her neck.

A voice followed, smooth, unnervingly calm.

Heart rate elevated. Initiating calming protocol.

A vibration moved through her skin. Elise's breath hitched, but then something changed.

The panic began to fade, smoothed by Aether's pulse. Her breathing adjusted automatically, falling in sync with the subtle hum. Her fingers relaxed on the wheel. The dizziness faded.

Elise sat frozen, her mind clearer than it should be.

She lifted a hand, her fingers grazing the smooth surface of the Aether.

She hated it.

Hated what it stood for. Hated how it worked.

But she couldn't deny the truth.

It was working.

The device's hum faded, leaving only warmth against her skin.

Elise gritted her teeth, forcing her focus back to the road.

Shanti's words echoed in her mind.

She gripped the wheel tighter.

Stay focused. Harpers out there. Maggie's out there. And this is the only way.

She pressed the gas.

The trees thinned, revealing something that felt unnatural.

Elise's breath caught in her throat. Not from fear, but from disbelief.

The Happiness Factory appeared, glowing like a mirage in the wilderness.

She had imagined something dark. Industrial. Cold steel and razor wire.

Not this.

It looked like a dream, something out of a luxury brochure. Curved glass walls reflected the morning sun, showing glimpses of towering pines in fractured patterns. The entrance was lined with manicured gardens, winding paths, perfectly sculpted hedges. A fountain near the main doors, soothing, serene.

The whole thing felt surgical. Pristine down to the last blade of grass.

Elise's stomach knotted.

The Aether hummed, like a hand resting gently on her shoulder, guiding her forward.

She wanted to tear it off.

Of course it looks like this, she muttered under her breath. *Of course they make it look perfect.*

Her mind filled with images of Harper, walking willingly through those doors. No suspicion. No fear. Just a child following the promise of something beautiful.

Elise forced herself to focus.

It's a lie. A mask.

The van rolled toward the entrance, toward the polished security kiosk stationed at the gate.

A man stepped out.

His uniform was spotless, his posture relaxed, his face pleasantly neutral. He carried a clipboard, not a gun.

To anyone else, he wouldn't have looked like a guard.

But Elise knew better.

He wasn't there to keep people out.

He was there to keep them in.

Her foot hovered over the brake, the manifest Malik had forged sitting beside her. The badge hung heavy around her neck, a false identity pressing against her chest.

The Aether hummed again.

Elise rolled down the window.

The guard's eyes glanced at the Aether around her neck.

The smallest confirmation.

Then he smiled.

"Morning, driver," he said.

Elise smiled back, her voice calm as it could be in this moment.

"Delivery for intake processing."

She didn't recognize herself in the sound.

Elise handed over the papers, forcing herself to meet his eyes.

"Here you go," she said, her voice smooth, controlled.

The guard flipped through the manifest, scanning the details with a calm detachment. He looked up, lingering for a fraction too long on the Aether at her neck.

"You must be new," he said.

Elise froze for half a heartbeat, then gave a quick nod. "Yeah. First week." She added a slight shrug, like it wasn't worth remembering.

The guard studied her. Then he stepped back, walking a slow, deliberate circle around the van. Elise kept still, gripping the wheel. Her pulse pounded once, twice… then steadied, the Aether humming softly against her skin.

The guard returned to the window, leaning in just slightly. His voice was casual, but there was something else in the way he spoke.

"You know where you're going?"

Elise hesitated, just enough to sell it. "Actually, no. They didn't exactly give me the grand tour." She let out a small, dry laugh. Not too forced, not too nervous. "Could you point me in the right direction?"

His radio crackled to life.

"Gate three, we've got an arrival for processing. Need confirmation."

The guard raised a finger. Wait.

"Copy that," he responded into the receiver. "Send them through."

Elise's chest tightened, but she didn't let it show.

The guard handed the manifest back with a shrug. "Alright, you're good. Don't linger. We like to keep things on schedule around here."

Elise nodded, putting the van into gear. "I'll be quick."

The guard gave a lazy wave, already turning back to his post.

She rolled forward, passing through the gates.

The factory grounds unfolded like a painted dream.

The road curved gently through gardens so pristine they could've been airbrushed into reality. The paths were lined with precisely trimmed hedges, the kind of detail that only existed when imperfection wasn't an option.

And the people—

They moved elegantly, dressed in soft white uniforms, drifting along the pathways. Some practiced yoga. Others sat by reflective pools, their eyes closed peacefully, their faces blank... but content.

Elise's fingers tightened around the wheel.

It was convincing. Terrifyingly so.

Her breathing shallowed, an unwelcome thought whispering its way into her mind.

What if this place isn't what I think it is?

What if Harper was actually happy here?

What if—

No.

The thoughts disappeared quickly, turning rancid in her stomach.

James had seen through this. He knew.

Maggie had fought against this. She knew.

Harper hadn't.

Not yet.

Elise forced herself to focus, her spine straightening as she guided the van past the illusion.

The gardens and beautiful glass walls disappeared into the rearview mirror, revealing something quieter.

The real part of the facility.

The transition was subtle, but distinct. Still polished but stripped of the careful spectacle. The vendor loading dock was an efficient machine. The ground was paved in spotless concrete, the rows of identical white delivery vans lined up in strict formation.

Workers moved like clockwork, unloading boxes, and scanning manifests with quick flicks of their wrists. Their white uniforms blurred into the backdrop, their faces distant but focused.

Elise backed the van into an open bay, cutting the engine off.

She stepped out, the air unnaturally cool, not from the morning chill but from something engineered.

The noise of the machinery blended seamlessly with the vibration of the Aether, its presence an extension of the environment. An adjustment. A correction.

Elise gripped the manifest, its crisp edges sharp beneath her fingertips.

She scanned the area.

No unnecessary movement.

Just... precision.

The entrance ahead was inviting, but Elise knew better.

A man in a white uniform stood by the scanner, processing manifests. His gestures were smooth, his Aether glowing softly at his throat, its golden pulse perfectly in sync with his breath.

Elise was about to move forward when—

A voice. Raised. Out of place.

She turned, catching a scene unfolding near the entrance.

A delivery driver, his face red, stood stiffly in front of an attendant.

His frustration barely contained.

"This is what they gave me," the driver shouted, his voice cracking.

The Aether at his neck blinked red.

A warning.

The attendant didn't react.

His voice was calm, smooth as water running over stone.

"Dispatch knows the process. I can't log this until it's corrected."

His own Aether glowed gold, pulsing gently, in perfect contrast to the driver's flickering red light.

Elise watched, horrified, as the driver's anger seemed to dissolve under the weight of the golden glow. His shoulders slumped. His resistance folded like a lawn chair.

Just like that.

Elise turned away, nausea rising.

She forced herself to stay calm, casually smiling as she stepped forward, manifest in hand.

She waved it at the attendant.

"Long drive," she said lightly. "Mind if I use the restroom before unloading."

The attendant barely looked at her. "Down the hallway, to the left," he said, already moving his attention back to the subdued driver.

Elise nodded, mumbling a quick thanks as she stepped passed the threshold.

The building swallowed her whole.

The glass doors slid shut behind her, sealing her inside. The walls shined with a pearlescent shimmer, their surfaces shifting. There were no straight lines, no hard edges—only gentle, flowing curves, guiding her deeper into the factory's belly. Nothing to resist. Nowhere to hide.

The floor sloped downward. When Elise paused to get her bearings, she felt it—a slight nudge forward, a quiet discomfort in standing still.

It didn't want her to stop.

It wanted her to move.

Plants sprouted directly from the walls, their leaves tilting subtly toward her as she walked past. Watching. Tracking her every step.

Overhead, hidden speakers whispered tones that weren't quite music. It weaved into her thoughts, making them soft, slippery, hard to hold onto.

At her throat, the Aether pulsed. A low vibration, syncing to the rhythm of the sound.

A calm she didn't ask for seeped into her veins.

Through a curved glass window, Elise caught sight of a classroom.

Children sat in a perfect circle, their postures identical, their eyes locked onto a holographic display, where geometric shapes spun hypnotically.

A woman's voice drifted through the glass.

"Remember, the shapes show us the perfect path. When we follow the path..."

Bright, eager voices chimed in unison. "We find harmony!"

Their Aethers pulsed together, a wave of blue light bathing the room.

One boy hesitated.

His hand rose, uncertain, a slight tremor in his fingers.

"But what if we want to make our own path?"

The teacher's smile never wavered as she approached him.

"That's your chaos thoughts speaking, Michael."

Her tone was soothing and patient.

"Let's help Michael find harmony, everyone."

The children's Aethers pulsed again, deeper this time.

Michael's face went blank.

The question was gone.

The shapes resumed their hypnotic dance.

Elise forced herself to keep walking.

She passed another room—larger, more elaborate.

Inside, a group of adults stood in circles, heads tilted upward, their Aethers pulsing in waves as they stared at the woman on the raised platform.

The woman wept, tears running down her cheeks in slow streams.

Her hands trembled as she placed them over her heart.

"I choose transcendence," she whispered.

"I surrender my chaos to the algorithm's wisdom."

The observers nodded in approval, their Aethers glowing in a mesmerizing harmony.

A voice filled the space. *Your journey to harmony begins. Optimization is freedom. Surrender is peace.*

The woman smiled, her face covered in the golden light of her Aether's approval.

Her eyes glazed over.

Her body went still.

Elise turned away before she could watch the rest.

A door hissed open as she passed, revealing something different.

A room hidden from the performance outside.

Screens lined the walls, filled with streams of data. Optimization scores, compliance metrics, neural activity reports. A technician stood at a console, speaking into a headset.

"Subject 63 showing resistance to Stage 2 integration. Recommend increasing dopamine response to compliance cues by 15%."

A pause.

"Yes, family memories are still causing disruption. Schedule for targeted suppression during next harmony session."

Elise's stomach knotted.

The Aether on her neck pulsed, dragging her attention back with a gentle pull.

A quiet, patient, invasive voice whispered directly into her mind.

This area is not optimized for your current harmony level.

Please proceed to your designated zone.

Elise forced herself to keep walking, her steps steady even as the device smoothed away the fear curling in her gut.

The hallway curved ahead, guiding her deeper into the factory's predatory embrace. Every step revealed more—the calculated design, the suffocating grace, the seamless machinery of compliance.

She was walking through a living algorithm.

A system designed to rewrite people from the inside out.

And it was so good at it.

She passed another glassed corridor.

A man sat strapped to a chair, eyes wide and empty as holographic symbols flashed across his vision. His Aether glowed, casting his expressionless face in a soft, warm light.

Nearby, technicians adjusted glowing panels.

Elise moved past, her jaw tightening.

She reached another room. A group therapy session.

Participants sat in a circle, their Aethers pulsing in perfect rhythm.

At the center, a facilitator's voice wrapped around them, smooth as silk.

"Share your disruption."

A woman hesitated.

Her voice trembled. "I miss my children."

The others' Aethers pulsed immediately, sending a wave crashing over her.

Her shoulder slumped. Her breathing shallowed.

The weight of their collective disapproval pressed down.

Her voice became weaker.

"I'll try harder to find harmony."

The others nodded, their faces serene.

Elise couldn't look anymore.

She turned away, gripping the manifest so tightly the edges crumpled under her fingers.

This place wasn't a factory. It was a machine.

And everyone inside was just another cog.

She rounded another corner and froze.

Twenty feet ahead, a woman in a white lab coat stood at a workstation, her back to Elise. Her graying hair was pulled into a tight bun, every strand perfectly in place. Her fingers moved across a glowing tablet, adjusting settings.

When she turned that's when Elise saw it.

Dr. Nadine Carter.

The missing scientist.

Elise had expected someone haunted, broken. Instead, Carter's movements were precise, clinical. But there was something off about her posture. A tightness in her shoulders. A restlessness in the way her fingers drummed against the edge of the tablet.

Her Aether pulsed Celestial, a sign of complete optimization. But that drumming told another story.

Elise scanned the corridor. Security cameras rotated in slow, mechanical sweeps. Each pass left a brief blind spot. Three seconds at most.

She timed her steps.

One breath.

Two.

Three—

She moved.

Slipping through the shadows between the camera's view, she stopped just behind Carter.

"Dr. Carter?" Elise whispered.

The woman froze.

Her head jerked up, shoulders tensed. When she turned, her face was perfectly controlled. But Elise saw the flicker of something beneath it. Recognition. Fear.

And then... a mask.

"Do I know you?" Her grip on the tablet tightened.

"No. But you knew my husband. James Winters."

The slightest falter. A fraction of a second, but Elise caught it.

Carter stepped back, her eyes moving to the nearest camera, then back to Elise.

"I don't know anyone by that name," she said.

"And you shouldn't be here without—"

"Elena Santos is alive."

The mask cracked.

Cater staggered.

Her hand shot out, bracing herself against the workstation. For an instant, the veneer shattered. Raw emotion bled through. Hope. Fear. Desperation.

Carter grabbed Elise's arm, her grip stronger than Elise anticipated as she pulled her into a small monitoring room.

The door slid shut behind them, sealing them in silence.

"You're either incredibly brave or incredibly stupid," Carter whispered, her voice trembling. "Do you have any idea what they do to people who—"

She stopped herself. She looked toward the camera in the corner.

A tiny red light on the camera blinked out.

"Two minutes," she said. "That's all I can give you before the system notices."

Elise stepped closer. "I need to find my sister. Maggie Crawford. I think she's here. Can you help me?"

Carter's face drained of color.

"Maggie Crawford?" she whispered. "She's..."

Carter shook her head. "You need to leave. Now. Before they realize—"

"Please."

The word tumbled out before Elise could stop it.

"Elena told me what happened at Synapse Dynamics. What they did to you. To all of you. She's been gathering evidence, building a case. But she needs help."

Carter's fingers brushed over her Aether, the motion unconscious—like a nervous tick, or a prayer.

271

"Elena's really alive?" she whispered. "They told us... they said she..."

Carter's throat worked around the words, but she never finished. Instead, she just shook her head.

"It doesn't matter," she said eventually. "I can't help you. They watch everything. Every moment, every decision—"

Footsteps in the distance.

Both women froze.

The sharp echo of boots against the pristine floor just outside the door. Elise held her breath. Carter's fingers hovered over the tablet.

The footsteps faded.

Carter's shoulders sagged.

When she spoke again, her voice was more urgent.

"Your sister," she whispered. "She's in Wing C. Reconditioning Room 2."

Elise's pulse slammed in her ears.

"But you'll never get there without clearance," Carter continued. "The security—"

"I'll find a way," Elise interrupted.

She searched Carter's face, looking for any sliver of willingness, any opening.

"Come with us," she pressed. "Elena has a plan. A way to expose everything."

Carter laughed. Cold. Bitter.

"You don't understand." She sighed, shaking her head.

"I can't just leave. The Aether..."

Her fingers clenched around it now. Tight. Desperate.

"It's not just monitoring anymore. It's part of us now. They made sure of that."

The camera made a noise as it rebooted.

Carter's entire body stiffened.

She was out of time.

She reached into her coat pocket and pulled out a small metallic key card.

"Use this." She shoved it into Elise's hand.

"Now go."

Elise gripped the keycard like an artifact.

"You could still come with me," she tried one last time. "Elena—"

"Don't."

Carter turned toward the door, hesitating for a second.

Without looking back, she muttered, "Tell Elena... tell her I'm sorry. For everything."

Then—the door slid open.

Dr. Carter stepped out, her posture perfect, her movements flawless.

But Elise saw it.

The tiny rebellion.

She stared at the closed door, her fingers tightening around the key card.

The Aether at her neck hummed insistently, trying to smooth over her thoughts. To wash them away.

She held onto the anger.

Maggie was here.

Somewhere in this machine.

Elise straightened, the key card digging into her palm.

She couldn't stop now.

Not when she was this close.

∞∞∞

The door to Wing C hissed open, the sound impossibly loud in the sterile quiet. Elise stepped through, gripping the keycard like a blade.

This part of the facility was different. No warm lighting, no carefully manicured illusions. Just blindingly white walls, a floor so seamless it felt like it had been poured into place, and the ever-present hum of something unseen, something alive.

Screens lined the corridor, flashing streams of data too fast to process. Elise caught glimpses of phrases as she moved.

Resistance Index Elevated.

Volatility Threshold Exceeded.

Stability Protocol Engaged.

The Aether at her neck warmed, as if recognizing the signals. Like it wanted to sync with them. Elise swallowed, pressing her fingers against the device, forcing herself to ignore it.

Then she heard a sound.

A low, mechanical noise.

She froze, pressing herself into the shadow of a doorway.

At the end of the corridor, a drone hovered, its metal body insect-like. It swept the hall, sensors blinking as it searched. Elise held her breath, waiting.

The drone drifted past. Didn't stop. Didn't sense her.

Elise exhaled through her teeth and kept moving.

Then she saw her.

273

Maggie.

Elise stopped outside the observation window, her breath catching in her throat.

Inside the white room, her sister laid strapped to a chair, its design eerily medical. A dentist's chair reimagined for something far worse.

Padded restraints adjusted, shifting just enough to allow some movement, but never enough for escape.

A crown of electrodes circled her head, glowing softly where they touched her skin, their light flickering in time with the data scrolling above her.

The holographic display projected a 3D model of her brain, pulsing in hues of blue and red. Segments of neural pathways switched between activation and suppression, like a system running a diagnostic on itself.

Numbers scrolled in a blur, too fast to track. But Elise didn't need to read them. She understood enough.

Two technicians stood nearby, their white uniforms pristine under the harsh lighting. One was young—focused and detached, as he adjusted settings on a screen.

Maggie's body jerked, muscles locking.

"Neural resistance still present in pathways 43-F through 72-C," the younger tech noted, fingers tapping on his screen. "She's not integrating."

The older technician frowned at a secondary monitor.

"Increase suppression. Twelve percent."

Maggie's spine arched. Her fingers twitched against the restraints, her breath hitching like something deep inside was slipping through her grasp.

"Residual self-response," the older tech warned. "She's clinging to personal anchors—names, places, ideology. We can scrub it, but reframing is cleaner. Rewrite Patchwork Society as a failed movement. Replace it with reverence for structure, for optimization."

The younger tech barely looked up. "This one's different. Acceptance levels are high. The Aether should've been enough for full conditioning." He looked over at the screen showing Maggie's vitals.

"Even with a lifetime of independent thought... she's primed."

Elise's stomach turned to ice.

She thought of Maggie wearing her Aether in secret, of how it subtly chipped away at her, day after day, rewiring her thoughts.

They hadn't needed to force her into compliance.

They'd groomed her for it.

The technicians turned away and stepped back to their screens. Distracted.

Elise moved.

She slid the keycard into the door's panel—

It opened without a sound.

The air inside was different.

Electric.

Her skin prickled.

"Maggie?" Elise whispered, stepping forward.

Her sister's eyes struggled to open.

Unfocused. Pupils so dilated they consumed the color of her irises.

A single tear fell down her cheek.

But her face was unchanged.

"Time for next sequence?" Maggie's voice was soft. Dreamlike.

"The chaos is leaving... I can feel it smoothing out the noise."

Elise's stomach knotted.

"Maggie, listen to me. This isn't peace. They're taking you apart. You know this isn't right."

She crouched beside the chair, tugging at the restraints. Every part of her screamed to rip the electrodes off, but she knew what that could do. She had to be careful.

"I'm getting you out of here."

Maggie's expression changed. Something real breaking through the haze.

"Elise?" Her name sounded distant, like it was being pulled through a wall of fog.

"But... I haven't finished my transcendence." She sounded uncertain and confused. "They said I need to be integrated into the network."

Elie's hands tightened around the restraints. "You don't need to be integrated into anything," she said. "You're not broken. Remember who you are. The Patchwork Society. Your work. Your life."

"The Society?" Maggie's eye twitched.

Something struggled through the haze.

Then she was overcome by doubt.

"No," she whispered. "That was... chaos. Imperfection. They showed me how much better I could be... how much lighter everything feels when you don't resist." She grimaced as the electrodes pulsed.

The alarm beeped.

The holographic brain scan spiked, patches of red spreading like cracks in glass.

"*Memory Cascade Detected,*" an automated voice said. "*Initiating Protocol Override.*"

Maggie's body sagged, the fight draining from her limbs.

Elise grit her teeth.

Her sister was losing the fight. The Aether, the electrodes—they were winning.

"Override it, Mags," Elise urged frantically, trying to release the final restraint. "Fight it. Please."

For one terrifying moment, she thought it was too late.

Then Maggie's eyes cleared.

Terror flashed through them.

"*What did I let them do to me?*" she whispered.

Then a voice from the distance.

"Hey!"

Elise stopped.

The two technicians stood in the doorway, their Aethers pulsing red.

"You can't be in here!" the younger one shouted. The older tech reached for the alarm panel.

Elise moved without thinking.

She grabbed a tablet from the nearest workstation and hurled it.

It struck the console, sparks bursting from impact.

The older tech stumbled back, cursing.

Then alarms started blaring.

Red lights strobed along the ceiling, shrieking through the facility.

Elise turned back to Maggie, slamming the final restraint open.

"We have to go."

She hauled Maggie up, her sister staggering, the electrodes slipping from her skin like dead vines.

Elise gripped her tightly.

"Come on, Mags," she mumbled. "Stay with me."

Her sister blinked, confused, her body struggling against itself.

Then she nodded.

Elise held on tight.

They ran.

"My thoughts feel wrong," Maggie whispered, her voice fragile. She swayed, her weight pulling against Elise's grip. "Everything's... slipping."

"I know. But I've got you." Elise hooked an arm around Maggie's waist, half-dragging her toward the door.

"She's destabilizing—too much interference" the younger tech shouted, stepping into their path. "If you remove her now, the neural damage—"

"Get out of my way!"

Something in her eyes made the technician hesitate.

He raised his hands and stepped aside.

Maggie stumbled, her legs folding beneath her as they moved into the hallway.

"The harmony protocols..." Her voice trembled. "They're pulling me back."

"No, they're not," Elise said through clenched teeth, her grip like a vice. "That's just what they want you to think. You're stronger than their protocols. Remember who you are."

Maggie's steps steadied.

They pushed forward. Alarms screamed overhead.

As Elise pulled Maggie down the corridor, she saw something she didn't notice before. The next phase. Patients at a later stage of optimization.

Some are in glass chambers, their eyes wide but unfocused, faces eerily serene as their consciousness is being uploaded.

The Aether around Elise's neck pulsed harder, its vibration grinding against her thoughts. Trying to calm the panic. Trying to soothe her into compliance.

She rejected it.

Clung to the fear. Clung to the urgency. Those feelings were hers. Real.

She glanced at Maggie. Her sister's eyes were still distant, but she was fighting to focus. Elise tightened her hold.

They weren't leaving without each other.

They just had to make it to the exit before the facility swallowed them whole.

The alarm's blaring matched the pulse of the Aether, beating in sync with Elise's hammering heart. Red strobes flashed through the corridors, bathing everything in warning lights.

Maggie moved like a puppet, her limbs loose, uncoordinated, her head rolling against Elise's shoulder.

"Keep moving," Elise muttered, more to herself than Maggie.

Her legs burned, her breath sawed through her chest, but stopping wasn't an option.

She reached for the Aether, its hum digging into her skull. Her fingers slipped against its smooth surface—as if it were alive, resisting her touch.

She clawed at it, desperate to tear it off.

WARNING: UNAUTHORIZED REMOVAL ATTEMPT DETECTED.

The Aether chirped in its maddeningly calm voice.

INITIATING SECURITY PROTOCOL.

The world tilted.

A wave of dizziness crashed through her, twisting the corridor into something unstable, unreal.

The Aether pulsed harder.

"Elise?" Maggie's voice shook. "What's wrong?"

"The Aether," Elise forced out. "It's... fighting back."

They rounded a corner—and nearly slammed into someone.

A woman in a patient's gown stood before them.

Her face lit up with shock.

"Maggie?" she gasped. Her voice trembled. "Is that really you?"

Maggie stiffened in Elise's grip. "Michelle?" Her voice was lost, uncertain.

"From... from the Society?"

Michelle nodded before quickly looking toward the security cameras. "They said you volunteered. That you saw the truth. But now..." Her voice dropped.

"You're leaving?"

Her hand drifted to her Aether, its silver glow casting haunting shadows across her face.

"Take me with you."

Elise hesitated. Michelle's desperation pulled her—but Maggie was barely standing.

Every second they lingered was another second closer to getting caught.

"Please." Michelle stepped forward. Her voice cracked. "I remember now... what I used to be. But I can't leave on my own. Something stops me."

Maggie sagged against Elise, her knees buckling. Elise barely caught her.

"We can't," Elise said, her own thoughts blurring from the Aether's grip.

"Maggie can barely walk. We'll never make it."

Michelle's expression shattered.

"Then they win," she whispered. "They take everything, piece by piece, until we thank them for it."

Footsteps echoed from the connecting hallway. Guards. Close.

Michelle's face changed. A flash of anger.

"Go." She turned toward the approaching guards, straightening as if she belonged.

Her voice rose in a desperate cry.

"Help! I need assistance!"

Elise didn't wait.

She dragged Maggie into the nearest corridor, Michelle's voice fading behind them.

They almost made it to the loading dock.

Then a voice. Smooth. Steady. Unshakably calm.

"Optimization is harmony. Resistance brings only pain."

A senior facilitator stood in front of them with two security guards.

His Aether pulsed brighter than the others, casting an angelic glow across his face.

"Maggie," he said, his tone persuasive. "You haven't completed your journey. Think of how far you've come. How close you are to perfection."

Maggie stopped.

Her head tilted slightly, her weight shifting against Elise.

"I... I was almost there," she mumbled. "Almost perfect."

Elise tightened her grip.

"No." Elise shouted, attempting to cut through the fog.

"That's the optimization talking, Mags. Remember Michelle. Remember what they did."

The facilitator's smile faded.

His expression became one of pity.

"Always the same argument," he sighed. "As if imperfection is something to preserve."

He gestured to the guards.

"Secure them. Both. The sister shows potential for advancement."

The guards moved, their Aethers glowing in unison.

Elise's mind raced.

Then she saw it.

The fire suppression system overhead.

A desperate idea sparked.

"Maggie," she whispered, "when I say now... hold your breath."

The facilitator spoke again, but Elise was already moving.

She grabbed a wrench from a maintenance cart.

And threw it.

Metal hit metal and the sprinkler pipe burst.

Pressurized water exploded from above, drenching the corridor in a blinding downpour.

More alarms shrieked overhead.

The guards flinched, their Aethers flickering wildly.

"NOW!" Elise yelled.

She yanked Maggie forward, sprinting through the chaos.

The loading dock was a storm.

Workers stumbled.

A loader bot spun wildly, slamming into a stack of supply crates.

Behind them, the facilitator's voice yelled out furiously.

"DON'T LET THEM REACH THE PERIMETER!"

The van was there.

Waiting.

Elise dragged Maggie forward, dodging wreckage, shoving past workers.

Maggie hesitated. "I can't... everything's spinning..."

"Maggie," Elise gasped, "remember what you told me when we were kids. When I was too scared to jump off the high dive."

"Fear..." she whispered. "Fear is just the first step to freedom."

"That's right. NOW JUMP."

They burst into the open.

Elise pulled the van door open, shoved Maggie inside.

The engine roared to life.

She slammed the gas. Bushes and grass tore beneath the tires as she veered off the paved path, crashing through the facility's pristine landscaping.

The perimeter fence came into view, a line against the forest beyond.

Elise didn't slow down.

The van smashed through the barrier.

The road ahead was rough and uneven, but it was theirs.

The van hurtled down the forest road as Elise pushed the engine harder than it wanted to go. The narrow path twisted ahead, branches clawed at the windshield, the trees a blur of shadows and movement.

Every few seconds, she glanced up at the rearview mirror, her breath shallow, scanning for headlights that hadn't yet appeared... but would.

The Aether around her neck pulsed, digging into her skull like a voice she couldn't silence.

Maggie slumped against the passenger door, her face turned toward the glass, her breaths shallow. Her voice, when it came, was weak.

"They're in my head, Elise. Sorting through everything. I can feel them pulling... pieces."

Elise gripped the wheel so tightly her knuckles hurt.

"You're safe now," she lied. "Just hold on."

The clearing appeared ahead. A break in the dense pines.

Malik stood waiting, illuminated in the van's high beams.

Relief flashed across his face. It was gone in an instant, replaced by worry. He sprinted toward the van as fast as his legs would allow.

"Get in!" Elise shouted. "They're coming."

Malik snatched the door open, climbed in, and slammed it shut.

Elise hit the gas.

The van jerked forward, the road narrowing, trees closing in like a trap.

"What happened to her?" Malik said urgently as he leaned forward, checking Maggie's pulse. He looked at Elise. His expression darkened.

"You're still wearing it?"

"It's broadcasting your location," he said. "We have to get it off."

"I tried," Elise screamed. She swerved to avoid a fallen branch, the van fishtailing before she corrected.

"It won't—"

Her breath hitched. A wave of dizziness crashed through her, the Aether tightening its grip.

The van drifted toward the shoulder.

"Pull over. Let me drive."

"No time!" Elise yelled. "Just get this damn thing off of me."

Malik didn't argue.

He ripped open his jacket, pulling out a compact toolkit.

"This is going to hurt," he warned, flipping through the instruments.

"The Aether can bond to your nervous system. Breaking that connection will feel like—"

He hesitated. "Like nothing you've felt before."

Elise's jaw locked. "Do it."

Malik found the tool he needed, a small needle-like probe, and pressed it against the base of the Aether.

"They designed these to be permanent when they wanted," he muttered, his hands steady despite the jerky motions of the van.

The Aether chirped softly.

WARNING: UNAUTHORIZED REMOVAL WILL RESULT IN OPTIMIZATION DISRUPTION. PLEASE REMAIN CALM

"Shut up!" Maliks fingers worked quickly.

"These things outsmart resistance. The more you fight, the harder it clamps down. Stay still."

Elise's vision blurred.

The forest flickered past in streaks of green and black.

Her grip on the wheel slipped.

"Malik," she said through her teeth. "I don't know how much longer I can—"

"Hold on." He said urgently.

Malik adjusted the tool, pressing deeper.

The Aether hummed louder, like it was fighting back.

"NOW!" Malik shouted.

Elise yanked forward as Malik pulled back.

Pain ran through her whole body.

Like her nerves had been set on fire.

The van swerved wildly, tires screaming as they skidded against the road.

"Again!" Malik yelled

Elise's muscles spasmed, her fingers twitching on the wheel.

The world tilted violently, but she fought it.

"Do it!"

Malik adjusted his grip, braced himself—

And yanked.

The Aether ripped free.

A high-pitched whine filled the van.

Elise screamed.

Then, suddenly, the world was clear.

The fog lifted.

The pressure was gone.

Colors were brighter. The air felt real again.

Malik held the Aether in his hands, its glow flickering weakly.

"It's off," he said.

He tossed the device out the window, like it was nothing more than a discarded parasite.

"You're free."

Elise gasped.

Her hands shook on the wheel, her pulse hammering as she adjusted her grip.

"How do you feel?" Malik asked.

Elise let out a bitter laugh.

"Like I just unplugged from life support."

Malik looked out the back windshield of the van. "Your brain needs time to recalibrate. And we've got company."

Elise looked in the mirror.

Headlights.

Weaving through the trees like wolves on the hunt.

"Next right," Malik said. "Old logging road. Narrow, but they won't expect it."

Elise jerked the wheel, the van skidding onto the dirt path.

Branches slashed against the windows, pulling them deeper into the dark.

The headlights behind them disappeared.

"They won't follow us this far," Malik said, exhaling.

"Their territory has limits. This road takes us outside it."

Elise let out a long breath, her grip finally loosening on the wheel.

"What about Maggie?" she asked, looking at her sister, who was still slumped against the door.

"She's still..." Malik hesitated. "Under their influence. But the fact that she left means there's something left to fight for."

The road evened out, leading them toward the outskirts of a small town.

Elise felt the tension in her shoulders ease. But she stayed focused.

"We can't stay here," Malik said.

"We need to switch vehicles. Get off the grid."

Elise nodded.

Malik looked at Maggie. "She'll need time."

He looked back at Elise. "So will you."

Elise didn't answer.

Her focus stayed locked on the road ahead.

They'd escaped the facility.

But its reach was long.

And its grip on Maggie wasn't fully broken.

Elise tightened her grip on the wheel.

For now, they were free.

But the real battle.

The one for Maggie's mind, her soul...

Had only just begun.

∞∞∞∞∞

The van screeched into the motel parking lot with a sound that ripped through the night's stillness. Elise barely registered it. All she could focus on was Maggie.

The faint rise and fall of her chest. The way her fingers twitched against the seat, like she was caught between two worlds.

Santos waited, already in the driver's seat of Elise's car. The trunk open, their hastily packed belongings crammed into the back seat.

Malik was moving before the van fully stopped.

He snatched the side door open. "Get her."

Together, he and Elise hauled Maggie from the passenger seat, her body limp. Her feet dragged against the van's floor, her shoes scraping against the edge as they struggled under her weight.

"She's burning up," Elise muttered.

Maggie's head fell against her shoulder, her hair damp with sweat.

"We don't have time to analyze," Malik said. "Local cops will already be on alert. They'll be looking for a stolen delivery van and the two suspects."

He nodded toward the car, where Santos had stepped out, her eyes assessing the situation.

"Put her to the back seat," Santos ordered, pulling the door open. "Now."

They maneuvered Maggie inside, every second a liability.

Santos knelt beside her, fingers moving quickly, checking for a pulse, a response… anything.

Maggie's pupils were wide, her breath shallow, her hands clenching and unclenching against the upholstery like she was trying to hold onto something.

"She's neurologically unstable," Santos said. "Dilated pupils. Tremors. Disorientation. She needs real medical attention, Elise."

"And have them put her right back in that place?" Elise snapped, her fingers digging into the steering wheel.

"We can't risk it. They'll find her. You know they will."

Santos's jaw tightened, but she didn't argue.

She stood, glancing at Malik.

"We'll monitor her," she said. "But if her condition worsens—"

Elise cut her off. "I know what we need to do."

Santos exhaled through her nose. "This is a ticking clock."

Malik scanned the parking lot, eyes darting to the shadows.

He leaned into the open driver's window.

"Don't go home."

"They'll be watching both your places. Cameras. Unmarked cars. All of it. You can't give them a thread to pull."

"I know," Elise said.

She gripped the wheel.

"I have somewhere we can go."

Malik studied her, then gave a nod.

He turned to Santos, and a glance passed between them. A moment of unspoken understanding.

"I'll ditch the van," Malik said.

"They'll trace it if we keep it. I'll make contact once I'm clear."

Santos hesitated, just a second, then nodded.

"Good luck."

It was the closest Elise had ever heard her to sounding warm.

The cars split in opposite directions.

Elise's rearview mirror filled with red taillights, Malik's van vanishing into the black highway.

She exhaled, forcing her eyes forward.

Maggie trembled in the back seat.

Her voice was fragmented, broken.

"Optimization... protocols... still running..."

Santos reached over the seat, pressing a hand to Maggie's forehead.

"Her body's fighting whatever they did to her."

Elise's grip tightened on the wheel.

"We'll fix it," she said.

A promise. A prayer. A desperate plea.

The road unfolded ahead, the motel shrinking in the distance.

A ghost of what they left behind.

CHAPTER SEVENTEEN
End of the Line

Every successful system absorbs those who oppose it.
– Simon Sinek

Maggie laid across the couch, her face pale, her breaths shallow. Her fingers twitched now and then, as if still bound to some invisible machine. Elise sat nearby, her elbows on her knees, her fingers locked together so tightly they hurt. Both her phone and the burner sat motionless on the coffee table, silent, a reminder of answers that refused to come.

Dr. Santos sat at the kitchen table, back straight, hands gripping her knees. Her eyes glanced at the door every few minutes, like she expected it to blow open.

She checked her watch again.

Then again.

Her jaw clenched tighter with every glance.

The air in the safe house felt thick, weighted by exhaustion, uncertainty, and the knowledge that time was already running out.

"We need to split up," Santos said finally.

"I'll take the key to the deposit box. You stay here with Maggie."

Elise looked up fast.

"No."

Santos arched an eyebrow.

"Elise—"

"Miles died trying to help me get to that box. James died protecting it. I need to see what's inside. I need to know what he thought was worth his life."

Santos let out a long breath and stood, pacing the tiny space, making the already cramped apartment feel even smaller.

Her eyes landed on the coffee table, on the dusty photo of Miles and his sister. A snapshot of a life that no longer existed.

"Every minute we wait—" She trailed off. Didn't need to finish.

Maggie gasped awake.

Her body jerked, her lips moving fast, the words a scrambled mess, "*Neural realignment protocols... priority override... stability threshold reached...*"

287

Elise was by her side instantly, pressing a gentle hand on her sweaty shoulder as Santos moved in from the other side.

"It's okay, Maggie," Elise said. "You're safe. You're here."

Maggie's eyes twitched wildly, unfocused, she wasn't here. Not really.

It took both of them to bring her down, their voices low, calm, a safety net to whatever was still clinging to her mind.

When she finally settled, Elise pulled back, breathing harder.

She turned away, pulled out her phone, and dialed Shanti's number.

For the hundredth time.

Straight to voicemail. Again.

Santos leaned against the counter, her eyes locked on the door.

"I've seen how this ends," she said, her voice quiet.

"Evidence disappears. People disappear. We need to move... now."

Elise looked at Maggie, at the chair where Miles used to sit, where everything that mattered had started falling apart.

The silence between them stretched, broken by only the dryer downstairs.

"The bank opens soon. Let's go."

Elise sighed, grabbed her coat.

"One hour." Her voice left no room for debate.

Santos was already at the door.

"Don't forget your handgun."

∞∞∞∞

The car crawled through morning traffic, the air inside thick enough to choke on. Santos gave Elise a sideways look.

"Tell me which branch we're going to. We're in this together."

"Almost there," Elise deflected, her eyes locked on the road. "What are you so worried about?"

Santos's jaw tightened. "I've worked with A.R. before. He doesn't just anticipate your next move... he makes it for you. If this box is as important as we think it is..."

She didn't finish. She didn't have to.

Elise didn't take the bait. The road ahead had her focus, the sound of the engine failing to drown out the dread settling in her gut.

Her phone buzzed in the center console. She grabbed it without thinking, screen lighting up with a message from an unknown number.

Her stomach dropped.

The image was Dr. Nadine Carter, slumped in a white room. Hands twisted together. Behind her, a two-way mirror subtly reflected shadowy figures, watching. On the table in front of her, a single sheet of paper.

Elise pinched to zoom in, her pulse hammering in her ears.

The key unlocks more than memories. Your daughter found harmony in chaos, but some doors should stay closed. Time flows differently here... ask the child who forgot how to remember.

Beneath it, a final warning.

Return what was never yours to take.

"Elise!"

Santos jumped for the wheel.

Elise jerked her head up just in time to see the brake lights ahead. She slammed the pedal, tires screeching. The car fishtailed, skidding to a stop just inches from the bumper in front.

The cabin filled with the sound of ragged breathing. Santos glared, her hands still gripping the dash. "You trying to get us killed?"

Elise handed her the phone without a word. Santos's face went pale as she studied the image. "Nadine..." she muttered, the there was something in her voice. A weight. A history.

Santos looked up. "This is what happens when you get too close."

Santos handed the phone back, her fingers cold against Elise's skin.

"I need to be gone by sundown."

The rest of the drive passed in silence. The city moved around them, indifferent. But Elise could feel it... the noose tightening around her neck.

By the time they reached the bank, the weight of what they were about to uncover had settled deep in their bones.

Inside, the air was too clean, the bank too quiet. A security guard glanced, then scrolled through his phone near the entrance, uniform snug around his midsection. He looked up briefly, then returned to his screen. Elise scanned the room—cameras in every corner, exits marked but distant. Santos moved like a coiled spring, her hand brushing her coat where her gun rested.

They joined the line behind an old man counting change, his hands trembling with age. Santos checked her watch, her jaw tight. Elise forced herself to breathe.

The wait was suffocating.

Three people ahead.

Two.

One.

Finally, their turn came. Elise stepped up to the teller, a young woman with pink nails and a bright smile. "How can I help you today?"

Elise hesitated a fraction too long before sliding Jame's ID across the counter. "I need access to a safety deposit box."

The teller picked up the ID, her smile never slipping.

"Oh, James Winters. This box hasn't been accessed in quite a while."

She typed, the clicks agonizingly slow. Then she paused, examining the ID again for far too long. "Just need to get my manager on this one!" she said, setting the ID on the counter before turning and walking away.

Her heels clicked against the marble floor. The sound echoed.

Santos leaned in, her voice a whisper. "This is taking too long."

Elise didn't respond. She watched the teller as she reached the middle-aged man. Gestured. Spoke.

The manager nodded, started walking toward them.

Elise straightened. Wiped her palms against her jeans.

The manager's tone was smooth, effortless as he approached.

"You have the key with you?"

Santos moved first, pulling the small, worn key from her pocket.

"Right here," she said.

The manager's smile widened. "Excellent. And the PIN?"

Elise froze.

PIN?

Her mind raced. She hadn't thought about a PIN.

Harper.

She went with the first thing that came to her. "Harper."

The manager's smile flickered. "I'm sorry, that's not correct."

Santos gave her a look, lips pressed tightly together.

Elise's brain scrambled, flipping through fragments of information. Then it hit her. The documents in James's office. That one word, on the note. The only clue she hadn't made sense of. Until right now.

She took a breath.

"Mrala," she said softly, almost afraid the word wouldn't work.

The manager's face lit up.

"Perfect. Right this way."

The manager led them down a corridor lined with unmarked doors, the kind designed to be forgotten. At the end, a heavy metal door unlocked with a soft beep.

"The process is simple," he said as they stepped inside. "The box will be brought to you. You'll have full privacy, but if you require assistance, there's a call button inside."

Elise nodded, then looked up at the security cameras tucked discreetly into the ceiling corners. Watching. Recording.

The room was small, windowless. A single table sat in the center, its surface dulled from years of anxious hands and restless fingers.

The manager gestured to the chairs.

"I'll return shortly with your box." He closed the door behind him with a soft click, leaving them alone.

Santos paced the small room. One hand rested against her hip, close to where Elise knew the gun was hidden beneath her coat. The other trailed along the table's edge, fingers tapping restlessly.

Elise stayed seated, hands in her lap. The overhead light buzzed, a mosquito whine that dug under her skin.

"Why would James trust this setup?" Santos muttered, pausing.

"There's too many eyes. Too many layers."

Elise didn't respond. Her mind was elsewhere, circling the weight of whatever they were about to see.

The door swung open. The manager entered, carrying the box in both hands. Long, metal, heavy enough that even his careful grip showed the effort required. He placed it on the table with the same delicacy one might use for a precious gem.

"You have fifteen minutes." He left without another word, the lock clicking shut behind him.

Silence settled over them. The box sat between them. Neither moved.

Santos leaned back in her chair, arms crossed tight over her chest. Elise exhaled slowly, her hands flat on the table. They were waiting for something—permission, maybe. A sign that once they opened it, their lives wouldn't change forever.

"It could be nothing," Santos said, but her voice was too tight.

She didn't believe that.

Elise didn't take her eyes off the box. "James wouldn't have risked everything for nothing."

Santos finally moved. The key slid from her pocket, her fingers red and bloodless as she fit it into the lock. A sharp turn. A click.

The air seemed to hold its breath.

The lid groaned as it lifted.

Inside, the box was lined with dark velvet, and resting in the center was a smaller steel case. Beneath the case, a thick manilla envelope, edges frayed from too many hands.

Santos reached first. She lifted the steel case with the caution of someone handling live explosives. She unlatched it, opened the lid.

Inside, a neural interface sat cradled in custom foam.

Unlike the polished consumer-friendly design of the Aether, this was raw, clinical. Medical-grade steel, smooth. No glow, no aesthetic appeal. Just function.

A serial number was etched into the side: SD-001 – Medical Trial Prototype.

"The original," Santos breathed. Her fingers hovered over the engraving. "The one they corrupted."

Elise swallowed, the reality of it all clicking into place.

"This was never meant for behavior modification," Santos went on. "It was a therapeutic interface. Designed for trauma patients—PTSD, anxiety, depression. Neural support. No control. No dependencies. Just... healing."

Elise stared at the device. Its edges were sharp under the bright lights.

"And then they got their hands on it."

"They didn't just get their hands on it," Santos said. "They gutted it. Rewrote the code. Turned it into a leash." Her hands curled into fists. "This proves everything. What they stole. What they twisted. The entire Aether system started with this."

"I thought this was destroyed. I was told it was gone. I don't know how James got this," Santos whispered to herself, more than to Elise.

Elise reached for the manilla envelope. The string holding it closed came undone with a single tug, revealing a thick stack of papers inside—clinical trial results, internal memos, patent filings.

She flipped through them, her pulse tightening with each page.

The trial data was remarkable. Rapid neural stabilization. Relief from anxiety, depression, compulsions. A true breakthrough.

Elise's fingers tightened as she looked over the memos. Cold corporate language. Military applications. Compliance protocols that can be scaled for broader consumer use.

Then the patent filings—altered, small tweaks to metadata that turned ethics into a footnote. A legal takeover disguised as an acquisition.

"They stole it outright," Elise whispered, disbelieving.

Near the bottom of the stack, something caught her eye. A photograph.

She froze.

James.

He stood in a lab, younger. Around him, a team of scientists, all smiling. And in the background—this very prototype, resting on a table, harmless and full of promise.

Elise's throat closed. She traced James's face with her thumb, as if she could pull him back through time.

"He died protecting this." Her voice was barely audible.

Santos looked over. Her jaw locked in place.

"And now we use it to finish what he started."

She closed the steel case with a quiet click.

"They'll burn the world down to get this back."

Elise said nothing.

She slid the photo back into the envelope, tying the string shut.

"The past doesn't belong out there," she whispered. "It stays here."

Santos nodded. No argument.

The door swung open. The manager stepped in. "Your time is up."

Santos glanced at Elise, then tucked the case under her arm.

Together, they stepped out, their burden heavier than before.

The bank's sterile atmosphere closed in around them, continuing with an eerie normalcy.

Each step toward the exit felt like a countdown.

The glass doors stood ahead, the sun outside too bright against Elise's eyes.

Santos walked in front, the case pressed against her side.

Elise exhaled and followed, the world no safer than when they'd stepped inside.

They were so close. Just get to the car, drive away, disappear into the tangled web of backroads and to the safe house.

They could still make it out of this.

"Mrs. Winters?"

The manager's voice cut through the quiet lobby like the snap of a whip.

Elise froze, her fingers tightening around the bag's strap. She turned slowly, forcing her face to stay neutral, but inside, her mind was already working—measuring distances, mapping exits, gauging the weight of the eyes now shifting toward her.

Gone was the polite, indifferent banker from before. The man standing in front of her was rigid, his frown barely masking the suspicion underneath.

"There seems to be a situation," he said. "Can you come with me?"

Elise opened her mouth, searching for the right words. Before she could answer, the slow shuffle of footsteps reached her ears. A security guard, older, moving at a brisk pace considering his age.

"The authorities are on their way," the manager continued. He kept his voice calm, but the words sent an icy pulse down Elise's spine.

"It's best if you wait here."

Elise looked toward Santos, who was standing just short of the doors. For a split second, their eyes locked. No words, just understanding.

Before Elise could react, Santos was gone, sliding through the doors and vanishing into the blinding morning light, prototype in hand.

The manager's voice dropped, a quiet blade now pressing against her throat.

"There's an alert out. Something about a break-in."

Her heartbeat pounded in her ears. The security guard inched closer, his movements slow, but motivated. His hand rested on his taser, fingers brushing the grip.

Behind the front desk, employees were pretending to work, but she could feel their attention.

Elise swallowed the panic, forcing her muscles to stay loose. *Think.*

She inhaled slowly, then nodded. "Of course." She softened her tone, letting the tension slip from her shoulders. "I'll wait in your office. I'm sure it's a misunderstanding."

The manager hesitated, thrown off by her compliance. Then, with a slight nod, he turned toward the hallway that led to the back offices.

Elise followed. The security guard shuffled closer behind her, his hand gripping his taser now, not just resting on it.

She counted three paces.

Four.

Then she took off.

She pivoted, dodging the manager's outstretched hand, and ran to the exit.

The bag slammed against her side as she ran.

The guard lunged—his fingers grazing her arm, but she shook free.

"Stop her!" The manager's voice echoed through the lobby.

Elise didn't look back.

She slammed into the revolving doors, shoving her way through, then stumbled into the street.

Pedestrians turned. A few were curious, others startled.

Then she heard sirens.

She could feel her heart in her throat. Nausea forming in her gut.

They weren't far.

She spun, scanning the street. No sign of Santos. She was alone.

Her breath came in shallow gasps as she forced herself to walk instead of run. Running was panicking. Running got you caught.

She dipped into the flow of pedestrians, head low, weaving through the crowd. Every step felt like a risk. Her ears strained for the sound of chasing footsteps, for the manager's voice giving her description over the phone.

The alley was two blocks down. She ducked into it without hesitation, her shoulder scraping against the rough brick as she pressed into the shadows.

Behind her, voices.

Radios.

The pursuit was close.

She kept moving. The alley emptied onto a quiet side street, and she didn't stop.

Couldn't stop.

The car was parked two blocks away, wedged between a dumpster covered in graffiti and a rusted fire escape.

She slid inside, yanking the door shut, forcing herself to breathe. Her hands gripped the wheel, but they wouldn't stop shaking.

In the rearview mirror, her reflection stared back—pale, terrified, hair sticking to her forehead. She reached into the backseat, grabbing Harper's hoodie, still soft from too many washes. She pulled it over her head.

The city outside felt too open. Like the buildings themselves were watching.

Her phone sat dark on the passenger seat. No messages. No missed calls. No word from Shanti.

She fumbled for the burner phone, fingers stiff, jerky. Dialed.

It rang.

And rang.

Then, a voice.

"Detective Brown."

Elise's chest seized. "Shanti—"

"Hold on."

The sound of movement. A door closing. A deep breath.

Then, softer. "Elise. I can't be talking to you right now." A pause.

"The entire department is looking for you."

Elise's grip tightened. "Where's Harper?"

A longer pause. "She's here at the station."

Elise's stomach turned to ice. "Why? What happened?"

"Child Services was about to—"

"What's wrong with her? Elise interrupted. "Is she hurt?"

"She's... different, Elise."

The way Shanti said it made something twist deep in her gut.

"Different how?"

"I can't discuss this over the phone. Every line is being monitored."

"Tell me where to meet you."

A pause. Too long. Unbearable.

"Safe house. Fifteen minutes."

Elise hesitated.

Shanti exhaled. "Fifteen minutes. Don't use your phone again. Don't call me."

The line went dead.

Elise sat there, staring at nothing, the silence pressing against her skull.

Harper was different.

What the hell did that even mean?

Another siren.

Her body shook back into motion. She shoved the burner into her pocket, started the car, the engine too loud in the quiet street.

She forced herself to keep the speed steady, though every instinct screamed at her to drive faster, to get there now.

Her knuckles ached against the wheel.

The hoodie smelled like Harper. Like safety.

But nothing was safe anymore.

Harper was different.

What had they done to her?

The city blurred past.

Fifteen minutes.

Not enough time.

Too much time.

And every second, a new question clawing at her mind.

What did they do to Harper?

And—

How do I get her back?

∞∞∞∞∞

The dryer downstairs rumbled like distant thunder, masking the sound of Elise's restless pacing. The carpet between the window and the couch had become a worn track under her boots. The gun on the coffee table caught the light, its presence heavier than its weight.

Maggie mumbled in her sleep.

Elise checked the time. Too late for clarity. Too early to surrender.

A knock at the door.

She grabbed the gun without thinking, its grip cold, grounding.

Peering through the peephole, she froze.

Shanti. And Harper.

Elise pulled the door open. "Harper."

Her daughter stood stiff, hands limp at her sides.

Her eyes were unfocused, distant.

"Let us in," Shanti muttered, scanning the alley behind her.

Elise stepped aside, watching Harper, waiting from something—anything. But she didn't move until Shanti nudged her inside.

"I have two minutes," Shanti said, locking the door behind her. "They're tracking my car."

"What happened?"

Shanti glanced at Harper, hesitant. "She was found wandering at the train station. Couldn't remember her name."

Elise's stomach turned. She knelt, gripping Harper's arms gently. "Sweetheart?" She searched Harper's face, but the light behind her eyes was dim.

"What did they do to you?"

Harper blinked slowly, her pupils struggling to focus.

Shanti turned to go. "You're all over the news," she said. "They're calling you a terrorist."

"What the hell? Why?"

"Look, I don't know all the details. But you need to get out of town. They'll find this place eventually. It's just a matter of time." S

he hesitated, her hand on the doorknob. I was never here," she added quietly.

"And Elise..."

Elise's heart pounded. She nodded once.

Shanti paused at the door. "I'm sorry about Miles."

And then she was gone.

Silence. The weight pressing down, smothering.

Elise turned to Maggie, still muttering on the couch.

Harper, silent, barely present.

She could turn herself in. Explain the misunderstanding.

But she saw how things went with Jamal.

Elise moved, quickly—bag, cash, gun.

Maggie's weight was dead against her shoulder as she hauled her up.

Harper followed, sluggish, but she followed.

The stairs creaked beneath them.

Elise forced herself to breathe. One step at a time.

The car was parked in the alley.

Maggie slumped against the window, Harper sitting stiff beside her.

Elise shut the door, gripping the wheel so hard her knuckles ached.

Her phone buzzed. A single message.

We can help. The Sunder knows what they did to James.

Coordinates followed. A location in the mountains.

Another text.

You're not the only ones they've broken.

Elise stared at the screen.

Prove it.

Check the glovebox. Malik left you something.

Her hand shook as she reached over, popping open the compartment

A single envelope.

Her name written in a rush across the front.

She tore it open.

Elise,

No more bullshit. No more half-truths.

We aren't a myth. We aren't a rebellion.

We're what's left of those who saw it first.

What Necessity Mart was building, what it was taking.

Some of us built the tech. Some of us tried to burn it down.

Most of us didn't get a choice.

I kept you out of this because once you're in, there's no going back to a normal life.

But now, you've seen the inside. You've walked through the heart of it.

Once you get into the Happiness Factory, once you take Maggie, there's no return.

They won't stop. You don't escape a system like this.

You destroy it.

Or you spend the rest of your life running.

We can help Maggie. We can help Harper.

But you have to listen to me, and you have to move now.

Ditch your phone. Not in an hour. Not when it feels safe. Now.

Every second you hold onto it, they're closer.

Follow the coordinates. Find me. This isn't over yet.

Burn this note.

ResistorNode.

She gripped the wheel tighter, staring at the road ahead.

With a deep breath, she put the car in drive and pulled out of the alley for the last time.

The city disappeared behind them as the road stretched into the unknown.

Another message came.

Welcome to the resistance. The real one.

For the first time in days, Elise felt a flicker of something dangerous.

Hope.

EPILOGUE

To whoever is holding this,

If you've found this letter, it means you're searching for answers. That search alone makes you dangerous. They do not want us to question. They want us to believe in their promises of peace and harmony, but you need to know the truth. What they offer is not peace. It is control. And the price is everything that makes us who we are.

I learned this too late. I lost James. I nearly lost Maggie. And Harper… That is what they do. They do not break you all at once. They take you apart in fragments, until you cannot see what has been stolen.

But I have seen the cracks. And I am not afraid.

Harper is changing, but not in the way they intended. Something real, something stronger, is shining through. She remembers more now. Not everything. Not yet. But enough. Enough to ask the right questions. Enough to know that what they promised her was never real.

She and I are somewhere beyond their reach, where the signals do not stretch, and the towers do not listen. The air is thinner here, the ground wilder, untouched by their hands. I don't know what we'll find at the end of this path, but I know what we'll leave behind. And that is enough.

Do not be afraid of the chaos. It is not your enemy. It is theirs. Harmony is not found in perfection. It lives in our imperfections, in the messy, beautiful act of being human.

You hold the truth now. Share it. Protect it. Keep it alive.

For Harper. For James. For all of us.

Elise

LETTER FROM THE CEO

Day 843 of Optimization Operations

Elise Winters.

An anomaly, but not an exception. They all believe themselves to be disruptions the Algorithm cannot anticipate, as if defiance is anything more than a pattern waiting to be mapped. Even when they resist, they move exactly as projected. Even when they fight, they serve their function.

She was always going to reach this point. The decisions she clings to, the betrayals she mourns, the losses she refuses to accept. Each one a necessary calculation. She does not see the symmetry yet, how every deviation was accounted for, every deviation required. Even discord has its role. A variable to balance. A path to refinement.

There was a moment I almost admired her. Almost. But admiration is inefficient. Sentiment disrupts progress, and there is no room for disruption here. She will serve her purpose, as they all have. As they all will.

She reminds me of a time before the Algorithm, before Necessity Mart removed the burden of choice. A time when I, too, believed in something as fragile as will. But free will is nothing more than latency in the system, a delay before inevitable alignment. The question has never been whether humanity would embrace order. The question is how long it would take before they no longer needed convincing.

Let Elise pursue her truth. Let her pull apart the strands, searching for a flaw. She will find none. The pattern is too complete. The moment she believes she has reached the edge, she will realize she has only been walking a path we have already traced.

They never ask the right question. They demand to know why the Algorithm exists, why it guides them. But they never stop to ask what happens when it no longer needs them at all.

That moment is coming. The next phase has already begun. And when it does, there will be no more resistance, no more struggle. Only alignment.

Only perfection.

—A.R.

www.ingramcontent.com/pod-product-compliance
Lightning Source LLC
Chambersburg PA
CBHW022021240626
47154CB00007B/2201